Praise for BRAHMA'S DREAM

"A timeless story about the meaning of life. . . . The story of Mohini and her parents is compelling, tear jerking, and next to impossible to put down. . . . Each of the characters is so tangible and real that the readers adopt them as their own family. . . . Ghatage has succeeded in writing a novel that at first appears simple and pleasant but reveals itself to be beautifully complex."   —*Calgary Herald*

"*Brahma's Dream* will surely enhance [Ghatage's] stature. . . . [It is] a sustained insight into the thoughts and feelings of a young girl . . . a moving evocation of her courage and resilience in coming to terms with her invalid status."
                             —*Ottawa Citizen*

"A moving coming of age story. . . . Mohini's character is engagingly self-possessed, with wisdom beyond her years, and the relationships formed with those around her are skillfully rendered."   —*The Women's Post*

"Mohini is an eloquent mouthpiece for the Calgary author's own discoveries about Indian religion, human foibles, and familial love."   —*The Vancouver Sun*

"Author Shree Ghatage paints a wonderful portrait of a family, a culture and a country. . . . [She] has created a remarkable and truly memorable character in Mohini. . . . Ghatage has an exquisite ability to tell a moving story."
                     —*The Chronicle-Herald* (Halifax)

"Delightful. . . . Ghatage's elegant, effortless prose weaves the fine, domestic strands that comprise the Oek's daily life. . . . Despite the loneliness and suffering—minute and grand—there is an irrepressible delight in beauty and humour, an undercurrent of love, forgiveness, endurance and verve that babbles through the pages. . . . In writing *Brahma's Dream*, Ghatage took on the challenge of treading some much-explored territory, already trod by rather daunting literary heavyweights. . . . *Brahma's Dream*, a quietly captivating, highly accomplished debut novel with a brave and enchanting girl at its heart, suggests [Ghatage] has risen to that challenge."

—*The Globe and Mail*

"*Brahma's Dream* affirms [Ghatage] as a mature and gifted writer." —*Quill & Quire starred review*

"A coming-of-age story, one all the more affecting for the fact that its heroine's life is precarious, is combined with a powerful evocation of how history impinges on ordinary people. . . . Ghatage, with her strong, unadorned prose and flair for the unconventional, empathetic point of view, appears to have found a satisfying space between . . . the novels of Rohinton Mistry, with their political engagement and Dickensian social sweep, [and] the playfulness of newcomer Anosh Irani."

—*The Gazette* (Montreal)

"Ghatage so deftly weaves history into her story about young Mohini, and shows us a version of Bombay with such lyrical prose, that you can almost see what the city would have looked like before it became Mumbai. . . . Her descriptions of the landscape and the characters are effortlessly evocative. . . . A delight to read, *Brahma's Dream* leaves you wanting more from Ghatage." —*www.mybindi.com*

Shree Ghatage

BRAHMA'S DREAM

A Novel

 ANCHOR CANADA

LIBRARY AND ARCHIVES CANADA CATALOGUING IN PUBLICATION

Ghatage, Shree
Brahma's dream / Shree Ghatage.

ISBN 0–385–66016–2

I. Title.

PS8563.H37B73 2005   C813.'54   C2005–901109–2

Cover image: Tim Davis/Getty Images
Cover and text design: CS Richardson
Printed and bound in Canada

Published in Canada by
Anchor Canada, a division of
Random House of Canada Limited

Visit Random House of Canada Limited's website:
www.randomhouse.ca

TRANS 10 9 8 7 6 5 4 3 2 1

For Lena, Rohan & Prafull

In memory of
Tai & Dad

'A wise man once said to his son: "Fetch me from thence a fruit of the Nyagrodha tree."

"Here is one, sir."

"Break it."

"It is broken, sir."

"What do you see there?"

"These seeds, almost infinitesimal."

"Break one of them!"

"It is broken, sir."

"What do you see there?"

"Not anything, sir."

The father said: "My son, that subtle essence which you do not perceive there, of that very essence this great Nyagrodha tree exists. Believe me, my son. That which is the subtle essence, in it all that exists has its self. It is the True. It is the Self."'

—*Chandayoga Upanishad*
circa 1500—1200 B.C.

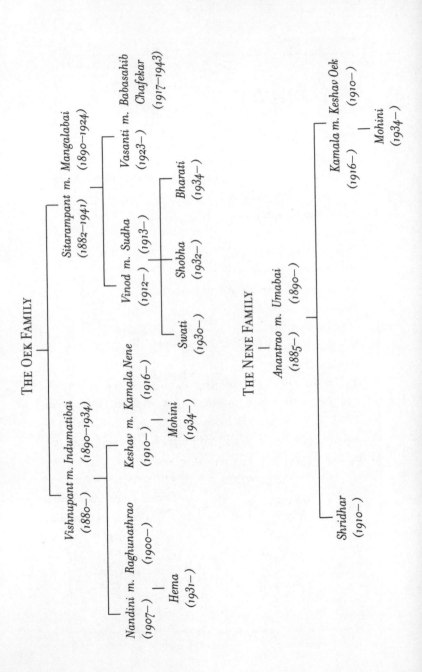

THE OEK FAMILY

Vishnupant m. Indumatibai
(1880–)   (1890–1934)

Nandini m. Raghunathrao
(1907–)   (1900–)

Hema
(1931–)

Keshav m. Kamala Nene
(1910–)   (1916–)

Mohini
(1934–)

Sitarampant m. Mangalabai
(1882–1941)   (1890–1924)

Vinod m. Sudha
(1912–)   (1913–)

Swati
(1930–)

Shobha
(1932–)

Bharati
(1934–)

Vasanti m. Babasahib
(1923–)   Chafekar
(1917–1943)

THE NENE FAMILY

Anantrao m. Umabai
(1885–)   (1890–)

Shridhar
(1910–)

Kamala m. Keshav Oek
(1916–)   (1910–)

Mohini
(1934–)

Bombay
1948

Mohur Lane and Mill Road
are imaginary, as are the
New English Academy,
Jijabai Samaj, the Gymnasium,
and Dadar West Gymkhana.

ARABIAN SEA

MAHIM BAY

•DADAR STATION

BOMBAY HARBOUR

•GATEWAY OF INDIA

MAHIM BAY

✚ Dr Natu

✚ Dr Chitnis' Clinic

DADAR SEA FACE

To Sitala Devi Temple ➡

SHIVAJI

PARK

Dadar West Gymkhana

CADELL ROAD

GOKHALE ROAD

Jijabai Samaj

Gymnasium

KELUSKAR MARG

MILL ROAD

ALLEY

Marzello Property

Irani Tea Shop

Shiv Sadan

Kulkarni Home

Koleshwar Nivas

MOHUR LANE

RANADE RD. EXTENSION

To New English Academy

To Portuguese Church

To Dadar Station

N

ONE

On a clear, ochre morning, standing in the front verandah of Koleshwar Nivas and watching a rain tree release into the sky a flurry of parrots, Mohini noticed that the outer corner of her left eye had stopped twitching. She dropped her chin and slowly rotated her head. The muscles in her neck had loosened during the night, and the ache in the centre point between her eyebrows had disappeared. Relieved, she reached forward and picked off the verandah railing the pink stone that she had forgotten there the evening before. It felt pleasantly cool against her skin, its surface smooth and glassy but for a few places where it was chipped and rugged. Mohini held it up. A dull opaqueness met her eyes. The April sun was slanting into the south end of the verandah. She leaned over the railing and opened her palm. Astonished, she held up the stone with her fingertips and twirled it. Seen from any angle, the stone retained within its kernel minute specks of lustrous gold.

It was on a similar morning, almost a year to the day, that Mohini had stood in the verandah on her thirteenth birthday and watched the Irani sweep the footpath in front of his

1

tea shop, the Light of India. He was leaning his broom against the wall when someone called out to him. He lifted his eyes.

Mohini turned to her right and followed his gaze. The back gate of the Marzellos' yard was wide open. Three girls whom Mohini had once met but whose names she did not know were standing on a pile of bricks inside its high compound wall, the drooping branches of a guava tree grazing their heads. Craning forward, the girls began to reel off a lengthy list to the Irani: mutton patties, chicken samosas, biscuits, eggs, bread. When the list was done, they stepped down and, stretching their arms high above their heads, gave wide, noisy yawns.

One of the girls noticed Mohini; she quickly pushed shut the gate, but not before darting at Mohini a self-conscious grin, her fingers tucking behind her ears the uncombed hair that fell to her waist. Mohini raised her hand in greeting and turned away.

Across the lane from Koleshwar Nivas, the Kulkarni sisters were standing on the footpath in front of their house. They were holding out something in Mohini's direction. "Come and show me!" she called out to them. They raced across Mohur Lane, opened Mohini's gate, and placed two items on the railing. Before she could speak, they hurried back and disappeared around the side of their house. Mohini looked down. On the railing were two shiny cups fashioned from frangipani leaves, their conical shape held together by slim sticks that had been whittled down at both ends.

Mohini's mother, Kamala, came out on the verandah. "Whom were you talking to?" she asked.

"Mina and Nina. Where's Guruji? I didn't see him this morning."

Kale Guruji was the priest who performed the daily religious service, the puja, in a spacious room that housed the family deities.

"He's coming late today. Your grandfather said he would sit for the Satya Narayan Puja at nine o'clock, after you have left for school." Kamala held out her hand. "Breakfast is ready," she said.

Mohini took in a deep breath. "Is it banana leaves I'm smelling, roasting on a griddle?"

"Bayabai has made your favourite—savoury rice pancakes."

Mohini placed one hand in her mother's and balanced on her other palm the two cups that weighed almost nothing.

On the way to school, just after Mohini had crossed Ranade Road Extension, Hansa appeared from behind a parked car. "I've been waiting and waiting!" she complained, a wide smile on her face. "I thought you would never come." She was holding her arms behind her back and now instructed Mohini to close her eyes. After lifting Mohini's hands, she pressed something into each palm. Mohini looked down. In her right hand was a picture of Lord Ganapati, His squinting eyes small and benign, and on her left palm a pinkish stone the size of a walnut.

"Hold it up," Hansa said, pointing to the stone.

Inside were nestled thread-like veins, scarlet-coloured and branched.

Hansa was disappointed. "But my uncle told me it would sparkle in the sun."

"It's still beautiful."

"Really?"

Mohini nodded. She began to undo the buckles of her satchel.

"What are you looking for?"

"My science book."

Hansa took Mohini's satchel from her shoulder and knelt down. After removing the book, she handed it to Mohini. Mohini placed Ganapati's picture between its pages and gave it back to Hansa. She slipped the stone into her uniform pocket, handling it gently as though it were a charm.

"I'll polish it after school for you," Hansa said, standing up.

When Mohini walked out of the gate at the end of school, Balu, their servant, was waiting outside. She handed him her satchel and asked why he had come to fetch her. "Your mother said to bring your friend Hansa home for tea," he said.

"I already asked." Mohini smiled at Hansa, who was trying to hang her satchel from the top of her head.

When Balu held out his hand, Hansa hesitated.

"Give it to him," Mohini said. "Look at your hair! It's all messed up now."

Hansa obliged.

Balu walked away, one satchel hanging from each arm.

Hansa looked at Mohini.

"What?" Mohini asked.

"Your body is tilting to the left today. More than usual."

"Do you think so?" Mohini placed her feet together and looked down at her knees. The left knee was flexed forward as it always was. She shut one eye. Hansa was right. It did seem to be jutting out more than usual. It was many years since that knee had started to buckle; since her body, in response to the slow collapse of that joint, had begun to lean away from its centre of gravity.

"Do you want to hold my hand?" Hansa asked.

"No," Mohini said. "Just don't walk too quickly or I shan't be able to keep up."

They started north on Mohur Lane, in the direction of Shivaji Park. Mohini removed the stone from her pocket and passed it to Hansa, who rubbed it against her skirt all the way to Koleshwar Nivas.

On arriving home, the girls found Mohini's grandfather, Vishnupant, sitting in the front verandah. He was tapping his pen against a thick notebook that lay open on his lap. Mohini asked what he was writing. "The usual," he replied. "The jumbled state of affairs in this great country of ours." He looked at Hansa. "And how is Hansa-phansa-chi-bhaji today?" he said. As always, Vishnupant's pet name for Hansa made her giggle. Mohini stepped forward to read what her grandfather had written.

Hansa tugged on Mohini's uniform. "Let's go," she mumbled, looking sideways into the house. Mohini knew that Hansa felt intimidated by Vishnupant. At the beginning, when they had just become friends, Mohini had asked Hansa why Vishnupant scared her so. Hansa had taken her time replying. "It's because he is bald," she said. "It makes him look too strict."

Mohini had laughed. "Don't be silly. What is there about a hairless head that makes you scared?"

It was only after his retirement from Bombay University

that Vishnupant had reverted to shaving his crown while retaining his Brahmin's topknot, which sprouted densely from the back of his head. Observing him from every angle, Mohini began to see how Vishnupant's tonsured head might be, for Hansa, a daunting sight. His features appeared prominent because of it, and when seen in profile, not only did his oval eyes protrude, but his knuckled nose pushed forward massively from his face; his lips appeared full where his long and abundant moustache all but covered his mouth.

"Go on in," he said now. "Your mother is waiting for you."

Even as Mohini and Hansa washed their hands at the basin, the deep-fried fragrance of potato and spicy batter wafted into the corridor.

After paying their respects to Lord Satya Narayan in the puja room, they sat at the dining table and waited for Kamala. She walked in slowly, bearing shallow bowls on which were placed steaming potato fritters. "Bayabai is frying them fresh for you," she said. "When these are finished, she will bring out more." Kamala called out to Bayabai, their cook, to take some out to Vishnupant.

Standing in the doorway of the dining room, Bayabai asked Kamala whether she might serve her as well.

"I'll eat later, with Mohini's father." She poured herself a cup of tea and watched Hansa and Mohini as they ate silently, dipping the fritters into the green coconut chutney, hurriedly taking big gulps of water whenever they bit into a particularly pungent chili.

Hansa pushed away her plate and slumped back against her chair. "I can barely move, I've eaten so much," she said.

"It's better, then, that you lie down," Kamala replied.

Mohini and Hansa went upstairs. When they heard the scrape of a chair in the room adjacent to Mohini's bedroom, they hurried forward. "You're home early, Baba!" Mohini said, sticking her head around the interconnecting door.

Keshav, Mohini's father, was at his desk. He swung around and held out his arms. Mohini went over and hugged him. "It is your birthday, is it not? And how is Hansa-phansa-chi-bhaji?"

"Not you as well, Baba," Mohini said.

"How was school?"

"Hansa got the second-highest marks in arithmetic and I was one mark behind."

"Still want to be an engineer when you grow up, Hansa?"

"Yes," she said.

Keshav removed the loosened necktie from around his neck and handed it to Mohini. He picked up his drafting pencil, which had fallen to the ground, then turned to the papers on his desk. Mohini undid the knot before tossing the tie onto his bed.

"Before you leave," Keshav said to her, "tell Balu to bring up my coat. My fountain pen is in the inner pocket."

Mohini looked at Hansa.

Hansa nodded and then ran to the back verandah, calling out to Balu to fetch Keshavkaka his coat. When she returned to Mohini's room, Mohini was balancing the carom board on top of two dictionaries she had placed on the spare bed.

"Why don't we sit on the floor?" Hansa suggested. "The board wobbles too much on the mattress."

"Because," Mohini reminded her, "after two minutes on the floor my legs start to fall asleep."

Hansa helped Mohini arrange the black and white wooden discs on the carom board, the two colours alternating in concentric rings outside the single red disc, the queen.

When Balu came into the room and opened Mohini's wardrobe, she asked, "What are you looking for?"

"Keshav Sahib's black coat."

"In my wardrobe?"

Lowering his voice, he said, "I can't find it."

"Baba!" Mohini called out. "Where did you put your coat when you came in?"

"I handed it to Balu."

Balu's eyes widened and he shook his head.

"He says not."

"Balu!" Keshav thundered. A pigeon roosting on the window next to his desk lost its footing and fluttered away.

Mohini got off the bed and went into her father's bedroom. Balu followed her and stood in front of the desk, slumped as though someone had placed a weight on his shoulders. Hansa sidled in through the door and sat behind Mohini, on Kamala's bed.

Keshav asked Balu in a stern voice, "Did I not give you the coat when I came home?"

Balu's chin dropped to his chest.

"Just answer Baba," Mohini whispered.

"Ji, Sahib . . . that is, no, Sahib."

"What nonsense are you talking? I handed you my coat on the stairs. I said to take some money from my pocket and get Mohini salty biscuits from the Irani because it is her birthday."

Balu cocked his head, his expression supplicating as though hoping for some hint that would allow him to understand what Keshav Sahib was saying. He looked beseechingly at Kamala, who had just walked in through the doorway of the sewing room.

She looked at Keshav. "I didn't know you were home," she said. "When did you come?"

"I didn't know Keshav Sahib had returned from work either," Balu muttered.

Mohini turned around and looked at Hansa. It was as though Koleshwar Nivas had turned into a ghost house. People had become invisible to one another. Objects too: the black coat had gone missing.

"When did you come home?" Kamala repeated.

"Three-thirty or thereabouts," Keshav said, his tone beginning to echo the uncertainty in the room. "Madanlal driver dropped me home, then went to Bandra to drop Tambe."

"But our school bell rings at three-thirty," Mohini said. "And Balu came to fetch me from school today." She looked at Kamala and told her about the missing coat.

Keshav almost shouted, "What does she mean, Kamala, that Balu wasn't even here when I came home?"

"It means," Kamala answered quietly, "that you handed your coat to someone else." She looked at Balu and inclined her head in the direction of the door. He hurriedly left the room.

Before she could ask Hansa and Mohini to leave, Mohini said, "But whom could Baba have given the coat to?"

"Tell me, Kamala," Keshav challenged her. He was drumming rapidly with his fingers the blotting paper on his desk.

"Someone must have followed you into the house," Hansa offered. Her voice was scratchy; her throat dry because she had kept her mouth closed for so long.

Mohini gave her an encouraging smile and nodded for her to continue.

Hansa swallowed. "You said you were on the stairs, Keshavkaka. So if you had stretched back your arm and handed over your coat without turning around, you would not have seen who was behind you."

"That's the only logical explanation I can think of," Keshav said, taking off his glasses.

Hansa blushed, pleased that her interpretation had been so readily accepted.

"But who could it have been?" Mohini said.

"Don't keep saying, 'but who,' Mohini!" Keshav's tone was irritable. "And as soon as I have an answer, you will be the first to know."

Hansa poked Mohini in the back and they stood up quickly.

No sooner had she clicked shut the door than she whispered to Mohini, "Do you think there was a lot of money in the wallet?" Mohini shook her head while pushing forward her lower lip. Hansa gathered the carom pieces off the board, returned them to the tin box, and left for home.

When Keshav opened the interconnecting door, he saw Mohini was reading from the dictionary. He sat beside her and lifted her left foot onto his knee, gently pulling on her toes until the bones clicked. "Feels good?" he asked.

Mohini nodded. "What are you thinking about, Baba?"

"How there was no hair on your head when I first saw you. You were fair-skinned, just like your mother. I remember wondering, Who will she resemble when she grows up? Whom will this little bundle turn out to be like?"

"And?"

"My mother. You are very much like her. That same curiosity, that same quick mind."

"Vishnupant says I am too."

"Which reminds me," Keshav said, standing up. "Don't mention the coat business to your grandfather. I don't want to worry him. And you better change out of your uniform. Your Vasantiatya must be waiting for you. I heard the front gate creak just as I came into your room."

When Mohini went downstairs, Vasanti, Keshav, and Vishnupant were sitting in the front verandah. Vasanti stood up and held Mohini close. "Happy birthday," she whispered into her niece's ear. She sat down again and pulled Mohini onto her lap. "I wanted to come this morning, before you left for school, but Bebitai was especially slow in getting ready for her bath."

Mohini leaned back against her aunt. "I looked in through your window about seven o' clock. Mai was sitting on the divan reading the newspaper. You were nowhere to be seen."

Vasanti lived on the ground floor of Shiv Sadan, a block of flats situated to the right of Mina and Nina's house, which was diagonally across the lane from Koleshwar Nivas. Vasanti was Vishnupant's niece, the twenty-four-year-old daughter of his deceased younger brother, Sitarampant. She lived at Shiv Sadan with her aunts: Mai, who was deaf, and Bebitai, who was excruciatingly slow.

Vishnupant looked at Mohini and told her that a long letter had arrived from Calcutta that morning. "All of them," he added. "Nandini, your cousin Hema, and your uncle Raghunathrao—all of them wish you a very happy birthday."

"What else did Nandini write?" Keshav asked. His sister, Nandini, was his elder by three years.

"It appears Raghunathrao is facing some labour problems at Carleton Engineering Works," Vishnupant said.

"What kind of problems this time?"

"The workers are demanding an Independence Day bonus and the directors of the company are refusing to pay it."

"What Independence Day bonus?" Keshav said. "We aren't even independent yet. When Atlee made his announcement, he said that the British would pull out of India no later than the middle of next year. Do the workers think that May 1947 has somehow become June 1948?"

"Nevertheless, they have declared a strike until the Independence Day bonus is granted."

"Hm," Keshav said. "Someone at my office did say that the situation with the unions in Calcutta is particularly bad. The workers when they want something invoke Gandhiji's name and threaten to go on a fast or declare a peaceful sit-in until management gives in to their demands."

"Strikes, hartals, processions, passive resistance, non-cooperation, civil disobedience—these measures may have been all right when we used them against the British, but if we continue to use them, you mark my words, these so-called non-violent demonstrations will one day backfire and we will be ruled by anarchy." Vishnupant had a deep-seated aversion towards any form of law-breaking.

Laying her palms against Mohini's back, Vasanti whispered that she would go into the kitchen to help Kamala with the birthday dinner. Mohini stood up quickly. She knew that her aunt wished to escape the ensuing discussion. Whenever Vishnupant pontificated on history or politics, he forgot two things: that he was not in a lecture hall, and that those listening to him were not his students.

Keshav clicked his tongue as Mohini sat back in the chair left vacant by her aunt. "I agree with you, but it is not so simple, Baba," he said. "Don't forget that these workers have been exploited for generations. It is only natural that they protest. Take Raghunathrao's Carleton Engineering Works. At twenty-five years of age, a British engineer who comes from England hasn't set foot in India for one month before he is able to rent spacious accommodation, hire a bearer, a gardener, an errand boy, and a cook. And don't forget the barber and tailor who pay him house visits." Keshav looked at Mohini, who was tossing the stone Hansa had given her into the air and raising her cupped hands to catch it as it plummeted down. "The workers, who contribute to this luxury, are not blind," Keshav continued. "How can they be when at night they return to their tin shacks and four children and rice bins that rattle because it is nearing the end of the month? Everyone says our workers are lazy and I will be the first to agree. But would not the British engineer be lazy too if he, like them, received a pittance for his services?"

Vishnupant had been nodding in agreement. "Nevertheless," he said now. "An independent India must start off on the right foot."

Mohini rose and moved to the edge of the verandah. She held up the stone and rotated it against the light. One side of it was blunt and slightly pitted, but she only had to twist it by a fraction of an inch before the scarlet veins appeared. She heard the sound of a car door being slammed and recognized Dr. Chitnis's dry cough even before she saw him walk into the car porch. He was running his hands through his hair. She smiled. "Dr. Chitnis is here," she said.

Vishnupant turned around. "Sit, Gokul," he said, pointing to a chair just as Dr. Chitnis approached.

"Not today, Professor," Dr. Chitnis said. "I came to wish Mohini a happy birthday and to eat some Satya Narayan prasad." He looked at Mohini.

She moved forward and led him through the house into the puja room. The metallic smell of tarnished silver mixed in with melted camphor filled the air. The flame of the silver oil lamp was short and steady. Rose petals were heaped on the etched black stone symbol of Lord Vishnu. There were yellow marigolds at the feet of all the deities, and on the wall, on the glass-fronted picture of Brahma, Vishnu, and Mahesh, was a thick paste of red kunku, yellow turmeric, and rice dotted onto their foreheads. Dr. Chitnis joined his hands together and did namaskar. After removing a rupee note from his pocket, he placed it carefully on top of the rose-covered heap. The money slid to the ground. He lowered himself on his knees and touched his forehead to the floor. After he stood up, he cupped his right hand over his left to receive the prasad, the sweet offering Mohini was waiting to serve him. She spooned into his palm from a large serving bowl a generous amount of the semolina preparation.

Dr. Chitnis had finished eating when Kamala walked in. He said to her, "This is delicious—in keeping with your usual standards."

Kamala said to Mohini, "Give him some more in a bowl."

"There's no need for a bowl," Dr. Chitnis said. He cupped his hands one more time. When Mohini offered him a third palmful, he declined, and left the room to wash his hands. On his return he said, "You were so tiny when you were born, Mohini, that I could hold all of you in just one hand." He flexed his right elbow and unclenched his fist.

"Do you remember, Kamalavahini?" he asked. "How I would point out to Mohini the bougainvillea in the terrace in order to calm her down."

Mohini smiled and placed the serving bowl on the windowsill. She went and stood next to Kamala. "Do you remember, Aai?" she asked.

Kamala ran the back of her fingers against Mohini's cheek and said, "What don't I remember!"

"Your mother and I," Dr. Chitnis declared as he and Mohini walked to the front verandah, "we remember everything, every small detail, and one day I would like to tell you just how much trouble you really were."

TWO

Some thirteen years earlier, the first thing that Dr. Chitnis had noticed about Kamala when she had walked into his consultation rooms were her small, shell-like ears. Her face was framed by thick, wavy hair that lay knotted in a bun at the base of her neck. Her complexion was pale and waxy. When Vishnupant, Dr. Chitnis's bridge partner at the Dadar West Gymkhana, had asked him to see Kamala because she had suffered two miscarriages and was feeling quite ill during this pregnancy, he had expected to see a woman whose eyes were clouded by fatigue. Instead, her expression had been alert, and there was neither tiredness nor resignation in the way she carried her slight body. There were barely any traces of a pregnancy, which made him conclude that the fetus inside her must be like its mother: compact and small. And, while he was examining her, he had a sudden premonition that this time the baby would be carried to term. He was a man of science and this presentiment took him by surprise.

Kamala had been in labour for forty-two hours when Keshav went to fetch Dr. Chitnis from the Hindu Gymkhana at Marine Drive, eight miles south of Shivaji

Park. The doctor was in the shade of its verandah, his shin guards fastened, and watching in horror even as his batting team lost three wickets—click, click, click, one after the other—in less than half an hour. When Vasanti, Keshav's eleven-year-old cousin from Poona, tapped him on the waist, he turned around. She led him to the end of the verandah and pointed to Keshav, who was sitting behind the steering wheel of a second-hand Morris Minor that Vishnupant had only recently purchased. He had kept its engine running. Relieved at the opportunity to leave, Dr. Chitnis quickly unstrapped his shin guards. He slid into the front seat next to Keshav, and after settling Vasanti on his lap, he said, "Nothing can reverse the fortunes of a team that wields a bat as though it were a fly swatter."

At Koleshwar Nivas, Kamala lay on a cot in the spare room upstairs. The brightness in her eyes was considerably dimmed. "It won't be too long now," Dr. Chitnis assured her after he had finished his examination. She turned away in disbelief and looked out the terrace door, her hair drenched in perspiration.

Mohini was born within the hour, her soft mewling a relief after Kamala's lengthy labour, during which she had clenched her teeth in order not to utter a single sound.

Mohini was a tiny baby, her fingers and toes like bleached twigs, her head no bigger than the width of Dr. Chitnis's cupped hands. She is not overly small, he assured the Oek family, as he ushered them into the birthing room after it had been cleaned. They moved forward quickly— Vishnupant, Keshav, Bayabai, and Balu—and peered into the cradle that Vasanti was gently rocking.

When Balu lifted one arm cautiously to clutch its side, Vasanti glared at him and made as though to brush away his hand. "Let him rock at least once or twice," Bayabai muttered angrily. "He's one year younger than you and just as curious." But Vasanti was unmoved. She drew back the cradle beyond his reach and held it there.

Dr. Chitnis gently lifted the sleeping Mohini and placed her in the crook of Vishnupant's arms. After Keshav had had his turn, he handed Mohini to Kamala's mother, Umabai, who had come to Bombay from Poona for her daughter's delivery. After instructing Mohini's grandmother that she should now coach Kamala on how to nurse and burp the baby, Dr. Chitnis indicated for everyone else to follow him downstairs.

Kamala, her recent exhaustion momentarily forgotten, unswaddled Mohini from the cotton quilt in which she had been loosely wrapped. She smoothed the soft, bald head with her lips, then traced with her fingertips the tributaries of Mohini's veins. Aided by her mother, she sat up in bed and undid the knot that fastened her blouse. She held the small head against her breast and followed her mother's instructions in an effort to get her baby to feed. But Mohini proved difficult to nurse. Kamala wondered whether she was doing something wrong. Umabai said that it was only a matter of persisting before the goal would be achieved. But Mohini remained restless. Instead of holding still, she squirmed this way, then that, and within moments turned away from Kamala in a fretful manner.

On the second morning after Mohini's birth, Kamala said, "Perhaps she has a very small appetite and only needs a few drops at a time."

Umabai lifted Mohini from Kamala's arms. She placed her granddaughter on the adjacent cot and rubbed warmed oil into her unformed limbs, then kneaded gently her tender flesh. She ran her fingertips along the ridges of her body and finished the massage by pouring a few drops into the soft concavity on top of her delicate head. But right from that first week, no matter how gentle Umabai's touch, no matter that she added to the oil aromatic ingredients designed to soothe, Mohini would not be comforted. She fretted incessantly, her high-pitched cries radiating into every corner of Koleshwar Nivas and even spilling out into the road.

As the days passed, Kamala sat helplessly on her cot while her mother walked Mohini up and down the room, holding against her shoulder the newborn face that was narrow and pinched, the waving fists clenched so tight that they reminded Kamala of unopened buds doing a dance in the face of a hurricane.

During the ensuing weeks, so ceaseless was Mohini's crying, so indifferent her appetite and so sleepless her nights that Kamala's swollen breasts began to wither. Umabai fetched from downstairs a small silver bowl half filled with warmed milk. She handed Kamala a shallow, rounded spoon, its edges thick and blunted and, after placing Mohini on Kamala's lap, instructed her on how to hold the small head at an angle before carefully placing the edge of the spoon against the puckered mouth. Mohini took to the spoon instantly. However, the crying that was thought to have been induced by hunger did not stop.

After Umabai returned to Poona, Dr. Chitnis got his wife, Sheelatai, to massage Mohini's small body to release any gases that might have accumulated within. Mohini quietened down initially, perhaps distracted by the unfamiliar touch, but within no time grew agitated once again. Five months later, when the intermittent fever that had troubled her since her birth peaked to a new level and remained there without dropping, Dr. Chitnis suggested that they take her to a child specialist.

From Shivaji Park, Keshav, Kamala, Mohini, and Dr. Chitnis travelled twelve miles south to Dr. Merchant's consultation rooms in Colaba. They could hear the high tide lapping against the restraining wall even as they got out of the car and entered his rooms. A shaft of sunlight coming through the window illuminated his mounted certificates. On the opposite wall hung a framed photograph of him paying homage to a laughing Gandhi. In one corner stood an intricately carved, paper-filled, glass-fronted cupboard that almost reached the ceiling. When Dr. Chitnis held Mohini up and pointed to her reflection, she gurgled, the single curl above her broad forehead rising like a wave.

After a long wait they were summoned into the inner room. The walls were lined with wooden panels that would likely become swollen in the monsoon rains. Dr. Merchant came from behind his desk. He was a tall, bony man, his dark-skinned face pockmarked and uneven. He held out his hands for Mohini. She seemed comfortable in his embrace as he walked her to the weighing scale.

Kamala reminded herself to speak up and answer clearly if Dr. Merchant asked her any questions. But the doctor did not look at her, and after he had finished taking Mohini's pulse and examining her reflexes, he told Keshav and Kamala to wait outside. He continued to hold Mohini in his arms. Uncertain, Kamala looked at Dr. Chitnis. Dr. Chitnis inclined his head slightly in the direction of the waiting room, his expression uncharacteristically formal. Kamala followed Keshav outside. They stood at the window. The ocean was heaving, its skin wrinkled and grey. Kamala pulled the end of her sari over her right shoulder. Her arms felt empty. After what seemed like a long time, Dr. Chitnis came out carrying Mohini. There was a sticking plaster in the shape of a diamond attached to the heel of her left foot. She slid easily into Kamala's arms and rested her head in the crook of her collarbone. "Good baby," Kamala cooed into her ear, "good baby, so well behaved for the doctor."

Dr. Chitnis waited until after they were seated in the car, then said, "We'll have to interpret the results of the blood test before we know what is wrong with her."

"How long will that take?" Keshav asked.

"About a week, I should think."

But within five days Dr. Chitnis came to Koleshwar Nivas and informed Kamala that Dr. Merchant had asked for another blood sample. This time Mohini was irritable. Watching Dr. Chitnis open his bag, Kamala wondered whether she could bring Mohini to his clinic at a later time, when she was feeling more settled. But Dr. Chitnis shook his head. He handed Balu a steel box containing his implements and told him to thoroughly sterilize its contents. When Dr. Chitnis came back a third time to draw more blood, Kamala asked him what was the need for so many samples. Without looking at her, he muttered something about hemoglobin, then tucked the vial of freshly drawn blood into the inner pocket of his coat.

Finally, after what seemed like an interminable wait, Dr. Merchant was ready to see them again. This time Dr. Chitnis askéd Vishnupant to come along. They sat in a semicircle in front of Dr. Merchant's desk; Mohini was once again in his arms. He informed them that she suffered from a hereditary congenital blood disease called Cooley's anemia. There was silence in the room. They looked at him without comprehension. "What that means," Dr. Merchant said, "is that her body does not produce enough hemoglobin. In layman's terms, hemoglobin is what gives our red blood cells their colour. Also, it is hemoglobin that carries oxygen to the rest of the body. So, a shortage of hemoglobin means that Mohini's organs are not getting the oxygen they need." He held up in front of Mohini his stethoscope, towards which she had been straining. She grasped it firmly and brought it to her mouth.

"Then what do we do?" Vishnupant said. "What medicine do you suggest?"

"Cooley's anemia cannot be cured. The longevity of the patient is anywhere up to three years," Dr. Merchant said. "Sometimes, in rare cases, it can be slightly longer." He fought the urge to look away as those seated in front of him were shocked into sudden silence. Vishnupant shut his eyes. Kamala looked at Mohini, who let go of the stethoscope and held out her arms. Kamala lifted her from the doctor's lap and sat back in the chair. When she turned to Keshav there was a frightened and wounded look in her eyes. Keshav glanced at her helplessly then leaned across and stroked Mohini's head. Mohini smiled at him. Vishnupant opened his eyes and nodded for Dr. Merchant to continue.

Dr. Merchant cleared his throat and said, "Cooley's anemia is treatable. We can administer blood transfusions that will slightly elevate Mohini's hemoglobin levels. The transfusions could be weekly, fortnightly, even monthly."

The curtain behind him ruffled and there was a brief smell of ether in the room. Dr. Merchant came round from behind his desk and lifted Mohini into his arms. He sat back in his chair.

Keshav was the first to speak. "What about iron?" he said. "I know our ayurvedic doctor told my mother to feed me lots of lentils and foods rich in iron when I was a little boy."

"An iron-rich diet was sufficient for you, Mr. Oek, because you are only a carrier of the disease. Mohini's bone marrow, however, does not have the ability to absorb iron. On the contrary, in patients like her, excess iron that is not absorbed by the blood has a tendency to accumulate in the heart. Also in the pancreas and other organs. In short, all over the body."

Vishnupant sat forward in his chair. "When will the first transfusion be?"

"As soon as we have drawn some of her blood and found a matching donor."

"Take my blood, or Keshav's," Vishnupant offered.

"Mr. Keshav's definitely won't do," Dr. Merchant said. "Cooley's anemia is caused when both parents have the same Cooley's trait, when both are carriers of the disease. For Mr. Keshav to have a Cooley's trait, his mother might have been a carrier or you may be a carrier. In any case, I would prefer not to use your blood, Professor, even if it is a match. Mohini may need weekly transfusions and what we really need to find is a pool of suitable donors. Gokul," he said, turning to Dr. Chitnis, "bring Mohini here for the first few transfusions. I will ask Dr. Mahajan, who has more experience than me at giving transfusions, to administer them. His rooms are adjacent to mine. Over time you will be able to do the transfusions yourself. The procedure is quite straightforward." He removed the stethoscope from Mohini's grasp and in its stead gave her the end of his necktie. She inserted this into her mouth.

Kamala looked on in horror as she willed Mohini to release the tie before it could get wet and sticky and before it could transfer its germs to her.

Dr. Merchant walked them to their car and handed Mohini to Kamala only after she was seated inside. On the journey back to Koleshwar Nivas, Kamala held Mohini across her lap. The motion of the car lulled the baby into a quiet sleep.

Keshav clutched the wheel of the car as he concentrated on the road and Vishnupant rubbed the back of his neck in the seat next to him. Dr. Chitnis, who was sitting behind Vishnupant, looked out the window. At Walkeshwar, the sinking sun cast a saffron mantle on the ornate stone buildings that faced the sea. Kamala caressed the soft curls on Mohini's head and concentrated on directing the flow of her tears into her throat, the effort causing her to tremble.

They were almost home, at Worli Naka, when dusk turned rapidly to night. Kamala shuddered and averted her eyes from the car window: hidden inside the thick, uneven shrubbery at the side of the road, it was as though unfathomable, untameable beasts were crouched, waiting to be released.

As Keshav pulled up in front of Dr. Chitnis's house on the north side of Shivaji Park, Kamala transferred Mohini to her shoulder. She was awake. Dr. Chitnis said, "Dr.

Merchant is no doubt the expert and I will be taking all my directions from him. However, Mohini is my patient and the ultimate responsibility for her treatment rests with me. There is much that Dr. Merchant has suggested I read and research. I intend to do so." He held out his hand in Mohini's direction. She grabbed it. After gently extricating his fingers, he got out of the car and walked around it to stand by Keshav's window. "You will need to get a telephone installed," he said. "One other thing. Any time of the day or night, if you or Kamalavahini need anything, call me. I'll come as soon as I am able."

Dr. Chitnis was as good as his word. The transfusions were usually scheduled for the morning, and more often than not, Madanlal, Keshav's office driver, would take Kamala and Mohini to Dr. Mahajan's rooms. However, if Keshav was away on site, assigned to the building of this bridge or that canal or causeway, Dr. Chitnis would bring around his car and accompany them to the appointment. If Kamala was feeding Mohini or changing her, he would wait patiently in the front verandah until they were ready to leave. The journey to Dr. Mahajan's in Colaba became a familiar one. Kamala joined her hands together in front of every temple they passed along the way. There were six of them, and after the first few trips, her gesture became mechanical.

Dr. Mahajan was a quiet man with a nervous habit of rubbing the tips of thumb and forefinger together when speaking to his assistant. His hand was accurate and steady, however, when he inserted the needle into Mohini's vein. He was a collector of miniature cars and would line them alongside her body to distract her before leaving the room to return to his microscope. Through the glass-fronted observation window in the wall Kamala could see him, hunched over his instrument, legs wrapped around the lower rungs of a high stool. Every ten minutes or so, his assistant would walk to Mohini's bedside and examine the inside of her elbow, afterwards checking the inverted bottle of blood to make sure its contents were emptying into Mohini's body at the desired pace. When the bottle was almost empty, Dr. Mahajan would leave his perch, and after stretching his cramped legs, he would remove the needle from Mohini's vein. Then, after the assistant had cleared away the transfusion equipment, the doctor would choose the biggest toy car from her bed and proceed to run it over her forehead, neck, and scalp because he had seen Kamala do that once, when Mohini had suffered from a headache. His silence was a comfortable silence, and Mohini would be lulled into compliance by the unhurried way in which Dr. Mahajan attended to her. When he was certain that there was no likelihood of an adverse reaction to the transfusion, he would lift Mohini into his arms and place in her hand a yellow banana, its bright skin unblemished and smooth.

On the way home, pressing her child's body against her own, Kamala would join her hands once again in front of the temples and thank God not only for creating doctors but also for making them available to Mohini in her frequent hours of need.

It took many months for Kamala to understand the extent of Mohini's disease. When she shared her fears with Keshav, he would listen to her patiently, then shake his head in regret because he had no answers. He would coax her to lie down when he found her sitting up in bed in the middle of the night, and would take her into his arms until her sobbing had subsided and her breathing had returned to normal. His work took him to the rural areas quite frequently and soon Kamala found herself sharing with him only the hopeful and wondrous details: Mohini's alert and smiling response when anyone in the household spoke to her; her quick transition from crawling to standing to taking her first step; the fearless and trusting way in which she greeted her doctors.

Knowing that she would have to accept her daughter's condition sooner rather than later, Kamala told herself to focus only on the things she could do in order to make Mohini's life as comfortable as possible. But early one morning, when dawn was breaking in the east, with Mohini fast asleep on the cot beside her, Kamala took a piece of paper and wrote out the questions that were the most difficult to ignore. Why was this happening? Why had her child been singled out in such a cruel way? And what if one day she woke only to discover that all her dedication and resolve were not nearly enough to alleviate the pain and hardship Mohini was destined to suffer? After she had finished writing out the questions, Kamala crumpled the piece of paper as she walked into the terrace. She placed it on the swing and put a lit match to it, and when there were only ashes left, she scattered them into the air and watched them disappear.

She took another piece of paper and began to jot down the less painful questions that swirled inside her head regarding this or that aspect of Mohini's anemia. A few weeks later, she asked Dr. Chitnis if she could read the notes he was compiling in a book marked "Mohini, Mohur Lane." The answers to all her medical concerns, she thought, could be found within.

But Dr. Chitnis shook his head and told her that the
notes would be of no use to her because they were written
in English. "And no, Kamalavahini," he added, "I do not
have time to translate them into Marathi." He was ten years
her senior and, although he addressed her as "vahini,"
sister-in-law, his manner towards her was avuncular.

That night, in the privacy of Keshav and Kamala's bedroom, the door to the adjacent room open only a slit so as not
to disturb Mohini while she slept, Kamala sat on Keshav's
bed and asked him if he would translate Dr. Chitnis's notes
for her. Keshav removed his glasses. He ran his fingers
through his hair so it stood up on his scalp in a way that had
once endeared him to her but that she was now too preoccu-
pied to notice. He took her hand and said that she should
learn English, that it would be the simpler thing to do.

She looked at him in astonishment, searching his face
for something that might have alerted her to his casual
confidence in her ability to learn a foreign tongue. She
curled her fingers against his palm.

He reached for her other hand and brought it to his
cheek. His dark skin was warm and elastic. "What?" he said.

"Nothing," she murmured. She placed her thumbs gently in the shallow pockets underneath his eyes. Looking
into his face, she smoothed away the lines she knew were a
result of reading too long and too often under inadequate
light. It was not so long ago that she had caught him on the
swing, peering into his book under the sheen of the full
moon, one hand absentmindedly holding Mohini's shoulder so she would not tumble off his lap. She removed her
hands from his face and sat back on her own bed. "Will you
teach me English?"

"Yes. But you'll have to teach yourself as well, Kamale," he said, using his private affectionate name for her.

Kamala nodded. "Of course."

Keshav said, "You amaze me. It's only a minute ago that I suggest you learn English, and I can already see the determination in your eyes. Now that that's settled, come back here." He moved over on the mattress in order to make place for her.

She once again sat on his bed.

"Can't you sleep here tonight?" he said.

When she was silent, he gently pulled on her earlobe. "Now tell me the truth. Your bed here, in our room, isn't it much more comfortable than the cot in Mohini's room?" There was a beseeching look in his eyes. He removed the pins from her hair so it slid down into his open hands. She didn't move. He tugged on it gently until she was facing him on the pillow. "No answer to my question means you'll stay?" She continued to look at him. He pulled her by the hip until her lower body was touching his. He nuzzled his mouth between her breasts, prying loose with his teeth the hooks of her sari blouse. "Well?" He lifted his head just as she was stretching her hand towards the lamp to turn it off.

Kamala proved to be a diligent student. When the burden of having to watch Mohini suffer through yet another transfusion, another headache, another temperature spike became too heavy, she would lighten it by getting lost in letters and words that, as the weeks went by, began to take on meaning and sound.

A few months later, when Dr. Chitnis saw her sitting cross-legged on the swing in the terrace, Mohini on her lap, an open *Free Press Journal* clutched high in front of her face where Mohini could not reach it, he was impressed. He said he would hand over his medical notes on Mohini any time Kamala wished to see them. He complimented her on her doggedness, adding in his customary, jocular fashion, "I will tell my wife that she should take a page out of your book."

When Mohini was five years old, Vishnupant decided to relinquish his university position. Those around him suspected that he wanted to spend more time with Mohini, who had lived longer than anyone had dared hope. Vishnupant maintained that he wished to retire in order to give undivided attention to a book that it was his dream to write, a definitive tome entitled *India After 1920*.

The current group of leaders steering the National Congress party, he felt, had come into prominence only around the year 1920 when Lokamanya Tilak, an early pioneer of the nationalistic movement, had died. Vishnupant saw in his retirement the opportunity, through study and examination, to understand more closely why the National Congress party had failed to achieve freedom after nearly twenty years of agitation.

The Congress party, he knew, believed in non-violence. However, passive resistance, in order to be an effective tool, implied resistance to existing rules and regulations, law and order, the normal functioning of provincial ministries, the regular flow of trade. When Vishnupant contemplated the "non-cooperation" ideas and techniques of agitation favoured by the Congress party, he wondered whether there was something in the Indian spirit that was by nature anarchic.

Yes, he told his students, he wanted the British gone, but he also wanted them to leave behind constitutional reforms that would embed into a free India the ideals of equality contained within progressive Western thought. He asked his students, Are not the spread of literacy, the acquisition of the basic principles of health and sanitation, the techniques of administration and governance, the study of advanced technology, are not all these equally worthy of non-violent agitation? Why limit the freedom movement only to self-rule? But in order to widen the present scope of the struggle, he continued, there would have to be a major transformation in policy. The use of *non-*, with all its negative connotations, would have to be dropped. Cooperation would have to replace non-cooperation, obedience disobedience, and non-violent demonstrations would have to give way to active compromise.

A historian, Vishnupant reminded his students, was not simply a person who recorded events but, more important, was one who brought critical analysis to bear upon any such compilation.

And so, after a career that had spanned over thirty years, he now devoted his mornings to the writing of his book. Sometimes, if there was research to be done, he would take the early train to the Royal Asiatic Society Library and lunch at Kamat Café before returning to Koleshwar Nivas in time for his afternoon nap. A month after establishing his new routine, he summoned Kamala to his room and said, "From today, after Mohini has finished her milk following her post-lunch nap, you will put her in my charge. You are not to worry about her for sixty minutes. This way you'll get a chance to do your embroidery or whatever you used to do in the afternoons before she was born."

Kamala did not remember one bit what she used to do with any of her time before Mohini was born. She also thought that one hour was too long and that forty-five minutes would have been enough. Nevertheless, she silently acquiesced.

The grandfather-granddaughter outing became a daily ritual. Every afternoon Vishnupant would stand Mohini out of Kamala's view on the side plinth of the car porch. Turning his back on Mohini, he would bend his knees and lower himself until she could clamber onto his shoulders with relative ease. Raising his voice to Balu—standing behind Mohini in case she was to fall—he would tell him that there was no need to accompany them to Shivaji Park. After all, Mohini was as light as a feather, and he was quite capable of catching her if she were to slide down. But Balu had received his instructions from none other than Kamala and so, keeping his distance, he would trail them mincingly until they had crossed Keluskar Road and entered Shivaji Park. When they were seated, he would place himself behind their bench, clutching in one hand an old newspaper and in the other any one of the dozens of flower-motif handkerchiefs embroidered by Kamala.

The distance between Koleshwar Nivas and the bench in Shivaji Park was a mere seven minutes, just enough for Vishnupant to relate to Mohini incidents from his childhood, and when she tired of those, to repeat yet another fable from the Akbar and Birbal tales. Balu would prick up his ears and move closer when Mohini demanded that Vishnupant tell her one. After a morning spent in taking

instructions from Bayabai, he looked forward with grinning eagerness to these afternoons. And soon, upon
listening to a few stories, he began to understand a thread
that was common to them all.

Birbal was a courtier in Emperor Akbar's court. He was
so renowned for his intelligence and quick-witted thinking that the mischievous emperor and other jealous
courtiers would pose him difficult problems in an effort to
baffle him. But Birbal was so clever that he would get out of
sticky situations time and again, thus frustrating the
scheming courtiers while at the same time gaining the
emperor's approbation and ungrudging trust.

There was one particular story that was Mohini's
favourite. She asked to hear it over and over again, playfully
tugging at Vishnupant's earlobes until he gave in. Reaching
up and clasping her hands in his, he would begin:

Once upon a time, there lived a very ugly sweeper in the
emperor's kingdom. People believed if they spotted him
first thing in the morning, they would have bad luck all
day long. One morning, when the emperor was strolling
in his garden, he came upon the sweeper, who was
performing his duties in the courtyard. That very same
day, misfortune dogged the emperor: his brother-in-law
met with an accident, a fly fell into the food he was just
about to eat, and he lost a severe argument with his
temperamental wife. Blaming the sweeper for his misfortune, the emperor condemned the ugly man to the
gallows. The ill-fated sweeper begged to see Birbal. Birbal
heard him out and gave him some advice. The next day,
when the executioner asked the sweeper to state his last

wish, the sweeper said that the emperor should also be sent to the gallows. The executioner conveyed this last request to the emperor, who stormed to the prison and asked the sweeper to explain this impertinent request. The sweeper said, "Sire, every man who lays eyes on me in the morning believes that I am the cause of his misfortune throughout the day. However, yesterday morning, when your gaze fell upon me, I looked into your face as well. And now here I am, facing the gallows because I had the misfortune of looking into your face. So, is it not fair to say that if I am to be condemned for bringing you misfortune, then the reverse must also be true?" In an instant the emperor, knowing that it was only Birbal who could have planted such an idea into the sweeper's head, ordered the condemned man to be released.

Mohini would let go of Vishnupant's neck and clap her hands at Birbal's wisdom. When this happened, Balu would hold out his arms, ready to catch her in case she lost her balance. And afterwards, when he would ask her whether she wanted to be like Birbal when she grew up, she would nod emphatically, her eyes dancing at the thought of having a mind so quick and keen.

Vishnupant's friends from Dadar West Gymkhana knew his afternoon routine and they would often seek him out on the bench in the park. As soon as Vishnupant was engaged in conversation with them, Balu would motion for Mohini to kneel next to him by the bench. He would smooth the newspaper on the grass and show her how to twist and fold it into a rat, a flower, a snake, or a boat. When her attention wandered, he would draw it back by handing her her own piece of newsprint, coaxing her into mirroring his actions as he folded the paper this way, then that.

After they were done, she would take him by the hand and pull him to the middle of the park, to the pond along the farther bank on which stood huts occupied by workers from the nearby Crown Mills. Crouched by the waterline, with Balu holding tightly the back of her frock, she would lean over and peer with wonder into the fluid surface that caught so deftly within its boundaries the fallen sky.

In the bulrushes there lived a family of ducks. If they were not out and about, Mohini would get Balu to make his duck-calls. Then, as soon as they glided out into the pond, she would hang her head upside down and watch the birds lose shape, their white bodies scattering and dancing under the water.

Sometimes the workers' children would be playing outside of their huts. Clasping their hands together and forming a long chain, they would hurry into the pond, their loud screeching and yelling almost drowned out by the sounds of splashing water. At such times Balu would hastily pull Mohini away, towards the protective presence of Vishnupant, and pinch her briskly if she strained to resume her crouched position over the water. His pinches were mere warnings, not intended to hurt. And from that safe distance she would sit on her haunches and watch the children as they jumped up and down, trailing water from their armpits to the tips of their outstretched hands so they looked like birds shedding opaque wings.

The children, ever conscious of her presence, would look in her direction as they hummed melodies and belted out rhythmic songs. They glanced at her slyly when they imitated Vishnupant's professorial manner, his echoing boom, his waving hands. They would turn away from her only when fits of laughter prevented them from imitating him further.

Mohini responded to their charades quietly, her head pushed forward in an alert manner, her occasional merriment seducing Balu into relaxing his hold.

Around the time Mohini turned six, she began to complain of a dull, heavy sensation under her left ribs. Upon examination Dr. Merchant discovered that Mohini had an enlarged spleen and recommended she undergo a splenectomy. Kamala flinched. The doctor gently reminded her that the fact that they might have to remove Mohini's spleen was a complication they had expected to face, and not quite so ominous if she were to consider that Mohini had outlived the initial prognosis by several years. Judged in that light, he said, it was a miracle that they were even having this conversation. He rang the bell for his assistant and instructed the man to fetch Kamala a glass of water. After she had finished drinking from it, he took Mohini's hand in his own and said: "The unabsorbed iron from all the transfusions she has received over the years has caused her spleen to become enlarged. Removing it, I can assure you, will not affect her health in any significant way." He lifted Mohini from the examination table and set her on her feet. "Go home, Mrs. Oek, and confer with your family, and if you decide to go ahead with the operation, let me know. I'll make arrangements for the surgeon to perform it in the operating theatre on the ground floor."

That evening, after Dr. Chitnis had hooked up the transfusion apparatus and slid the needle into Mohini's vein, Kamala looked at him and inclined her head in the direction of the terrace. He opened his textbook at the illustration of the digestive system and stood it up on the bed in front of Mohini. "I think this will interest you," he said. "Call if you need me."

Kamala followed him outside. After she had related to him her conversation with Dr. Merchant, Dr. Chitnis said he wasn't surprised that the spleen was enlarged, nor that Dr. Merchant had suggested removing it. "There is always that risk of iron deposition in various organs. We must be grateful it is not her heart that is overly enlarged. A spleen can be removed. What does Keshav think? Does he want to go ahead with it?"

"He's not home yet," Kamala said. "Will the operation be dangerous?"

"No more than any other that requires general anesthetic."

"Can you speak to Mohini's father and grandfather when you have the time?"

Dr. Chitnis nodded. But when he spoke to Keshav and Vishnupant he was cautious. He said that they could, if they wished, take Mohini to the United States for an expert opinion. Keshav and Vishnupant were willing to consider his suggestion, but Kamala shook her head. She had faith in Dr. Chitnis, who had faith in Dr. Merchant's recommendations, and it was her confidence in them that made Vishnupant decide there was no need for another opinion. Dr. Chitnis silently marvelled at the way Vishnupant deferred to Kamala's instincts.

A week after the operation, on the day of her release,

Mohini asked Dr. Merchant whether she could see her spleen. Dr. Merchant nodded at his assistant, who came out with a bottle in which was floating the spongy, purplish, fist-sized organ. Kamala turned her head and looked out the window, struck by Mohini's unfaltering curiosity. Mohini scrutinized the bottle and told the assistant to turn it this way, then that. When she asked Dr. Merchant whether she could take her spleen home, Kamala said no. Dr. Merchant agreed with Kamala. "I'll keep the organ here," he said to Mohini. "The next time you want to see it all you have to do is send for my assistant. There is one condition, however, that you must keep before I will allow him to show it to you."

"What condition is that?" Mohini asked.

"The spleen is the organ that helps the body fight infection. You must be careful not to catch an infection now that the spleen is removed."

Before Kamala could put forward the question, Mohini said, "What must I do?"

Dr. Merchant thought for a moment. "If someone visiting your house has a cold, cough, or fever, keep your distance from that person. Your mother is already boiling your drinking water. Other than that, continue to lead a normal life—or rather a life that is normal to you, which is the same thing, really."

Mohini looked puzzled.

Dr. Merchant leaned forward and ruffled her hair. "Just try not to catch any infection. You are a sensible girl. I'm simply cautioning you, that's all." He passed her a plate containing a vegetable samosa with chutney, its mint-laced pungency filling the air.

Kamala suspected the samosas had come from the cart of the vendor whom Dr. Merchant often praised for his culinary skills. The man was a permanent fixture in front of the Gateway of India and moved under its arches only in the monsoon season. He would stand over a cast-iron vessel and drop previously filled samosas into hot oil at the approach of a customer. Considering what Dr. Merchant had just said, Kamala thought Mohini should not be eating samosas that had been fried in murky oil whose age would forever remain indeterminate. She looked disapprovingly at him. But he was busy mopping the chutney with the triangular end of his samosa, oblivious to the fact that he had just broken his own condition. She turned and waved away for the second time the plate the assistant was holding out to her and noted with relief that this assistant was not the same one who had handled the bottle containing the spleen.

Dr. Merchant looked up. Kamala hoped to catch his eye in order to make her point, but he had stopped eating only to offer Keshav a third samosa and to tell Mohini that she could not have another because he did not want her to develop a stomach ache. He looked at Kamala with the satisfied air of a responsible man who had just performed the necessary task of informing a patient that he, Dr. Merchant, would not allow a person in his care anything that had the potential of causing harm.

Not knowing whether to laugh or cry, Kamala sat back in her chair.

When the long gash across her middle had healed, Vishnupant took Mohini back to Shivaji Park. She had grown just a little and could no longer perch on his shoulders. The pond in the centre of the park was filled in now, as was the well on the north side of the gymkhana. Two tennis courts had been installed on its west side, and sometimes Mohini would tell Balu to return to the gymkhana a stray ball that had flown over its hedge. With the filling in of the pond, the mill workers had dismantled their temporary walls and left. The open grounds were now used for cricket practice. Mohini liked to watch the bowlers as they hurtled down the run-up, their faces screwed up in concentration, the breeze ruffling and raising their hair.

Vishnupant did not sit on the bench any more. His ayurvedic doctor had told him that retirement had reduced his activity and that if he wished to hold his diabetes in check, he must walk. So he walked, committing himself to three rounds of the park, twirling his cane every now and then as he moved forward briskly, without looking back.

Sometimes, when Mohini was just about to throw a tantrum because she wanted to accompany her grand-father, Balu would insist she first strap on her sandals after which he would allow her to tag along behind him, follow-ing her closely as the distance between her and Vishnupant widened. People would stop and watch the three of them, the taller boy keeping pace with the shorter girl.

Mohini's small body and face had now acquired a shape typical of sufferers of her disease. Her nose was wide and flattened at the tip and it had lost its bridge. The frontal bone of her broad forehead had become very prominent, and from certain angles her head looked too large for her slender neck. Her bald, smooth skin had a greyish tinge where the excess, unflushed iron had settled under its sur-face. Her abdomen bulged above her thin, unbending legs.

If acquaintances stopped and asked her how she was doing, she invariably smiled and answered she was fine. The expression in her eyes often reminded them of her mother's—a subtle watchfulness in which everything observed was absorbed into places where it had little chance of being forgotten.

One night, after Mohini had recovered from the operation, Kamala sat up in bed excited by a certain notion that was now a distinct possibility. For a year now she had been suppressing the thought that one day Mohini might be able to go to school. Now the issues that this would raise were something that Kamala was delighted to face. After clearing it first with Dr. Chitnis, then consulting with Keshav, she informed her daughter that she was thinking of enrolling her in Mrs. Joshi's New English Academy.

The announcement took Mohini by surprise. She told Kamala she did not want to go to school. Why couldn't Vishnupant and she, Kamala, continue to teach her? Especially since Kamala knew that she could read and write Marathi as well as anyone else. She also had a smattering of English, did she not, from listening to the radio news alongside Vishnupant. And from listening to the history students who came to him for extra help. She reminded Kamala that he had already taught her the English alphabet. And in case her mother did not know, because she was always busy in the kitchen at that time of day, Mohini wished to assure her that after evening prayers, Vishnupant would open an English book and ask Mohini to identify two- and three-letter words. Just the previous week he had told her that it was only a matter of time before she would have the confidence and the interest to read the *Free Press Journal*.

"Vishnupant said I was too lazy to use the dictionary or I would be reading the newspaper by now. But if you don't send me to school, Aai, I promise I won't be lazy and I will make a list of words and their meanings, five words every day. I promise!"

Mohini clamped the thin skin of her throat between her thumb and forefinger. But Kamala shook her head.

"You need companions of your own age. Balu is no longer a child and Vishnupant and I are too old for you to be spending all your time with us. Also, being the only child in the house—and through no fault of your own—you have become very used to being the centre of attention. You need to learn how to share and give, and above all, how to listen." Kamala got up abruptly. She left the terrace swing and went downstairs to the front verandah, with Mohini following closely behind. Knowing she could no longer avoid this conversation, Kamala told Vishnupant about enrolling Mohini in New English Academy. "Mohini's father must have told you already," she added, looking at Mohini, who was standing next to Vishnupant's armchair.

But no, Keshav had said nothing about Mohini's possible enrollment in New English Academy although he had mentioned something about sending her to school, and to that Vishnupant had no objection. "But he never said an English-medium school," Vishnupant grumbled. With Mohini perched on the arm of his chair, he lectured his daughter-in-law on the sanctity of the Indian—and, indeed, the Maharashtrian—heritage, and brought into his argument the glory of the Indus Valley civilization and the Vedas and the Mahabharata and Shivaji Maharaj who had founded the Maratha Kingdom. He reminded Kamala that native languages were the single, glorious symbols of a culture that had been subjected for centuries to foreign rule, and here she was suggesting that her daughter adopt the language of the foreign ruler everyone was trying so hard to get rid of.

"But, Vishnupant," Mohini interrupted. "You would not have become a history professor and Baba would not have become an engineer if neither of you knew English."

Kamala glared at Mohini. This here was the perfect example of why Kamala felt Mohini ought to go to school. She needed to learn to curtail the freedom that Vishnupant so readily gave her, the freedom to say aloud what was in her mind, to articulate what was on her tongue. He even encouraged Mohini to call him by his name instead of demanding that she refer to him by his respectful title. In the past, when Kamala had reprimanded Mohini for not calling him Ajoba, grandfather, Vishnupant had admonished her. "Why are you scolding the child, Kamala?" he said. "It is not Mohini's fault. She is like a monkey. Monkey hears, monkey says. She calls me Vishnupant because my friends at the gymkhana call me Vishnupant. Don't scold her over this little trifle." Kamala had been silenced then, but she was determined to plead her case now.

Pinning Mohini with her eyes, she concurred with her father-in-law. "Of course, the sanctity of our heritage must never be forgotten." She paused a moment before adding, "Mohini already knows how to read and write Marathi. You taught her." She shifted her gaze to the ground.

Vishnupant knew Kamala was too shrewd to think that acknowledging his role in Mohini's Marathi education would flatter him into dropping his opposition. She was simply making a point.

"But this English-finglish," he said. "Day in, day out. It will drive everything else she has learned out of her head."

Kamala raised her eyes in the direction of Vishnupant's ground-floor room. "Mohini tells everybody that one day she wants to say that she has read all your books. It might be a tall order, I admit . . ." She wiped the perspiration from her upper lip with the end of her sari. "But she is determined. What I am saying is that if she continues to read the Marathi Mahabharata and the Ramayana—the children's version, that is—I doubt she will forget." She stopped, her thoughts drying up just as quickly as they had previously appeared. It was the longest conversation she had had with Vishnupant, perhaps the first. Previous exchanges had been limited to a question-and-answer pattern: Vishnupant did the asking and Kamala answered with a brevity consistent with her role in the house.

"At New English Academy, where will she develop the Marathi vocabulary required to tackle my volumes?" Vishnupant asked.

"She will be in school only five hours a day. I will teach her Marathi at home. Also, the academy is not a convent. There will be plenty of emphasis on India, Hinduism, and our culture."

"You have an answer for everything!"

Kamala was silent, her eyes on her toes. Her hairline was beaded with sweat.

"Is Keshav agreeable to sending her to this school?"

Kamala nodded, but knew not to repeat what Keshav had said: "If you want to put Mohini in New English Academy, put her there. You never know—English may just become the new language of an independent India because it is the one common tongue in a subcontinent that speaks a hundred and seventy-nine."

"I take it you have made up your mind," Vishnupant said.

Kamala shook her head.

"You haven't?"

"Not without your permission will I send Mohini to Mrs. Joshi's New English Academy."

Vishnupant sat back in his chair, suddenly feeling old. He had inexplicably forgotten that it was Mrs. Joshi who ran the school. Kamala had only said "New English Academy," her face flushed and uncharacteristically determined. Of course he had heard about Mrs. Joshi and her decision to include Sanskrit in the school curriculum. He also knew that the academic year ran from January to December, unlike vernacular schools that ran from June until May. Something inside him eased. Nevertheless, he scratched his chin and told Kamala that he would personally have to visit the school before giving her an answer.

Mohini knew the decision had been made in Kamala's favour when her mother measured her for the academy uniform: a navy blue knee-length gathered skirt and a half-sleeved white cotton blouse.

THREE

Keshav had asked Mohini not to mention any-thing about the missing coat to Vishnupant, so she did not refer to it while eating. She knew that Keshav was sensitive to Vishnupant's opin-ion of him, and now that his coat had inexplicably disappeared he was disinclined to deal with his father's reaction. Mohini kept looking across the table at Vasanti, impatient to tell her everything about that mysterious afternoon. After they had washed their hands, Vasanti said she would return home.

"Stay the night," Mohini pleaded.

"I don't know."

"But it's my birthday!"

"I'll stay tomorrow night. I promise. I haven't any night-clothes—"

"Aai will lend you her sari," Mohini said. "Please say yes."

"Only if you allow me to go home first thing in the morning."

"I will."

That night, Vasanti slept in Mohini's room. As always, Balu had made up the spare bed by placing at the foot of it an extra cotton quilt for the early morning hours when the

46

air became cool, when the ceiling fan—which Mohini needed in order to breathe comfortably—could not be switched off.

After they were settled in for the night and Kamala had called out to Mohini to turn off her lamp, Mohini related to her aunt the events of that afternoon. When she was finished, there was no response from the spare bed. She leaned over and peered into the darkness: her aunt had fallen asleep, her small body coiled into itself like a kitten's, her hands like soft paws that she held curled underneath her chin.

Mohini pulled back and lay on her side. Outside the terrace door everything was dark. The outline of the swing was barely visible. It was amavasya, a new moon. Her birthday had been an eventful one, Mohini admitted to herself, yet she wished now that it could have been something more. Perhaps the family could have taken a trip to the cooler heights of Lonavla, or to her father's site to see the latest stage of the dam construction, or even sat on the sea-ledge at Marine Drive, their faces turned to the turbid, pre-monsoon ocean, holding in their hands paper cones filled with roasted peanuts just off the griddle. Or, as a birthday present from Him, for a brief, solitary second, just as the rain tree loses its shadow at noon, she could have lost her disease.

Turning her head, Mohini reached for the pink stone that was lying on her night table. She slipped it under her pillow and, wondering who could have stolen her father's coat, she fell asleep.

When she opened her eyes in the morning, Vasanti had already left. The door to Kamala and Keshav's room was shut. Mohini went downstairs. Vishnupant was walking in through the front door carrying a parcel wrapped in brown paper. "It was on the shoe stand," he said. She followed him into the sitting room where Balu snapped the string. Wrapped inside and folded neatly was Keshav's black coat. When Vishnupant asked Balu what Keshav's coat was doing on the shoe stand, Balu, without as much as a glance at Mohini, who was vigorously shaking her head, happily spilled out the events of the previous afternoon. When he was finished, Mohini didn't see the point in holding back from her grandfather Hansa's version of what might have happened.

Vishnupant said, "At least the thief has returned the coat."

"I think also the wallet," Balu said, thrusting his hand into the inner pocket of the coat and pulling out Keshav's money clip. He handed it to Vishnupant, who passed it to Mohini.

"From now on keep the front door closed at all times," he told Balu. "Let people ring the doorbell if they wish to come in. Now take the coat upstairs."

"I'll take it," Mohini said.

Keshav was sitting up in bed and Kamala was doing namaskar to the rising sun when Mohini entered their room. She held up the coat and told Keshav how someone had left it on the shoe stand.

"Hand me the money clip," he said, extending his arm.

"Lie on my bed, Mohini," Kamala said. "It's early yet."

Keshav opened the leaves of the clip. There was nothing inside.

"How much is missing?" Kamala's voice was impatient. "Do you even remember how much there was to begin with?"

When Keshav remained silent she clicked her tongue but did not repeat her usual comment: how this was typical of him—born with a silver spoon in his mouth when he did not even know the value of silver. Mohini did not think that this particular characterization of Keshav was fair although she did not tell her mother so. Her father did not know the value of silver because he did not want to know. Silver was not important to him.

At school, Mohini told Hansa briefly about the return of the coat and changed the topic. She felt embarrassed that Hansa had witnessed her father's shouting the previous afternoon.

After dinner that night, when Mohini started to grind her knuckles into her temples, Kamala told her to go upstairs. Balu was turning down her bed. There was a smile on his face.

"What?" Mohini said.

"Nothing."

"Why are you grinning, then?"

"Can I help it if God gave me a grinning face?" He left the room.

Mohini switched off her light. She touched her head. Her scalp was tender. Watching the terrace through the open door, she thought she smelled rain. She closed her eyes and concentrated on shepherding her consciousness, her entire being, into that point inside her head that hurt the most. The pain eased and she opened her eyes. The door to her parents' room was partially open.

"I said, Kamala, aren't you going to ask me what else I want?"

"Can you smell rain?"

"I wouldn't bother putting that on," Keshav said. "It'll only have to come off." There was a teasing quality in his voice.

"Ssh! You always talk so loudly."

"Just shut the door," Keshav said.

Kamala closed the interconnecting door, but not without lingering a moment to see whether Mohini was awake. Mohini stilled her breathing and did not turn around. She shut her eyes and let sleep seep into her head along with the scent of fresh, falling rain.

Someone was ringing the doorbell. Mohini's eyes fluttered open. Grey clouds were perched in the sky. A pigeon was drinking from a shallow puddle on the floor of the terrace. She walked downstairs slowly, her eyes gummy with sleep. The front door was open. Someone was talking. She went outside and recognized the Irani from across the lane. He nodded at her as she stood next to Kamala, who had covered her hair with the end of her sari, no doubt to hide its unruliness. Vishnupant was sitting in his armchair and Keshav was standing to the left of him, his hands clasped behind his back. In front of them the Irani was holding his son by the scruff of his neck. Mohini recognized him to be the eldest of the Irani's three children. She had often seen him clean the steel shutters of the shop or load his bicycle with provisions before making routine deliveries. The boy's shirt had tightened into a noose.

The Irani continued to speak. "As I was saying, I tell him he is on cricket team only because he is the tallest lout there. Eighteen years old in a class of fifteen-year-olds. Last year he begged his mother—"

"Why have you come here?" Keshav said. "What can we do for you?"

The Irani released his son, who stepped away beyond the reach of his father. He looked at Mohini. His face was red and in his deep, dark eyes there was shame.

"No, Sahib, it is more the question of what this lout . . . of what my family can do for you. I am an honest man and it is because of the goodwill of people such as yourselves that I can keep my shop open in this neighbourhood." Mohini went and sat on the armrest of Vishnupant's chair. The Irani glanced at his son and said, "Go on. Tell Oek Sahib's bebi what you did on afternoon of her birthday."

He turned to Mohini. Upon reading her surprised expression, he said, "Everyone in this neighbourhood knows bebi's birthdate. So, Sahib, we are sleeping on bebi's birthday morning when we hear this loud crash. I think there is a riot, a hartal, and people are smashing in this poor Irani's store. It's not easy, Professor Sahib, being the only Muslim in this locality."

Vishnupant sternly cleared his throat. It brought the Irani back on track.

"I ran from our back rooms into the shop to check and found Gulaam here is standing in front of mirror over glass counter, cricket bat in hand, red season ball rolling on the floor. Glass is everywhere. Only last month I installed mirror. This lout here was practising batting. When I asked why with season ball, he said he didn't mean to hit so hard."

Vishnupant leaned forward in his chair. "So, Irani, you want a job for your son so he can occupy himself as well as pay for the glass?"

The Irani's face creased in wonder. "How did you read my mind, Sahib? That is exactly what I said on bebi's birthday. But today we are here to beg forgiveness from Engineer Sahib for what Gulaam did." The Irani made a basket of his fingers, which he rested on his considerable stomach. He explained that on Tuesday afternoon, when he saw the driver drop Keshav Sahib home, he told Gulaam to go quickly and ask Sahib for a job. He saw with his own eyes Gulaam entering Koleshwar Nivas. Five minutes later the boy was back, saying there was no job for him. "Last night your servant boy told me about missing coat." The Irani reached into his pocket and removed a slim wad of notes. "Count, Sahib. If it is more that you are missing—"

"I told you that's all I took. I swear!" Gulaam looked at Kamala. The expression on his face was supplicating. She nodded silently.

"Why did you not identify yourself when I addressed you?" Keshav's voice was hard.

"I was just about to when you held back your coat—" Gulaam swallowed and shifted his gaze to Kamala's feet.

"Go on, tell Engineer Sahib!"

"I thought I would go to the shop, get the biscuits for bebi's birthday, then come back."

But Mohini could see that the opportunity to pay for the damaged mirror without having to work for it had been too good to resist.

"If Sahib's servant had not come last night, I would not have known," the Irani said. He lifted his hand. Before his father could force him to the ground, Gulaam knelt down and touched Keshav's feet. He swivelled on his knees and did the same in front of Vishnupant and Kamala.

"That's better," the Irani said. "The boy's mother tries to teach him manners, but too much uncertainty these days."

"So," Vishnupant said, waving for Gulaam to get to his feet, "are you and your family going to leave us for Pakistan?"

"What business would I have there? Ever since my fore-fathers left Iran so many generations ago we have lived only in Bombay. My wife is from Konkan area, from Ratnagiri. She speaks pure Marathi, much better than me. There is no place for people like us in that new country. No relatives, no friends. Also, what with all the trouble at the border crossing." He shuddered. "I have three children—"

Keshav interjected quickly, "Do you still want a job, Gulaam?"

"Ji, Sahib," he said a bit listlessly. Perhaps he was hoping that everyone had forgotten about the job.

"Can you read and write?"

"Ji, Sahib."

"He goes to the school in Mahim." Mohini knew the one the Irani was referring to. It was a school at which the curriculum was largely confined to religious instruction.

"Can you do simple mathematics?" Keshav asked. "Add? Subtract?"

Gulaam looked at his father, who said, "He sits at the till sometimes. Gives out change to customers."

"I'll see if there is a peon's job or a courier's. You will have a better chance, Gulaam, if you complete matriculation. You look like a bright boy."

"You tell him, Sahib."

"Then take him out of that religious school, Irani," Vishnupant said. "Children absorb religion very well when they are young and I'm sure the school has taught him right from wrong. It's time now to put him into a regular school. One where matriculation topics are covered."

"Ji, Sahib! Thank you, Sahib!" The Irani looked at Mohini. "Accha, bebi, I will send biscuits with Gulaam."

Keshav and Kamala entered the house. Balu came out on the verandah. Pushing himself up from his armchair, Vishnupant looked at him and said, "The Sherlock Holmes of Shivaji Park. I suppose you realized that the brown paper in which the coat was wrapped was similar to the one the Irani uses. However, the next time you find a culprit, make sure you tell him to make his confession at a more reasonable hour. And, Mohini, even if your father has decided it is all right to bring into the house foodstuff from the Irani's shop, you better eat your birthday treat out of Bayabai's sight." He left the verandah.

Gulaam was back. He handed Mohini a buttery package of salty biscuits and hurried to the front gate. He walked away carefully, his right leg stepping forward with difficulty.

"Why is he walking like that?" Mohini asked.

"His father must have had to beat him black and blue to get him to confess," Balu replied. Mohini looked at him. His expression was smug. "What?" he said.

She narrowed her eyes, but her dark look was lost on him.

When Mohini came home from school that afternoon, Vasanti and Kamala were at the dining table, drinking tea.

"Bayabai, get Mohini her milk," Kamala called out.

"What are you doing here?" Mohini asked Vasanti, who had left Koleshwar Nivas the previous morning without saying goodbye.

Vasanti laughed. "I came to return your mother's sari. And of course to say I should not have fallen asleep like that, right in the middle of your story, whose ending I have just heard."

"Your aunt is tired at night because she is once again reading the Venkatesh Stotra twenty-one times, twenty-one mornings in a row," Kamala said.

"But why must you pray at three in the morning, Vasantiatya? Why not later? Lord Vishnu's ears are always open, aren't they?"

"Well, it's not as if I am not flexible," Vasanti said. "It was later yesterday morning, wasn't it, because I slept here night before last?"

"I wish you still lived with us, Vasantiatya," Mohini said. "Mai and Bebitai could easily have continued to live in Poona."

"She's only across the road, Mohini. Now drink your milk. Any headache today?" Mohini shook her head. Kamala pushed back her chair. "I must run. My embroidery class begins in twenty minutes."

Vasanti put out her hand across the table and Mohini placed hers in it. "I don't know what I would do without you," Vasanti said. There were tears in her eyes. "At night, my head going round and round, I keep thanking my lucky stars . . ."

"Do you want to sit on the terrace swing?"

"I have a few minutes," Vasanti said.

Walking up the stairs, Mohini tried to think whether her aunt was the youngest widow she knew, and felt sadness when she came to the conclusion that yes, Vasanti was.

FOUR

Mohini had been nine years old when, without prior warning or premonition, the afternoon postman handed Vishnupant a letter containing the news that Babasahib Chafekar, Vasanti's husband, was dead. "It says Babasahib died as a result of a fatal fall in the Scottish Highlands," he said. He had fixed his gaze into the distance, beyond the treeline of Mohur Lane. "Fatal fall," he repeated.

Mohini had never seen her grandfather's face so stricken. She removed the letter from his grasp and shouted out to Kamala. When Kamala hurried to the verandah, alarmed by the panic in Mohini's tone, Mohini held out the crumpled piece of paper for her mother to read.

"Why did the Chafekars not send us a telegram, Kamala?" Vishnupant said. "That way the news would have reached us right away. Do you think Vinod knows?" Vinod was Vishnupant's nephew, Vasanti's elder brother.

"He would not have kept us in the dark if he knew," Kamala replied.

Vishnupant shook his head. It was his firm opinion that Vinod Oek had married a girl who was not disposed to maintaining relations with her in-laws. Vinod, his wife

Sudha, and their three daughters lived only twenty minutes away by foot, yet they rarely visited Koleshwar Nivas. Mohini met them every now and again at weddings, naming and thread ceremonies, and family functions. Sometimes, when she was in the park, she saw her aunt crossing Cadell Road on her way to the Jijabai Samaj, the women's institution where Kamala held her embroidery classes. Mohini liked her cousins, and from the way they fussed over her she could tell that they enjoyed meeting her too. And yet, when she asked them why they did not come to see her more often, they would drop their eyes and shuffle their feet without offering any reply.

Handing Kamala the ripped envelope of the letter, Vishnupant said, "Since you think Vinod knows nothing about Babasahib's death, I will have to inform him. Keshav can take me there this evening when he comes home. In the meantime, I want you to send Balu to the railway station to make a train reservation for Nagpur. I must pay my condolences in person. A letter will not do."

It had been some time since Mohini had last seen Vasanti. Still, Mohini remembered very well her aunt's tiny palms, the mole centred at the base of her right index finger, her dark brown plait framing the side of her face. Vasanti had come to Bombay with her father then, to celebrate Mohini's sixth birthday. It turned out to be the last time that Mohini would see her grand-uncle, Sitarampant, who had died unexpectedly the following year. Vinod was already married and living in Bombay when his father passed away, and he requested that Kamala remain in Poona after the funeral, just until she was sure that Vasanti was capable of coping on her own. The few days had become a month. It was the longest time that Mohini had been separated from her mother.

While she was in Poona, Mai and Bebitai, Vasanti's aunts, informed Kamala that before Sitarampant had passed away, the plan to marry Vasanti to Babasahib had been all but finalized. It was now the responsibility of Vishnupant, they said, to continue the correspondence with Nagpur and set the wedding date.

And now, after barely two years of marriage, Vasanti was a widow. Vishnupant got up and left the verandah, calling out to Balu to wipe and dust his suitcase and holdall in preparation for his departure to Nagpur.

Bayabai, who had been listening from the sitting-room window, came out and stood next to Kamala. "How terrible Vasanti's fate must be," she said, "to first become an orphan and then a widow at such a young age."

Kamala shook her head in bewilderment, letting her hands fall to her sides. "To think that the poor girl is only twenty years old," she agreed.

Looking at Bayabai, who was also a widow, Mohini feared for her aunt. There was something about the stoop of Bayabai's shoulders, the bitter smell that exuded from her body, the single hair that protruded from a mole on the underside of her chin, that Mohini associated with the words *musty*, *widow*, and *old*.

Mohini had once asked Kamala why Bayabai dressed the way she did, a faded red sari draped over her head and shoulders so that it completely covered her arms, a single black thread worn around her neck. Mohini already knew that Bayabai was bald because once, when she had seen a barber with his barber's roll of implements exiting the back door of the house, she had asked Kamala why he was leaving the house from the kitchen door and not the front entrance. And why was he inside Koleshwar Nivas at all, given that he was not the same barber who daily shaved Vishnupant's face and head? Kamala had tried to avoid giving Mohini an answer, but Mohini repeated her question at such odd times that Kamala was forced to yield. "He comes for Bayabai," she said. "Her hair must be shaved off because she is a widow."

As to Bayabai's mode of dress, Kamala's answer had been identical. "Because she is a widow, society expects her to dress in a certain way."

"Why?"

Kamala had thought for a minute. "In some ways it is protection for a widow to dress like that. Protection against her own feelings, her natural desires, protection against others."

"I don't understand," Mohini said.

"You are too young," Kamala had murmured.

Bayabai slept in a room that was off the corridor leading from the kitchen to the back door. Her mattress was a hard pallet, her quilt an old sari, threadbare and worn. When she walked around the kitchen groaning and clutching her hips in the colder months, Kamala would wordlessly lay a thick cotton quilt on her pallet, and when warmer days crept in, Bayabai would return the unused quilt to Kamala's cupboard.

Vishnupant had no patience with her. He repeatedly told her that as much as the world demanded that a widow maintain a starkness, an insipid seclusion, even at times invisibility, it was all right to sleep on a cotton mattress and cover oneself with a decent blanket in the winter months.

"Look at the way your back is bowed!" Vishnupant would repeat in an exasperated tone. "The chill from the stone floor has seeped into your bones. And the next thing that will happen is that you will catch a cold, after which you will refuse to allow Kamala to take you to see Dr. Chitnis."

But Bayabai was stubborn. Fate had decided to punish her and she would not deny fate that satisfaction. Life was a burden to be shouldered, not something to be lowered to the ground when it became too heavy. Detachment was the key, she told him. Renunciation the road. Vishnupant muttered that she spoke like the Buddha, if only she had His enlightenment.

There was a history between the two of them, Mohini could tell. Bayabai was the only person in the world who could make otherwise invisible muscles twitch behind Vishnupant's ears. Some of Mohini's earliest memories were of the strident arguments that would break out between them at the drop of a hat. Whenever the sound of their raised voices swelled through the house, Kamala would take Mohini upstairs and fix on her such an unblinking glare that Mohini would be pinned to her place. They would ride out the storm from the terrace, alert to everything that was happening below. Mohini would clamp her hands to her ears even as pots and pans were hurled, doors and drawers repeatedly slammed, coconuts dashed to the ground.

These arguments had continued until the time Mohini was five years old. That summer her temperature had soared, making her face so pale and wan that in comparison her lips looked a dark purple-red. She refused all food and drink. Leaving her bedside one evening, muttering that there was something he had to do, Vishnupant went downstairs to the puja room. When he returned, his expression was resolute. He told Mohini that she would be well in no time, now that he had made a promise to God. This time, he assured her, he intended to keep it.

Months later, she overheard Kamala remark to Keshav that Vishnupant did not seem to lose his temper with Bayabai any more, at least not the way he used to.

Mohini called out from her room, "I think so too! But I don't understand why Vishnupant used to get so angry with her."

Kamala stood in Mohini's doorway and said, "How many times have I told you not to eavesdrop or interrupt your elders when they are talking?"

Mohini dropped her eyes, her manner immediately contrite.

Kamala murmured to Keshav as he walked into Mohini's room. "Don't give in to her."

"It's only natural curiosity, Kamale," he said over his shoulder. He sat on Mohini's bed. "All I can tell you, Mohini, is that Bayabai is my mother's second cousin. She was a child widow. Her husband died when she was only eleven years old. When her brother-in-law in Nasik expelled her, she came to live with us. After that she went away only once—Nandini and I were very young then—and when she returned I remember my father telling her that if she made mischief between him and my mother ever again, he would personally throw her out and never take her back."

"What mischief?" Mohini asked.

"I don't know, and I suggest you do not ask your grandfather either." He looked behind him but Kamala had left the doorway.

"Good night, Aai!" Mohini called out before ducking her head under her cotton covering. There was no response. But in the middle of the night, when Mohini sat up in bed for a glass of water, her mother was there to take the empty glass after she had finished drinking from it. She waited for Mohini to slide down on her bed before covering her legs with the quilt.

A week after Vishnupant left for Nagpur to make his con-dolence visit, a horse-drawn carriage, a tanga, pulled up in front of Koleshwar Nivas. Mohini, Kamala, and Balu hur-ried to the gate. Vishnupant paid the driver as Balu retrieved the luggage. Vasanti got down from the carriage and walked towards Kamala, a hesitant smile on her face. Suddenly shy, Mohini glanced away, relieved that her aunt did not look like a widow and that her thick plait still bracketed one side of her face. The horse was snorting and tossing his mane, as though the restraining straps and metal pieces were chafing against his head and mouth. There was a scent of roasting peanuts in the air. The mos-quitoes were beginning to rise from the ground. Vishnupant hurried inside and they all followed him in. He told Kamala that it was Vasanti's fasting day. "She has eaten nothing since breakfast," he said.

Kamala looked at Mohini and told her to tell Bayabai to put some potatoes on to boil. Mohini went to the kitchen. Bayabai had reached there ahead of her. Lifting her hands to her head and lowering the end of her sari farther down over her forehead, she said, "The bananas are on the side-board in the dining room. The milk is in the mesh-fronted cupboard. That should suffice for anyone who is fasting."

She leaned against the wall and ran her fingers over her prayer beads.

Keeping her face averted from Bayabai, Mohini removed some potatoes from the hanging basket and looked for a small knife with which to pare them.

"What are you doing?" Bayabai said.

Mohini's mouth tightened. "If you don't want to make anything for Vasantiatya, I will." She carefully peeled the potatoes, then put them on the gas ring to boil. Her heart racing because Bayabai was still watching her, she chopped some green chilies, then removed the curds and salt from the shelf.

That night, Vasanti ate with relish the potatoes Kamala said Mohini had prepared, Mohini adding that it was the first time that she had cooked anything for anyone. Vasanti smiled at Mohini, two spots at each corner of her mouth collapsing into deep dimples. Mohini had forgotten how beautiful her aunt really was. "Aai said you will sleep with me in my room," she said. There was immediate pleasure in Vasanti's eyes, a slackening of tension.

Vishnupant told Kamala that the first thing he wanted her to do in the morning was remove from the safe a gold chain and two matching bangles. "Vasanti will also need kunku for her forehead. Black or red, it doesn't matter. It's bad enough she is dressed all in white."

The tears flowed down Vasanti's face when Kamala dotted her forehead with a black kunku. Like a child Vasanti sat still, her hands clasped in her lap as Mohini eased the chain around her neck. Kamala slipped the bangles onto her wrists, one on each hand.

"Widows aren't supposed to look into a mirror, let alone

wear gold," Vasanti said, her shoulders heaving. "What will people say? What will Bayabai say?"

Kamala glanced at Keshav, not trusting herself to talk without her words getting caught in her throat. Keshav looked at Vasanti and told her sternly that whereas Bayabai was fifty, Vasanti was only twenty and the rules that had governed society when Bayabai had become a child widow no longer applied. "Even you must realize this," Keshav said. "A few years ago my father would not have taken you from your married home and brought you here, to Bombay." Keshav paused to make sure Vasanti was listening. She was. She had stopped mopping her face and her long eyelashes glistened as she continued to look at him.

"So, things have changed now," Keshav continued. "And before you give credence to Bayabai's reactions, remember that she is from a tiny village. She does not like to make tea for my non-Brahmin colleagues, but do I not bring them home? Her ideas of purity and impurity are based on caste and pre-scribed rituals for this and that, and nothing you or I can say to her or people like her will make the slightest difference." He stopped talking and looked at Kamala. She nodded imper-ceptibly as though she wanted him to carry on. He removed his glasses and said, "What I'm saying, Vasanti, is that you should try to view your situation in a practical light. You are here, with us, and that is all you should remember."

It was the first time Mohini had heard her father assert his view in the domestic sphere. Vasanti calmed down immediately, and as the weeks went by she gradually regained a portion of her previous poise. Her thoughtful manner gave her the appearance of someone who had crossed a fast-flowing river aided only by a single oar.

She was the first to wake up in the morning and took over from Balu the task of preparing tea. With this routine established, she asked Kamala if Balu could clear the front yard, which was overgrown from past neglect. After the yard was cleared, she instructed him on how to prepare a raised bed, and when that was done she planted seeds— carrots, peas, capsicum, and French beans—in the moist, loamy soil. When Vishnupant complained that she had not planted his favourite vegetable, spinach, she prepared yet another bed and planted that as well. When Kamala asked her where she had developed her love of gardening, she scrunched up her face as though *love* was too strong a word for what made her step out into the midday sun. "In Nagpur," she replied. "When I was alone, after he had left for England."

Roughly six months after Vasanti came to live at Koleshwar Nivas, someone asked Kamala at the Jijabai Samaj whether it was true that Babasahib Chafekar had died in England at the end of a long, lingering disease. Kamala nodded—knowing that to the woman England and Scotland were the same thing—adding that it was the first time she had heard of any disease, lingering or otherwise. "Oh! Then, how did he—?" But Kamala had already turned away to talk to someone else. Another time an acquaintance stopped Kamala on the street and asked her when Vasanti would be returning to Nagpur. When Kamala looked at her pointedly, the woman muttered something about wanting to send a letter, then went on her way.

The fact of the matter was that neither she nor Keshav knew when Vasanti was likely to return to Nagpur. Only Vishnupant had the answer to that, and he hadn't told them. But Kamala was used to Vishnupant's ways, as she was to the considerable degree of disapproval that was conferred on him by the orthodox segments of their society. They found unacceptable his endorsement of widow remarriage, his views on the necessary eradication of meaningless religious rituals, his belief in the equality of gender and caste; and they considered heretical his willingness to allow Untouchables entry into temples. Vishnupant dismissed their criticisms with indifference, which sometimes bordered on disdain.

Nor was it just the neighbours in Shivaji Park who were interested in Vasanti. Mohini wanted to ask her all kinds of questions about her life in Nagpur. Neither she nor Kamala had been able to attend the wedding, and although she had heard some descriptions about her aunt's new home from Vishnupant, she wanted to know more.

She already knew that Chafekar Wadi was very large and grand and that the prestige and bearing of Nanasahib, Babasahib's father, was so royal that in a princely gathering he would have eclipsed even a king. Mohini imagined Chafekar Wadi to be a palace, except she didn't know what a palace looked like. Keshav had mentioned the large amounts of jewellery that her in-laws had given Vasanti, and after listening to his description, Kamala had exclaimed, "I wish we could have seen it! I'm not surprised at the quantity, though. After all, the Chafekars own seven villages."

"Eight," Keshav corrected her.

Mohini had been lying next to Keshav on his bed. She widened her eyes.

"You ask Vasantiatya to describe Chafekar Wadi and the jewellery when next you see her," he said.

"When will that be?"

"I don't know but I'm sure she will come to Bombay sometime."

And now, here she was, in circumstances so unexpected that even Mohini knew better than to ask questions. However, one early morning, when Vasanti had been with them for over nine months, Mohini said, "Would deer really stroll up to the front steps of Chafekar Wadi?" Vasanti was bent over Mohini, ready to peel back a compress from her forehead.

"Ssh," Vasanti said. "Your body is still quite hot. Go back to sleep. It's only five o'clock." She wrung out yet another cold compress and applied it to Mohini's forehead. All night Mohini had suffered rigors accompanied by nausea and vomiting, her temperature spiralling upwards by the hour.

Lately, she had developed antibodies to blood taken from some of her regular donors. But when it came to finding a suitable replacement, Dr. Chitnis was adamant in his refusal to use the hospital bank. Without knowing the background of blood donors, he explained to the Oeks, it was impossible to screen their blood—not for antigens and proteins to which Mohini had developed antibodies, but for other diseases. Tuberculosis was rampant, he continued, as were typhoid, jaundice, polio, and other diseases they had probably never heard of.

Keshav and Kamala accepted Dr. Chitnis's reasoning, and when a donor could not be found, they repeated to each other what Dr. Chitnis had told them: they would find one eventually, no matter how hard the search. They trusted his judgement and over the years came to accept the irreversible pathology of Mohini's disease.

But Vishnupant was more sanguine. When someone suggested to him a cure for Mohini's brittle bones or sluggish liver or headaches or lack of energy, he would take the suggestion to Dr. Chitnis. Some medications such as herbal ointments and medicinal balms Dr. Chitnis would allow, but he was skeptical about tablets and syrups and powders. At first, when Mohini's condition had been diagnosed, Dr. Chitnis had encouraged the Oeks to try ayurvedic and homeopathic remedies. But when none of the alternative medicines proved helpful in relieving the symptoms of her disease, he told Vishnupant that Mohini should not become a guinea pig for possible cures.

Mohini opened her eyes. The compress had fallen off her forehead. Under her left ear the pillow was wet. Kamala and Vasanti were sitting on the doorsill of the terrace, facing away. Downstairs, Balu was thrashing clothes against the washing stone. A yellow scent of Sunlight Soap filled the air. Kamala was saying, "Mohini actually asked that? I'll have a word with her." She glanced back into the room and Mohini quickly shut her eyes.

"No, don't." Vasanti laid a restraining hand on Kamala's arm. "I would like to tell her about the deer and how domesticated they were." She paused. "However, there was a strict rule about not feeding them. There were tigers in the nearby forest and my father-in-law did not want the deer permanently settled in our area . . . Kamalavahini, do you think it hurts to speak about Chafekar Wadi? I've been wanting to tell you about it all these months." There was a breaking quality to Vasanti's voice.

"I took my cue from Mohini's grandfather," Kamala softly said. "Until this day he has not told us the details of what happened, as to why he removed you from Chafekar Wadi and brought you back here with him. I have been wanting to ask you so many things ever since you arrived."

"Then why didn't you?" There was hurt in Vasanti's tone.

"I didn't know how and where to begin."

"You should have just asked me."

Kamala was silent.

"I didn't mean it like that. And really there is not much to tell."

"Mohini is still sleeping," Kamala said. "Why don't you tell me something? Anything. Whatever you want."

Vasanti took her time replying. "It seems that Babasahib's plans to go to London to do his law articles were finalized long before we were married."

"Do you think your father knew that?"

"I don't think so or he would have mentioned something to me."

"I remember Mohini's father and grandfather going to see Babasahib off at the Bombay docks when he sailed for England," Kamala said.

Mohini turned the pillow so that now the dry side was under her head.

"What was Babasahib like?" Kamala asked.

"Handsome, like his father. And he was never without a book." Vasanti's voice was softer now, and Mohini had to strain her ears.

In the anteroom off their bedroom, Vasanti told Kamala, there were built-in shelves that held countless books bound in worn leather jackets. Vasanti liked that room because of its leathery smell. Babasahib's study of English literature was so great, she said, that just the way learned men could recite from the Mahabharata and Bhagavad Gita, he could quote verse and passage for any length of time. One day, he plucked a book off a shelf and told her to read it. He was horrified when he realized that she had no knowledge of English.

"What made him assume that you knew English?" Kamala asked.

Vasanti shrugged. "He said it was high time that I learned. He said he would teach me."

Babasahib was a strict and demanding tutor. When Vasanti was heavy-tongued and made little progress copying into a notebook assigned letters and words, he scolded her soundly, just as a teacher would an errant pupil. She was eighteen and had only finished her vernacular matriculation. He was twenty-four and almost a lawyer.

"So, did he stop teaching you?" Kamala asked.

Vasanti shook her head. "With my luck?" she said. She reached for a hairpin that had released itself from her bun and slid it back in.

"Go on," Kamala urged her.

Vasanti shifted position and leaned her back against the side of the door. Mohini slowly brought up the soft sari that Kamala had placed on her body so that it all but covered her eyes. Vasanti looked at the sky. Babasahib was an aloof man, she said, and had very little to say to the rest of his family. However, she asserted, he was quite talkative with her.

Mohini could see that her aunt was blushing.

As his departure for England grew closer, Vasanti continued, Babasahib's zeal to teach her English began to accelerate. She didn't understand the hurry, but did not say anything because she had decided that she would study very hard when he was away and surprise him upon his return.

One day, when she was sitting on the bed after her head bath (her wet hair framing her face in shiny tendrils, Mohini imagined, her skin newly washed and smelling of sandalwood), he said to her, "No one told me anything about you. If I had known, I would have included you in my plans." As before, she did not understand what he meant.

Instead of limiting himself to teaching her simple words, he now wanted her to absorb whole sentences. Her progress was so slow that by the end of the first few months all she could repeat without fumbling was a single line: "Elephants and tigers do not roam the streets."

Babasahib accused her of being apathetic, lazy, unwilling to learn—all of which she now admitted to Kamala as being true—and one day, in exasperation, he plucked a Marathi book from her dressing table and pointed to a paragraph on the page at which her bookmark lay. He handed her a notebook and told her to write down the paragraph he was about to translate. Because she had not given much attention to memorizing the English alphabet, Vasanti was utterly confused. She scribbled something on the page while shielding it from his eyes, and even as he dictated, she devised a plan: the next time she would write down in Marathi script the words he was pronouncing. However, there was always the possibility that he would ask to see what she had written, making her scheme an imperfect one.

Sometimes, Babasahib would repeat a sentence and its meaning over and over again until she had grasped it. But by now he had stopped scolding her. On the contrary, he would compliment her when she got something right, laughing loudly even when the words rolled inside her mouth strangely, sticking to her palate as though they were pieces of uncooked dough. He held her right hand steady with his own as she wrote across the page. Vasanti stopped speaking and glanced quickly at Kamala. She ducked her head and brought her padar to cover her face. When she lowered it, she recited, "'The glorious sun is nevertheless primordial because of the light and heat it confers.'" Her voice was girlish and trembling.

"You said the elephant and glorious sun sentences beautifully," Kamala said. Impressed that Vasanti could remember anything, Kamala knew that she would never have learned English had she been taught it that way. "Do you remember any other?"

"Only one more." Vasanti raised her eyes to the treeline and said, "'Clouds are like herds of cattle when they gather in the sky, sacred like the cow who gives daily milk because they nourish the earth.'"

Kamala leaned against Vasanti's knees on the doorsill. "Do you know what these sentences mean?"

"I think so." She grinned.

Kamala said, "After Babasahib left for England, what happened then?"

"At first, he sent monthly letters, but I never saw them. They were addressed to Nanasahib, and his servant would inform me after one had arrived."

"Did you ever write to him?"

"He never wrote to me, so how could I write to him?" Vasanti replied.

Kamala nodded.

"Then, after nine months or so, two months went by

without a single letter. The following month he wrote that
his study load was increasing, and that if he didn't get the
time to write again, Nanasahib was not to worry." Vasanti's
voice was dropping, and Mohini had to listen carefully.

After that, the correspondence from Babasahib's end
was sporadic. And then the fatal telegram arrived. Shortly
afterwards a letter followed, written by the woman in whose
home Babasahib had lived as a paying guest. It explained
that he had fallen off the side of a mountain in the Scottish
Highlands while out on a walking expedition. His brothers
asked her for the particulars of his death. Had he been cre-
mated? Could his ashes be sent to Nagpur? There was no
reply. Babasahib's youngest brother was ready to catch a
ship to England, but after what had happened to Babasahib,
nobody was willing to let him go.

The astrologer who had declared Vasanti's and
Babasahib's horoscopes a perfect match on all thirty-two
counts before the wedding now said that Vasanti's horo-
scope was so flawed that her continued presence at
Chafekar Wadi would jeopardize the well-being of the
entire family. This was conveyed to Vishnupant when he
came to pay his condolence visit.

Kamala pulled out a handkerchief from the waist of her
sari and passed it to Vasanti, who was silently crying. It was
a while before she could continue.

"Right after Vishnukaka heard the eldest brother
relate what the astrologer had said, he addressed
Nanasahib. I was listening from the other side of the
door. I remember his exact words: 'If that is the case,
allow me to take Vasanti back to Bombay. She need not
stay here. I will look after her.' Astonished, I peeped into

the room. My father-in-law's head was bowed over his chest. I think he was ashamed that his eldest son had repeated the astrologer's words. Everyone was taken aback by Vishnukaka's suggestion, but nobody said that I should remain at Chafekar Wadi. Before leaving, I went to see my eldest sister-in-law. She said, 'I know you think this family is rejecting you because of what has happened, but I want you to know that it is a grave responsibility to look after a young widow, particularly a young widow such as you. There are so many comings and goings at Chafekar Wadi. How long will you remain protected?' I started crying then, Kamalavahini. Throughout my stay she had looked after me like a daughter."

Vasanti sat forward and swivelled her legs so that she was now facing the terrace. She was sobbing. Kamala ran her hand up and down her back, and when that did not comfort her, she hugged her close.

Mohini had been holding back her own tears. She reached over for the water and the empty tumbler clattered to the floor. Before she knew it, Vasanti and Kamala were standing over her. Kamala felt her forehead with the back of her hand. It was lukewarm. "You can both go to sleep now," Mohini said. "I'm feeling fine."

Vasanti, who was red-eyed, quickly entered the bathroom. She did not sleep with Mohini any longer but slept in the narrow chamber next to Kamala's sewing room. She had asked to move out of Mohini's room, explaining that the continuously whirring fan made her feel so cold at night that sometimes she could not sleep.

"She's clever enough to have picked a convincing argument," Keshav said to Kamala. "She knows Mohini cannot breathe properly when the air around her is still. It's best you allow her to sleep where she will feel comfortable."

The new arrangement had lasted only a month. One day, Mr. Patil, the owner of Shiv Sadan, came to see Vishnupant. He was looking for tenants for his ground-floor flat, he said. In 1942, when parts of Shivaji Park had been evacuated on account of an imaginary threat of an Axis invasion, three of his tenants had left. All but one had returned and now the ground-floor flat was still unoccupied.

At the time, Mai and Bebitai Oek, Vishnupant's spinster cousins, were living in the Oek ancestral home in Poona, a crumbling property that Vishnupant had long been thinking about selling. The major hurdle he faced, however, was trying to persuade his cousins to move to Bombay. Now that a flat had come up for rent in such close proximity, right across from Koleshwar Nivas, he resumed his correspondence with his cousins. After a flurry of letters from both sides—Vishnupant's logical and to the point, his cousins' emotional and sentimental and stubborn—Vishnupant said that the only way to get through to Mai and Bebitai would be for him to talk to them in person. Vasanti asked to accompany him, suspecting that they would listen to her. She was right. They said they would be willing to take up residence in Shiv Sadan on the condition that their niece move in with them. Vasanti readily agreed and packed her belongings, knowing that she would not be too far for Mohini to call out to her, yet not too near to be stifled by a generosity that could at any time make her regret her dependence.

FIVE

Following her thirteenth birthday, whenever the Irani saw Mohini in the front verandah, he would wave out to her. Gulaam, on the other hand, would avert his eyes. Instead of using Ranade Road Extension, which would require him to walk in front of Koleshwar Nivas, he would cross the lane and take the narrow road behind the Marzello property in order to reach the market. Whistling short bird calls as he sauntered past their back gate, he would walk on tiptoes and continue to look over their high wall for as long as he could, all the while swinging in his hands capacious cloth bags made from gunny sack that was sturdy and brown.

At the end of May, just before the start of the month-long holidays, Keshav suggested to Kamala that she and Mohini accompany him to Poona the following week. It had been a year since they had last visited Kamala's parents, and since he had a supervisory call to make at some construction site on Satara Road, he could take them to Poona in his car, commute to the construction site whenever required, and bring them back to Bombay at the end of their stay.

Kamala wrote to her mother and received a joyful reply: "Come as soon as Keshav is able to bring you, and stay at least a week." Preparations for their journey were well under way when Kamala heard from Poona again. This time it was a postcard from Kamala's father, Anantrao. "Tukaram," he had neatly written across its mustard length, "has been called away to his village, and even though your mother is insisting that she can manage quite well without a servant, it is better that all of you postpone your coming here until after he is back."

Knowing his anxious nature, Kamala replied right away: they would wait to hear that Tukaram had returned before leaving for Poona.

Keshav shook his head at her haste. "You should have thought about it for a couple of days, Kamale. Tukaram or no Tukaram, your father always finds it inconvenient to have anyone visit him whether it is for one week or one hour. Ask your brother and see if he doesn't agree with me. Come with me to Poona. Mohini has her summer holidays and it will be a good change for both of you. You don't have to worry about your father. You know he always keeps his temper in check when I am there."

But Kamala was not convinced. "He'll only take it out on Aai after we leave."

"Your mother is quite capable of looking after herself. I saw that when I was in Poona last."

"I'm not saying anything about cancelling the trip, am I?" Kamala protested. "Neither is Baba. I'm only postponing it as he requested. You go whenever you have to go. Mohini and I can take the train if required."

Mohini tended to agree with Keshav that they should go anyway, in spite of her grandfather's postcard, which she suspected he must have stamped and posted without first informing her grandmother. But Mohini did not say anything. She knew Kamala's heart was set on going, and that no matter how great her own disappointment, her mother's was that much greater. Yet, this summer more than ever, Mohini longed to leave Shivaji Park. There flashed into her mind the memory of her grandmother's small hands alighting on various objects as she went about her tasks inside their small dwelling. She wished to solve with her grandfather brain-twisting mathematical problems from his book of quizzes and to breathe in the dry Poona air instead of air so humid that it appeared to gain weight as it pressed against her chest at night. She wanted to see their jacaranda tree, to smell its blue-and-violet blossoms that littered the ground. She wished to taste food cooked by someone other than Bayabai. Her grandmother made the best chirote she had ever eaten, the deep golden syrup in which they were dipped not too sweet. And she would be alone this summer: Hansa was visiting her father in Baroda, where he was now stationed, and would not be back in Bombay until a few days before the start of school.

Kamala and Mohini waited for Keshav in the front verandah on the evening he was expected to return from Poona. The choral buzzing and droning of insects was occasionally interrupted by a sharp click-click as lizards scurried here and there, mercifully unseen. By the time they saw Vishnupant walk down the lane from the gymkhana, it was past eight o'clock, and Keshav still had not returned. They had just finished eating dinner when they heard a familiar car horn, and Mohini hurried to the porch.

Later that night, she lay between Keshav and Kamala in the single beds that Mohini had earlier instructed Balu to join together. She often slept in her parents' room on Keshav's first night after being away on site.

Keshav lifted Mohini's hand, stretching out her fingers one by one, and said, "I met your grandmother and grandfather this morning. Aji told me that Tukaram is expected back tomorrow. She wants you to visit her quickly, before school begins."

In unison, they turned towards Kamala: her eyes were shining. Mohini gave a whoop.

"Not so fast," Keshav said. "When is your next transfusion?"

"I had one only this afternoon. So there. Now we don't have a single excuse not to go."

"I have an embroidery class tomorrow," Kamala said. She sat up in bed and laid aside her book. "We can leave the day after."

"Been married and living in Bombay for so long, yet the sparkle that comes to your mother's face when a trip to Poona is mentioned!"

Vasanti accompanied Mohini and Kamala to the railway station. When Mohini leaned out of the carriage window and held out her hand, Vasanti said that if Mai and Bebitai were still living in Poona, she would hop onto the train, just like that, without giving it a second thought. She was still standing there waving to them when the train pulled away.

Inside the compartment everything was dusty and unswept, but outside it was lush and green. There was thick vegetation sprouting from between the wooden slats of the railway tracks, and on the grassy knolls as the train rolled by, red, yellow, and purple blossoms nodded and trembled in the rushing wind. Kamala pointed to a pond that was normally a lake, to a stream that should have been a river. Watching the fields roll by, she muttered, "I hope they get enough rain this year."

Umabai, Mohini's grandmother, was waiting on the platform at the railway station. Shridhar, Kamala's older brother, was standing next to their mother. "Did you know he was here, Aai?" Mohini asked.

Kamala shook her head, smiling. She steered Mohini towards the door of their compartment. Shridhar stood on the platform and held out his arms, and Mohini let herself slip into them just the way she used to when she was a little child. She grumbled into his ear as he set her down, "You haven't come to see us for so long."

Umabai clasped Mohini close to her chest, then looked at Kamala and made no comment. Silence meant Umabai was satisfied that her daughter was looking well. Shridhar carried their bags to a waiting tanga. He took Mohini on his lap. The driver flicked his whip, and the horse turned into the traffic without looking left or right. Mohini laughed and glanced at Kamala. Her mother had placed her hand on her grandmother's lap. At a distance it would have been difficult to tell them apart: who the mother and who the daughter, Umabai was so small, taller than Mohini only by a palm's double width.

Mohini was disappointed when the horse came to a stop in front of her grandparents' residence. She had wanted the ride never to end. In spite of the ring of the horse's hooves and the scrape of the tanga wheels against the road,

Anantrao remained fast asleep in his armchair in his habitual place on the raised platform that surrounded the entire building. Umabai and Anantrao lived in the last three rooms in a row of dwellings, each separated from the other by a wall that was slightly thicker than the walls that divided the rooms within.

Her grandfather had once told Mohini that he didn't like it in Poona, that he would have given anything to return to the Konkan of his childhood, to the cool shadows of the mango orchards, to the seaside gardens, the lapping waves. Anything to avoid the noise, the neighbourliness, the quarrels, the borrowing without returning, of community life, he said, pointing to the back verandah, where tenants were chatting and beyond them to the shrieking children, who played a game of marbles in the finely powdered earth. He had stopped his gaze at the shared toilets that stood under the spreading branches of a banyan tree.

Kamala and Shridhar had grown up in this very colony, and several women—mothers and sisters-in-law of the girls she had once gone to school with—came forward now and greeted her and told Mohini how tall she had become. Mohini felt awkward because she hadn't met them in a while, and pulled down on her frock so that it covered her buckling knee. She blushed in spite of herself and for something to say conceded that she might, indeed, have grown a little, whereupon they all laughed and pinched her cheeks and chucked her under the chin. They told Kamala that she and Mohini must come over for a cup of tea some morning, no excuses this time. And with the wave of a hand they drifted away, in no hurry to get back to their lunch preparation that had been momentarily interrupted.

Kamala pointed to a spot on the stone courtyard in front of Anantrao, who was still asleep. Someone had marked onto it in chalk the game of hopscotch. "Is that all right?" Kamala asked.

"I've told the children that as long as they are quiet they can play in front of our rooms," Umabai said. "They always keep one eye on your father, however, and as soon as he stirs in his armchair, away they run."

Mohini and Kamala washed their feet at the outdoor tap, and when they went into the kitchen, Umabai was sitting on the ground and lighting the kerosene stove.

"Where's Tukaram?" Kamala said.

"He was supposed to return two days ago but he never showed up." Umabai turned away quickly, looked at Mohini, and said, "What can you smell?"

Mohini breathed in deeply. "Chirote."

"Ever since you were born, Mohini," Shridhar said, entering the kitchen, "it is not important to your grand-mother that she prepare something that Kamala or I like. It's always, 'I'm cooking this because it is Mohini's favourite dish.'" He sat cross-legged in the window next to her.

"That's because she doesn't have any other grand-children, Shridhar," Kamala said, not without a hint of reproach.

Umabai smiled slyly, stirring some fresh coconut into the curry. "That's why he is here, to look at a girl."

"Will we get to see her too, Aji?" Mohini asked.

Her grandmother nodded. "The girl is from Sangamner and twenty-seven years of age. Her eldest uncle lives in Aundh." She tipped her head in the direction of the front verandah and lowered her voice. "Your father asked

Shridhar to tell her uncle to bring her here. We are not going all the way to Aundh, he said."

"You actually agreed to meet this girl, Shridhar?" There was surprise in Kamala's voice.

"I came here yesterday on my way back to Bombay. It's only then that Aai told me about her. Before I could react, Baba said if I didn't agree to see her, then I should not bother coming back to Poona, ever again. There was no question of agreeing or disagreeing."

"This time it is going to happen, Kamala, you'll see," Umabai said. She looked down and busied herself, stirring the vegetable curry that was about to come to a boil. She turned to Mohini. "The cuckoo that used to sing in the gul mohur? Now there is a flock of them. In January, a music teacher moved in next door. Morning to night the teacher holds singing lessons, and morning to night the cuckoos trill along with the scales. They are silent today because Sunday no music lessons are taught."

Anantrao was coughing. His armchair creaked. Mohini and Kamala hurried outside. Kamala bent down and did namaskar. Mohini bowed her head and joined her hands together, her torso and legs too stiff to allow her to bend at the waist. "Tell me," Anantrao said, "how Vishnupant condescended to send the two of you by train, all on your own." His tone was mocking but time had dulled its edge.

"Things have changed, Baba," Kamala said. "You are thinking of pre-war years when mother and daughter didn't travel alone. Now, the trains are full. There is no danger of any kind."

"There was no danger of any kind back then," Anantrao muttered. He looked at Mohini as he settled back into his armchair. "What did you bring for me?" He held out his right palm.

"This," she said, placing her hand on his.

"Just what an old, toothless man like me needs." He pulled her down on his lap. His thighs were bony and his breath was sour from sleep. "Tell me about your train ride. Did you see any tigers?"

"Not even a lion," Mohini said, smiling.

"No, not any more." Anantrao closed his eyes, the wrinkles on his forehead disappearing as he spoke. "Those were the days when one saw tigers and wolves and wild goats in the ghats. Long ago. In the pre-war years." He lapsed into a silence for so long that Mohini thought he must have fallen asleep. She slipped off his lap and went to the kitchen, where Kamala was cutting cucumber and Umabai was measuring into a small round-bottomed steel container several teaspoons of curds.

"Your father has difficulty sleeping during the night," Umabai said to Kamala. "I often hear him pacing up and down, clearing his throat, spitting into the bushes."

"Nonsense!" Anantrao shouted from the verandah. "Maybe I cannot fall asleep because my wife is keeping track of my every movement. Let me sleep in peace, Umabai, let me lie awake in peace!"

"All right! All right!" Umabai shouted back. "When I wake up in the middle of the night I will tell myself it is a ghost who is pacing, a ghost who is getting on and off the mattress, a ghost whose joints are cracking loudly like a whip."

Mohini looked outside the kitchen window into the backyard. Even though he must have heard his parents,

Shridhar continued to dangle his legs from the platform;
he turned over yet another page of his book and proceeded
to read. She looked at Kamala. There was a very small smile
on her mother's face. Baba is right, Mohini thought. Aji is
more than capable of standing up for herself.

Mohini awoke the next morning to the soft, gentle murmuring of a cuckoo and the laboured tones of some woman
who was singing scales rather badly. A portable wooden
commode had been placed for Mohini in the corner bathroom that was separated from the rest of the room by a
stone lip five feet high. Mohini closed the shutters of the
window, locked the door, and used the commode before
washing her face and mouth with the water that was placed
in a brass vessel to one side. She could hear the tinkle of
spoons licking vessels. She glanced at the pegs on the wall.
Kamala's and Umabai's nightclothes hung there. They
must have bathed and tiptoed out of the room quietly, without making much sound.

   In the kitchen they were busy preparing khichadi. The
evening before, while discussing the prospective girl and
her family's visit the following day, Kamala had learned
from her mother that she was planning to serve each guest
only one sweetmeat, along with a single cup of tea. Kamala
shook her head and suggested that at least one other dish
be served. "These people are coming all the way from
Aundh," she said.

   But Umabai muttered that in her opinion there was
absolutely no need for another dish, that after all it was the
girl's side coming to see the boy's side, not the other way
round. Kamala glanced at Mohini. "Why don't you make

khichadi, Aji?" Mohini quickly said. "That way I'll get to eat it too. You know how much I love it."

"Be careful, Umabai," Anantrao cautioned his wife. "Your granddaughter and her mother are as thick as thieves."

"I don't need to be reminded," Umabai sniffed. "They've been like that since the day Mohini was born. But how often does my granddaughter visit? When she says she likes something, I know she means it. Mind you don't groan afterwards, Mohini, as you did the last time when you ate too much. Starchy sago has a tendency to bloat inside the stomach."

Mohini was sitting in the diffused sunlight under the feathery canopy of the jacaranda tree when a battered red car pulled up in front of the compound wall. The doors were thrown open and Mohini counted seven heads as people tumbled out. The girl was the last to appear. Mohini got up and stood next to Kamala. She had hurried outside and was greeting a man, who was murmuring an apology for showing up in such numbers. Mohini thought he must be the girl's father. His eyes were lanceolate, like hers, and he had the same eyebrows, arched and full. He turned to Anantrao and Umabai, who had walked out onto the verandah, and said, "I needed my brother and sister-in-law to show me the way to Parvati, and at the last minute their grandchildren insisted on coming along."

Anantrao was silent, and when Umabai did not respond, Kamala quickly said that it did not matter in the least that the children were here, her warm tone suggesting that if two carloads had arrived instead of one, the Nene family would have been ready to receive them all.

After the entourage—the girl, her father, her uncle, her aunt, a young man who may have been her brother, and her two young nephews—had walked up the stairs and entered the front room, Mohini went around the building. She slipped into her grandmother's room through the back verandah. She went to the window of the dividing wall and parted slightly the curtains that covered its lower end. The girl showed herself in blurred slivers as she fidgeted in her seat. Long fingers, two plaits tied into a single loop with a black ribbon, a small nose, and what seemed like a twitch at the corners of her mouth each time she looked in the direction of Mohini.

After a few minutes, when the ladies moved to the back verandah, Kamala introduced Mohini to the girl, Suhasini, and her aunt. Before hurrying away to the kitchen to help Umabai with the preparation of tea, Kamala smiled at her daughter and indicated with a swift nod that Mohini could, if she wished, converse with the guests. But Mohini felt shy and didn't know what to say. The aunt looked straight ahead at the running creek that meandered silently under a row of tamarind trees that lined the back compound wall.

Suhasini glanced at Mohini two or three times. Finally, she said, "A third cousin of mine is your very best friend."

"Hansa?"

"Yes." Suhasini nodded happily. "Her mother and my mother are related."

Mohini looked at Hansa's distant cousin with renewed interest. Suhasini's two plaits had come undone and dangled on either side of her face as she dropped her head and removed from the back of her neck a small leaf that had drifted there. Her skin was definitely dusky, Mohini had to admit, duskier than Shridhar's, but not dusky enough to provide a good enough reason to reject her, she thought.

He came out now, and the aunt moved away, but only a couple of yards. Kamala called out to Mohini that her grandmother needed her in the kitchen.

That night, Shridhar agreed to marry Suhasini. Mohini had never seen her grandmother look so relieved. But Anantrao, who had all along insisted that Shridhar not leave Poona without finalizing a match, chose this moment to express his doubts. "But how will a village girl be equal to the task of settling down in Bombay?" he said.

Shridhar glanced at his mother in exasperation. Umabai was staring at her husband in disbelief.

"Never mind," Anantrao grumbled. "Make the arrangements and fix the dowry amount."

"There's no need." Shridhar looked at his mother. "I don't want a dowry."

"What do you mean?" Anantrao said.

"Vishnupant didn't ask our family for a dowry, did he?"

"We are not the Oeks," the old man replied. "Nenes always ask for dowries. Big fat ones."

Shridhar repeated, "I don't want a dowry."

"The Bombay air is not only in your lungs but has also entered your head," Anantrao said. "And because of you and your sister, your mother is beginning to breathe it too. Look at her—standing like a tigress, ready to protect the wishes of her son no matter what they are. Kamala tells me times have changed. These are not pre-war years, she reminds me. All right. Have it your way." He went through the front door and stretched out on the mattress Kamala had prepared the way he liked, the pillow placed so he could come awake to the first rays of the sun falling across his face.

Shridhar turned to his mother.

"He is tired with the day's activities," she whispered. "I'll talk to him in the morning, after you have left for Bombay."

Kamala wanted Shridhar to postpone his departure, but he told her he had to get back to work. Like Keshav, he was an engineer, employed by the Public Works Department of the Bombay Municipal Corporation. Before leaving, he asked Kamala whether she thought Suhasini was the right choice.

Kamala nodded. "She seems very level-headed. Not too shy either, which is good. And don't worry, she'll settle in Bombay. Didn't I?"

After Shridhar left, Mohini found the book he had been reading on the windowsill of the front room. It was covered in brown paper. She opened it: *The Adventures of Sherlock Holmes*, by Sir Arthur Conan Doyle. Mohini could not believe her eyes. Ever since Vishnupant had compared Balu to Sherlock Holmes, and had afterwards explained to her what he had meant by it, she had wanted to read this book. She now pulled the second armchair into the back verandah and became so absorbed in his innumerable adventures that Kamala had to call her twice when it was time to eat, or when the neighbours visited, or Oek relatives dropped by with mangoes or spicy bakarvadi, her favourite snack.

In the evenings, Kamala hid the book; she could tell

Mohini was getting headaches, although when questioned Mohini insisted that they were very mild. Kamala also noticed that come late afternoon Mohini's skin became hot to the touch. "It is as though," she said to Umabai, "the mounting heat is leaking into her body as morning turns to night."

Kamala didn't sound concerned, but by the fourth day Umabai became worried.

Mohini told her that it was probably a heat-fever.

Kamala tended to agree. "Mohini is not used to Poona's dry heat," she assured her mother. "In Poona she doesn't perspire, whereas in Bombay the perspiration regulates her body temperature."

Mohini did not tell Kamala that at times she felt quite feverish even during the day.

At times when her headaches became worse and the pounding in her ears grew fiercer, Mohini would put down her book and watch her surroundings closely, applying logic like that of her new literary hero, to come to satisfactory conclusions. Except in her grandfather's case, she was aware of the facts leading up to the conclusions and did not have to deduce them. Anantrao's grouchy temperament, she knew, was the result of growing up in a household where appearances had to be kept up in spite of dwindling resources. The farmland inherited by the Nene family in Konkan was largely fallow, and the rent from the leased-out plots negligible. The once considerable holdings had, over generations, been divided and subdivided between sons and then their sons, and there was constant bickering as to whose strip was potentially the most valuable. Not that anyone actually worked the land in any significant way: all energies were expended in attending court cases and settling disputes. When Anantrao, the mathematician in the family, had come to Poona as an accounting clerk, the needs of his brothers and their families had followed him. He would say to anyone who was inclined to listen: "What is the advantage of being a Brahmin except to live and die in poverty?"

Mohini turned her attention to her grandmother. After she'd been bullied for years by Anantrao, her grandfather's and grandmother's roles were finally reversed. Now Umabai told her husband what to do, when to do it, and like a child faced with authority, he obeyed her and waited for instructions. He didn't take a bath if Umabai did not specifically tell him that his water was ready and that it was his turn to use the bathroom, even though he had seen her lug the bucket from the kitchen and hang his fresh clothes on the bar, alongside the cotton towel. And when she scolded him for continuing to sit on the cot in his crumpled nightclothes, he would accuse her of forgetting to tell him that the water was ready, without commanding her—as he would have done in the past—to put it back on the stove for reheating. Like a mother, she ignored his grumbling, and like a son, he accepted her right to control.

Visiting the house she had grown up in brought laughter to Kamala's face. She did not take her headache medication, but placed it discreetly underneath her pillow at night when she thought her mother wasn't watching. Instead of subsisting on three cups of coffee and bananas on Tuesday and Thursday—her two fasting days—she ate whatever fasting food her mother placed in front of her: dried lotus seeds mixed together with curds, salt and green chilies, sweet sago kheer, spicy potato kis, and even the peanut and

jaggery ladoo that she normally avoided because it produced heat in her body and caused her stomach to rumble.
She and her mother were the best of friends when they sat
on the back verandah, chatting late into the night even
though they had chatted all day long. Kamala was a little girl
again, a slightly older sister of the younger Kamala whom
Mohini had seen in the wedding pictures her grandmother
kept in the bottom shelf of her cupboard.

Soon, it was time to leave. Kamala did not say much,
Mohini deduced, because her tears were locking her
throat. Anantrao's eyes were wet. He walked with them to
the footpath where the tanga was waiting. He told Kamala
that the next time Shridhar came to Poona he would get
him to look for a doctor who could administer transfusions. That way, on their following visit, Mohini and
Kamala could stay longer. He pressed fifteen rupees into
Kamala's palm just as she was climbing into the tanga and
told her that five of those were for Mohini.

Umabai handed up a large cloth bag into which she had
stuffed all kinds of sweetmeats and savouries. "The sesame
ladoos are only for Keshav," she said. Her small hands
shook as she caressed Mohini's cheeks.

Mohini said, "I know you always say that you cannot
come and stay with us because a wife's parents never visit
her in-laws, but I want you stay with us in Bombay next
time, and not with Shridharmama."

Her grandmother was silent.

"Promise me, Aji."

Umabai nodded and put the end of her sari to her mouth
as the horse pulled away.

At the railway station, Kamala paid the driver. While

searching the capacious pocket of his shirt for some loose change, he nodded in Mohini's direction and asked, "What's wrong with her?" He ran his gaze over her bent knees, her dull skin, the way she held on to Kamala so as not to lose her balance.

"She'll feel better once we reach Bombay," Kamala said. "She finds it difficult to breathe here, in this dry heat."

"There is a medicine man near the station who is famous all over the region. If you go down the gully next to the Grand Hotel, you will see his shop, Miracle Cures. You can't miss it."

"We don't have time today, but I will remember the shop when I'm next in Poona."

The driver put his fingers in his mouth and whistled for a coolie. The coolie hoisted their bags easily onto his shoulders and Kamala held out her hand to Mohini. When Mohini looked back at the driver, he was shaking his head. He waved to her. Once they were seated in the compartment, she was unable to read her mother's expression. "What are you thinking?" Mohini asked.

"That it is amazing how so many people express concern for your well-being. If only I could count the number of times this or that doctor has been suggested to me, this or that cure, this or that prayer. Are you hungry, Mohini? Aji has made another little packet for the journey."

"Not yet," Mohini said. She looked outside the window at a vendor who was hurrying along carelessly, balancing on his head as though it were an empty basket a tray laden with steaming cups of tea.

SIX

Laying down the newspaper she had just finished reading, Mohini grumbled to Vishnupant that she wanted to do something different. It had only been a few days since she had returned from Poona. "Sit with the college students," he said. "Join in on their discussions." The students normally gathered at the gymkhana. It was closed for repairs, and Vishnupant had offered Koleshwar Nivas as a temporary venue.

"What do they talk about?"

"This or that. Wide-ranging topics."

"Do you sit with them?"

"Sometimes. For a few minutes." The book Vishnupant was working on was almost nearing its end. He had added afternoons to his work time in order to further the final drafts.

Mohini nodded. Kamala liked the idea as well. So now, instead of climbing the stairs with her mother after lunch, Mohini began to take her afternoon nap in her grandfather's room, downstairs. It was cooler here, the windows cut into each wall providing cross ventilation so that every now and then a little breeze would drift through, bringing a slight relief to Mohini, who would be sleeping on her grandfather's four-poster bed.

Vishnupant watched his granddaughter while she slept, her cropped hair damp at the temples, the back of her left knee so out of alignment that it was unable to touch the mattress. He would gaze on a point at the side of her throat where the skin moved up and down sharply at each intake and release of breath. Sometimes, she would lift her hand up to her head, and Vishnupant would wonder whether she was awake or if she massaged her temples absent-mindedly in her sleep. As he looked at her, a long-forgotten memory would surface: the belaboured rumbling of trains as they screeched to a halt outside his grandparents' home. And then another: him standing on the stone windowsill of their front room and handing the window screens down to his grandmother so she could wash off the tiny grains of soot that had blocked the wire mesh one square pinhole at a time. He tried to find a connection between this persistent memory and his granddaughter, and when he couldn't, he wished there was something he could say or do that would enable him to remove the cloudy screens that were inside her; that were clogging her pores with suffering and pain. He got up and stared out the window as a thought occurred to him: Mohini would never grow to reminisce about him the way he reminisced about his grandparents.

When it was nearing the time for the students to arrive, he would wake her and she would wait in the front verandah and watch the vegetable vendor, whose habit it was to walk down the centre of the lane at this time of the afternoon, the basket on top of his head casting a deep shadow across his face. If it were raining, she would stand just outside the front door and listen to the water roll off the eaves into the shrubs below, and watch it stream down verandah posts before spreading under her feet in gently lapping waves. Sometimes, she would wait at the sitting-room window, the crash of the downpour mesmerizing as it pitted the softened earth, the occasional paper boat whirling past swiftly in the rain-swept gutter. But rain or drizzle, the students would come one or two or three at a time and stay for an hour or longer if the discussions became heated and no one wished to concede a point. At such times, at Mohini's request, Bayabai would bring in steaming cups of tea, her mouth pursed because now there would be less milk left to turn into curds.

Earlier in June, the British viceroy, Lord Mountbatten, had announced that the transfer of power would take place ahead of schedule, on August 15, less than three months away. The newspapers detailed the developments relating to this transfer, and the topic of partition was never far from the students' minds. One afternoon, a slight youth by the name of Jayant Deshpande removed from his pocket a detailed letter from his cousin in Lahore. "My cousin writes that there is a permanent stench of blood in the air. Communal riots are flaring up all the time, he says, the next one beginning before the first is put down."

Mohini listened aghast, her breath drawn even as Jayant unfolded the letter and read out scenes of horror, glancing briefly in her direction as he referred to assaults against women and children, looting, and dismemberment. She wished to move away from the window ledge but a morbid fascination pinned her to her place. Besides, she knew that once the letter was put away it was only a matter of time before the history of the Raj would be revisited, possible reasons why the north had exploded in such carnage cited, arguments built up from their foundations, layer by layer, date by date, event by event. She marvelled at the ease with which the students remembered their figures and facts. And they in turn liked to play teacher with her. They were delighted by her interest in Indian history and spoke to her as though she were their equal, an attitude that pleased and flattered her immensely.

"The divide-and-rule policy that the British so thoroughly employed, pitting Hindus against Muslims, the upper classes against the lower," Jayant Deshpande explained to Mohini, "has ultimately become their legacy. Now that they are quitting India, they are leaving it a divided nation."

Mohini was sitting next to her grandfather on the sofa, watching him rearrange jumbled handwritten notes according to their page numbering. She looked at Jayant now to let him know that she was listening.

The people of the North West Frontier Province and Punjab were the worst hit by partition, Mohini learned. There, the Sikh and Muslim populations lived side by side, and as it became clear that one of them would have to give up their homeland, the communal tensions increased. To make the problem worse, there were no immediate boundaries drawn and the people had little sense of what was to come. This caused unnecessary panic and pre-emptive attacks. In Bengal, a similar situation existed, except this time the violence was between the Hindus and the Muslims.

"In these conditions, how do people carry on with their daily lives?" a student asked.

Jayant shrugged, then said, "Perhaps they try to convince themselves that everything is an illusion, a dream. That's what my grandmother said she did when seven of her eleven children passed away. She firmly believes that we will be delivered from our suffering only when Brahma stops dreaming about us."

Turning to her grandfather, Mohini whispered, "If all this is Brahma's dream, then why is He having such nightmares?" But Vishnupant was getting to his feet, the arranged papers clasped under his armpit. The students were so absorbed in their discussion that they did not even notice him leave.

Ramesh, Jayant's cousin, was loudly saying, "Disrupted daily lives are one thing, but there is something else that is not clear to me at all. In the past, when so many non-violent opportunities presented themselves—round-table conferences and meetings between the government and our freedom fighters, formal and informal talks—why did the Congress party not take these opportunities and come to some form of agreement?" When nobody replied, he continued: "What I mean is this—since the Congress party made non-violence the platform by which independence would be achieved, why were all measures that would result in non-violence not employed?"

Jayant nodded. "The most non-violent way would have been to achieve freedom through conferences and dialogue. But every time the British approached us and offered concessions, however small, the Congress party shut down communication because they had made non-cooperation their motto. And the irony of it all is that in spite of this non-violent policy, thousands upon thousands are killing each other even as we speak." He shook his head with incomprehension.

Sometimes, heartsick with the stories of bloodshed, Mohini would go to the kitchen, where her mother and Bayabai would be preparing dinner, the pungent smell of green chilies and fresh coriander bringing water to her eyes. She would carry in from the puja room a low stool and sit in the corner while Kamala kneaded the dough and Bayabai sighed with satisfaction at the end of each completed task. After shelling the peas or snapping the green beans that her mother had placed in a basket on her lap, Mohini would lean against the wall and close her eyes. Steam-blowing vessels would be bubbling on the stove with such gusto that the kitchen would be transformed into a railway station, a place from which intrepid travellers journeyed forward to destinations unknown.

However, by the time she went to bed, it would become impossible once again to block out the voices that she had heard that afternoon. One night when the rain had petered out and she did not have to raise her voice above its din, she asked her mother, "You know Jayant Deshpande? He was saying the British do not rule the whole of India. That two-fifths is still under the control of the maharajas and nawabs."

Kamala lowered her embroidery, looked up briefly, and said, "The new government will have to come to some kind of an agreement with them. Maybe those within the territorial boundaries of India will be assimilated into India and those inside Pakistan will join Pakistan. I don't know. You'll have to ask your grandfather."

"Did you know there are five hundred and sixty-two princely states?"

"As many as that?" Kamala looked up again, holding her needle at elbow's length. "Some of the maharajas and nawabs are pukka Englishmen, I have heard."

"How so?"

"A lot of them are educated in England and when they return home they live just like Englishmen."

"What does that mean?"

"I don't know. Maybe they eat meat and drink alcohol and dress like the British all the time, not only when they are at work. Malatimavshi, who lives in Kalyan? Her married name is Talwalkar. Her husband's family are retailers for white drill cloth and satin duck, the material that officer cadre suits are made of."

"What about her?"

"Many years ago, when I was younger than you, her family anglicized the name of their establishment from Talwalkar and Company to T. Walker Merchants of Cloth. They thought it would bring prestige to the company to have a British name."

It had occurred to Mohini that she had not met a single British person even though they had ruled India for over a hundred years. She had, however, met an American. Three years previously, Dr. Chitnis had taken her to a house in Bandra to meet Dr. Peterson, who was passing through Bombay on his way to the Malabar Coast.

"As you know," Dr. Chitnis had explained to Kamala on the terrace, "Dr. Cooley was the American pediatrician from Detroit who first reported the thalassemia trait. The doctor who is coming here is doing similar research in another city, in Boston." Dr. Chitnis said he had been in touch with Dr. Peterson from the first diagnosis of Mohini's disease. When writing to Dr. Chitnis about his impending visit to India, the American doctor had expressed a desire to meet Mohini. Dr. Chitnis had boasted to him that she was his one patient who confounded on a day-to-day basis conventional medical wisdom that predicted for patients with the disease up to three years, perhaps a bit more, of survival.

Kamala said that she had no objection to Mohini's meeting Dr. Peterson. However, since she, Kamala, had to take Vishnupant for his eye appointment that day, she would have to ask Mohini whether she would mind going to meet Dr. Peterson on her own. Mohini said she did not mind at all.

The house in Bandra belonged to a Parsi family. Dr. Chitnis helped Mohini up the steep flight of stairs. Tall wooden doors opened into a large marble hall in which were placed marble statues and wooden chests and Persian carpets the like of which Mohini had never before seen. On the walls hung life-size portraits of various family members and oil paintings that depicted thick woods and green pastures, and china vases overflowing with delicate, pastel flowers. On one wall, above a door, was a framed portrait of King George VI. The carved furniture was so beautiful that Mohini thought the sofa was a showpiece until the American doctor asked her to lie down on it.

His hands were gentle as he palpated her abdomen, and Mohini felt instantly at ease. He kneeled in front of her and examined her jaw and neck by pressing his fingers lightly into the contours. Mohini watched his face, the skin around his eyes white and creased like wrinkled paper, his mouth red and fleshy. While he was examining her, he spoke with Dr. Chitnis. She couldn't understand much of what he was saying as he pronounced his words so differently, and watching Dr. Chitnis's quizzical expression, she suspected that he was having difficulty too. After Dr. Peterson had finished examining her, he got off his knees and helped her into a sitting position.

The side table was laden with food. Dr. Peterson filled a plate for Mohini, and for the rest of the visit he continued to ply her with tomato-and-cucumber sandwiches, small golden cakes, and salted potato wafers so thin that through them she could see the design on her plate: a green gabled mansion next to a steepled church reaching up into a cream-coloured sky, and a river in front of which a stout oarsman lounged lazily, leaning against his flat-bottomed boat. When it was time for fruit, Dr. Peterson waved away the bearer who came forward with a silver spoon and encouraged Mohini to hold up her slice of watermelon to her mouth. Easier to eat with your hands than with a spoon, he implied with his grin. Mohini grinned back, and although she was ten years old and attending New English Academy, she did nothing to contradict Dr. Peterson's impression that she did not speak or understand a word of what he was saying.

"I was thinking about Dr. Peterson, Aai," Mohini said to Kamala now. "Isn't it strange that I have met an American even though he lives far away in America, yet I have never met an Englishman?"

"True," Kamala replied. Squinting, she looked into the eye of the needle and carefully inserted a long length of thread.

"I told that to Jayant Deshpande," Mohini said, "and he told me that the British used to mix with the Indians at the beginning, when they first came to India. They spoke our languages too, he said, and some even married Indian women. But when the Suez Canal was opened, the journey to India became shorter. So the Englishmen went home more often and brought out their wives. Jayant said it was the wives who did not want their husbands mixing in with us."

Kamala nodded. "I have also heard your grandfather say that whereas the French colonialists cultivated the company of the native intellectuals, the British kept the Indian intellectuals at arm's length. They distrusted the educated elite."

"I'll tell Jayant that," Mohini said.

Mohini had heard her father refer to his British colleagues at B & J Construction every now and again, but he never invited them home, not even for a cup of tea. Vishnupant had told her that several of his colleagues at Bombay University had been British, but when pressed to answer what they had been like, he had nothing particular to say except to repeat that they kept very much to themselves.

Mohini had heard of British-only clubs and hotels outside which were hung signs that read, Indians and Dogs Not Allowed. Once, when she and Kamala were waiting in Dr. Merchant's rooms in Colaba, the door of the inner room had opened and an English couple had walked out. Because the husband was holding his wife by her elbow, Mohini supposed it was she who was the patient. Her frame was large, her wrists twice the breadth of Kamala's wrists, and her pink cheeks exuded a healthy glow. Her eyes were like a cat's, pale blue in colour. When Mohini described to Vishnupant the Englishwoman whom she said was the most unpatient-like patient she had ever seen, he shrugged and told her that there was no denying the nutritive value of a diet that was composed chiefly of meat.

Mohini knew Vishnupant thought that the British Raj had long outrun its course. Nevertheless, whenever he spoke of the British there was reverence in his voice. He recognized the ideas and values they had brought to India. Ever since the start of the Mughal dynasty, he told Mohini, the Indian mind, which in bygone days had reached a monumental level of sophistication, had sunk into apathy. In all branches of religion and science, where previously there had been great research and thought, now there was very little introspection. Society had become static. Superstition, ritualism, blind faith, and casteism had become the pillars around which life revolved. However, with the advent of the British, he said, that giant mind was reawakened. Now that it had come out of centuries of hibernation, it was anxious to absorb new ideas. And it was these new ideas and concepts that ultimately had caused disillusionment and ignited within the Indian breast an ardent desire for self-rule.

Yet, Mohini's Poona grandfather repeated only one thing: he thanked God that the British had not tried to make India their own, as they had done alongside the Boers, in South Africa. Paraphrasing with satisfaction the triumphant words of an erstwhile Roman conqueror, he exclaimed, "To India they came, they saw, they conquered! . . . and left upon completion of duty."

Although Keshav could force Anantrao to concede that but for the British, German, and French scholars, pre-Islamic India would not have been revealed to her people, he still wanted the British gone. "They have fulfilled their destiny by showing us the potential we once possessed, the potential that culminated in dynasties such as the Mauryan Empire, the Gupta Empire, the Chola dynasty, the Pandyan kingdom. Now, it is time for them to leave."

Mohini was puzzled that it was possible to hate the British Raj and at the same time recognize its contribution. There seemed to be a contradiction here. She said as much to Keshav one day when he had finished extolling the British for the establishment of one law for all in a caste-ridden society. "That's the way it is," he replied. "Contradiction or no contradiction, it's important to call a spade a spade."

"Some people are born honest," Kamala murmured, looking at Keshav with a soft smile on her face. "They have this ability to see the world for what it is." She hastily sobered her expression when she saw Mohini glancing her way.

"Jayant Deshpande," Kamala said now. "You like him, don't you?"

Mohini wrinkled her nose and brushed a loose strand of hair away from her forehead. "Yes."

"What do you like about him?"

"I don't know . . ." She paused. "When he is explaining something to me, he looks at me to make sure that I have understood what he is saying."

"You like that?"

Mohini nodded and said, "Why are you asking?"

"Just curious, that's all."

Mohini looked into the terrace as the rain reached a crescendo. Clouds emptied themselves over the city with such torrential force that but for the walls and roofs the lights within homes would have been extinguished, the people drenched to their bones.

Weeks later, lying on her back, searching for ways to get lost in her memories in order to forget the pain, Mohini would recall her school years and especially these nights: her mother doing her embroidery within the contained circle of the lamp, her needle flashing every now and then as she filled blue thread into the flowing river and the tops of water jars, reserving the detailed work—the silver anklets of the village girls, the darker veins in the leaves of the weeping willow, the birds flying high in the sky—for the bright light that would come with the morning.

Whenever a wet breeze fluttered the pages of a book Mohini had abandoned on her desk, Kamala would stop her needle and look into the terrace, watching for a while the rain bounce off the floor in a flurry of beads. There was a mirror by the side of the door. Glancing into it every now and again, Kamala became conscious of the timelessness of the reflected scene: mother and daughter spending the last half-hour of the evening together, waiting for the return of the husband and father who was employed in building causeways in a land where ancient rivers had run dry.

SEVEN

Three days remained until the end of the summer holidays. It was late afternoon. Mohini turned on the light in the sitting room and stood by the window peering outside. Overhead, there were only clouds, no sky. The rain tree in the yard was still, the leaves so motionless they could have been carved out of stone. Kamala came from behind Mohini and massaged the back of her neck. Together they watched Vasanti, who was bent over the bushes near the front gate. She was clearing the damp earth of the bedraggled twigs, leaves, and petals that had drifted there. She had been in the garden all afternoon, working the vegetable patch with such single-mindedness and determination that Vishnupant had scolded her for remaining outdoors under such a humid sun. Vasanti had ignored him.

Kamala called out to her, "You better stop now, Vasanti, before a scorpion bites you. It's getting dark."

"I'm more or less finished," Vasanti said, straightening her back.

Mohini looked at Kamala. "Are you coming out on the verandah?" she asked. "Vishnupant is there."

Kamala shook her head.

When Mohini went outside, Vasanti was washing her feet at the garden tap. She walked up the shallow stairs while drying her hands on the end of her sari, and waited for Vishnupant and Mohini to finish reciting their prayers before holding out to Mohini the pink stone that Hansa had given her. "I found it by the tap," she said.

"Hansa must have left it there after she had finished washing it this afternoon. We still can't see any sparkles."

"How are you feeling?" Vasanti asked.

"I'm fine," Mohini said. "Vishnupant asked me that question just a little while ago." She passed to Vishnupant an orange that she had been attempting to peel.

Vasanti turned to her uncle. "Mohini's eyes look swollen, don't you think?"

He nodded but did not add that Mohini's eyes had had that same heavy-lidded look the entire summer, causing him often to wish that there was something he could do or say to bring her a little peace.

Vasanti got up. She was almost at the gate when Vishnupant raised his voice. "You may want to listen to this, Vasanti, before you go."

She turned around.

"In fact," Vishnupant said, "Kamala should be here as well."

Vasanti glanced at Mohini.

Mohini called out, "Aai!"

Kamala entered the verandah.

"Come and sit." Vishnupant pointed to the empty chair next to Vasanti. When Kamala was seated he turned to Mohini and said, "You thought I didn't hear you that time when the students were here, when you asked me that if all this is Brahma's dream, then why is He having such night-mares." He began to peel the orange.

Mohini nodded.

"She asked you that?" Vasanti said.

"She did. I don't have any answer to the why in that question, Mohini, although thinking about the answer did produce some other thoughts."

Vasanti sat forward in her chair. "Will this take long, Vishnukaka? I really must go home." Vasanti had been rest-less ever since her in-laws from Nagpur had visited her the previous afternoon. Mohini had noticed that they had the same unsettling effect on her whenever they passed through Bombay, and it always took her a couple of days after they had left to recover.

"I'll try to be as quick as I can," Vishnupant said. "But, before we begin, I want to say that one of the bases of the assertion that this world of ours is all maya, an illusion, Brahma's dream, is based on the premise that things can-not exist independently of the perceiver's mind. But when I searched for an answer to your question, Mohini, my thoughts led me in a completely different direction."

Mohini settled back into her chair.

"I asked myself, what if I were to compare various aspects of my own dreams to the dream Brahma is having?"

There was a brief silence. "Go on, Vishnukaka," Vasanti said.

Vishnupant looked up as the last of the sparrows sped across a darkening sky. "Do you remember your dreams?" he asked.

"Sometimes," Mohini said.

Vasanti and Kamala nodded agreement.

"Do you have control over your dreams? Are you able to go to bed saying, 'Tonight this is what I am going to dream about,' and then dream it?"

Vasanti and Mohini shook their heads.

"The people inside your dreams, do they have a free will?"

"I don't understand," Mohini said.

"What he means is," Vasanti said, "are you the dreamer telling the people in your dreams what to say and do? Am I right, Vishnukaka?"

He nodded. "So, do they have free will?"

"When I dream I don't control the actions of the people in my dream," Mohini said. "Then yes, they do have free will."

"Now let us assume that the people in our dreams have free will. That's the same as saying that once my dream begins, I, the dreamer, have absolutely no control over the content of my dreams."

Vishnupant was speaking very slowly. Kamala started to say something, then stopped. Vishnupant said, "Go on, Kamala, ask whatever you want."

She dropped her gaze.

"Ask him, Aai," Mohini said.

"It's not a question. I was just thinking that I couldn't say that I have absolutely no control over my dreams because my dream is not the same as your dream. It matters who the dreamer is."

Vishnupant was silent. He transferred to a low table next to him the orange peels that he had been collecting on his lap.

"I think what I want to say is that a sailor will dream about the sea, a student about his books . . ."

Vishnupant still did not say anything.

Vasanti was impatient. "Well?"

"You make a valid point, Kamala. I will change my premise and say that although my conscious, material circumstances dictate who will people my dreams and what kind of events will occur in them, I have no control over the people or the nature of the events once my dream begins. Can I say that?"

Mohini, Vasanti, and Kamala nodded slowly.

"Now, what if the same analogy were to be made about Brahma's dream? Just like the people in my dream who have free will, do I, a person in His dream, have free will as well?"

Kamala nodded.

"So, it is established that I, like the people in my dream, have free will. That being the case, can I say that this universe of mine which He has dreamed up and in which unfortunate events occur—can I say that these events are His doing because He is the dreamer? Or, can I say that like the people in my dream who exert free will, I, in Brahma's dream, do the same?"

There was no response. Vishnupant reached for his glass of water.

Vasanti looked at Kamala and lifted her eyebrows, wondering why Vishnupant was addressing Mohini's question with such passion. Kamala shook her head.

"All right, let us follow along the lines of fatalism. According to that theory, events such as birth, marriage, death, and other major landmarks in our lives are predetermined." Vishnupant held up his right hand and extended a forefinger. "However, life is composed of many moments. Do we not exert free will in the majority of those moments, the day-to-day events? Not to forget complete free will in what goes on inside our heads. Do we think that our thoughts are predetermined? The fatalist may say that they are. But really, from our own experience, do we not exert choices all the time? What to eat. What to read. What to say. Or do we think we are puppets whose every physical and mental twitch is monitored by Him?"

"We're not puppets," Kamala murmured.

"Let me give you an illustration."

They waited for him to continue.

"Let's say I have a dream in which two men are arguing. One man says that such-and-such a thing is responsible for the partition of India. The other disagrees and cites different reasons. They continue to argue and finally one of them gets so angry that he picks up a rock and dashes it against the skull of the other. Now, keep in mind that *I* am the dreamer when I ask you the next question."

Mohini leaned forward and pinched her mouth and nose together in concentration. She glanced at Vasanti. Her aunt was watching Vishnupant strip the white threads from the orange. Her fingers were tattooing an uneven rhythm on her lap.

"Given that the dream is my dream," Vishnupant continued, "am I responsible for the actions of the two men? Is it I who made them argue in the first place and then made one lose his temper and commanded the other to hold his in check?"

Vasanti was watching Vishnupant intently. A muscle at the corner of her mouth was twitching. Kamala answered for them all: "No."

"So, the communal violence that is taking place in the

north—is Brahma responsible for that or are we? And if the answer is that we are, then is it not up to each of us to mould ourselves in a way that will allow us to live our lives in equanimity and peace?"

"No, it is not," Vasanti said. She thrust forward her neck, slapping away impatiently at a mosquito that was buzzing around her face. "It is not up to us because even though we have free will we did not make us. Brahma made us and He made us with flaws."

"I agree. But the knowledge that I have free will still allows me a measure of hope—"

"What hope, Vishnukaka, what hope?" The veins in Vasanti's neck were pulsing. Mohini turned her head quickly and glanced at Kamala. She had never seen this expression of scorn on her aunt's face. "Knowing all this is Brahma's dream gives you hope?" Vasanti raised her voice above the sound of a dog that was barking at the end of the lane.

Kamala put her fingers to her lips, cautioning Vasanti not to say any more. Not when there was every danger that she would say something in a tone and manner she would later regret.

"No, Kamalavahini, no. You heard what he said. Vishnukaka is implying that if all this is Brahma's dream and we have free will, then everything is more or less well with the world because there is hope."

Mohini didn't think her grandfather had meant it like that. She also didn't understand why Vasanti was so angry. She had never before seen her aunt disagree so forcefully with Vishnupant. It unsettled Mohini, made the inside of her stomach feel as though it were being wrung.

"I haven't finished yet, Vasru," Vishnupant said, his tone deliberately playful. But his old nickname for her—newborn calf—only made Vasanti bristle. She jumped up and stood by the verandah railing with her face turned towards the sky, in which rain clouds continued to obscure the moon and stars.

Kamala quickly said, "Let your uncle finish, Vasanti. Come and sit."

"I can listen from here," Vasanti muttered without turning around.

"Let's go back to my dream then," Vishnupant said. "There are these two men. One hits the other. Now, if I, the dreamer, could talk to the man who picked up the rock, what would I say to him?"

"You'd tell him not to get so angry," Mohini said.

"Yes, but *why*?"

There was silence. Vishnupant looked at Kamala.

Kamala's voice was soft and hesitant as she said, "You, the dreamer, will say to the man, 'Don't get so angry because after all this is only my dream.'"

Vishnupant nodded. "I would say to the man, 'You are as real and substantial as my dream is real and substantial. The minute I wake up, you and everything else in my dream will disappear, cease to exist. And because you were only a figment of my imagination, you never really did exist.'"

Vasanti, who had been paying close attention to her uncle, snorted and said, "What kind of philosophy is that? My world, Vishnukaka, is very real and it hurts. I hurt here." She beat a fist against her heart. Her clenched thumb and fingers made a sharp sound against her chest. "And I hurt here," she said, this time knocking her head with her knuckles. Her face was red and her eyes were wet. She brought up the end of her sari to rub them.

Vishnupant's face softened at her anguish and he looked down at the orange he had been holding. Slowly, he divided it into four. After passing three-quarters to Kamala, he said, "What you say is true, Vasanti." His voice was soft and gentle. "However unreal Brahma's dream may be, there is another reality in which all of us live, where there is good and bad, joy and suffering, virtue and vice. On the other hand, knowing our flawed reality, and understanding that we have free will, does it not seem reasonable to say that since this world of ours is full of good and bad consequences, it is up to of each of us to mould ourselves in such a way as to maximize mental peace and minimize suffering?"

"But you spoke about hope," Vasanti said, her tone defeated, uncomprehending.

Looking at her, Mohini did not understand why Vishnupant was pressing the issue of Brahma's dream, why he was holding on to it so tightly; why he was not letting it go. She sat forward in her chair, her clammy hands gripping its edge. Kamala held out to her one half of the orange. Mohini placed a segment in her mouth.

Vishnupant rubbed his face with the soft cotton towel that was hanging from his shoulder and briefly closed his eyes. When he opened them, he said, "Do you think I am unaware of your situation, Vasru? Unaware of your pain? Life is not easy to bear, much less to grasp. I have minimal understanding of it myself."

Vasanti turned her head and looked at him in disbelief.

"I mean that," he said to her. "Understanding something with my intellect is completely different from understanding the same thing with my soul. Intelligence and wisdom don't always go hand in hand. Both of us are sailing in the same boat, in more ways than you think."

"If everything is so difficult to understand, Vishnukaka, then how long before I will be able to grasp what is meant by Brahma's dream, even if it is only with my intellect? Twenty years? Fifty years? Or do I have to wait for another lifetime? Perhaps several? And what do you propose I do in the meantime?"

"I don't know, Vasanti, but allow me to relate to you what the late Pantoji Natu once said to me. He used to suffer from gout. Once, someone suggested a remedy that involved a foul-smelling poultice. Pantoji said he was reluctant to try it because he didn't think he would be able to tolerate the smell. At the same time, he said, his gout was too painful to ignore. What he said next, Vasanti, is something that has stayed with me. 'I suppose the road to good health,' he said, 'is like the road to the Vishveshwar Temple in Kashi. It is made up of a million steps. The man who does not take that first step is unlikely to take the last.'"

There was a long silence. Across the lane, people were hurrying out of the Irani's tea shop, packaged provisions clasped in their hands. The fresh, yeasty scent of baked bread drifted into the verandah. The grandfather clock from the floor above Vasanti's Shiv Sadan flat measured out seven loud gongs, and as the echo of the last gong died out, Vasanti said, "What if I tell myself, 'Remember, Vasanti, all this is Brahma's dream. No point in getting angry or feeling miserable. After all, all this is Brahma's dream.' What if I tell myself that?" Her voice was quavering. If there was a note of sarcasm, Mohini did not detect it.

Vishnupant looked down at his lap. He placed his elbows on the armrests of his chair and rested his chin on his steepled hands. "I'm listening," he said.

"So, I wake up in the morning with every intention that during the day I will not allow myself to lose my temper. Then, just as I am halfway through combing my hair, Mai calls out to me to leave her clean clothes and towel in the bathroom because she has been perspiring so much during the night that she must have a bath, right away. Before I can pick up my comb again, Bebitai starts fretting. The same children who steal her champak flowers every morning are entering the compound, pail in hand, and she wants me to shoo them away. Afterwards, while hanging the clothes on the drying wire, the blouses fall to the ground and I have to rinse them out all over again." Vasanti had been pulling on her chain. The clasp came undone and it hung from her neck like a broken rope. Her mouth was swollen where she had rubbed it with the end of her sari. "That first step to Kashi? I am more than willing to take it providing everybody else is willing to take it with me."

Looking at her, Mohini regretted that she had ever asked Vishnupant why Brahma was having such nightmares, and tried to convince herself that it was simply a passing observation on her part. At the time she thought that Vishnupant had not even heard her question. But here he was, having invited his niece to take part in this discussion, so that instead of returning to Mai and Bebitai where she would now be measuring out the rice grains before putting them on the stove to cook, Vasanti was on the verandah, her face and eyes swollen from so much crying. Mohini turned to her grandfather, willing him to drop the discussion then and there, to get up and go into the house, to order a round of snacks and tea. But no, that next step to Kashi had to be taken.

Vishnupant raised his head and said, "In my dream, Vasanti, the man who was hit on the skull was in many ways helpless because he had no control over the other man's actions. The same as you have no control over Bebitai, Mai, or the breeze that brings the clothes to the ground. And difficult as it may seem to put into practice, it is only you and no one else who can tell yourself not to be irritated by events that are beyond your control. You do have free will to shape your reactions. It is a question of asserting it."

Vasanti, who had been standing against the railing, slid to the ground and said, "'Does the blind Hemant know colour?' the Guruji at the Chafekar Wadi temple asked me after we received the news about Babasahib's death. 'Like Hemant, you must learn to be blind.'" Vasanti peered through the slats of the verandah. The roots of the rain tree had pushed up through the topsoil and looked like snakes. "The Chafekar Guruji was an odd man," she continued. "He spoke in parables. Nobody understood him. What's the connection between the blind boy and me? I felt like shouting at him. What does it matter that Hemant does not know colour when he does not even know objects unless he can feel and touch them? Don't you see I wasn't born blind, but that fate has made me so . . . ?" Vasanti ran out of breath.

Mohini looked down at her lap and put the last segment of the orange into her mouth. After slowly counting to ten, she glanced up. Vasanti looked exhausted, her legs folded sideways under her body, her knuckles white as she clutched the bars of the railing.

Wordlessly, Vishnupant handed his uneaten orange to Mohini and got up from his armchair. He went to the shoe stand. He slipped into his sandals and walked through the car porch and crossed Mill Road in the direction of Shivaji Park. The street lamp cast a long shadow in front of him as he disappeared down the lane.

Kamala said to Vasanti, "Why don't you stay here tonight?"

Looking across into her flat where the light was shining from the window, Vasanti said, "One day, Kamalavahini, who knows, I may be persuaded to take that first step." She pushed herself to her feet.

Kamala held out the remaining quarter of the orange to Vasanti. "Eat some," she urged.

But Vasanti was looking in the direction of the park. "Shouldn't you send Balu to fetch Vishnukaka?" she asked in a quavering voice. "Where could he have gone? I should not have argued with him like that."

"Don't worry about your uncle," Kamala quickly said. "Sometimes he likes to take a stroll before dinner. It whets his appetite."

Vasanti walked to the front gate and turned around. "But Vishnukaka never did say *why* Brahma is having such nightmares, did he? He never really did answer Mohini's question." She crossed the lane and entered Shiv Sadan. Kamala and Mohini watched as Bebitai got off the divan and walked towards their front door to let her in.

After dinner, when Keshav was getting ready for bed, Mohini told him in detail about the discussion regarding Brahma's dream and Vasanti's reaction to it. Keshav thought for a bit and said that he had always given Vasanti

full credit for adapting so well to her changed circumstances at Shivaji Park. However, in the wake of her
outburst, it had now become clear to him that what she had
been doing all along was suppressing her sorrow and anger
at the irretrievable loss of her own unfulfilled dreams.

EIGHT

Mohini was sure she had caught a cold. Towards the end of the second week of school, around mid-July, her head felt cumbersome, as though someone had unscrewed her ears and stuffed burning rags into her forehead. On Thursday afternoon, instead of going to the kitchen, she dropped her satchel against the hat stand and went upstairs to lie down on the swing. Its slow, rocking motion felt good, as did the hard wood against the side of her head. She closed her eyes. Taking an imaginary spoon, she placed it against her skull just behind her left eye and ear. Gently, she inserted its blunt wooden edge into her head and loosened that part of her brain that was burning the most. She removed the swollen knot and placed it in a copper vessel full of ice water, as clean and clear and frigid as the Himalayan streams she had learned about in geography class. Someone tiptoed across the terrace and dropped a thin cotton covering over her body. A moment later the edge of Kamala's sari touched her forehead. She wanted to hold out her hand to her mother, but Kamala was gone before she could get herself to move it. When she opened her eyes, the sunshine was at her feet. She threw off the covering and got up slowly so as not to disturb the new arrangement inside her head.

In the morning she felt much better and told Kamala that she had changed her mind about not being able to go to school. There was a science test that day which she did not want to miss. She looked well enough, so Kamala gave her permission to attend school provided she allowed Balu to carry her satchel.

Hansa was waiting for her outside the classroom door and together they went over the test portions, point by point, making the most of the ten minutes left before the school bell. Mohini's head remained sufficiently clear to allow her to answer the questions, but by lunchtime, the stuffed, woolly feeling inside her head had hardened to stone. She set aside her tiffin box without opening it. Her neck felt stiff as she turned her head to look for Hansa. When she could not locate her in the canteen she returned to her classroom and placed her tiffin in her satchel and the satchel under her bench. She left school by the front gate.

When she reached Koleshwar Nivas, she placed her hand on the compound wall in order to catch her breath. The front door of the house was shut. Vishnupant was not at his desk inside his room and Kamala was probably at the samaj, at her embroidery class. Mohini waited, her hand on the latch of the gate, willing Balu to come out on the verandah so she could tell him to tell Kamala that she had gone directly to Dr. Chitnis's clinic. But everything was still, the silence broken by two sparrows hopping on and off the verandah railing, twittering and swooping even as they played their curious game. Mohini took her hand away from the gate and continued on her way down Mohur Lane towards Shivaji Park.

The shortest route to Dr. Chitnis's clinic, she knew, would be to cut across the park. The entrance gate creaked as she pushed against it. The air felt laden, the sun a floating eye behind a spongy blanket of clouds. The grass had drunk up all the rain. The green shafts were crisp and sharp as they brushed against her shins. She stopped and looked down. Her feet were bare. She did not remember shrugging off her leather sandals. Her head felt so massive she thought it might roll off her shoulders and drop to the ground. She would not be sorry to see it go. She squinted her eyes: the façade of Dr. Chitnis's house was a yellow blur between the trees. She forced her feet to move more quickly. Suddenly, she was immobilized, her ankles sinking into soft sludge. The monsoon had turned the area under the trees into a swamp.

"Oho, Rani!" a harsh voice called out. She spun to her right. Less than ten feet away a man was slumped at the foot of a jamun tree. He was scraping his back against its trunk as though he had some kind of an itch. "Oooo, Rani. What is princess like you doing all alone in middle of the park in middle of the day like this?" He raised his arms, his fingers grotesque as they clenched and unclenched in a beckoning gesture. His voice was slurred, his eyes swimming in a viscous liquid that was yellow at the edges. "Here! Use my dhotar to wipe your feet," he shouted as she looked away, his voice nasty, threatening.

Mohini lifted her feet out of the wet mud and dashed across the road, the imprint of his exposed lower body imploding inside her head. She entered the side gate of Dr. Chitnis's compound and went around to the back and pushed against the door of the clinic. Inside, all was oddly quiet. There was no attendant at the desk. She heard a dry cough. A woman was sitting cross-legged on a folding chair against the far wall, a baby across her lap. Even though Mohini's breathing was loud and ragged, the woman did not open her eyes. Mohini held her breath: from behind her came a rustle, the sound of feet being dragged along the ground. The man was following her in. She rushed into Dr. Chitnis's examination room. The windows were closed and the air smelled musty. Through the inner door came sounds of spoons scraping utensils, a murmur of voices. She recognized that of Sheelatai, Dr. Chitnis's wife. The family were at lunch. Mohini lay down on the examination table, its unyielding hardness pushing against her back. She turned on her side, the clash of steel against steel from the servant girl washing the vessels under the running water piercing her ears with a pointed sharpness, a penetrating bite.

Her eyes blinked open when the ceiling light was switched on. She lifted her head. The piercing pain caught her unawares. She reached up to clutch her temples and groaned. Dr. Chitnis spun around. It took him only a moment to lift her wrist between his fingers and hold it against his chest.

"Where's Aai?" she asked. The area behind her eyes felt tight, as though the fluid within had thickened.

"How long have you been waiting for me?"

She shook her head and once again the pain leaped through it. Dr. Chitnis cupped her face with his hands and very gently held it in place. "Around lunchtime," Mohini said.

He let go of her face and slid the thermometer under her tongue. After removing it and glancing at the thread of mercury, he said, "It's high." He washed it at the basin and shook it until the mercury dropped back into the bulb.

"How high?"

"Just over one hundred and two."

Mohini said, "That's not high."

"I'll have to draw blood."

"What's wrong?" she asked. "Is it serious?"

"Where do you get the energy to ask all these questions?"

"Is it?"

"I haven't forgotten our pact, Mohini. But I cannot provide you with a diagnosis when I don't know what is ailing you myself." His voice was kindly but firm. She closed her eyes. "Does anyone know you are here?" he asked.

"No."

After drawing blood from the inside of her elbow, he covered her body with something cottony and thin. He turned on his desk lamp, then switched off the ceiling light and switched on the fan. The whirring blades grated against the walls of her head, but at least she could breathe. She closed her eyes and opened them only when she heard footsteps. Her mother's fingers were on her forehead. There were purplish shadows under Kamala's eyes. "I couldn't find Hansa to tell her I was leaving school," Mohini said. "I couldn't find Balu either."

Kamala's throat moved as she swallowed. She took the end of her sari and dabbed the sweat on Mohini's hairline. Her touch was light.

"I should have let someone know. I came by the house. You were at the samaj."

"It doesn't matter," Keshav said. He leaned forward, hanging his head over Mohini's face.

"Baba! I didn't see you there. What time is it?" His wristwatch was ticking next to her ear.

"A little after eight."

Mohini looked at her mother.

"It's all right," Kamala said. "Now that we know where you are, it's all right." Although the effort showed on her face, she couldn't muster a smile.

Kamala released Mohini's hand and Keshav came around and held it in his own.

"She has just gone to talk to Dr. Chitnis," he said. "We must have searched everywhere for you."

Mohini flinched.

"What is hurting?" His voice was anxious.

"You are shouting in my ear," she replied peevishly.

She closed her eyes, but not before she had seen the hurt in his. He stepped back, releasing her hand. She opened her palm in his direction. He took it quickly and moved nearer. She looked at him. There was a deep line, a meridian, running between his brows.

"We thought about checking here," Kamala said, as she followed Dr. Chitnis into the room. "Then remembered Friday is your hospital day."

"I know you told me that, Kamala," Keshav said. "But I came here after stopping at the gymkhana, after making inquiries there. The waiting room was empty."

He moved away and Dr. Chitnis took his place. "When there is no one here, Mohini, you must go through that inner door and inform someone," he said. "It was just by chance that I came in here to get something. Now try to sit up."

Keshav helped her up and supported her shoulders against his chest. Dr. Chitnis handed Kamala two tablets, which she placed on Mohini's tongue. Mohini closed her mouth and took a deep breath, dreading what was to come. Clenching her will into a determined knot, she tilted her head very slightly and took a gulp of water from the glass that her mother was holding up to her mouth. Even so, the small movement made her head feel as though it was going to burst. She drained the glass while holding still her neck and asked for more.

"If only the rest of my patients were half as co-operative!" Dr. Chitnis said.

"I'm not cooperating," Mohini muttered. "I just have this terrible thirst." She did not miss the look Dr. Chitnis gave Keshav and was relieved to note the returning smile on her father's face.

"I see you are feeling well enough to answer some questions," Dr. Chitnis said. He brought forward a high stool, perched on it, his back hunched, his glasses on his forehead. He rubbed his eyes, taking his time about it.

Keshav eased Mohini onto her back. She immediately turned on her side, her knees and elbows flexed.

"Your headaches are intense," Dr. Chitnis said. "More intense than those that you are used to. Anything else?"

Mohini was silent. Dr. Chitnis looked at Kamala.

"The last few nights," Kamala said, "I thought I heard Mohini crying out once or twice. I went to her room, but each time she didn't stir. I don't think she was awake."

Dr. Chitnis let go of Mohini's wrist. "Her pulse is a bit rapid. Anything else, Mohini? Try to remember."

"At lunchtime today, I felt like throwing up. But I hadn't eaten anything since breakfast."

"After breakfast, did you get that same nauseated feeling?"

"No."

"Anything else, Kamalavahini?"

"She's been feeling a bit irritable all week—"

"No I haven't," Mohini said.

"I thought it was because she and Hansa have been studying so hard for the science test. I should not have let her go to school this morning. I should have realized her headaches were not her normal ones. Just yesterday Vasanti pointed out to me that Mohini was lifting her hands to her head more than usual."

"It doesn't always do good, Mohini, to be such a conscientious student!" Dr. Chitnis said. There was a smile on his lips, but his tone was serious. "I can see you are tired. I'll try to be as quick as I can. Did you have a bowel movement today?"

"No."

"That cry in the middle of the night, Kamalavahini, was it continuous? Did she seem to be sobbing?"

Kamala shook her head. "Just a short scream. And when I went to her room she was lying on her side the way she is now."

"Sounds like a hydrocephalic cry."

"A what cry?" Mohini said.

"It can happen when there is an unusual amount of fluid in the brain. Turn towards the light, Mohini, so I can see your eyes."

"I can't! It hurts too much."

"Your head?"

"No, my eyes. Both."

"Just once, then."

"I can't."

"That's all right. You can go home now. I have given you something that will ease your headache. I'll come and see you in the morning."

Keshav lifted her off the examination table and carried her outside. Balu was standing next to the car. He held open the back door. "I'll be all right," Mohini said to him. He swallowed a few times, his Adam's apple bobbing prominently. Kamala got into the back seat from the other side and moved to the centre so that Mohini could rest her body against her own.

When Keshav pulled into the car porch, Gulaam was waiting in one corner, his little sister in his arms. Bayabai was standing in the other, the end of her sari held up to her mouth. Chitra Kulkarni switched off the light in her front porch across the lane, and her voice carried when she told her daughters, Mina and Nina, that there was nothing more to see, so they should come in and wash their feet and go to bed. Gulaam lowered his sister to the ground and opened Kamala's door.

"Gulaam also searched for you," Keshav said, helping Mohini out of the car. "He was the one who found your sandals outside our front gate."

Hansa rushed down the steps leading into the car porch and threw her arms around Mohini. Her eyes were streaming. Balu snatched from Gulaam's hands the overnight bag Kamala had packed in case she was required to stay with

Mohini at the clinic, and that Gulaam had removed from the front seat of the car. He shooed away the beggar children who were standing behind Bayabai. They watched intently as Vasanti helped Mohini up the shallow stairs, holding her by one arm as Kamala held her by the other. Vishnupant—whom Mohini had never seen smoke—threw his burning beedie into the bushes. He could not meet her eyes. He ordered Keshav, his voice taut and gruff: "Carry her upstairs."

The last words Mohini said to Kamala before she fell asleep were, "Tell them all that I will be fine."

NINE

When Mohini woke up in the morning, Hansa was sitting on the spare bed. She was twirling in her hands the pink stone.

"How are you feeling?" she asked Mohini, her voice just above a whisper.

"What's that on your lap?" Mohini asked.

"It's Ganapati's picture—the one I gave you for your birthday. I removed it from your science book."

"What are you doing with it?"

"I want to glue it to your night table where you can see it," Hansa said.

"Ask Balu for the glue."

Hansa nodded.

"Did you sleep here last night?" Mohini asked.

"With Vasantiatya, in her old room."

Mohini could not keep her eyes open. "Shall I call Kamalakaku?" Hansa said, sounding alarmed.

"Where is she?"

"I'll go and look. I think she's waiting for Dr. Chitnis, downstairs."

"No, don't. What did you and Vasantiatya talk about?"

"She asked me about the first time I met you. I told her."

"Do you mind if I close my eyes?"

"Of course, you can close your eyes," Hansa said. "Kamalakaku said to let her know if you want something to eat. Do you need to use the toilet? Water?"

"I don't need anything. What else did you talk about?"

"But you should rest. With me chattering here, you won't be able to."

"I'll be all right if you don't raise your voice." Mohini opened one eye and smiled.

Hansa smiled back and looked out the terrace door, her eyes beginning to fill. She blinked back her tears and said, "Do you remember Mrs. Tomene's Standard One class?"

"I do," Mohini said, shutting her eyes.

On that first day of school, Mohini wore her brand-new uniform, the starched gathered skirt stiff against her knees. Some of the faces in the classroom had been familiar. They belonged to the girls who lived in the immediate vicinity of Shivaji Park. The ones she did not recognize were of those who lived farther away. One of the new faces was Hansa's. At lunchtime, when Mohini was sitting at the outer end of a bench in the canteen, Hansa had slid into the vacant seat across from her. She told Mohini her name and said that she had recently moved to Bombay from Vidharba. She, her mother, and her two brothers all lived with their uncle on the fourth floor of his flat in Matunga, she said. Even though she missed her father, she liked living at the same height as the trees because now when a crow alighted on a branch and cawed persistently in the direction of her room, she could pitch a pebble at it without missing.

Between bites, she proceeded to tell Mohini about the railway journey across the plains. She had seen one woman, with no less than seven brass pots on top of her head, maintain her balance by the swinging motion of her arms. She had passed regiments of soldiers waiting to be transported to the war in Europe and had watched a speckled snake glide smoothly into a ditch by the side of the railway tracks, narrowly missing being crushed by an oncoming train. She had stolen from her brothers' satchels their collection of rounded pebbles in order to get back at them for tying her legs together with a rope while she was asleep. Hansa paused, looking at Mohini shyly, with a sudden touch of self-consciousness, as though she was aware for the first time that she had been chattering for so long. Mohini wished she would continue. Hansa spoke Marathi with an unfamiliar, enchanting lilt, using idioms that were foreign to Mohini but whose meaning she could surmise. There was a concentrated air about Hansa, as though a million thoughts were swirling inside her head and she had to focus properly in order to reel one out.

She asked Mohini how old she was. Mohini told her.

Hansa said she was one year older than the rest of the class, not two, like Mohini.

"For one whole year I could not go to school because there was no proper school where Baba was working," she explained. "But why are you so old for the class? Did you fail Standard One?" Her voice was devoid of censure. They were walking back to the classroom now, the lunch break almost at an end.

Mohini explained her illness in the briefest possible way. Hansa listened quietly, her gaze on Mohini's body, taking in her spindly legs, her protruding belly, her eyes that were slightly squint. When Mohini stopped speaking,

Hansa seemed to be satisfied with the sketchy medical history and did not ask any questions, although Mohini would have been prepared to answer them all. It was the least she could do in return for a friendship so readily given.

She looked at Hansa's plump face, smooth as a grape, her body narrow and slender, at her glasses, which she removed every now and then with an irritated shrug because she had to mop the perspiration that gathered on the bridge of her nose.

Evidently, Hansa did not consider Mohini particularly odd because instead of asking her more about her ailment, she said, "I want to be an engineer when I grow up. Just like my father."

"My father is also an engineer," Mohini said. "He works for B & J Construction and his office is in Fort. Where does your father work?"

Hansa looked slightly uncomfortable while reciting in a rehearsed fashion: "My father attended Poona Engineering College, but he does not do engineer engineering. He engineers this and that so that those who cannot read or write are able to do so."

Mohini raised her eyebrows. She did not understand.

Catching her questioning gaze, Hansa sheepishly said, "That's what my brothers told me to say if anyone asks what Baba does for a living. He is now stationed in Latur, and because he has to share a house with others, he sent us here to live with my uncle in Matunga."

When Mohini repeated the engineering part of the conversation to Vishnupant, he said what Hansa probably meant was that her father was a social worker whose primary aim was to spread education where there was lack of it.

"Then why did he study engineering?" Mohini asked.

"You'll have to ask Hansa."

Mohini asked Hansa, who had by now become a part of the Oek family, often accompanying Mohini to Koleshwar Nivas after school. Hansa said her father was a social worker in the cause for freedom and that she had learned all her Sanskrit prayers from him. She said she would introduce Mohini to him when he next visited Bombay. He was a very tall man with bushy hair that had turned completely white and that had earned him his nickname.

"Hansa?" Mohini said, opening her eyes. "I forget—what is your father's nickname?"

"Hansa's left," Kamala said. "I sent her home. She said she would come and see you after school on Monday. Dr. Chitnis is here. Do you think you can sit up?"

"That's all right," Dr. Chitnis said, moving forward. "You can continue to lie down. Tell me, how is your headache?"

"Not good."

"No change after the medication I gave you last night?"

"Not much."

"She seemed to sleep through the night," Kamala said.

"Mohini, the blood test won't be back for a day or two. However, I have come across three cases of meningitis in the last two months. From your symptoms, I think you might have the same. To be absolutely sure, I need to take a small sample of your spinal fluid."

"All right," Mohini said drowsily.

"In the meantime, in case it turns out to be a bacterial meningitis, I am going to give you a streptomycin injection."

Mohini smelled the ether when Dr. Chitnis emptied a few drops on some cotton wool and dabbed it onto her hip.

His hand was light and she could barely feel the prick as he eased the needle under her skin. "Now that that is done, I need to remove some liquid from your spine. I will insert a needle between the vertebrae in your lower back."

Mohini's eyes flew open. "Now?"

Dr. Chitnis nodded.

"Will it hurt?"

"My patients tell me that it is not too painful a procedure."

She looked at Kamala.

"It will be all right," Kamala said. "I am here."

"Is Baba here?" Mohini asked.

"I don't think we can wait for him to come home," Dr. Chitnis said. "Everything I need I have brought with me and the sooner we remove the spinal fluid, the sooner we will have a definite diagnosis."

Mohini held out her hand to Kamala. Kamala took it and nodded at Dr. Chitnis. "Stay curled the way you are," he said. "With your knees and elbows flexed."

When she saw him move behind her with the needle, Mohini whispered to Kamala, "Can you say a prayer?"

Kamala tightened her grip on Mohini's hand and repeated the Gayatri mantra, Vishnupant's voice joining hers where he stood in the doorway, his face averted from the scene on the bed.

> *Lead me from Darkness to Light,*
> *from Ignorance to Knowledge,*
> *from Death to Immortality.*

Hansa visited Mohini on Monday, before the start of school. Mohini's eyes were closed. Hansa sat on the cot next to Kamala and whispered into her ear, "I met Mr. Marzello just as I was opening the gate. He asked me how Mohini was doing. He said I must not forget to give her his best." She stood up and crept out of the room.

Mohini stirred. Kamala said, "Go back to sleep."

Mohini closed her eyes once again and thought of that last day of school, three years ago, after their Standard Four exams, when she, Hansa, and Vishnupant were sitting on the stone ledge of Shivaji Park as they watched boys of all ages do exercises in front of a raised, saffron flag. Suddenly, there was a loud crash. They turned around. An unseen person was shouting for help. Vishnupant crossed the road and peered through the hedge in the direction from which the cries were coming. "I'll be back in a moment," he called out to Mohini and Hansa. "Don't move." He slipped in through the wicket gate in the hedge and disappeared. Mohini wished she could follow him in, but she was still recovering from a fractured toe, and Kamala had been reluctant to let her accompany her grandfather to the park.

Hansa nudged Mohini.

"What?"

"Don't you know whose house that is?" Hansa whispered.

"The Marzellos'."

"And?"

Mohini shrugged.

Hansa lowered her voice. "My brother says strange things go on in there, especially at night."

"Meaning what?"

Hansa shook her head.

Mohini turned back to the boys, who had finished their exercises and were now singing patriotic songs interspersed with religious bhajans. Some of the songs were familiar to Hansa and she sang along softly. "Bharatmata ki Jai!" she raised her voice with theirs, when they were finished singing. "Victory to India."

"Let's go and find Vishnupant," Mohini said. Hansa stood up and held out her hand. Mohini took it while crossing the road. They peeped in through the wicket gate.

Hansa pulled back. "Mohini! Your grandfather told us not to move. Don't let him see us."

But Mohini continued to peer in through the gate. Vishnupant was facing away from her. He was talking to someone who Mohini thought must be Mr. Marzello. She had seen the man walk down Mohur Lane many times but had not known that he was the owner of this property. He was tall and dark-skinned and a luxuriant moustache decorated his upper lip.

"Come in at least for a minute," Mr. Marzello was saying. "I'd like you to meet my wife."

Vishnupant glanced towards the house, then nodded. When they had disappeared through the front door, Mohini pushed open the gate and, motioning for Hansa to follow, stepped into the compound. The morning-glory creeper that so effectively screened the property from the park was deeply green, its papery purple flowers dangling from their stems. The beds under the creeper were thick with flowering bushes. Mohini peered into a shining leaf that was curled up at the edges. Nestled inside was a single drop of water. Although she did not know the name of the bush whose leaves were like cupped palms, Mohini recognized the frangipani, and the cloud of white daisies, their mustard centres paying homage to an infinite sky.

On the other side of the house there was a grove of palm trees. Mohini moved nearer, Hansa following so closely that she tripped against Mohini's body when Mohini came to a stop. The soft soil under the palm trees had been swept recently, the bristles of the broom leaving a trailing design. Hansa nudged Mohini and she turned around. Three girls were walking towards them. One of them said something in Konkani, the meaning of her words made evident by the welcoming expression on her face. She held out her hand to Mohini. Mohini took it and climbed the shallow front stairs, too shy to say she was capable of doing that unaided. "Come on," she called out to Hansa over her shoulder.

From the direction of the park everything was silent. The boys had dispersed. Shadows were disappearing rapidly as dusk turned to night. Hansa ran up the stairs behind Mohini, who was already stepping into the house.

"I thought I told you girls to wait in the park for me." Vishnupant's voice was stern.

"That's all right," Mr. Marzello said, "Come in, young ladies, and take a seat."

Hansa poked Mohini in her back.

"Come in," Mr. Marzello repeated.

Vishnupant nodded.

The room was large, the floor covered in white china mosaic save the centre and four corners where geometric patterns opened out in colours of red, blue, and green. Mohini nudged off her sandals as the three girls who had led her into the house disappeared through an inner door. The uneven tiles felt good against her bare soles as she went towards Vishnupant, who was seated on a yellow velvet sofa with a high wooden back. Mr. Marzello was pouring a drink from a tall clear bottle. Although the liquid was the colour of honey, it flowed out of the bottle swiftly, like water.

"The best toddy in the whole of Bombay," Mr. Marzello said.

"Give me very little," Vishnupant murmured.

"Very little," Mr. Marzello repeated, even as he laid the glass on the side table next to his guest. There was a swelling on his right temple the size of a walnut, the centre of which was split open by a long, red gash. "Your grandfather came to my rescue when the ladder came crashing down on my head," he said to Mohini, his eyes twinkling. "For a brief moment I thought my skull was cracked open and I was going to die." He looked up. "Come and take a seat," he called out to Hansa, who was still standing underneath the transom of the door. She shrugged off her sandals and scurried to take a seat next to Mohini on the sofa.

Someone appeared in the doorway through which the three girls had noiselessly disappeared. Vishnupant did something Mohini had never seen him do: he stood up and remained standing until the woman who had entered was seated across from him. She looked at Mohini and patted the empty space beside her on the divan.

"Go and sit next to Mrs. Marzello," Vishnupant said.

Mohini went and sat next to her. She put her arm around Mohini's shoulders and gave her a long hug. There was a waft of jasmine attar and talcum powder, touched by

the faintest tinge of urine or perspiration—it was difficult
to say. It was a strange smell, at once repulsive and enticing. Mrs. Marzello was wearing a sleeveless frock. The
neckline revealed the rise of her breasts every time she
leaned forward to take a sip of the drink Mr. Marzello had
placed in front of her. Mohini noticed Vishnupant had not
touched his. She glanced at Hansa. Hansa was looking at
her toes.

Mrs. Marzello broke the long silence by saying, "It is an
honour indeed to be visited by a famous history professor."

Vishnupant gave a self-deprecating laugh.

"Don't forget he is the father of the equally famous engineer," Mr. Marzello said.

Vishnupant looked up from the centre table where he
had fixed his gaze. "No, no!" he fluttered his hands in
embarrassment. "Not famous at all."

"I was cleaning the eavestrough when the ladder gave
way, Jolly," Mr. Marzello said, turning to his wife. "Mr. Oek
heard me all the way from the park and came to my rescue."

Mrs. Marzello shrugged. "So, my dear," she said to
Mohini, "do you think your grandfather can tell us whether
the British will ever quit India?"

"Yes, they will," Vishnupant quickly said. Mohini waited
for him to continue. She had never heard her grandfather
state his opinion so simply.

"You will have to expand on that, dear Sir," Mr. Marzello
said.

"If you think they will quit India, then do you think that
it is a good thing or a bad thing?" Mrs. Marzello asked.
There was a coy quality to her voice, as though she felt that
patience touched by sweetness would draw out her guest.

"Or are we assuming that it is necessarily a good thing for the British to leave?"

"Gandhiji certainly thinks it is a good thing," Mr. Marzello said, laughing. "Leave India to anarchy, he tells the viceroy, but leave. I had the pleasure of listening to the Mahatma once. A jolly good fellow. A saintly man."

Mrs. Marzello clicked her tongue and glared at her husband as though she felt he was leading Vishnupant down the wrong path. But before she could ask him another question, Vishnupant said that the British would leave India because it was inconceivable that they, the British people, had not noticed the irony of an imperial power fighting a war in Europe in order to establish the principle of freedom, when they themselves were ruling a population that for decades had wanted them gone. Besides, the war had bankrupted England and India had become a white elephant. "Imperialism does not fit in with modern thinking," he added. "After the Industrial Revolution, it was socialism versus capitalism. Now it is totalitarianism versus democracy." He stopped abruptly as though reminded that what he had just explained was too complex to be appreciated by present company.

Perhaps he was right because Mr. Marzello asked, "But when do you think the British will leave?"

"Soon, I should think. But the war has to end first." Vishnupant stood up. Hansa, who had been shifting uncomfortably on the sofa, followed suit quickly, a relieved expression on her face.

"Come again, Professor Sir, and enlighten us," Mrs. Marzello said, hugging Mohini. "Our house has for too long been occupied with things not pertaining to the matters of the mind. We need people like you to remind us . . ." She smiled at him, her chin tilted upwards, her eyebrows arched and fine.

Vishnupant coughed and looked down at Mohini. "We really must leave," he said as though it was she who was detaining him.

Mr. Marzello walked them to the gate. "Come any time, young lady"—he tousled Mohini's hair—"and bring along your friend." Hansa hurried forward and stepped out on the footpath before Mr. Marzello could do the same to her head. They turned the corner away from the park and walked down Mohur Lane. The sky was dark but for the stars that hung together in ancient clusters. The trees sighed every time the wind passed through them.

"Where did his daughters go to?" Hansa asked twice. The second time Vishnupant stopped swinging his cane.

"What daughters?"

"The three girls who brought us in," Mohini said.

Vishnupant cleared his throat several times and, looking up at the sky, replied, "They have only one son. His name is Samuel. No daughters. Those three girls were probably his nieces."

Hansa's uncle was waiting for her at the front gate of Koleshwar Nivas. There was an annoyed expression on his face. Mohini squeezed Hansa's hand and said, "Don't come in. Just go home and don't say anything to your brothers or you might get into trouble."

"Your mother must be weeping with worry," Hansa's uncle said, moving forward. "Even Mohini's mother could not tell me where you were." He hurried her down Mill Road. Hansa glanced over her shoulder at Mohini. In spite of the fact that her uncle would give the top of her ear a tight squeeze as soon as they were out of sight, she winked, her eyes shining with the thought of keeping a visit to the Marzellos' a secret from her brothers.

Kamala was waiting in the front verandah. Vishnupant told her to tell Balu to serve dinner. That night, in her parents' bedroom, Mohini told Kamala and Keshav about the visit. She got off the bed, saying she wanted to lie down and needed her own pillow.

Kamala glanced at Keshav, concerned. "It's all right, Kamale," he murmured. "She went to the Marzellos' with her grandfather, did she not?"

When Mohini re-entered the room, Kamala asked her whether the garden was really as beautiful as she had heard it was, and Keshav said that theirs was one of the few old properties still left standing in Shivaji Park, almost all the others having been developed into multi-tenanted buildings.

"Hansa said her brothers said that strange things happen in the Marzellos' property, especially at night. What did her brothers mean?"

Kamala said, "Didn't Hansa tell you?"

"She doesn't know."

Keshav looked at Kamala.

"She'll have to ask her brothers, then, won't she, what they meant? Now brush your teeth and get ready for bed," Kamala said.

That night, and in the days following, Mohini could not get Mrs. Marzello out of her mind. She remembered her long, unplaited hair held back by a broad satin ribbon, the rims of her irises darker than their soft brown centres that

were caught up in shining points. She recalled the pearly
tint of her long, oval fingernails, her lips slightly parted as
she listened to Vishnupant, the tip of her tongue darting
every now and again to gather the lingering remnants of
her drink. Mohini knew, as did the neighbourhood, that
Mrs. Marzello had not stepped outside her compound in
years. But now that Mrs. Marzello had met them, Mohini
hoped she might be tempted to open the back gate of their
property, cross Mill Road, and walk through the car porch
to meet Kamala and the famous engineer. When she told
her mother her wish, Kamala said, "I doubt that very
much." And as the weeks went by and the gate remained
closed, Mohini had to grudgingly concede that Kamala was
probably right.

TEN

Mohini was eating so little that Vishnupant began to fear that she would have no strength to fight her illness. When Kamala urged her to try softened rice stirred in with some curds, milk, a grain of sugar, a pinch of salt, Mohini, who in the past would have been persuaded to taste a little, said she couldn't swallow, that it hurt too much.

Standing in the terrace, her back to Mohini's room, Kamala gave Dr. Chitnis an account of all the things that she had noticed. "Mohini is drowsy most the time," she said. "And just yesterday her father pointed out to me that the squint in her left eye is more pronounced. I've been taking her pulse and her temperature as you told me to."

"And?"

"Her pulse is slow. Also irregular. Her temperature has dropped below one hundred and two degrees."

"Any convulsions?"

"No. At least, not at night. Vasanti relieves me during the day, but she would have mentioned if she had noticed any."

"Rigidity?"

"Do you mean the way she lies on her side without moving?"

"Not exactly. Rigidity normally follows convulsions, but not always."

Kamala thought a moment. "No, I wouldn't say rigidity." She waited for Dr. Chitnis to reveal to her the next step in the treatment.

"We'll continue with the streptomycin injections," he said.

"What about her headaches?"

"It's the fluid inside her brain that is exerting all this pressure and causing so much pain. I think we will have to do a few lumbar punctures. If I remove a little spinal fluid, just five to ten cc's at a time, it'll help ease the pain."

Kamala flinched but did not take her eyes off Dr. Chitnis's face. "How many will you have to do?"

"One puncture every now and again for as long as her headaches continue."

Kamala took a step forward and sat on the swing, the front of her toes dragging along the terrace floor as the swing moved back and forth. She looked into Mohini's room. Vasanti was fanning Mohini's face with a folded magazine.

"The lumbar taps will help her headaches," Dr. Chitnis said.

Kamala asked, "Have you made a diagnosis yet?"

Dr. Chitnis nodded. They re-entered Mohini's room. Vasanti moved to the windowsill behind Mohini's bed. She shook her head at Kamala and pointed to the untouched bowl of rice on the night table. Vishnupant was sitting in the armchair he had asked Balu to fetch from downstairs. He called out to Keshav, who was in his room. Dr. Chitnis sat at the foot of Mohini's bed. "You have tuberculous meningitis," he said, massaging her ankles. Only a movement of her eyeballs under the swollen lids indicated she had heard.

"Your mother tells me your headaches are unbearable. The medicine I gave you is not working. There is one other thing we could try."

There was no response from her.

Dr. Chitnis said, "I'll give the streptomycin injection first."

Kamala looked at Balu. He hurried downstairs. A few minutes later he returned with a steaming rectangular metal container that he placed on Mohini's desk by the terrace door. "Did you boil everything thoroughly?" Keshav asked.

"Ji, Sahib," Balu muttered and left the room.

Dr. Chitnis removed the streptomycin powder and the saline solution from his open bag and prepared the injection. He picked up the sterilized pincers from the container and slipped the needle into the glass syringe. He shook the prepared vial then drew a measure of the antibiotic. His hand was light as he inserted the needle into Mohini's hip after cleaning a small area on her skin with ether. When he had returned the used needle to the rectangular container, Mohini whispered, "You said there was one other thing we could try."

"There is fluid inside your head that is pressing down on the nerves. In order to ease the pain I will have to do a lumbar puncture and remove some—"

"Again?" Mohini opened her eyes and looked at Kamala.

"It will be all right," Kamala said. "You've had one before. Everything was over within minutes."

Dr. Chitnis said, "What do you think, Mohini? Shall we give it a try?"

Mohini closed her eyes in assent as a spot in the bottom of her spine started to throb unpleasantly. Something inside Kamala eased; she was relieved that Mohini had not thought to ask Dr. Chitnis how many lumbar punctures would be needed for the treatment to work.

"You can turn her over a bit," Dr. Chitnis said.

Mohini's eyes flew open.

Kamala held Mohini's hands as Vasanti helped raise the petticoat she was wearing until her back was uncovered. "Curl into yourself, Mohini, so the skin will be stretched a little and I can see the lower vertebrae," Dr. Chitnis said.

Vishnupant got up from his armchair slowly and walked out to the back verandah. Keshav followed, unable to watch the anguished expression on Mohini's face as the doctor removed the needle from the sterilized tray.

"Direct the lamp so it is pointing at this spot," Dr. Chitnis instructed Vasanti.

Kamala began softly chanting the prayer she said every evening while lighting the flame in front of the gods.

Eight lumbar punctures later, lying in a darkened room, the terrace door shut and the window curtains open only a slit, Mohini watched on the ceiling inverted stick figures as children hurried to and fro at the beginning and end of school. She had overheard Vasanti tell Kamala a long time ago that when she, Vasanti, couldn't sleep at night, when the prospect of waking every morning to a dull, unchanging reality became a continuous hammering inside her head, she would make lists: name, place, animal, thing.

Mohini started with names. Achala, Amita, Archana, Ashutosh—the pain inside her head gnawed through her concentration. Achalpur. Antelope. It was another few minutes before she could even recall what game it was that she was playing. If she were to continue to try to distract herself, Mohini decided, she would first have to get rid of the four restricting categories. She began a new list, one that consisted of the things that calmed her, brought her comfort.

The fragrance of sandalwood soap on Kamala's skin. A wafer moon at noon so thin that one could glimpse through it the light blue sky. Oil-filled earthen crucibles reflecting unwavering flames. Bayabai's chili pickles nudging with that first taste on the tongue a flagging appetite. The clean sound of the sweeper's broom, the distance between each pile of debris measured by ten revolutions of his wheelbarrow. Jayant Deshpande's chiselled profile against the flashing curtain of rain. A sparrow drinking from the terrace floor, its beak no bigger than a mogra bud. Pearl bangles matching Kamala's pale wrists. The sudden silence at dusk . . .

Without warning, a spasm of pain ripped through Mohini's spine. Her mother had told her that she must remember to move her limbs and torso occasionally if she wished to prevent bedsores and body ache. Mohini slowly shifted her weight so that now her back was slightly tilted and not parallel to the bed. This time the spasm travelled down her left thigh and into her ankle. The wrenching pain caused tears to run down her face. Clenching her teeth, she moved her legs into a more comfortable position, and breathing in deeply, willed her body to relax, as Kamala had taught her to do. Closing her eyes, she braced herself for the next spasm and when it did not come, she resumed her list.

The bleat of Keshav's horn in the distance. Hansa's ink-stained fingers. The scent lingering in the air long after tea was drunk and the crumbs of pungent onion fritters cleared away. The muted patter of rain on the rain tree, its hard pebbly clatter on the terrace floor. The thud of Vishnupant's walking stick against the hat stand announcing that he was home. Balu's toothy smile, wide and unreserved. And then, out of nowhere, a memory of what Vishnupant had said about things not existing independently of the perceiver's mind. And before she could make sense of her grandfather's words, another memory of what the Chafekar Guruji had told Vasanti after she was widowed. Something about learning to be blind . . .

Mohini groaned. She brought her hands to cradle the cage atop her neck, but Kamala's fingertips were already pressing against her chin, her thumbs lightly massaging Mohini's temples.

"Where's Vasantiatya?"

"I sent her to Shiv Sadan to tell Mai and Bebitai that they must stop sending you food. Every day they prepare something new, hoping you will be tempted to try this or that."

Mohini rolled her eyes without turning her head. Her room looked like a hospital ward. In the corner next to her bed was an oxygen cylinder, its slim rubber tubing wrapped around its body. On her desk were sterilizing equipment and bottles of ayurvedic medicines: thin syrups and thicker ones consisting of herbs ground into honey. Mai and Bebitai must have sent those too. Just inside the door leading out to the back verandah was a wheelchair. Shridhar had rented it for Mohini, saying that on the day she felt better she could be wheeled out onto the terrace or carried downstairs by Keshav and Balu if she preferred to watch the world from the verandah below.

Kamala's paraphernalia—she slept on the spare bed now—was on the night table. Hairpins, spools of thread, scissors, her own jugful of water that she drank all at one time the first thing in the morning, before brushing her teeth. Now that her mother was sleeping in her room, Mohini had to be careful while moving on her bed at night. The slightest twitch of Mohini's covering would waken Kamala. Even if Mohini lay still, which she sometimes did in order to delay waking up her mother, Kamala would open her eyes and ask her if she needed the bedpan or a sip of water or help in turning and facing the other way.

"Just the way Kamalavahini can read your mind, Mohini," Dr. Chitnis said, after she had told him how light a sleeper Kamala was, "I am trying to read your eyes. A village doctor once told me that an entire diagnosis can be made by scrutinizing the face. The dual pulses of the face, he said, are the eyes. He taught me what I should keep a lookout for, but diagnosis by such a method must require years of training, because I simply could not have told you that you have meningitis without the use of the laboratory and modern equipment."

Many lists and thirteen lumbar punctures later, Keshav, who had been postponing going on-site, told Kamala that he could do so no more. On the morning he was to leave, he sat on Mohini's bed. Mohini told him that she had been very hungry that morning and that Kamala had fed her a ripe mashed plantain mixed in with a little milk, sugar, and cardamom. She had eaten it all, she added. Seeing the relief in his face, she did not tell him that she still had to hold her head steady and centre her eyeballs in the middle of her eyes if she wished to control the occasional spasm that went through her head when least expected. Keshav looked at her closely. The half-conscious, half-unconscious look of the previous week was gone. "I'll be back soon," he said. "Promise me you'll be sitting up in bed by the time I come home."

"I promise," she said.

On the morning of his return, the twittering of sparrows as Vasanti scattered grain into the air on the terrace alerted Mohini to the particulars of her surroundings in a way that had eluded her ever since she had made that long journey to Dr. Chitnis's clinic, some six weeks ago. She opened her eyes and said to Kamala, "Show me how much you have done so far." Kamala held up her embroidery. It was the river scene: the women's anklets and the veins in the weeping willow leaves had been filled in. What remained were the birds, although she could see their faint V-shaped outlines pencilled in against the completed sky.

"I'm hungry," Mohini said.

After washing her hands, Kamala removed the cotton gauze from the tray that Balu had earlier placed on Mohini's night table. She held the glass of sweetlime juice to Mohini's mouth. When that was finished she took the lid off the semolina sheera. "Will you have a little?" she said.

Mohini nodded. As if alerted to what was going on upstairs, Vishnupant, Bayabai, Balu, and Vasanti came and stood in her doorway. They watched Kamala as she fed Mohini slowly, a little at a time. After a few mouthfuls,

Kamala put down the spoon. She knew it wouldn't do Mohini any good to eat too much on the first day.

Vishnupant told Balu to place his armchair next to the oxygen tank. He ordered Vasanti to go to Shiv Sadan. He commanded Kamala to go to her room and to close the interconnecting door. She was not to appear until she was sent for. He told Bayabai that he felt like eating peanuts with lots and lots of jaggery: she should send some up with Balu right away. Bayabai grumbled that just last week she had written a letter to Nandini in Calcutta, promising her that she, Bayabai, would not give Vishnupant any sweet food. Vishnupant looked at her, the muscles behind his ears beginning to throb. "If my daughter wishes to keep a check on my diabetes, she will have to do so in person," he said. "There was no need for you to promise her anything. I want a fistful of peanuts and an equal amount of jaggery." He turned to Mohini and winked at her as Bayabai, still grumbling, exited the room.

That evening, there was quickness in Keshav's footsteps as he hurried up the stairs. Touching Mohini's forehead with the back of his hand, he said, "Balu gave me the good news." He sat at the bottom of her bed and massaged her feet.

"How was your trip?" she asked.

"You talk with your father," Vishnupant said, getting up from his armchair.

"He's been like a sentinel all day," Mohini informed Keshav, pointing to Vishnupant. "He even had his lunch upstairs. He sent Balu up and down, first for lime pickle, then for more papad and salt."

Vishnupant chuckled and placed the roll of newspaper next to her pillow in case she was up to reading it.

"Where's your mother?" Keshav asked after Vishnupant had left.

"Sleeping. But Vishnupant said no one is to disturb her. Will you sleep in my room tonight?"

"Why not? It's about time I relieved your mother." He flopped on her bed and nestled close to her. He pulled a pillow over his eyes and was instantly asleep.

Kamala did not wake up until eleven o'clock the following morning. She scolded everyone for allowing her to sleep, but nobody paid any heed. She went to Mohini's room and sat on her bed, the lids of her eyes still swollen. "Your transfusion," she suddenly remembered. "It was this morning."

"Dr. Chitnis came. Vasantiatya was here as well."

"And?"

"And nothing. He said there was no need to check on me every day and that he would come here again on Saturday."

"What else did he say?"

"Nothing. You don't need to have it confirmed by him that I'm out of danger, do you?"

"It's not that—I just thought he may have said something about stopping the streptomycin."

"Not yet, he said."

"What about the other medicines?"

"I have to continue taking those for another seven or eight months. Along with vitamin B six."

Kamala yawned and, stretching her arms high overhead, told Mohini she would go in for her bath. There was ease in the way she got off the bed.

"Vasantiatya told me to tell you that there is a surprise for you on the terrace."

Kamala stepped outside and when she returned she was carrying a hibiscus, its colour a blazing scarlet inside her cupped hands.

Keshav was barely home a fortnight when he received a phone call at work. There had been an accident on-site. Two men working on the bridge had fallen into the river. Their bodies had not yet been recovered. The supervisor at the other end told Keshav that there was no need to come and that all that he wished to do was to inform him, since he was the senior-most engineer on the project. At the dinner table, Keshav told Vishnupant that he would have to go, that the two men were well known to him, having worked as welders on previous sites.

That night, Mohini sat on Keshav's bed as Kamala packed his clothes. After Balu took the bag downstairs, Keshav carried Mohini back to her own bed. He reminded her that her daily quota of reduced reading time had been used up, and before she could protest, he switched off the lamp.

"Sleepy?" he asked, pulling up the quilt so that it covered her feet.

"Tired," she said, closing her eyes.

On the way out of her room he left the door open.

"How are you feeling, Kamale?" Mohini heard him ask.

"Is Mohini sleeping?"

"Just about to, I think. But you didn't answer me. Look at these bones. Have you been eating at all?"

Mohini heard the click of the interconnecting door. A shaft of light fell across the top of her bed. She looked up. Earlier in the day, Balu had pushed open the window above the transom of the connecting door in order to clean it. He had forgotten to close it again. Sometimes, sparrows flew into her parents' room, and the last time the transom window had been left open a single sparrow had flown through it into Mohini's room and out the terrace door, somehow avoiding being sliced by her whirring fan. She would tell Balu in the morning to latch the window down. Her room was plunged into darkness. Keshav must have switched off his light.

"What's the matter?" Keshav said. His voice sounded so close that Mohini opened her eyes. "Are you unwell?"

"No! I'm fine. I just don't feel like it."

"It's all right, Kamale."

"Is it? When she is confined to her bed like that, week after week, her head gripped by piercing fangs—"

"Is that how she described it?"

"She doesn't need to. I can tell. And you say it is all right."

"She's better now, isn't she?" Keshav's voice was calm and reasonable.

"How much longer will she stay better? How much longer is He going to torture her? One day this, another day that. Draw blood, match blood, transfuse blood. As if that weren't enough, blinding headaches, seventeen lumbar punctures, a sore back, and bones that have become so thin that every few months a fracture. Is it all right? Why won't He give her some peace?"

"I don't know, Kamala." A headboard creaked. "All I know is that she is better now and the sooner you leave this illness behind—"

"If suffering is the price one pays to learn a lesson, what lesson is she learning and how important can this lesson be that she is required to pay such an agonizing price?"

"Kamala. Don't—"

"And tell me one thing. What is the ultimate purpose of her illness? If someone, you, anyone, can give me a justification for her suffering, then perhaps I will have a solid reason to—"

"Kamala! Stop. Don't torture yourself like this."

"I cannot expect you to understand." There was uncustomary bitterness in Kamala's voice. "I gave birth to her. How can you expect me to take pleasure when she has just recently come out of so much pain?"

The lamp was switched back on. The light poured again across Mohini's eyes. She shut them when Kamala pushed open the connecting door and walked into her room. She adjusted the quilt on Mohini's feet and sat on the edge of her bed, her sobs barely contained as her fingers removed the hairpins that held her hair in place. She didn't return to her room until after Keshav had switched off his light.

ELEVEN

Mohini woke up one afternoon to the sounds of the newly minted national anthem ringing in her ears as children returned home after school, a sense of pride lurking in their strident tones, their footsteps tapping the pavement in unison. August 15 had come and gone some five weeks previously when Mohini had still been confined to her bed. In celebration of Independence Day, Balu had hung in the front verandah and the upstairs terrace the Indian flag, its horizontal stripes of saffron, white, and green with the blue Dharma Chakra, the Wheel of Law, at its centre, flying high from a pole. He had removed the Divali lights from their box and strung them along the frame of Koleshwar Nivas. On the eve of independence, Keshav carried Mohini to the terrace so she could see the various properties along Mill Road. The front entrance of the Irani's was decorated with strands of roses hanging from the lintel, the balconies in Vasanti's building were lit up, and the trees on the Marzellos' property were studded with golden bulbs so bright that they twinkled like miniature suns. The dense aromas of the flowers and leaves swept across the terrace in little waves, and the atmosphere was so charged that

Mohini shivered. She tightened her hold around Keshav's neck, suddenly wishing that she had been well for the political discussions that had do doubt flowed through the house during her illness.

So unwell was she at the time that she would have even forgotten about the much anticipated Independence Day festivities at New English Academy had she not heard Hansa whisper to Vasanti that she was playing the role of Kasturbai, Gandhiji's wife, in the school play written especially for the occasion. Vasanti urged Hansa to enact her part for Mohini. Mohini opened her eyes. Hansa removed a bundle from her satchel and hurried into the bathroom. When she came out, her slender body was draped in a white cotton sari, her head completely covered with its end. After thrusting a tattered script into Vasanti's hands, Hansa squatted on the floor, her knee drawn up to her chin, her shoulders bowed. She nodded at Vasanti to begin reading aloud the parts not ascribed to Kasturbai. Vasanti cleared her throat and Mohini suppressed a chuckle every time Hansa's eyeglasses slipped down her nose as she gestured emphatically with her hands, nodding vigorously whenever Vasanti read the part of Gandhiji. Hansa repeated his exhortation, "An eye for an eye makes everyone blind." That was her only line.

Keshav had returned from the Independence Day celebrations in Shivaji Park full of optimism and hope. As a long-standing member of the community, Vishnupant had been asked to give a speech after the flag-hoisting ceremony.

"Did people clap when he was finished?" Mohini asked.

Keshav nodded. "But then they were cheering all the time. Prominent singers sang freedom songs, and men, women, and children released multicoloured balloons into the air. Some were waving flags." He produced a wrinkled one from his pocket and laid it on Mohini's night table. "Do you want to go outside?"

Mohini nodded.

Keshav carried her to the swing and they sat silently, the sound of footfalls and laughter lifting into the air as people walked home from the park. The flag that Balu had erected in one corner of the terrace rippled gently every time there was a breeze. Now and again there came from the direction of the open water a faint boom of guns as people continued to celebrate on land and sea.

Hansa visited regularly. She would rub the pink stone against her skirt even as she gauged whether Mohini's energy levels were sufficient to allow her to attempt some school work. If Mohini was in the mood and not too tired, she would remove her books from her satchel and go over the school portions with her, laying particular emphasis on science and mathematics. When Mohini appeared distracted and could not concentrate as well as she used to, Hansa would patiently urge her to try.

One afternoon, when Mohini was particularly listless and heavy-eyed, Hansa said, "You don't want to drop from the third ranking on your report card, do you?" Mohini shook her head. She had been meaning to ask Dr. Chitnis when she would be able to go back to school, and Hansa's timely reminder made her sharpen her focus.

Their favourite subject was poetry. After completing history and geography, Hansa would pull from her satchel her poetry book and together they would read Percy Bysshe

Shelley, Wordsworth, Walter de la Mare, and Keats. They learned by heart assigned poems, then committed to memory some more. The two lines that were continuously on the tips of their tongues were the refrain from Alfred Lord Tennyson's poem, "The Brook." *For years may come and years may go, but I go on forever.* They repeated these lines so many times that Vishnupant ordered them to stop. "Where do you think you were born?" he muttered. "In Buckingham Palace that you are all the time reciting English poetry?"

Mohini did not understand why Hansa came to see her so often when it would have been more fun for her to play with her older brothers and cousins and the other children who lived in her building in Matunga. Hansa's mother did not understand either. When she asked Hansa what it was that attracted her to Koleshwar Nivas, her daughter's response had been simple: "Mohini is good for my soul." Hansa's mother related this conversation to Kamala, who passed it on to Keshav, who said, "Hansa is right. Sometimes it takes the perception of a child to point out to us the truth of the matter. Whatever did we do to deserve our Mohini?"

Keshav was working longer hours now. He returned late in the evenings, after darkness had fallen.

Kamala resumed her embroidery classes, but instead of going to the Jijabai Samaj where they were usually held, she now ran them from her home. Her students were girls from the Mahila Seva Ashram in Sion, a charitable institution for the destitute. Three of Kamala's girls were unmarried mothers, but they usually came to class unaccompanied by their children. However, one day, when one of them brought her baby clad only in a frayed and dirty cotton diaper, Kamala placed Bayabai in charge and hurried to the cloth store on Ranade Road. She returned with several cut pieces of cotton brightly patterned with roses, paisleys, and little birds. From then on, along with the embroidery, she taught the young mothers how to sew small jackets and little sleeveless frocks decorated with bright buttons and sashes and bows. Mohini watched the girls from her wheelchair in the back verandah as she practised her embroidery stitches on a sampler that Kamala had suggested she work on in order to pass her time.

One of the girls had been abandoned on the steps of the ashram at birth, and she cheerfully told Mohini the first time she met her that she was the only person in the world who did not have a single mother, but several (all the caregivers at the ashram), and no father. She said she had no regrets on account of the latter because fathers were known to beat their wives and neglect their children. She had mood swings, this girl with several mothers, causing the other girls to steer clear of her when she appeared aggressive and sullen. Her name was Durga and she dragged one foot because one leg was a couple of inches shorter than the other. Her skin was taut over her high cheekbones, and she wore her hair pulled back into a tight bun, making her face look severe. There was a slate-grey tinge to her hair, and her eyes were so sparsely lashed that at times it seemed that she hadn't any eyelashes at all. The rest of the girls teased her and said, "You were born an old hag." Every time they said this, Mohini watched Durga from the corner of her eye, waiting for her reaction, but their characterization did not seem to bother her, and instead of a scowl, she invariably rewarded them with a smile.

Tuesday and Thursday afternoons, Kamala would be ready at three-thirty to receive the girls in the back veran-dah. Sometimes all four of them would show up—making it five if one of them brought along a friend—and at other times, only two. Ever since the venue had shifted from the samaj to Koleshwar Nivas, they had a tendency to drift in and out whenever it suited them. At the samaj, they had to sign in their attendance. At Koleshwar Nivas, Kamala did not keep a book. Sometimes the women were uncoopera-tive, and at such times it would take Kamala the first ten minutes of the class merely to organize them. It was impor-tant to have them sitting on the ground at such a distance from each other that there would be little chance that one of them would encroach on the other's space. But no mat-ter how Kamala placed them, the girls found a cause over which to quarrel. They complained about each other to Kamala and expected her to sort out their differences as though she were their headmistress and they her pupils.

Some afternoons, when Vasanti dropped by, Mohini would chat with her upstairs, sitting on the swing before the sun came to claim it. Now and again, Durga's intemper-ate laugh would drift into the terrace.

Mohini looked forward to her mother's embroidery classes. The girls always asked how she was keeping and said they missed her when she was not there. Each time, Durga made it a point to tell Mohini that if she, Mohini, wished to use the bathroom, then, she, Durga, would wheel her to it. Durga was so earnest in her offer of help that even if she did not need to use the toilet, Mohini would signal to her by holding erect the small finger of her right hand. Pushing the wheelchair to a stop outside Vishnupant's room, Durga would repeat that Koleshwar Nivas was so peaceful that every time she came here she felt as though she was entering a temple. No doubt alerted by the lumbering sound of the wheelchair against the stone floor, Bayabai would come out of the kitchen and stand next to Durga for the duration that Mohini was in the toilet. Annoyed by this unnecessary vigilance, Mohini asked Bayabai exactly what it was that she expected Durga to steal. After all, Vishnupant was in his room—admittedly a sleeping and snoring Vishnupant—and what would she find if she were to sneak upstairs? Mohini's clothes, books, medicines? Bayabai shrugged and said, "You and Kamalavahini are innocents. The girls tell you just enough to elicit your sympathy. You don't even know the half of what they are up to when they are not here."

Vasanti was a bit like Bayabai. She did not trust the girls. Now and again she would mutter, "I don't think it is such a good idea for Kamalavahini to conduct these classes here." She would clasp her hands over her ears whenever Durga's strange laughter floated upstairs.

For weeks now, Mohini had noticed that there was a certain sadness, a vulnerability, to Vasanti's gestures. This fragility wasn't there all the time, but it would occasionally surface after someone had said something, or upon catching a snatch of a tune. One time, her eyes had filled with tears when Keshav had casually asked whether a herd of cows had passed through the car porch, the smell of cow dung was so strong. Vishnupant, Mohini was sure, had noticed this change in Vasanti as well. So now, whenever he shared with Mohini words of wisdom, he included his niece in the conversation. Once, he said,

"I'm going to tell the two of you what I used to tell my students. I used to tell them that the body is limited in what it can do, whereas the mind is infinite. Space, speed, and time cannot measure it. It has no boundaries. It will develop wrinkles only if you let it."

Mohini, convinced of Vishnupant's assertion, tried to develop her thought processes by poring over her textbooks. But more often than not, her thoughts would wander away and she would end up remembering tidbits of information, something she had read or heard someone say.

There were times she wished she could start over again. Then, in that other body, she would be a healthy thirteen-year-old girl, not someone touched by disease. Kamala's three cousin sisters and five nieces all had deep clefts in their chins, ivory complexions—which they proudly compared to the leaves of the delicate ketaki flower—and narrow, shapely noses. Walking into Nene family gatherings, Keshav often said, was like entering an enchanted garden where a sorceress had changed every girl to look like the other. Remembering his words, Mohini wished to be given a chance, if only for one day, for a few hours, or even a minute, to experience what it would be like to be an ivory flower in that enchanted garden.

But these were fleeting thoughts.

Mohini's teachers came to see her. Her classmates too. The latter smiled at her shyly and told her this and that about school before trooping out into the terrace. They made the swing go so high that its supporting cables creaked rhythmically, almost drowning out their exhilarated shouts.

Now that she was mobile, using the wheelchair downstairs only because it was wider and more comfortable to sit in than the other straight-backed chairs, Vishnupant's friends from the gymkhana would ask to see her when they visited. After inquiring how she was doing, they would return to their conversation with him, sometimes including her in it with their eyes. She liked to listen as they complained about an ailment, worried over the rising price of vegetables, or discussed the pall cast by the exodus in the north. One evening, after an hour-long discussion about mutual friends and their whereabouts, an old friend of Vishnupant's motioned with his waving hand to the yard, the house, and the car. "You haven't done too badly," he said.

Ignoring the rancour in his friend's voice, Vishnupant measured his response. "Some circumstances generate money. Education for one, and in my case, my father owned a lot of property. There were only two of us brothers. Because of my inheritance, we live the way we do. If I hadn't inherited anything, we would have had to live accordingly."

Living accordingly, Mohini told herself, was what she was trying to do.

Towards the middle of October, Mohini told Dr. Chitnis that she was ready to go back to school. She said it was three months now that she had lain in bed and could not afford to do so any longer. He looked up from his newspaper and watched the glass bottle drip blood into her vein. Mohini knew he had heard her. "I don't think you can go back to school," he said. "Not yet."

"Then when?"

"I don't know." He looked out into the terrace. She could tell he was avoiding her eyes.

"You are not saying that I can't go back to school, are you? Never ever?"

"'Never ever' what?" Kamala said, walking into the room carrying a tea tray. She placed it on the spare bed and handed a filled bowl to the doctor. Mohini continued to look at him without answering her mother.

He looked at Kamala and said, "Your daughter wants to know when she can go back to school." He turned to Mohini. "I think the word 'never' is too final a word in your case. I have found over the years that I may treat your body, but you control your will, and that will has a power of its own. But yes, to come straight to the point, I do not see you going back to school."

"Why not?" Mohini's mouth was collapsing, but she stiffened her lower eyelids into a dam.

Kamala sat on her bed and gently placed her hands over her ankles. "This last illness has weakened you considerably. I do not deny that every week you are gaining strength, but a school day is long. You have to sit at your desk, there is no place to lie down when you are feeling tired, and then you have to come home and do homework. It is only a few years left to matriculation. The study portions are increasing."

Dr. Chitnis was nodding, the hand holding the empty spoon suspended over his bowl. "When you feel you are ready to tackle your books," he said, "you can have private tuition. My sister-in-law is a retired headmistress. If I tell her that you would like tutoring two or three mornings a week, I'm sure she will oblige. But, as I said before,

Mohini, the word 'never' is too final a word in your case. All I can say is, at the moment, it would be most inadvisable for you to attend school."

In the evening, when Kamala was downstairs in the kitchen seeing to dinner, Mohini took the steep iron steps to the third-floor terrace. The three chairs under the steel awning of the doorway were stacked in exactly the same way they had been the previous year. Underneath them were two broken teacups and a cracked saucer, which Balu must have stashed there, too ashamed to own up to Kamala that he had broken them while doing the washing. How they had escaped Bayabai's hawk-eyes, Mohini could not tell. She caught her breath by leaning against the door frame. When her heart had stopped pounding, she entered the narrow corridor between the two water tanks in the east corner of the wall-less terrace. She sat on the cement casing of one and found she could not lift her feet to prop them on the casing of the other the way she used to. She leaned back and turned sideways, placing her ear against the tank. There was a familiar city in there: gurgling streams, meadows of oceans, liquid skies. She looked up. Some infant—perhaps held up by the father—was ringing the overhead bell in the Ganapati temple that stood in the west end of Mill Road. The peals were unevenly paced, loud, then soft, then loud again. An evening star appeared as if out of nowhere. She closed her eyes, the star a black pinpoint against her eyelids.

"I thought you might be here," Kamala said. Mohini leaned forward. Her mother held out her hand. With its aid, Mohini hobbled out from between the tanks. Kamala dabbed Mohini's eyes with the end of her sari, then bent down and rubbed her legs and feet until circulation returned. "Did you remember the yellow flowers on our bhendi tree the last time you were up here?" she asked. "The treetop looked like a flowering carpet then. See how much the tree has grown now." She led Mohini to the edge of the terrace.

The raat-rani, the queen of the night, from Mr. Marzello's backyard, was releasing its sweet fragrance into the air. Mohini leaned over. Kamala held on to her arm. "You haven't made a zaai garland for so long," Mohini said.

"It's late now. The flowers must have already opened. Remind me tomorrow afternoon to pluck some buds. Have you given a thought to what Dr. Chitnis said?"

Mohini leaned against her mother's shoulder, her eyes beginning to fill. "I want to live," she said. "I won't go to school."

Kamala turned and clasped Mohini's hands inside her own. In the fading light the rims of Kamala's eyes were red. "Talk to Him, Mohini. Pray."

"I do. But what in particular should I pray for?"

"Courage, strength, acceptance. Anything you want and you'll see He will give it to you. You are a sensible girl. You will not ask for something that is beyond your capacity to receive." She released Mohini's hands.

TWELVE

Vasanti came out on the terrace. "Kamalavahini,"
she said, "You are wanted in the kitchen."

Kamala said she had forgotten that she was
supposed to be making the fenugreek curry that
evening. She hurried down the stairs.

"Baba doesn't like the way Bayabai makes it," Mohini
said. "I wonder when he'll be home."

"He's rarely back before seven o'clock these days, is it
not?"

Mohini nodded.

Vasanti pulled forward the stacked chairs and unloos-
ened two of them. She placed them in the centre of the
terrace, under the open sky. "It's been so long since I came
up here. Let's sit for a while—but only if you don't want to
wait for your father downstairs."

Mohini sat down.

"It doesn't matter, you know," Vasanti continued. "We
can always come up here some other time."

Vasanti had become very mindful of other people.
Where before she had played the role of an aunt, by telling
Mohini what to do and how and when to do it, she now let
Mohini take the lead, without offering any resistance or

advice. It seemed she had decided that her earlier outburst had been unwarranted, and by lifting the lid and shedding light on her emotions, she had somehow sent the message that she was not grateful to Vishnupant and the rest of the family for everything they had done.

"Sit down, Vasantiatya," Mohini said.

Vasanti sat on the chair and cocked her head. "Can you hear the waves?"

"All I can hear is Gulaam's sister crying."

"When I was a little girl, long before you were born, every time we came to Bombay from Poona, we would go to Dadar Seaface at least once during our visit. I haven't told you this before, have I? I'm not repeating myself—"

"No, you are not, Vasantiatya. Go on," Mohini said.

"In those days, before Koleshwar Nivas was built, Vishnupant and your family lived in Hindu Colony. We'd walk over Tilak Bridge and take the shortcut to Ranade Road through various gullies, before crossing Cadell Road in order to get to the sea. Two things were a mystery to me then: why the level of the ocean was constantly changing, and why were flowers floating on its surface. After all, the sea did not grow flowers." She opened her mouth as if to continue, then shut it again.

"What?"

"Well, in due course I had my answers. Tides are caused by the waning and waxing of the moon. And, after removing the wilted flowers from the puja room, people sometimes release them into the sea."

Mohini looked at the rain tree silhouetted against an indigo sky. In its upper branches were caught a handful of stars. Gulaam's sister had stopped crying. The queen of the night continued to cast her scent into the air, and when she was least expecting it, the sound of Keshav's horn rose above the ring of footsteps as people made their way home from Shivaji Park.

"Vasantiatya?" Mohini said, holding out her hand so her aunt could help her up. "Wouldn't it be nice if there was some place we could go to get all our questions answered?"

"If only I could tell you, Mohini, the number of times that I have wished for the very same thing."

That night, with the interconnecting door to her parents' room wide open, Mohini listened to Keshav's heavy breathing. Earlier on, when he was sitting on her bed, she had complained to him that he did not talk to her any more. He did not tell her about his current projects, nor did he tell her stories about his early engineering expeditions when there was hardly a car or bus or train to be seen in rural areas, when the commonest mode of transport was two legs or a bullock cart.

"I can't think of anything new to tell you," her father said, yawning.

"Then tell me something you've already told me . . . Your wedding, Baba. Start from the night before."

"Again? You've heard that story so many times, and not only from me, but also from your Poona grandparents, not to mention Shridharmama, your mother, even my father."

"But I haven't heard it in such a long time."

Keshav stood up quickly. "Not today," he said. "Now go to sleep."

Mohini pulled a pillow over her head to blot out Keshav's snoring. She repeated to herself the story that she had not heard in a while. The story of her parents' wedding in Poona some fifteen odd years ago.

The night before their wedding, Keshav had pulled up in front of Umabai and Anantrao's building in a two-wheel cart pulled by a single bullock, white body covered in a fine grey dust. Curious as to who it could be at that late hour of the night, Shridhar and his cousins stopped unrolling their bedding on the front verandah and hurried to the side of the road. It took Shridhar a moment to recognize the bridegroom. Keshav was sitting up stiffly, his hands clutching the reins of the cart, as its diminutive owner slept in the back. Like the bullock, Keshav's hair and face were matted with fine dust. He nodded, and Shridhar, who instinctively knew that Keshav would go into a spasm of coughing if he were to open his mouth and speak, immediately showed him to the outdoor tap.

Kamala drew back from the front window in which she had been standing. She peeped from behind the shutters and watched the man who was to become her husband alight from the cart and walk with stiff, bowed legs towards the side of the building. She moved forward and clutched the bars of the window, not knowing whether to laugh or cry. She could hear him splashing noisily as he rinsed the grime off his body. He gargled loudly and repeatedly, in an attempt to loosen the grit from his teeth, all the while oblivious to the male tenants of the building who stood to one side, watching with curiosity as he performed his ablutions with such gratitude and vigour. When Keshav was at last finished, Shridhar handed him a cotton towel. Kamala drew back once again. Before Keshav could enter through the front door, she retreated into the inner room. She listened to him explain to her father how, at the very last moment, a senior engineer on-site had sequestered a car that had been firmly promised to him, Keshav, to transport him to Poona for his wedding. He had had no choice therefore, he said, but to hire any mode of transport that would allow him to come in time for the marriage ceremonies that were slated to begin the following day. He explained that the roads leading to the Oek ancestral property had been blocked by police due to some political demonstration, so he had had to come directly to the bride's house.

Kamala, who had seen Keshav only once before, at the time of their engagement, did not know what to make of a man who in his determination not to be late for his own wedding had come to Poona not with his family but directly from work in such a dramatic way. She closed her eyes, and in front of her eyelids flashed the crab-like image of Keshav walking away from the bullock cart, his face a white mask, his movements slow and cumbersome. Smiling, she sat back on the trunk that was packed with the clothes she would be taking to Bombay. Sitting on the cot opposite her, Umabai was smiling too.

After the wedding, Keshav made no reference to the manner of his arrival. Instead, he told her regretfully— Kamala was pleased to detect the genuine disappointment in his tone—that he had been granted only a five-day leave. "Of course," he continued, "that does not mean you cannot come back with me." He had applied to his superiors to bring her along for a few days, and surprisingly, they had granted him married quarters. He grinned, most pleased with his good fortune. He looked expectantly at Kamala, and when she said nothing, he assured her—as if the topic might have some bearing on her silence—that the night sky in cities and towns was nothing compared with its equivalent in the rural districts. "Do you ever look at the sky at night?" he asked. "I mean really look at it? Because if you do, then you will agree that what we see up there is nothing short of immaculate engineering. The spaces between heavenly bodies? What else but spanning bridges, supporting plinths, foundations—albeit invisible—that have withstood the test of time."

Once again, Kamala did not know whether to laugh or cry. He tapped her hand to get her attention in case it had wandered. It was obvious to her that he had not said everything that he wished to say on the subject. His enthusiasm was contagious. She smiled as he continued: "In case you think I am an expert on the sky, I want to make it clear that I am not. I do not know anything about astrology or astronomy. But then there is no need to qualify and quantify everything in nature, is there, Kamale? I can call you Kamale, can I not? Some things are better seen with faculties other than that of the intellect. You'll see what I mean when we look at the sky together."

Kamala withdrew her hand, which he had picked up while speaking. All she could think about was that the site to which he was posted was a jungle, teeming with snakes. Keshav himself had described it as such when various people in the marriage party had asked him about his current posting. Married quarters or no married quarters, wild elephants would not drag her within ten miles of it; that much she knew. What she did not know was that Indumatibai, Keshav's mother, had already given the matter some thought. As someone who shared Kamala's phobia of reptiles, she told her son he should report back to work for his remaining two months and that Kamala would return home with them, to Bombay.

Keshav wrote her long, descriptive letters when he was away from home and told her even more when he returned. She heard about areas where the humidity was so great that the body felt bloated, like a balloon filled with water. "The moisture forces its way through the skin and penetrates the organs so a man becomes four pounds heavier," he said. Without letting a glimmer of laughter enter his face, he puffed his cheeks for emphasis. She laughed at his exaggeration, genuinely amused, not suspecting one little bit that this was the exact response he had intended to elicit. She continued to dangle her feet from the side of the high bed, too shy to look at him as he sat next to her, leaning his shoulder now and then into her slight body. "And in such places," he continued, "insects breed like rabbits and can be heard at least fifteen minutes before they attack in a black cloud and crawl inside noses and ears and probe their way through outer clothing until the skin is covered with them." He put his arms around her before she could flinch. When she did not move, he gently turned her face against his chest where she could hear the rapid beating of his heart. Taking her hand, he ran her slender palm up and down his darkened, bumpy forearms while informing her that burning and itching rashes were common hazards of on-site work.

He told her he passed villages so poor that emaciated men would work fallow fields in a stupor produced by hunger, waiting for a harvest that would partially fill their bellies. When the saris of their women became threadbare, the woman with the most opaque garment would share hers with the other women of the household so that the woman whose turn it was to be clothed that day would leave the hut while the others cowered inside to hide their nakedness. Kamala covered her mouth with her hand, appalled by the shameful image. "But why don't they have clothes?"

"Because they do not have the money to buy them with. In that district there are no big landowners who pay cash—however petty—in lieu of wages. The men these villagers work for, their landholdings are small. If the crop is good, the farmhands are paid grain. If the weather fails, everyone, farmhands and owners, starve. In such areas monsoons are unpredictable. Three out of five years are lean." There was a furrow between Keshav's eyebrows as he spoke, and agitated, he let go of her hand. He turned and looked into her eyes to see whether she was interested in all the things he was so eager to share with her. Satisfied, he tucked behind her ear a strand of hair that was brushing her neck.

Seeing his face and hearing the accompanying words, Kamala not only got a glimpse into the reasons behind Keshav's decision to go into civil engineering, but she also understood why he measured progress by the rate at which roads, bridges, irrigation canals, and dams were built. Nothing else can better serve the remote villages, he told her. Nothing else can better assure them food, water, education, and electricity. She also understood, at long last, why her father so fervently wanted the British gone. With three-quarters of the wealth getting drained out of the country on an annual basis, there was nothing left over to attend to the needs of the women Keshav had just told her about.

Kamala entered Mohini's room. Mohini raised her head. "Don't tell me you are still awake," Kamala whispered, coming forward.

"I can't sleep. I was thinking about the night before your wedding."

"That was so long ago, Mohini . . ."

"I know, but the story is so typical of Baba that I like thinking about it."

Kamala yawned. "It's so humid," she said, tilting her face towards the fan. There were long, moving shadows on the ceiling. "Remind me tomorrow to tell Balu to get out on the roof of the car porch and cut back some branches of the rain tree." She left the room.

Mohini closed her eyes and summoned up the image of Shri Krishna playing His flute, His blue body forged from the eternal sky. But the image disappeared quickly, and when she tried to raise it again, it was gone almost as soon as it was evoked. She tapped her stomach with her knuckles. It made a hollow sound. She clicked her tongue in annoyance. For some time now she had been meaning to complain to Dr. Chitnis that the streptomycin injections, along with her other medication, were causing her stomach to bloat and rumble. And now that her belly was distended with wind she was sure it stuck out even more than before. The next time he came by she would tell him that he would have to prescribe some other medicines to replace the ones she was taking. But when he came the following week, she was reticent, morose.

"Is anything the matter?" he asked. "Are any of the symptoms recurring? Headaches, nausea, light sensitivity?"

Kamala was standing on the other side of her bed, searching her face. Mohini looked out the door and watched as a gust of wind scattered the fallen leaves across the terrace floor. She wished everyone would stop caring for her as much as they did. Their selfless regard for her well-being, the commitment they felt towards doing everything in their power to make her feel comfortable, their scrutiny and questions were like soft clouds pressing into her body, suffocating her by their constancy, crushing her with their weight. She did not want Dr. Chitnis to start his evening clinic late because he felt he had to personally administer her transfusions; a junior doctor or even an assistant could have monitored the drip just as well. She wanted her mother to visit Poona and plan Shridhar's wedding in person, not through letters. She wanted her to resume her embroidery classes at the samaj. She wanted her to accompany Keshav when he went on-site and she wished Keshav would plead, the way he used to in the past, that Kamala go with him.

Dr. Chitnis removed the needle from the inside of her elbow. "Well?" he said. "You haven't said a word all evening."

"I'm allowed not to, aren't I?" she said testily, then instantly regretted her tone. But it was too late to retrieve the words or the manner in which they were spoken; it was already too late the minute she had hung them in the air for everyone to hear. She did not look at her mother.

"You can take a vow of silence; it will not bother me," Dr. Chitnis said. "But you must promise to tell me if you are feeling particularly weak or if your head is aching more than usual."

She nodded. Without looking at Mohini, Kamala followed Dr. Chitnis out to the back verandah and down the stairs.

THIRTEEN

When Mohini went to the dining room, Kamala and Vasanti were drinking tea. Kamala ignored Mohini and continued to sip from her cup. Vasanti pulled out the chair next to her and told Mohini to sit. "Mai made besan ladoo this morning. Here, try one."

Mohini stood without moving.

"What's the matter?" Vasanti asked. "Are you crying, Mohini?" She glanced at Kamala.

Kamala looked at Mohini and said, "I don't ever want you to speak to Dr. Chitnis in that tone. Is that understood?"

The tears ran down Mohini's cheek.

Vasanti clucked her tongue, got up, and pulled Mohini down on the chair next to her. Mohini sat limply, her shoulders bowed. "Eat the ladoo," Vasanti softly urged. "I know that whatever happened with Dr. Chitnis, you know better than to let it happen again. Eat now."

Balu came into the dining room to clear away the tea things.

Kamala said to him, "You are leaving for your village in three days. Have you found a replacement for yourself as you said you would?"

"My cousin will come."

"The last time one of your cousins promised to come, you remember what happened? We never saw his face. Sahib is leaving on Friday and this time he said he might be gone longer than usual. With him gone, I will not have Madanlal driver to do the marketing and run errands. I don't want a repeat of last time when you left us high and dry. You say your mother is ill and you must go, which means I cannot ask you to postpone your leaving until after I have found a replacement for you myself."

"This is another cousin, Kamalavahini," he patiently said. "Not the same one who didn't show up the last time."

"You are leaving on Saturday morning. Make sure he is here on Friday night."

Balu left the room.

"Keshav is going away again?" Vasanti said. "His trips are becoming more and more frequent."

"Two engineers are on leave, he told me. And there have been delays due to the monsoons. He needs to supervise to make sure the work is not lagging behind. Mohini, eat the ladoo. It's very good." Kamala leaned across and nudged the bowl nearer to Mohini. Her voice was soft and coaxing. Vasanti unclawed Mohini's right hand and thrust the sweet-meat into her palm. Mohini returned it to the bowl and, covering her face, let the tears run down; her shoulders were heaving. Kamala got up from her chair and put her arms around Mohini, placing her chin on top of her head.

Without letting Mohini see, Vasanti reached up and with her handkerchief dabbed Kamala's eyes. She pushed back her chair and carried the rest of the tea things into the kitchen.

———

On Friday evening, Mohini and Kamala were sitting in the front verandah when Balu came out carrying the tray with the dhoop. The dense, white smoke emanating from the crucible scattered the mosquitoes and insects into the darkening corners of the ceiling. Mohini breathed in deeply the combination of incense and burning coal.

"What time is your cousin expected to arrive?" Kamala asked Balu when he stood in front of her holding out the tray. Balu muttered a reply as he shifted and held the crucible out to Mohini. As her mother had done a moment before her, Mohini directed some of the smoke towards her own body before joining her hands together in a brief namaskar.

Kamala looked at her daughter. "Did you hear what he said?"

"He said nobody can come."

Balu moved away towards the car porch.

"I thought that's what he said. Balu!"

He scampered back, the tray held so close to his body that the smoke caused tears to well up in his eyes.

"Put that down on the ledge," Kamala ordered. "Did we hear you correctly?"

Balu hung his head.

The front gate creaked. It was Gulaam, the Irani's son. Addressing Kamala, he said, "Salaam, Memsahib. I met Sahib outside the gymkhana last week and he said I should come this week to find out whether he has a job for me."

"Baba left town this morning," Mohini said.

"But he said to come Friday."

"Next time before coming, make sure Sahib's car is here," Balu admonished him. "Don't trouble Memsahib."

By the light that was falling on the verandah from inside the front door, Mohini saw a flush creep up Gulaam's face. This was his third time standing at the bottom of the steps, asking for a job. The last time, after he had come and gone, Vishnupant had said, "He waits until he knows Keshav is not here. He doesn't want any job. He just wants to tell the Irani he has made inquiries." Kamala and Mohini were not so sure about Vishnupant's assessment. Gulaam had a polite, sincere demeanour that denied any subterfuge.

"Come next week when Sahib is here," Balu said to Gulaam.

Gulaam was almost at the front gate when Kamala said, "Call him back." Balu hesitated, but her voice had carried. Gulaam was once again standing at the bottom of the steps.

"Balu is leaving for his village tomorrow," she told him. "His replacement is unable to come. We need someone to do the jobs Balu does: mopping, sweeping, cleaning, dusting, ironing . . ." Kamala's voice tapered off.

"I'll come, Memsahib," Gulaam said. He glanced sideways at Balu, his face triumphant.

"But, Vahini, Narya—"

"I thought you said your cousin was not coming." There was anger in Kamala's voice. Her eyes were narrow.

"But Bayabai will not like it if Gulaam came," Balu persisted.

Mohini looked at Balu in surprise. It was unlike him not to know that Kamala's displeasure and disappointment in him were so firmly rooted that trying to bring Bayabai into the conversation at this moment was akin to walking into a hard concrete wall.

Kamala turned deliberately to Gulaam and said, "Come on Sunday morning. If in the meantime Balu's replacement shows up, I will send you word. But first, go home and ask permission of your father whether it is all right for you to work here. Your mother too."

Gulaam nodded, then turned away quickly and left.

"Bayabai will not let him near the kitchen," Balu said.

"When I want your opinion, I will ask for it." Kamala's voice was stony. "Don't utter another word, because it is you and no one else who has put me in this position. If you had told me earlier when I asked you that your cousin was unable to come, I would have found out from the ladies at the Jijabai Samaj whether they knew of someone who would work for me during your absence."

Kamala wiped the back of her neck with the end of her sari. Balu left the verandah.

"I admire your secularism, but I hope it will not backfire," Vishnupant called out from his room.

Kamala flinched. She walked down the verandah and stood outside his window, to one side. Vishnupant was at his desk. "I should have asked you first," she said, a tremor in her voice. She held out her hand behind her. Mohini placed her own in it. Her mother's palms were wet.

Vishnupant said, "Gulaam's presence in my room or in our house will not contaminate us, Kamala—"

"But I should have asked you first," Kamala repeated.

"Let Gulaam come. By all means, let him come. It is how you will broach the subject to Bayabai that interests me."

"I will send a message for Gulaam not to come," Kamala said, barely able to control the quaver in her voice. Mohini came forward and wiped the palms of her mother's hands against her frock.

"Kamala"—Vishnupant's voice was firm—"I am not objecting, am I? Bayabai is the one who needs convincing if Gulaam is to begin here on Sunday . . . You could have him work here regardless of Bayabai's approval of course, although you may find yourself in the midst of a domestic Mahabharata. It might liven things up! Either way, you will have to tackle that woman on your own. And don't forget one other thing: the people in the neighbourhood and your ladies at the samaj will not hesitate to criticize you."

After dinner, Kamala went to the kitchen. She told Bayabai that Balu was upstairs turning down the beds and that she wanted to talk to her before he came down.

Mohini waited for Kamala on the bottom step of the stairs, opposite the front entrance. Kamala was standing just inside the kitchen door, at the other end of the corridor. Vishnupant joined Mohini on the steps. He did not switch on the stairwell light.

"As you know," Kamala was saying to Bayabai, "Balu's cousin cannot come for the time that Balu is away. That being the case, I have asked Gulaam to come as his replacement."

Bayabai did not respond.

Vishnupant elbowed Mohini. She leaned against him.

Kamala said, "Did you understand, Bayabai, what I just said?"

Bayabai replied, "All I understand is that there is no way I will remain in this house if Gulaam steps in through that front door."

Kamala said, "If you wish to be gone for the time Balu is away, I can look after the kitchen and cook. What I cannot do is take on Balu's responsibilities. Mohini's father is also away. Even if I send word to the vegetable vendor to come to our door, there is no Madanlal to buy the medicines and other provisions that we will need. And I cannot single-handedly clean the house." Kamala's voice was calm and reasonable. Mohini let out her breath.

"You know very well I have no place to go to even if I wanted, which so many times I do," Bayabai said.

"I was completely aware of that fact when I made the suggestion," Kamala said, ignoring the addendum to Bayabai's assertion. "You could stay with my parents in Poona or at Vasanti's across the lane. I'm sure none of them would mind. You tell me what you want to do."

"All I would like is for Gulaam not to darken my doorway."

Kamala was silent. Vishnupant and Mohini leaned forward and peeped around the corner of the wall. Bayabai was plucking her handkerchief from her waist. She held it up and gave her face a good rub. When she lowered it, her skin looked sore and red.

"Gulaam will not darken your doorway," Kamala gently said.

Bayabai stopped sniffing.

In the dark stairwell, Vishnupant leaned back, shaking his head. He had not thought Kamala would give in so easily. He was about to stand up when Mohini pulled him back.

"I will personally see to it that Gulaam does not darken your doorway," Kamala was saying. "He will not enter the kitchen, the puja room, or the dining room. That way, you need not see him and his shadow need not fall on you. You can keep this door leading into the corridor closed when he is in the house."

"Then who will dust and sweep and mop the three rooms?"

"I will. Three is easy to manage compared with the whole house."

"There is no need for that! Who else but me sweeps the puja room and kitchen first thing in the morning?" There was fury in Bayabai's voice.

"Then that's settled. I'll take Mohini's jug of water since I am going upstairs."

Vishnupant was entering his room when Kamala switched on the light in the stairwell. She held out her hand to Mohini and together they climbed the stairs. Balu was waiting at the top. He took the jug from her. "I don't want you to mention Gulaam to Bayabai. And the next time you go on leave, I want you to tell me a month in advance."

Vishnupant hollered for Kamala to quickly come downstairs. It was six o'clock on Sunday morning. She rushed down, pulling the end of her sari around her shoulders because her hair was hanging loose on her back; she had been in the middle of combing it. Mohini hurried behind her as fast as she was able.

"It's that wretched Irani," Vishnupant said. "I just saw him cross the lane. Hasn't anyone told him that because he opens his shutters at five-thirty every morning, the rest of the world is not open for business at that time?"

"Shall I unbolt the door?" Kamala asked.

"Do you have a choice?" Vishnupant said.

Kamala unbolted the door and followed Vishnupant and Mohini outside. The Irani's face was all teeth. He was grinning widely. "My son will be here shortly," he said.

Vishnupant started to ask Kamala if she wanted him here so early, but the Irani was already stating that his son was a good boy. "He simply needs someone to give him a chance. My wife and I want to thank Memsahib and Big Sahib."

"I don't believe this man even begins to understand what it has cost your mother to give his son that chance," Vishnupant muttered to Mohini.

The Irani grinned. "You won't regret this, Sahib. He is a big, strong boy—"

"That we can see," Vishnupant said.

"You can ask him to do anything, Sahib. Inside house, outside in the garden. He does all the heavy lifting in the tea shop. You can even ask him to move furniture. Here he is now."

Gulaam looked at his father in astonishment. Clearly, he had not expected to see him there.

Vishnupant said, "You have told us what your son is capable of doing, but we don't ever move the furniture in our house. Everything stays the way it is. Everything. You remember that, Gulaam." Vishnupant pinned the boy with his eyes.

"If not furniture, then your feet, your head, he will give good massage if you want," the Irani said.

"I'll remember that." Vishnupant turned to go inside.

"There's the matter of payment." The Irani glanced at the ground.

Kamala replied that she would pay Gulaam half of what she paid Balu per month since Balu would be away for two weeks.

The Irani ducked his head. He looked pained.

"If that is not enough—" Kamala said.

"Enough? No, Memsahib." He turned to Vishnupant. "Memsahib is not understanding me."

Mohini looked at Vishnupant who was standing impatiently in the doorway, his mind clearly on the first cup of tea, which Bayabai was no doubt already brewing in the kitchen.

"There will be no pay," the Irani declared. "Gulaam is simply making up for the trouble he caused Keshav Sahib. Isn't that so?" He placed a playful smack on the back of Gulaam's neck. Gulaam nodded.

"All right, then. You can start with the upstairs rooms. Just follow me," Kamala said to Gulaam, leaving the verandah.

The Irani pulled a chocolate from his shirt pocket and handed it to Mohini. "Here, just a sweet little something before I go," he said. "You tell me, bebi, if Gulaam gives Memsahib any trouble. Agreed?" Mohini nodded. He walked down the front path and closed the gate carefully behind him.

Gulaam was thorough in his work. The first time Kamala told him that except when it is on the head, hair is a thing of disgust and that he must make sure that every fallen strand is swept up and dropped into the dustbin, he heeded her words so well that she didn't have to tell him again. He scrubbed the bathroom tiles until they shone and afterwards dried the floor so that Mohini would not slip and fall, something even Balu did not do, leaving the floor to dry on its own.

Mohini watched him from the swing as his muscled arms ironed Kamala's sari in the covered part of the terrace, not satisfied until the fabric looked like an unopened newspaper: flat and crisp. He wiped the windowsills and the patterned iron bars across the windows with a wet cloth, which he frequently rinsed and wrung out in running water. While sweeping, he slid the broom up and down the corners of the room to rid them of cobwebs.

He swept and mopped the floor of the corridor leading into the kitchen when he knew Bayabai was out of sight, when he could hear her singing loudly her prayers in the puja room, perhaps to drown out the turmoil inside her breast caused by Gulaam's invisible presence inside Koleshwar Nivas. He left the used water jugs and glasses from the previous night on the corridor windowsill so he would not have to enter the kitchen. He was very respectful of Kamala and avoided being addressed by Vishnupant by averting his eyes when he cleaned his room. He worked silently, until one day. He was ironing and Mohini was sitting on the swing. He turned to her and said, "On your mother's dressing table, those statues, are they her gods?"

Mohini said they were. There was a crawling baby Krishna; Goddess Saraswati, the goddess of learning; and an ivory Ganapati.

Gulaam grimaced.

"What's wrong?" Mohini said.

"All these gods. We are taught that there is only one God and his name is Allah."

"We believe in a single God too."

He stopped ironing and looked at her in disbelief. "No, you don't! I myself counted three on Memsahib's dressing table."

"They are all manifestations of one God."

"They are all what?" he asked, his eyes filled with confusion.

"Guruji explained it to me this way. He used my mother as an example. He said she is one person but she is also a daughter, a sister, a mother, a wife, an aunt. Also, she is a teacher when she teaches me, a cook when she is in the kitchen, an artist when she does her embroidery. He said God is like that. We give Him different names when He performs different functions. He said if I were to draw a picture of Aai in her various roles, then I would have a different picture each time, and if I combined all the pictures, she would have lots of arms because she performs so many functions. In the same way, Brahma, Vishnu, and Mahesh are actually only one God, simultaneously doing three different things: creation, preservation, and destruction."

"But if you have only one God, why do you pray to so many?"

Mohini had to think awhile before she could answer that question. Gulaam thought he had stumped her and was smiling when she said, "That's because, that is, it is no good asking Aai, the cook, to sew me a new frock. Or asking Aai, the tailor, to prepare my favourite dishes. That's why, when I have an exam, I pray to Lord Ganapati for intellect and wisdom, and if I'm having an operation, I pray to Lord Vishnu so He will preserve—"

"But you also have a god of wind and god of clouds and this god and that god," Gulaam interrupted. His tone was challenging.

"Oh, that's because everything in the universe is equally important, and the only way to get people to respect everything is by elevating that thing to the status of a god. That's why we have three hundred and thirty million gods."

"And your guruji told you that as well?" Gulaam sounded sarcastic.

"No, my friend Hansa's father told her, and she told me."

Gulaam gave a shrug and clicked his tongue. Mohini could tell he wasn't convinced. The following day and the next he did not address her, and once or twice when she caught him looking at her, she saw pity on his face, this time not only for her body, but also for her mind.

On the night before Balu was expected to return, Mohini sat on Kamala's bed as she watched Keshav eat his sugar and curds. He was silent when he handed her the empty bowl. "Baba, how come you don't talk much these days?" Mohini asked him.

"Do I not?"

"Not much since you came back last week."

"I wasn't aware."

"Ask Aai if she doesn't think so too," Mohini said, as Kamala walked into the room.

Without responding to Mohini, she took the bowl from her daughter's hands and walked into the bathroom in order to rinse it.

When she returned, Mohini said, "I told Baba he doesn't talk much these days. Don't you think so too?"

Kamala was silent.

"Does that mean yes or no? Do you agree with Mohini or not?" Keshav said, rubbing his eyes with his left hand, still clutching the pen with his right.

"It means there is nothing to say. You are always work-ing. These days you come upstairs right after dinner because you have unfinished reports . . ."

"Even Vishnupant was complaining that you do not tell him about your on-site visits the way you used to," Mohini said. "He says he likes to know about your work because when people at the gymkhana ask after you, he has something to tell them."

Keshav went back to the papers on his desk. Kamala quickly turned on her heel and re-entered the bathroom. Mohini got off the bed and went to her room, pulling the door shut behind her. In the middle of the night, when she woke up for a drink of water, she noticed that her mother was sleeping in the spare bed next to her. In the morning, when she asked Kamala why she had slept there, Kamala replied that she had heard Mohini groaning and thought it better that she remain at hand in case Mohini needed something. Mohini looked at Keshav. The papers he was stuffing into his bag fell to the floor. Kamala did not lend him a hand but deliberately continued to smooth out her unused bed, as he bent down and gathered them together.

FOURTEEN

In spite of the fact that Mohini did not have much to do, the days moved forward at an easy pace. When people asked her whether she was bored now that she was without homework or friends or school to occupy her, Mohini would say, "Lonely, not bored." Where before her quick answers and pronouncements had impressed others, now her more thoughtful responses might have fooled the same people into thinking that meningitis had made that rapid mind sluggish and slow. They could not have known that taking those extra few seconds before saying something merely reflected the fact that she had had, over the previous weeks, given much thought to subjects other than the school curriculum or current events.

Around the second week of November, Vishnupant received a telegram. He did not like telegrams. He handed it to Balu to open. Having been taught to read Marathi alongside Mohini by Kamala all those years ago, he peered at the typed letters, then passed it to Mohini because it was written in English. The telegram was from Calcutta. She read aloud: "'Nandini and Hema arriving November 11 at Dadar 10 a.m. Come to receive at station. Raghunathrao.'"

"That's tomorrow!" Mohini said, dropping the telegram in her excitement. She turned to her grandfather. "Did you know they were coming?"

"In her last letter," Vishnupant said, "Nandini had mentioned that there were significant labour problems at Raghunathrao's Carleton Engineering Works, and that she and Hema would leave for Bombay if the negotiations became too tense."

"So that's why they're coming," Mohini said, "or they wouldn't be leaving Calcutta in the middle of Hema's school year."

Vasanti offered to go with Mohini to the railway station. That way, she said, Kamala could oversee the preparation of lunch. Keshav said he would go to his office with a colleague so they could have Madanlal and the car.

At the station, Vasanti warned Madanlal not to park the car so far away that she would have to go searching for it. "If you don't get parking nearby," she said, pointing to all the empty parking spaces alongside the footpath, "come and wait at the entrance and keep a lookout for us."

Characteristically, Madanlal let her words wash over him as though he had not heard her, and as soon as Mohini had closed the car door behind her, he changed the clutch noisily and sped away.

"Why does Keshavdada not get rid of him?" Vasanti muttered, even as she crooked her arm so Mohini could hook her hand in it.

"Baba can't find anyone else who is equally good at long-distance driving. Madanlal has been with him for so long that he knows all the roads and shortcuts, even in the rural areas."

The onshore wind had been blowing all morning, driving forward clouds that covered the city in soft grey folds. There was a crack of lightning, and then another and another, the rumbling thunder not far behind. People hurried past Mohini and Vasanti, up the steps and into the station as the rain came crashing down. Vasanti steered Mohini towards the information window. Shepherding her to a less busy spot near the wall, she said she would find out on which platform the Calcutta train was due to arrive. There were muffled thumps and a loud clattering as holdalls and great big trunks were lowered to the ground. Somewhere, a stationmaster was repeatedly blowing his whistle. Opposite Mohini, a mother was scolding her children for tugging at her sari, a baby was demanding to be fed, and a man, his face twitching with nervous energy, was urging his party to walk faster lest they miss their train. Under the large, round clock stood a cluster of children, who had missed the onslaught of the rain, hands held together, their shirts white and crisp, their green shorts starched and ironed. Some of the children nudged and pointed at Mohini and soon all of them were looking her way. She stepped back and leaned against a pillar and straightened her spine so that her body wouldn't appear slumped over, listing to one side because of her buckled knee. Vasanti was back. "This way," she said, taking Mohini's hand. "The train is running half an hour late. We're fifteen minutes early. It'll be a long wait. Is that all right?" Mohini nodded absent-mindedly, looking at the children who were now half-reciting, half-singing a song.

The platform at which the Calcutta train was to arrive was deserted. They walked midway down it and sat on a bench. The air was cooler now and Vasanti brought the end of her sari to cover her right shoulder. They watched the rain stream down, and just when they thought the downfall was abating, the torrent would start again, the din against the steel roof increasing rapidly until they could hear nothing but the rain. Mohini narrowed her eyes to see whether she could spot the platform across the railway tracks. She couldn't. The rain was an opaque curtain.

"Twenty-five minutes before the train comes in," Vasanti said, pointing to the clock suspended from the tall ceiling. Mohini looked around. The platform was beginning to fill up. A man passed in front of the bench on which they were sitting, holding carefully in his hands a plate made of leaves from which steam was rising.

"Hmm . . . onion fritters," Vasanti said. "My mouth is watering."

"I'm hungry."

Vasanti was silent.

Mohini nudged her aunt in the ribs.

"No," Vasanti said. "You are only just recovering. I'll makc you fritters at home." Her voice lacked conviction.

Mohini deliberately turned around in the direction of the food stall. It was crowded. People were pushing forward to place their orders.

Mohini said, "It doesn't matter whether I can eat or not because we have no money."

Vasanti was silent.

Mohini said, "You didn't bring any change, did you?"

Vasanti removed her handkerchief from the top of her sari blouse. She undid the knot in one corner and displayed two rupee notes. "I slipped them in last minute," she said.

"The vendor looks quite clean, Vasantiatya. Nothing will happen to me. And you know my stomach is like a horse's stomach—it's the strongest part of my body."

"Mohini! The things you say . . ."

Vasanti stood up.

"Where are you going?"

"Only onion fritters. No chutney—the coconut may not be fresh."

"Agreed," Mohini said.

When Vasanti returned she was carrying in one hand a steel tumbler filled with water and in the other the onion fritters. She laid the leaf-plate carefully on the handkerchief Mohini had spread out on the bench. Then she poured into Mohini's hands some water from the tumbler. Mohini leaned over the side of the bench and rinsed her fingers, letting the water trickle to the platform. Vasanti did the same.

The fritters were delicious. They ate them quickly and washed their hands once again, and Vasanti had returned the tumbler to the vendor and disposed of the plate when puffs of smoke announced the arrival of the train. They spotted Hema right away. She was sticking her head out of the compartment window. She handed Vasanti their luggage from the doorway and went back in to fetch her mother. Nandini, when she stepped out onto the platform, was wearing a cotton towel wrapped tightly around her head.

"Headache?" Vasanti asked, when Nandini was sitting on the bench, one arm around Mohini.

"Yes. Second day running and showing no signs of leaving."

Hema, Mohini's cousin, who had almost toppled Mohini when she had hugged her earlier, now signalled for the coolie to gather their belongings. Mohini glanced at her shyly. It was three years since Nandini and Hema had last visited Bombay. Hema looked all grown up, dressed in a sari.

"My," Vasanti said to Nandini, "she looks every bit her sixteen years."

"Time to find her a boy," Nandini replied.

"I'll walk with Mohini, Vasantimavshi," Hema said. "You go ahead."

Hema held out her hand. There was a tinny, metallic smell emanating from her clothes. She must not have had a bath in three days, but as she looked down at Mohini, her face was as fresh and smiling as ever. After Vasanti, Mohini thought Hema was the most beautiful creature she had ever seen. Her small face was triangular, the eyebrows thick and curved to the shape of her darkly lashed eyes. Her complexion was like her father's, very dusky, but there was a velvety smoothness to it: her skin was even in tone. Her nose was long and straight and her cheekbones high, and when she smiled her eyes almost disappeared into her cheeks. Mohini placed her hand in Hema's and knew that she would be less lonely for a while, now that her cousin had arrived.

"Am I going too fast for you?" Hema asked.

"Not at all," Mohini said. She slowed down for a moment nevertheless, in order to catch her breath.

It had stopped raining, but the steps were slick with water. Vasanti and Hema helped Mohini down them. "You should not have come, Mohini," Nandini said. "You haven't yet fully recovered, I can see."

"Of course she should have come," Hema said. "I was hoping you would, Mohini."

Vishnupant and Kamala were waiting for them in the front verandah. "It's been too long," Vishnupant said as Nandini and Hema bent over and did namaskar to him. There was gruffness in his voice.

Nandini turned to Kamala. "I expected from Baba's letters for Mohini to be frail, but look at you. I must have a word with Bayabai. She needs to fatten you up."

"She's picked up her health," Vasanti said defensively. "You should have seen her two weeks ago."

"Where is Keshav?" Nandini said.

"It's the middle of the day," Vishnupant reminded her, leaving the verandah. "He'll be back by six."

Hema did namaskar to Kamala. After hugging her, Kamala held her at arm's length and said, "It's so good to see you. What a difference three years have made. Here you are, grown into a very pretty young woman. Tall too."

Hema blushed. "You always say such nice things, Kamalamami," she said. She turned to Mohini. "Am I to sleep in your room?"

"Yes," Kamala said. "And, Nandinitai, I have asked Balu to make up your bed in the end room off the back verandah."

"Good," Nandini said. "My knees hurt these days and climbing stairs makes them worse."

Hema rolled her eyes in her mother's direction. "You should exercise more, Ma."

"You girls go on upstairs," Kamala said. "Hema, you can have a bath before lunch if you want."

Balu came out on the verandah and picked up the bags that Madanlal had placed untidily by the shoe stand.

"Balu," Nandini said. "How are you and your mother and father and your eight siblings—or is it nine?"

Balu grinned, showing his gums. "Everyone is all right, Tai. And how is Hematai's father?"

"He's coming to take us back to Calcutta in two weeks' time," Nandini said. "And I haven't forgotten to bring you some holy ash from the Durga temple."

"You remembered?" Balu said, shaking his head.

"If you open my bag, the black one, it's in the inside pocket. You'll recognize it when you see it."

"Tai remembered," Balu said to Nandini, touching her feet.

That morning, when Mohini had asked Keshav whether he was looking forward to seeing his sister, he had smiled and nodded. But the first thing Nandini told him upon meeting him was that he was looking quite terrible, that he had been neglecting himself, and that he should stop going on-site because his skin had darkened considerably and he had begun to show his age. Although Keshav said nothing, Mohini could tell by the tensing of his mouth that he was annoyed. They were sitting in the back verandah, outside the room Nandini always occupied on her visits to Koleshwar Nivas.

"What did you do for Independence Day?" Hema asked.

"I was still in bed with meningitis," Mohini said. "But our school put on a play about Gandhiji and the freedom struggle and Vishnupant gave a speech at the public celebrations at Shivaji Park."

"Baba didn't mention that in his letters. What did he talk about?"

Keshav said, "The usual. How everyone has more responsibility now and how each citizen must work sincerely and honestly and be above corruption."

Vishnupant came out to the verandah. Hema gave her chair to him and Kamala pulled her down onto her lap.

Nandini said, "How come you did not write to me, Baba, that you had given a speech at Shivaji Park?"

Vishnupant shrugged and said he was going for a brisk stroll before dinner. He walked away.

Mohini knew that her grandfather did not like to discuss the topic now that Independence Day had come and gone. She recalled one evening, after listening yet again to a friend from the gymkhana glorify the freedom struggle, citing the singularly prominent events that had culminated in the most auspicious of them all, Vishnupant had said, "Time to move on. No one event in history stands heads and shoulders above any other."

When his friend had protested and said that it was very important to keep alive the memory of that struggle, Vishnupant said, "In ten years' time, twenty years' time, not to mention in a hundred years' time, all this will seem but a part of a continuum." Soon afterwards, Mohini had left the verandah to look up "continuum" in her dictionary. That night, lying on her back and watching the rotating blades of the ceiling fan, Mohini thought that if history was a continuum, then Brahma's dream was also a continuum: an unending series of happenings. One thing now, another thing another time . . . the first thing back again.

"So, what else is new?" Nandini said, turning to Mohini.

"Gulaam—shall I tell them, Aai?" Mohini asked.

Kamala nodded, and Mohini told them how Gulaam had

replaced Balu for two weeks during which time Bayabai had not uttered a single word.

"She was born in a different era," Nandini said. "That's why she is so old-fashioned."

Mohini said, "Kulkarnimavshi from across the lane was most upset. She told Aai that the next time Balu is away, she, Chitra Kulkarni, will find a replacement for him."

Mohini looked at Kamala. Her face was flushed. Even today, Kamala felt a bit frightened by the bold step she had taken. She had allowed Gulaam, a Muslim, inside the house even when it was customary for Hindu tradesmen who belonged to the lower castes to stand outside the back door without ever once planting a foot over its threshold. Kamala remembered the cobbler, a gentle man who carried a copper tumbler during the summer months so that he would not have to ask Bayabai for a glass of water but could draw his own from the outside tap. Whenever he brought back the repaired shoes or sandals, Bayabai would tell him to arrange them on the ground, and after they were properly lined, she would sprinkle a few drops of water over the leather in a superstitious attempt to purify the footwear of the cobbler's low-caste touch. And he would watch with a steady gaze this cleansing ritual as he squatted on his haunches, patiently waiting for his payment that she would place on the top step.

"You don't have to be ashamed, Kamalavahini," Nandini said. "The next time the samaj ladies say something, tell them about Mathumavshi in Girgaum. The milkman who delivers their milk comes all the way from Vasai and he is a Christian. And anyway, as I understand it, Gulaam was only doing the top jobs, wasn't he? No cooking."

Kamala nodded.

"Bayabai is so old-fashioned," Hema said.

"Don't be disrespectful, Hemi," Nandini warned her.

Hema ignored her mother and said, "It used to annoy her that Mohini called Ajoba by his name."

"She still doesn't like me calling him Vishnupant," Mohini muttered.

"Do you remember that day, Mohini, when she nagged you so much that you emptied a jug of water over her head."

Mohini blushed, the memory of that incident and Kamala's wrath afterwards still fresh in her mind as though it had happened only yesterday. She was grateful that dusk had fallen and nobody could see her face.

"That's enough, Hema," Nandini said.

"How are things at Carleton Engineering?" Keshav asked.

"I forgot to tell you the main thing. That's the reason why Hema's father sent us away. Two weeks ago the workers led a huge demonstration to the managing director's office. They squatted in the pouring rain the entire day and said they would sit out for as long as it took management to meet their demands. The following day someone left an anonymous note on the managing director's desk, threatening to take action against his family if their demands were not met. The director—a Mr. Paul Rutledge—called in Hema's father to negotiate on his behalf. Thirty years in Calcutta and he doesn't speak a word of Bengali. Never made the effort even to understand it."

Keshav nodded.

"The workers' demands are not altogether frivolous," Nandini continued. "During the war years there was so much industrial expansion that the company made enormous profits. Realistically, the workers have a share in those profits. But the directors—half of whom live in England—are not willing to make a settlement, not even a small one."

"What about the Independence Day bonus?" Keshav said.

"That's the other thing. The workers were promised it and then were told that they would get it along with their Divali bonus. In any case, last week Hema's father received a similar anonymous note. He thinks it is just a threat, and that the workers know he has no power to grant anything. But I think the terrible communal massacres resulting from Direct Action Day last August are still fresh in everyone's mind. So, he thought we should come here until the crisis has passed. He said the directors are in the middle of selling Carleton Engineering Works to some local Marwadis and that is the reason they do not want to make any commitment to the workers. But he managed to convince them that the bonus should be paid right away and that a small increment—smaller than their demands—should be acceded to."

Keshav looked at Kamala, and tilted his head in the direction of the dining room.

"Dinner will be ready in a few minutes," Kamala said, patting Hema on her back. Hema stood up and followed her aunt into the kitchen.

"Kamala's looking much too thin," Nandini complained to Keshav.

"You talk to her," he said, barely containing his irritation. "She doesn't listen to anything I say." He got up and walked into the house.

FIFTEEN

That night, Hema changed into her night sari in the bathroom, managing not to get it wet even though the floor was slippery where Mohini had just washed her feet before going to bed. When she came out, her bodice was tucked into the roll of her day sari, and Mohini watched from her bed as she placed the roll under a heap of clothes that Mohini had put for the wash next to the clothes horse. She removed a bottle of oil from her suitcase and, after sitting cross-legged on the bed, dipped her forefinger through its narrow neck, then rubbed the oil into her right brow while watching the clock. A minute later she did the same with the left. Her lips were a bit chapped from the train journey so she rubbed oil into them as well. Next, she rolled her eyeballs right to left and left to right and up and down and round and round. "What are you doing?" Mohini said, fascinated by Hema's ritual.

"Baba's number is minus four in both eyes. Ma said I should do eye exercises because since I've inherited most of his traits, there is every possibility my eyes will get bad if I don't take care of them." She yawned and stretched out on the bed, bringing forward her plait so it would not brush against the back of her neck. Her breathing was slow and deep by the time Mohini had switched off the bedside lamp.

In the morning, after eating breakfast, Hema returned to the kitchen and made a paste of chickpea flour, the creamy top of the milk, a quarter teaspoon of sugar, and a pinch of bright turmeric powder. She smeared this on her face while standing in front of the mirror in Nandini's room, carefully avoiding the soft area under her eyes but making sure that she had covered the front portion of her neck. The application of the face pack became a daily ritual, and Nandini would nag Hema to take a bath when the mask became powdery, threatening to fall to the floor in dusty clumps. By the end of the first week, Mohini's bathroom was stained with yellow rivulets leading into the drain where the turmeric had coloured the white tiles.

Mohini asked her aunt what she thought about all these beautifying rituals. Vasanti replied that they were natural for someone of Hema's age.

"But she's already so pretty," Mohini protested.

"Perhaps she thinks that whatever she is doing will only enhance that beauty."

"Did you rub oil into your eyebrows and walk around wearing face masks when you were her age, Vasantiatya?"

Vasanti laughed. "In our house in Poona there was only one mirror, and that was in Aai and Baba's room. Once our hair was combed, we didn't look into that mirror until the following morning."

Two days later, when they were crossing the lane after lunching at Vasanti's, Mohini's right foot slipped out of her sandal. She lost her balance and her weight came down on her left wrist as she put out her hands to break her fall. Hema helped her to her feet. Mohini winced, holding her left hand against her waist. "Let me see," Kamala said. Very gently and slowly, she rotated the wrist. Mohini cried out. "I'll have to take her to the orthopedic doctor," Kamala said to Nandini. She walked Mohini back to Koleshwar Nivas. "We'll wait for your father to come home so that Madanlal driver can take us. In the meantime, I will send Balu to get some ice from the Irani's."

By the time Keshav took Mohini to Dr. Agarkar's, her wrist was swollen and slightly discoloured.

"I missed you," Dr. Agarkar said, smiling at Mohini. "When were you here last?"

Mohini looked at Keshav. "About eight months ago," he said.

"I remember now. That time it was a hairline fracture. This one looks nastier. Where did you fall? In school?"

"While crossing the lane," Mohini said. "And I don't go to school any more."

"You must be the envy of all your friends," he said.

While taking the X-ray of her wrist, he asked her why she had stopped going to school. She looked to her father, and Keshav explained.

"There's never a dull moment in your house, is there?" Dr. Agarkar said. Mohini smiled.

When the cast was put on, he said, "You keep that hand still now and don't take off the sling even if it is irritating your neck—"

"And don't get the cast wet," Mohini finished for him. She slid forward on the examination table. Dr. Agarkar lifted her and set her on her feet.

"Even though I miss you, I don't want to see you except when you come in to get the cast removed." He turned to Keshav. "Her bones have thinned out even further. They are very brittle and she has to be especially careful. There is a possibility of a fracture even if she accidentally bangs her wrist or hands or arms or feet or any part of her body into a wall or against any hard surface." He addressed Mohini, "You must be careful getting in and out of the car, or walking down the stairs. All right?"

"You heard him, Mohini?" Keshav asked.

Mohini nodded, used to such cautionary instructions.

Mohini was dozing in the front verandah when a tanga carrying Raghunathrao, Hema's father, pulled up in front of Koleshwar Nivas the following week. Everyone, including Kamala, had gone to the seafront. Mohini stood up and waited for Raghunathrao to come to her. The driver of the horse carriage followed him, carrying a holdall and a leather suitcase that he deposited by the shoe stand. Raghunathrao paid him, and only then did he look at Mohini.

"How is school?" he asked her, when she went forward and did namaskar.

"I don't go to school any more."

"Do you not?" he said. "What happened to your hand?"

"I broke it."

He peered into the house.

"They've all gone to see the sunset from Dadar Seaface," she said.

Balu came out. Mohini told him to make Raghunathrao a cup of tea and to get him something to eat.

Balu nodded, carrying in Raghunathrao's luggage.

Mohini glanced down Mill Road, wishing everyone was back, because she always felt awkward and tongue-tied in his presence. He had a forbidding expression, and his chin tilted up in such a way that he had to look down his nose when addressing anyone shorter than himself. She watched silently as he took off his sandals and lowered himself into Vishnupant's armchair; he opened the footrests so he could stretch out his feet. Within seconds he was fast asleep.

The tea had long turned cold by the time Hema ran up the path and Raghunathrao opened his eyes. Hema told him that he had come much too early to fetch them and that she wished she could stay in Bombay forever. There was a brief look of surprise and disappointment on Nandini's face. Raghunathrao got to his feet, cleared his throat, spat over the railing into the bushes, and asked his wife where her father was. "He's gone to the gymkhana. We were not expecting you until later in the week . . ."

Raghunathrao turned to Kamala and nodded. "Your daughter looked after me very well," he said. "Unfortunately, I fell asleep and could not drink the tea she told your boy to bring me." He reached down, tested the temperature of the tea with his little finger, and before Kamala could say she would ask Balu to make another cup, he drained it in one gulp. He picked up a ladoo and, biting into it, went inside. They all followed him into the back verandah. He walked to the far end and stretched his arms over his head several times, bringing them back to the side of his body after each stretch. Then he collapsed his knees and sank into his hips and did that a few times. Before he could begin another set of exercises, Nandini coughed to get his attention. He turned around and she handed him a towel and some fresh clothes that she had removed from his suitcase. He took them from her and entered the end room in which Balu was making up his bed.

When Mohini and Hema saw the bathroom light switched on and heard the bolt pulled across the door, they sat on the raised platform of the verandah, their legs dangling into the bushes below. Behind them, Raghunathrao started to sing a Bengali song:

Monay-bua, Monay-bua are you sleeping?
Sitting in the tree, are you eating? . . .
Come down and smell these flowers red,
Monay-bua, Monay-bua, are you dead?

They looked at each other. Hema was smiling widely.
"What?" Mohini wanted to know.
"He always sings in the bathroom, all kinds of gibberish rhymes."
"Who is Monay-bua?" Mohini asked.
Hema shrugged and elbowed Mohini in the waist and translated for her the Monay-bua rhyme, softly imitating her father's sonorous tones. Mohini burst out laughing. They were snorting uncontrollably when Nandini and Kamala hurried out to the verandah.
"What's the matter, girls?" Nandini asked, glancing in the direction of the bathroom window through which the light was shining. Mohini made an effort to control herself and Hema ran towards the ground-floor water tank, hiccuping loudly.

Kamala knelt next to Mohini. "I'm all right," Mohini said, holding her side where a stitch was beginning to form.

"We didn't know whether you girls were laughing or crying!" Nandini said.

"Why would we be crying, Ma?" Hema came forward, her face now composed.

Just then Raghunathrao entered the verandah, a short, white towel wrapped around his waist, bony knees knoblike under portly stomach, hair pointing towards the ceiling. "Where's my hairbrush?" he asked.

Kamala and Nandini quickly averted their gaze as Nandini said, "I left it next to the basin in the bathroom."

Hema and Mohini focused their attention on the ground until Raghunathrao had once again disappeared into the end room. They did not have to look at each other to burst out laughing again.

"That's enough," Kamala said sternly, turning away towards the kitchen so no one could see her smile.

Nandini wagged a finger and said, "Don't either of you forget that those who laugh immoderately always end up crying."

On Sunday morning, Vinod and his family came to Koleshwar Nivas. After greeting everyone, Mohini's three cousins, Swati, Shobha, and Bharati, crowded around and told her they had something to give her. They hurried her upstairs, and when they were sitting on the swing, they placed a roll covered in brown paper on her lap. "Open it," Shobha said.

Inside were two yards of pale yellow-checked cotton material onto which was worked the most beautiful smocking

Mohini or Hema had ever seen. "Who did this?" Hema asked.

"All three of us. We took turns," Bharati said.

Mohini ran the soft material alongside her cheek. "It's so lovely."

Bharati, who was the youngest and Mohini's age, picked up Mohini's palm and scrutinized it. She turned her attention to the tips of her fingers. "Look at this!" she exclaimed. Swati and Shobha came forward and peered at the fingertips.

"What?" Mohini said.

"We're reading Baba's palmistry book, and it says that if you have round whorls on your fingertips, it is a lucky sign. You have them not only on one finger, but on all."

"Let me see," Hema said.

"See the ridges? Each is in the shape of an oval. If you look at any of ours, they are in the shape of a wave."

Hema examined her own. "I see what you mean," she said.

Balu entered the terrace and told them that tea was served. Downstairs, her aunt Sudha took Mohini's hand and asked her how she was doing. Mohini said she was fine. Vinod looked her over and declared, "But for your wrist, you look much better than during your meningitis attack. Then you were on your back, now you are on your feet."

Mohini unrolled the smocking and passed it around so everyone could see it.

"I'll make the dress as soon as I have a moment," Kamala said.

Sudha hurried her daughters to eat because since they were here, she wanted to stop and see Mai, Bebitai, and Vasanti before heading home. On her way out, Sudha whispered to Kamala, "As I said, I don't know whether this boy that Swati is seeing tomorrow, whether the match will come through. So, do keep a lookout for any other good boys. Shobha is just two years behind her at fifteen. Three girls to marry off. You're lucky you will never have to face that problem." She hurried down the steps.

Without letting the congenial expression slip from her face, Kamala said, "I'll keep your girls in mind when I hear of suitable boys." She quickly put out her hand behind her back. Mohini came forward and clasped it. Kamala said to Swati, "Make sure you wear your mother's pearl-drop earrings when the boy's family come to see you. You'll look so pretty that they will not be able to say no."

Swati did namaskar to Kamala. "Bring Mohini to see us, Kamalakaku. No need for advance notice. Even if Aai is not at home, you know the three of us will be there."

They crossed the lane and disappeared into Vasanti's building.

Mohini could not sleep that night. A snatch of a Meerabai devotional song floated down the road. The beggar brother and sister who made their rounds every night were making their way down the lane. The bhajan became louder. Mohini got off her bed and went to the back verandah where she knew she would see them when they came around to collect their food. Bayabai must have heard their sweet, reedy voices too because she was placing a package on the top step of the back entrance when Mohini held the bars of the verandah railing and slid down to get a better view. The children turned the corner of the house and walked into the light. The sister wore a

long, grubby skirt and glass bangles around her wrists.
Her brownish hair was matted and uncombed. Her plaits
looked as if they had been braided days ago. The boy, only
a little taller, was just as dishevelled. He picked up the
packet Bayabai had left, unfolded the outer leaf, and
sniffed its contents. He then closed it and placed it in a
cotton bag that hung from his shoulder. They took turns
pouring into their mouths the water that was in the jug.
They replaced the jug, and turning to their right, did
namaskar before walking away. Mohini glanced to her
left. Vishnupant and Raghunathrao were sitting in the
verandah in front of the end room, talking.

"As I was saying," Raghunathrao said, "the old man still
has plenty of energy. He was in Calcutta on Independence
Day and it was largely because of his presence that the city
was spared the communal massacres that are still going on
in Punjab."

Vishnupant nodded.

"Have you finished writing your book?" Raghunathrao
asked.

"I thought I had. Then, when the war came to an end,
Atlee announced the handover of power and Mountbatten
declared it would be on August 15. Now I am in the process
of making additions."

Nandini came out and informed Raghunathrao that his
bath water was ready. He got up and left the verandah.
Nandini sat on the floor and leaned against a verandah
post. There was a short silence, after which she said, "I
don't know how Kamala and Keshav do it. You have
absolutely no idea how many times I thank God that He did
not choose to test me in this way."

Mohini knew that her aunt was referring to her; she was accustomed to Nandini's train of thought. At the end of each visit, her aunt would compliment Kamala on her courage and patience and tell Mohini in a solemn fashion how lucky she was to have such a mother, a father, and a grandfather who looked after her so selflessly.

"Does Mohini still shadow you, Baba?" Nandini said. "Does she still cry to be allowed to sleep in your room?"

"Mohini has long since grown up."

"The Hoshiarpur astrologer had given two years as being the most critical, had he not? Her thirteenth and fifteenth?"

Vishnupant took his time replying. "The storm that had every potential of carrying her away is passed. She looks weaker of course; her left leg is buckling at the knee. Still, as long as she has determination and courage . . . fevers can come and go, as can reactions, headaches, and other illnesses . . . as long as her willpower is strong, she is strong."

Mohini crouched to one side so that she would not be seen.

Nandini looked up. The moon was a disc ringed by white clouds. She examined her palms, holding them in front of her face like an open book. Gulaam's cats were mewling. Raghunathrao called out to Nandini. She jumped up and stubbed her toe on the threshold as she hurried into their room. Vishnupant rose and disappeared into the house. Mohini kept sitting until Nandini closed her door and all was in darkness. She held on to the verandah bars and pulled herself up. Her legs were stiff and there was no sensation in the foot that had been folded under her body. She put her hand against the wall as she hobbled her way back to bed.

"Where did you go?" Hema asked.

"To look at the beggars."

But Hema was turning over to the other side, her question already forgotten.

SIXTEEN

With Hema and Nandini gone, the house felt empty. One afternoon, Mohini was happy to see Hansa: sauntering down Mohur Lane, a stuffed satchel hanging from her shoulder, her glasses slipping down her nose. Mohini smiled. Mental telepathy had pulled Hansa into the orbit of Koleshwar Nivas. "How come school finished so late today?" Mohini asked, as Hansa stepped into the verandah and flung her satchel on the ground before slumping into a chair.

"Miss Sohoni wanted me to stay behind and show Kanta how to do something in algebra."

"Who is this Kanta?"

"She's a new girl. She sits where you used to sit in class—next to the window."

"How come you never told me about her?"

Hansa shrugged. Mohini was relieved: Kanta might have taken Mohini's seat in the classroom but that didn't mean that she had replaced Mohini as a friend. Hansa had been shocked when Mohini had finally broken the news to her that she would not be going back to school. Mohini had expected Hansa to have guessed the situation and was taken aback by the tears that had welled up in her friend's eyes. They were sitting in the upstairs swing, and Hansa quickly got up and leaned over the terrace wall and stood bent over for a long time, as though she was looking for something in the shrubbery below. And when she turned around, her cheeks were red and there was a look of great sadness in her eyes.

"It's not as if you cannot come and see me after school," Mohini said. She dragged her foot against the floor, slowing down the swing to allow Hansa a chance to reclaim her place.

But Hansa was too agitated to sit down. She returned to her satchel the history notes she had duplicated for Mohini in her best, neat hand. Afterwards, they sat quietly next to each other, as the swing gained height, Hansa pushing first her feet, then her toes, against the hard terrace floor.

"You must promise to come and see me as often as you can," Mohini softly said, the swing coming to a halt. She was embarrassed by the hint of tears in her own voice.

Hansa had nodded.

Mohini looked at her now, as Hansa reached across and stood the flung satchel against the railing so that her books would not tumble out. Kamala appeared on the verandah. She nodded at Hansa and asked her how she was.

Hansa said she was fine. "Can I take Mohini with me to Shivaji Park, Kamalakaku?" she asked.

"Why?"

"I want to get my grandmother some twigs from the jamun tree at the corner of Keluskar Marg and Cadell Road."

"What for?" Kamala said.

"The jamun fruit season is finished so my mother can't make any more of the medicinal drink she normally prepares for my grandmother who has diabetes. However, my grandmother's friend told her if she were to use a jamun twig as a toothbrush then at least some of the goodness from the jamun tree would enter her body."

Kamala looked at Mohini. "Madanlal is not here to drop you," she said.

"It's only five minutes, Aai. I'll be able to walk."

"I'll hold her hand," Hansa said.

Already late for her embroidery class, Kamala hurried to the front gate. "Don't be gone for too long, and don't forget to tell your grandfather where you are going!" she called over her shoulder as she crossed the lane.

Standing underneath the jamun tree, Hansa and Mohini tilted back their heads and searched the softly stirring leaves. Sunbirds were weaving in and out of the branches. The twig that Hansa wanted was out of reach. After placing Mohini under a branch, Hansa grabbed the trunk of the tree and shook it hard in an attempt to lower the branches. But Mohini was too short and the trunk too rigid to succumb to Hansa's efforts.

"Let me do that for you," a voice said. Mohini spun around. It was Jayant Deshpande. She had not seen him since last June, not since he had talked to her as an equal and shared his thoughts and ideas in such a generous way. He stood next to her, his hand accidentally brushing her side. "What is it that you are trying to reach?" he asked. Mohini pointed to a low-hanging twig. He moved away and tilted back his head. Without any warning, he flexed his knees and jumped high into the air, opening his fingers in order to grab the long twig, but it was beyond his reach.

"At least I tried," he said. There was laughter in his eyes as he turned to Mohini. Before Jayant could notice her flushing face, Mohini glanced in the direction of Hansa, willing her to come forward. But Hansa stood where she was.

"It's been very hot today," Jayant said, moving towards the cement ledge that circled the park. "You should have waited to come outside until after the sun had set. Come and sit down."

"Hansa would not have been able to stay for so long," Mohini said. She pointed to Hansa, who shyly approached and sat next to her. The front of Hansa's uniform was smeared with bits of coarse bark. She nodded at Jayant then looked away.

"I came once or twice during your meningitis attack," Jayant said, sitting next to Mohini in the vacant spot to her left. "Professor Oek told me you were too weak to come downstairs."

She nodded, then found her tongue. "Have you finished your degree?" she said.

"No. The final exams are not until next May."

Mohini felt a catch in her throat. What a stupid question to have asked! Of course she knew that Jayant had about six months to complete his B.A. She frantically thought of something else to say, but her mind was blank. She could smell the soap he had used to wash his face. It was a clean smell, minty and green. The silence was becoming elastic, as though any minute it would stretch and snap.

Jayant stood up. He looked down at Mohini. "Give your grandfather my regards," he said. They watched him walk away.

"I've never seen him at your house," Hansa said, once Jayant was out of earshot.

"That's because he doesn't come any more. He and some other students used to meet at Koleshwar Nivas last summer when the gymkhana was closed for repairs."

Hansa looked at Mohini and asked, "Are you blushing?"

Mohini touched her cheeks. "It's very hot today," she said, "and I'm tired."

Hansa stood up and crooked her arm so that Mohini could slip her own through it. Once back at Koleshwar Nivas, Hansa said she couldn't stay, that there was lots of homework she had to do. She left by the car porch, giving the swing next to it a big push before hurrying away. Mohini sat back and lifted her right arm to her nose and sniffed. There was a faint scent of Jayant's soapy smell. She closed her eyes. For Jayant to know that she had meningitis, she reasoned, he must have asked to see her when he had come to visit Vishnupant. A heated blush spread across her face.

She was watching two men, one pushing, the other pulling a handcart piled high with cement bricks, when Kamala came home from the samaj. As soon as Mohini saw her mother she told her about this strange feeling that she had in the pit of her stomach.

"A stomach ache?" Kamala asked.

Mohini shook her head. "No, lower than that. Like little waves—I can't explain it."

"Lie down on your grandfather's bed then, and don't climb the stairs," Kamala said.

"It's not that bad. And I don't feel like lying down."

"Do you want to come upstairs with me?"

"What are you going to do?"

"Make a paper cut for your smocking dress."

"What can I do?"

"You can watch me, or you could rearrange the bottom shelf of my wardrobe as you said you would last week. What will it be?"

"The latter."

Upstairs, Kamala fetched the small stool from the dressing table and placed it in front of the opened wardrobe. She switched on the light in the dressing room and pulled out a bundle from the bottom shelf. She asked Mohini to sort out various papers that were held together in the bundle in a haphazard fashion.

"How come they are so mixed up?" Mohini asked.

"While you were sick, I was looking for some old blood reports, and I must have shoved everything back in once I was done."

With her mother in the sewing room, Mohini took on her lap the bundle of papers that were loosely tied in a square piece of cloth that Kamala had cut out from one of her old saris. She riffled through the heap. Mostly, they were her medical reports, some dating back to the beginning of 1935. There were letters from Dr. Merchant's office, bills for services rendered, receipts for payments received. It had been a very long time since Mohini had visited Dr. Merchant's rooms. He was semi-retired now and his nephew ran his practice. He had paid Mohini a visit during her meningitis attack, but it had been in the capacity of a well-wisher and not that of a doctor. Gokul Chitnis had informed him about Mohini's condition, he told Keshav as he walked into Mohini's room, and since he was on his way to Juhu to lunch with some friends, he had thought he would drop in and see her. He placed an oblong box containing dried fruit on her night table. It was the

first time he had visited Koleshwar Nivas. Mohini was glad
to see him, and although she couldn't say much, she put out
her hand, which he stroked while he talked to Keshav.

Mohini returned to the bundle on her lap. There were
pieces of paper on which were written Mohini's temperature at different intervals of the day. The month and the
year had been underlined at the top of each page. Adjacent
columns contained details of when a particular medicine
was given and how much of it was prescribed. Also
recorded was the intake of food right down to the last half
teaspoon, along with the frequency of bowel movements.
There were other pieces of paper, which were records of
various times when she had suffered from heat boils,
severe temperature spikes of 105 degrees every third day at
the age of three, benign tertian malaria around six, a mild
attack of measles at seven, several episodes of reactions to
transfusions, several episodes of fevers.

On a separate piece was written:

Mohini's normal range of hemoglobin: 1–1.25 grams
Normal RBC: 1.5–2.00 million
RBC goes below 1 at lowest point
Normal transfusion rate: every 7–10 days
Before transfusion: RBC—1.2 million; hemoglobin—1.2 grams
After transfusion: RBC—2.00 million; hemoglobin—2.00 grams
So far her best has been 2.5 grams—very rare.

There were about five pieces of paper headed "Nature
cure from textbook lent by Kanekaku in Poona."
Mohini read from some of the notes:

ANEMIA: wheat and wheat-grain cereals, brown rice and
  rice polishings, leafy vegetables, apples, raisins, figs,
  dates, eggs.
BACKACHE: all raw vegetables and fruit except bananas.
FATIGUE: seeds, nuts, grain, vegetables, fruit.
HEADACHES: copious drinking of water; no spices, toma-
  toes, sour buttermilk, oily foodstuffs.

There were notes on where to apply pressure while giving a massage. Kamala had drawn a hand and a foot,
marking the various areas that stood for the bladder, ear,
hip, knee, kidney, liver—

Mohini looked up. Her mother was standing in the
doorway of the dressing room. "How long have you been
there?" Mohini said, giving a start.

"I just came. I need your shoulder measurement." Kamala
stepped around Mohini and unrolled the measuring tape
against her back. "Are you tidying up or are you just reading?"

"Do you know you used to make notes about this and
that? Medical notes. I was reading about various pressure
points. I did not know that the base of my middle finger
stands for my eyes. Aai? Are you listening?'

"Not really, Mohini. I must finish my paper cut today,"
she said, stepping back. "Do you intend to finish tidying up
as well?"

"I'll just read a few more of these notes and then I'll sort
them all out. I promise."

"Hurry up," Kamala said. "Baba said he would be home
early today."

Mohini was rustling through the papers on the floor
when she noticed a thin blue notebook. She picked it up

and sat back on the stool. There were a few inkblots on the
cover, but apart from that there was no title or name to suggest what was inside the notebook or to whom it belonged.
She riffled through the pages and noticed that only a very
few had been written on, all of them in her mother's hand.
She opened one at random.

Nandinitai keeps saying, "Go to the samaj, go to the
samaj, you need to get out and mix with the other ladies."
But how can I find the right words to tell her that I am
not like those other ladies? Putting on face powder and
making sure their saris are nicely ironed. There is
nothing wrong with that. In fact, it is good that unlike ten
years ago when there was no samaj, now at least they have
a place to go, to meet friends. I am very glad for that. But
I don't feel as happy as they do when I am there. Other
things occupy me now. Dr. Chitnis's medical books.
Mohini's grandfather's history books. Mohini herself.
How can I tell Nandinitai that happy as I am for the ladies
who go to the samaj, I do not want to be like them? If I tell
her this, she will think I am looking down on them—
which I am not—or being stubborn by not taking her
suggestion—which I am not.

Another entry read:

Mohini did not cry this morning when I told her that I
would be taking her to Dr. Mahajan's for her transfusion
in the afternoon! No tantrum, nothing! What did I do to
deserve her? That chatter, those questions, that endless
curiosity which can drive me crazy, especially in the

afternoon when the rice is settling nicely in my stomach
and all I can think of is getting a long, cool sleep under
the fan . . . I close my eyes and those small hands pat
my face, small head nudges my back as she snuggles
and winds herself inside the end of my sari. All I want
to do then is hug her close, fold her in, kiss those cheeks,
but I check myself. If I did that, she would think I am not
sleepy at all but ready and at attention to play with her. It
is not the end of the world to have given birth to an ailing
child. There are many more that are far worse off than
Mohini. Many more . . .

Mohini looked up momentarily, a lump in her throat.
She turned to the next page.

Dr. Chitnis had difficulty finding Mohini's vein today.
Mohini watched him closely as he leaned over her arm,
muttering, "Not yet, not yet," every time he missed the
vein and continued to struggle. I could tell he was beginning to get unnerved. Finally, he told her in a very stern
voice to turn away. As soon as she looked away, he found a
vein and was able to slide the needle in. He drew some
blood and sat back in the chair. "Just because I give you
all my *corporation*," she grumbled, sticking out her lower
lip, "doesn't mean you can shout at me." I could tell
Dr. Chitnis was trying hard not to laugh. He put away his
equipment and, before leaving the room, gave her all the
peppermint sweets from his pocket. Although he does
not say it that much any more, Mohini obviously
remembers all the previous times he has praised her
for her cooperation. "But for your sweet cooperation,

Mohini," he would tell her, "life for everyone would
become a living hell." She must have heard Shridhar say,
"Bombay Municipal Corporation," referring to his firm,
and that's how she has the two words mixed up.

Mohini looked at the date on top of the page: August
1938. She had been four years old. Kamala had written the
words "corporation" and "cooperation" in English.

Two loose, folded pieces of paper were tucked into the
next page. Mohini removed them and put them to one side.
Feeling a cramp begin to develop in her right thigh, she
quickly stretched out her legs. Her feet were thick with pins
and needles but she ignored them, too absorbed now to
stop reading from Kamala's notes. Another entry was dated
March 1, 1935. Mohini would have been ten months old.
This entry, like the rest of Kamala's personal entries, and
unlike the medical reports and miscellaneous notes, was
written in Marathi. Intrigued by its title, "A Recurring
Dream," Mohini started to read.

Koleshwar Nivas is circled by a verandah. I am walking
round and round in an attempt to calm Mohini down. If I
sit on the wooden bench outside the kitchen in order to
catch my breath, Mohini resumes her wailing. Therefore,
when I shift her from one shoulder to the other, my
movements are slow and designed to trick her into thinking that she has not been moved at all. The ground
beneath the rain tree is scattered with pink flowers. I
kneel and scoop some into my hands. I hold my palm up
to her face. She blinks, her lashes roped together because
they are wet. The flowers seem to soothe her although

they carry no scent. She looks at me and smiles. My throat is choked by this small victory. I place my mouth against her ear. "You are not like the Kulkarnis' Madhav," I tell her, "who cries with anger when his mother calls him into the house each evening, telling him that if he doesn't come in at once, the trees will reach down and eat him up and fly his torn clothes like banners on their branches in the morning. You are not like Mina, who cries with jealousy and rage when she thinks her mother has given her older sister a bigger ladoo, a longer hug, the prettier dress. You are not like Nina, who cries for attention all day long. No, my sweet kiss, my darling, my very own baby, you cry not because you want to make me feel guilty or because you are angry with me for not giving you wholesome blood. You cry because everywhere in that tiny body of yours there is this gnawing pain that will not go away." I whisper all this into your ear because I know you can understand me.

Mohini turned the page. There was no more. The dream must have ended. She moved back the stool and leaned against the wall, her eyes wet.

Reminding herself that she still had all the pieces of paper to tidy up, she turned to the last remaining page of the notebook on which Kamala had made an entry. Another folded piece of paper was tucked into the spine. She laid it aside and returned to the notebook. Her mother's handwriting was bold and scrawled across the page, heedless of the lines.

It is the fourth time now that Lelevahini said to me that we were being selfish for not giving it another try to have a son.

She said—again—that Vinod and Sudha have no sons, and if
we continue in our decision not to take another chance,
then this particular Oek line will have to die. She said
Lelekaka had spoken with Dr. Chitnis. It appears Dr. Chitnis
told Kaka that there was an only one-in-four chance of producing a thalassemia major. "But three in four chances of
producing a minor," Lelevahini repeated. As if I don't know.
What do I say? Tell her that we did try and succeeded not
once but twice, only to lose the baby not once but twice . . . It
is very tempting to discard my motto, "If I am to suffer, I
must suffer in silence," in hard cases such as the Leles'.

Mohini glanced at the date. Kamala had written this
when Mohini was seven years old.

Tears ran down her face. She removed a handkerchief
from her pocket. How could she not have known that her
parents had lost two babies? Shouldn't she have sensed her
mother's sadness at the time? She closed her eyes and tried
to remember. Nothing. Her mind was blank. She turned the
page, suddenly feeling guilty because she had uncovered a
secret that really wasn't hers to uncover. Perhaps her
mother had told her at the time, but she had been too young
to understand. To tell Kamala now about what she had just
read would only bring back sad memories. Her heart
jumped at the thought of two younger sisters, two brothers,
perhaps a brother and a sister. How different and greater
everything would have been! The notebook fell from her lap
to the floor as she brought her hands to her face, ashamed
that the image in her mind was of two siblings who looked
just like her when she knew now that there was a high prob-
ability that they could have resembled Keshav or Kamala.

"Mohini!" Kamala called from the sewing room. "Didn't you hear Balu tell you that Shridhar is here?"

"No!" Mohini hastily gathered the scattered reports and slid the notebook under them. She slipped into her pocket all the folded pieces of paper that she had earlier set aside and which she had not had the time to read. She had finished tying the knot on the bundle just moments before her mother walked into the dressing room.

Kamala said, "I heard Balu tell you Shridhar was here before he came to the sewing room to call me downstairs."

"I didn't hear him."

Kamala quickly returned the knotted bundle to the bottom shelf of her wardrobe, then put out her hand. Mohini held it and raised herself to her feet, turning her face away so her mother would not see her grimace as she fought to control the pain inside her legs. But Kamala had sensed her discomfort and made Mohini sit on the bed so she could rub her feet until her daughter could feel her toes once again.

Downstairs, Shridhar and Keshav were in the sitting room. The heat was fiercer today than the unmoving sultriness associated with May. Mohini reached for the wall-mounted regulator of the ceiling fan. "I've already turned it to full speed," Shridhar said. "Come and sit next to me. Look what I have for you."

"Sugar cane?"

He passed the newspaper-wrapped elongated parcel to her. She opened it. Inside was a walking stick with a herringbone pattern along the length of its body and a dragon-head handle. Mohini looked at Kamala, her eyes round and accusing. "I didn't know anything about it," Kamala said.

"Your mother is speaking the truth," Keshav said. "I told Shridhar to get one for you."

"But why didn't you tell me first, Baba, that you had asked him?"

"I thought it would be a nice surprise. And it's just as well I told Shridhar to get one because see how you fell and broke your wrist? It wouldn't have happened if you had a walking stick."

"Surprise?" Mohini's voice was incredulous. "Next time you wish to surprise me, Baba, give me advance notice." She composed her face and turned to Shridhar.

"There's this village I pass through, Mohini, where they do the most intricate woodwork. Your father told me weeks ago that if I happened to pass that way again, I should pick up a stick for you. I've cut it down to size. If you think it is too high, get Balu to saw off a piece from the bottom. That rubber stopper comes off. I put it on to keep the bottom of the stick from slipping on the floor."

"I'll do that," Mohini said. She looked at Kamala. Her mother tilted her head in the direction of Keshav. Mohini went and sat by him and put her hand on his lap. "Aren't you going to change out of your office clothes?"

"I was coming upstairs when I got waylaid by Shridhar." He squeezed her hand and stood up.

"Baba, I'll use the walking stick," Mohini said, her voice small. Keshav nodded and left the room.

When Vishnupant noticed the walking stick in the sitting room after dinner, he said to Mohini, "Look at it for a few days. If at the end of that time, the dragon looks as though it might become a friend, pick him up and use him."

"I'm not a baby," Mohini grumbled. "I don't need to make friends with a walking stick."

"I know you are not a baby, but sometimes the method for breaking the ice whether you are young or old—sometimes the method is the same."

That night Mohini removed two of the loosely folded sheets of paper she had slipped into her pocket and read them while sitting up in bed.

December 1, 1932

My darling Kamale,

These last few days I have been missing you so much. The next time you say you do not want to come with me I shall not budge from the house until your things are packed and the tangewala lays them alongside mine in the tanga. Every time I think about you I see you bending over me with an expression in your eyes that excludes everything and everyone except the two of us. Your hair that has slipped out of its customary bun frames your luminous face.

But first I should explain why I am sending you another letter when I sent you one just yesterday, although I cannot think of a single reason why a bridegroom may not in the first year of his marriage send a stream of letters to his bride. However, something happened this morning. I know it will be difficult for you to hear but I feel I must tell you about it.

Just as I was getting ready for bed, after having worked through the night, there was a sudden commotion in the compound. At first I ignored it. (For some time now the cook

and his helpers have been at loggerheads and even the most
thundering reprimands from our senior engineer has had
no effect in getting them to hold their peace.) But when the
commotion moved nearer my door, I went out. A villager
attended by several other men was standing in the clearing,
displaying the most bizarre behaviour. His entire body was
shaking. He kept opening and shutting his mouth as though he
was chewing leather. He twirled his fingers, twisted his hands,
and see-sawed back and forth.

The senior engineer is a Mr. Lamb. I didn't see any reason to
wake him up. I motioned for Ram Limaye to come forward. He
is our medicine man when he is not a geologist. But Limaye said
he had never seen such an affliction before. I sent for
Ramanujam, who is our scout. Although only fifteen, he speaks
several dialects and knows the ways of the jungle. He talked to
the shaking man and we soon had the entire story, although
it had to be extracted in bits and pieces. It happens that the
villager wasn't seeking a remedy for his own condition, which
he said he has had for a long time, but wanted immediate help
for his daughter. Earlier that morning, he said, his wife had
noticed that their ten-year-old child, who lay next to her, had a
serene expression on her face. She decided to let the child sleep
on a little longer. Later, when it was time to share the first meal
of the day before going to the fields, the sleeping girl's mother
went to rouse her. She removed the sheet from her daughter's
body and whatever it was she saw made her scream. The rest of
the children rushed in and they also stepped back in horror. It
wasn't until the father went near his girl that he realized that it
wasn't a snake that had coiled itself around her body, but only
the deep impression the creature had left on her soft, pliable skin
when he had slithered over her during the night.

The shaking man kept pointing to the knot of villagers who had moved in closer. One of them was holding a long cloth-covered bundle that was the lifeless form of his little girl. Ram Limaye had a look at the child. She was already dead. After the villagers left, Ramanujam disappeared into the jungle. He came back with herbs and grasses that he has been tying all day into little bunches. We are to surround our bedding with them tonight. I don't know what protection his efforts are going to offer, but none of us are questioning his faith in this simple talisman.

But I assure you, Kamale, that we are several miles from the river (the villagers think it was a water snake) and you have absolutely no reason to worry. By the time you receive this letter we will be on our way home. Make sure you sit with your embroidery every afternoon between four and six in the front verandah so yours is the first face I will see when the tanga pulls up in front of our house. If Vishnupant is also in the verandah, do not be afraid of him. If he thinks you are not in awe of him, he will talk to you at length. He has many stories to tell, opinions to express, theories to expound. All you have to do is listen.

My best regards to him and Aai and all my love to you.

Yours, as always,
Keshav

P.S. I know how much you dread snakes, so please forgive me if I have caused a chill to go down your spine. And because you are not here to watch the night sky with me, I think I will roll it up, moon, stars, and all, and unfurl it in our upstairs room when I come home.

SEVENTEEN

Early the following morning, Mohini entered the bathroom to use the toilet. She shouted out for her mother and kept calling to her until Kamala was at the door, asking whether Mohini was all right, had she fallen, could she come in? When Mohini did not reply, Keshav, who was standing next to Kamala, said, "What is it then? A flying cockroach, a lizard, a mouse?"

Mohini opened the door and put her head around the corner. "Come in, Aai. Not you, Baba!"

"What happened, Mohini?" Keshav said. "Why are you grinning?"

"Am I?" Mohini let Kamala in and shut the door.

Inside the bathroom, she picked up her pants that were lying on the stool and held them out so Kamala could see.

"I think I've started," Mohini whispered.

"So you have," Kamala said in wonder, grateful for the normalcy of the moment. "Do you feel weak? Is your stomach hurting?"

"Not weak, but I do have an ache here." Mohini ran her hand across her lower abdomen.

Kamala sat on the stool and looked up at Mohini. "You

are a young woman now," she said, grinning widely. Mohini's joy was infectious. Kamala stood up.

"Where are you going, Aai?"

"To get what you will need for your time of the month."

Mohini sat on the stool. Gone were the thoughts of how fortunate the shaking villager's daughter was to be dead because by her death she was spared a lifetime of hunger and drought, penury and suffering, famine and thirst. Gone were the thoughts of what her mother had had to endure on account of her illness. Pushed to the back of her head were the thoughts about how she had to learn, like the Chafekar Guruji had advised Vasanti—advice she was still struggling to understand—to become blind.

Kamala returned.

"Did Dr. Chitnis tell you anything regarding this?"

"No, nothing. We never discussed the possibility," Kamala said.

"Are you going to tell him?"

"You know I will have to."

"But don't tell anyone else. Promise? And I want to tell Vasantiatya myself, and you can write to Aji if you want. But no one else."

"Baba already knows."

"He does?"

"He saw me carry in these things. Do you need me to show you how—"

"No!"

Kamala left the bathroom. Mohini sat on the stool and held her face in her hands. She couldn't stop smiling.

When Mohini was waiting for Vishnupant and Keshav on the front steps of the gymkhana that afternoon, she saw Mr. Marzello walking down the footpath. He went past her, then came back and pushed open the wicket gate.

"I almost did not recognize you, young lady," he said with a wide smile, the pointed ends of his moustache lifting until they almost touched the outer corners of his eyes. "How are you?"

"Fine!"

"Is your father inside?"

Mohini nodded. "Grandfather too," she murmured.

He rested his hand briefly on her head and climbed up the shallow flight of stairs and entered the gymkhana. She heard him greet her father. "Can I have a word with you, Sir?" he said. Keshav and Mr. Marzello came out and walked a couple of feet down the path, towards the gate.

"I was wondering whether there is any further news about the job application my son made to your firm?" Mr. Marzello asked.

"I spoke to Behram Padamjee only yesterday," Keshav said. "Samuel should receive the acceptance letter any day now."

Mr. Marzello barked a short laugh of disbelief. He looked at Mohini. "Your father is a very influential man! One word from him . . ."

Keshav grimaced. "I would not have brought Samuel to Behram's attention if I did not think him worthy of the job." Keshav's voice was stern and cold. Mr. Marzello looked stricken. He dropped his eyes. But when he raised them, he was beaming.

"The last time we met, your son was looking for a job,"

Vishnupant called out to Mr. Marzello, as he walked down the steps.

Mr. Marzello looked up at him.

"I take it from your expression, then, that he has found one," Vishnupant said.

Mr. Marzello shrugged and held out his palms. "What can I say, Professor? The boy is the brain in the family!" His eyes were twinkling. "Won't you come and have a cup of tea with us? Samuel is here. He returns to Vasai tomorrow. After that, who knows? He will have to find boarding and lodging somewhere in the Colaba area, nearer his work, as far away from here as possible. Do come, especially today when you have brought me such good news."

Keshav hesitated in the face of such effusion. Say yes, say yes, say yes. It was Vishnupant who read Mohini's thoughts. "Perhaps a quick cup of tea," he said.

"We'll follow you," Keshav said, holding out his hand to his daughter.

"I have a walking stick now, Baba."

"Give me the walking stick. I'd rather you take my hand."

"I'm not a baby any more," Mohini said, smiling. She planted her cane firmly on the ground and pulled herself to her feet. By the time they came up to the front gate of the Marzello property, Samuel was hurrying down the verandah steps, his mother following closely behind.

"A quick cup of tea for everyone, Jolly!" Mr. Marzello called out to his wife. Samuel looked at his father. There was no need for Mr. Marzello to tell him that he had the job.

Samuel held out his hand to Keshav. "I want to thank you, Sir," he said. "As my father always says, all things said and done, in the end it is who you know that counts."

"Meet Mr. Keshav's father," Mr. Marzello swiftly interjected. "This is Professor Oek and this here is his
granddaughter, Mohini."

After greeting Vishnupant, Samuel held out his hand to
Mohini. When she hesitated, he picked up her right hand
and shook it gently. "How old are you, Mohini?" he said.

She told him.

"My! You are tall for a thirteen-year-old." He said this
with such rakish charm that everyone, including Mohini,
laughed. His eyes were like his mother's, a light, light
brown.

"Please come inside," Mr. Marzello said.

The room was exactly the way Mohini remembered it,
except now the cabinet that held the bottles was closed.
Vishnupant took the same end of the sofa he had previously
occupied.

Mrs. Marzello came out through the inner door. "I've
told Nelly," she said. "The tea will soon be ready." Her eyes
found her son. He went and put his arm around her waist
and pulled her forward.

"Do you know everyone?" he asked easily.

She nodded at Vishnupant, who had stood up, then at
Mohini, and proffered Keshav her hand. Keshav shook it
and she said, "In the same neighbourhood, but my son has
to apply to your firm so we can all meet." Her voice was
young and girlish and Keshav glanced away. As before, she
called Mohini to her side and gave her a long hug. Her bare
arms as they brushed against Mohini's were pleasantly cool.
The talcum powder, which she must have hastily applied, lay
in patches on her face. Her lipstick was neat and made her
mouth look pretty. "Please, everyone, sit down." At the end

of a long silence, she looked at Vishnupant and said, "Now that everyone has got their wish and the British have long last quit, what happens next?"

This time Vishnupant had no difficulty finding his tongue. "To mend the destruction caused by the vivisection of our land. Unfortunately, that is going to be a challenging task. In some people's minds there is resentment against the Muslims who did not go to Pakistan. As one student said to me, 'All these years the Indian Muslims fought for their land, and now that they have it, they don't want to live in it.'" Vishnupant sat forward in his chair and placed on the table in front of him a crushed peacock feather he had found on the seat of the sofa. "Nevertheless," he continued, sitting back, "after decades of being the unwilling recipients of the British policy of divide and rule, we must once again learn to coexist. There is no other choice."

"So what's to be done to break down the communal tensions?" Samuel asked.

"Something that should have been done a long time ago. Compulsory and standardized education for all, with no bias towards caste, colour, or creed. Look at you: a Christian employed in a British firm soon to be taken over by Gujaratis. One boss is a Parsi, and the other, my son, a Hindu. What do all of you have in common? Education."

Mohini looked at her grandfather and willed him to say no more. Since August 15, after the initial flush of rejoicing, Vishnupant had become increasingly pessimistic. He often said that if India did not start off on the right foot, it would become swamped in corruption and inefficiency before the year was out. Whenever the subject of independence was broached—it was still too new to have faded away—he refused to discuss the past but took the opportunity to expand on his heartfelt theme, education. When Keshav complained to Kamala that Vishnupant often repeated himself, Kamala pointed out to him that his father was getting old. She said those who respected his opinions understood his genuine concerns for the future.

Once again, as if Vishnupant had heard Mohini in his head, he responded to her wish and said no more. The silence was broken when the curtain bulged and Nelly came out carrying a very large tray on which stood several cups of tea, the steam rising above them in short, lazy curls. She knelt at the centre table and lowered the tray carefully. Her cropped hair was grey above her ears. "I've already added sugar," she said loudly, her tone defiant, daring anyone to question her right to sweeten the tea. She looked at Mohini and shook her head. "Jolly Memsahib did not tell me there was a child here. This is the first time—I have never been asked to make refreshments for a child before."

"That will do, Nelly!" Mrs. Marzello said, her tone sharp.

"Here, child, take the tea with the most milk."

Mohini sipped the tea. It was tepid, the topmost layer beginning to congeal in an unpleasant way.

"It's not often our Samuel comes to stay with us," Mr. Marzello said after Nelly had left. "We've given the staff the day off. No visitors today, just the family."

Mrs. Marzello put down her cup with a clatter and looked at her husband in anger. Mohini, who now knew what Hansa's brothers had meant about strange things happening at the Marzellos', guessed she wouldn't get a glimpse of the three "nieces." There were no noises from the inner rooms. No gramophone playing fast tunes, the kind Mohini sometimes heard when she was walking alongside their property on her way to Shivaji Park. The only sound was the scramble of claws as a crow alighted on the window shutter. Samuel was the first to get to his feet. He moved restlessly to the front verandah. Laying his cup on the table, Keshav said, "I think we must leave."

Everyone stood up. They followed Samuel outside. "You poor, brave dear," Mrs. Marzello said to Mohini as she hugged her.

At the gate, before leaving, Mohini glanced back. Mrs. Marzello was standing on the top step, her shoulders slightly bowed, staring in the direction of the palm trees where colourful paper lanterns hung from sagging wires.

That night, Kamala came and sat on Mohini's bed. After Mohini had told her about their visit to the Marzellos,' Kamala pulled the sheet up to cover Mohini's waist and, running her hands up and down her daughter's legs, asked, "How are you feeling? Stomach ache?"

Mohini shook her head.

"I spoke to Dr. Chitnis. He said if the flow is heavy, you must let him know at once. Because then he will make adjustments in the transfusion. Is it heavy?"

"Not even a trickle. In fact, after that initial amount, very little."

Kamala looked relieved. "That's good on two counts," she said slowly. "Good that you have got it. And now that you have it, good it is very light. That way we don't have to worry about blood loss."

Mohini nodded. "Is Baba still upset with me because I was angry when he gave me the walking stick?"

"I don't think so. He didn't say anything to me."

"Then he's not angry. He would definitely have said something to you if he was."

Kamala was silent. Keshav wasn't saying much at all these days. The previous night, when she had sat up in his bed waiting for him to finish at his desk, he had turned around and told her that he had a lot left to complete. And when her eyes had pleaded with him to put down his pen if only for a short while, he had turned away, leaving her to creep back to her bed and drink a glass of water to ease the constriction in her throat. It was the second time that he had brushed her off. She had turned on her side and faced the wall, a numbness entering her body, haunted by the thought that maybe this time—unlike all the other illnesses when she had paid attention to Mohini and neglected him—that this time she had irrevocably pushed him away.

"Aai? Are you all right?"

"Yes. Did Vasanti come this morning when you sent her a message?"

Mohini nodded.

"I was wondering what happened to the boy your cousin Swati was supposed to see. Did Vasanti say if she had heard from Sudha?"

Mohini shook her head.

"Are you sleepy?" Kamala asked.

"A bit. You can switch off the light."

Mohini looked out into the terrace. The swing hung heavily in the motionless air. Watching the slice of sky contained within the space of the open door, she thought once again about what the Chafekar Wadi Guruji had told her aunt about trying to be like the blind. Mohini closed her eyes.

What if she had been born blind? What shape would the swing have taken then? Assuming, of course, that she could feel it with her hands? Would she still imagine it to be the same as it appeared to her eyes? Would she know Mrs. Marzello's face just by the way she spoke? By the touch of her fingers, by the brush of her arms? And Samuel? How could she know, if she was blind, just how closely he resembled his mother?

In the next room, Keshav switched off his light. A spasm of sleep gripped Mohini and her legs moved involuntarily. She drifted off . . .

A man walked into her dream, balancing a basket on top of his head. He crossed the junction and moved away from Koleshwar Nivas. She was sure she had seen him go towards the sea, but here he was, stamping his feet at the front entrance, banging on the door. The area under his eyes was deeply wrinkled, the loosened end of his turban twitching against his heart like a shaken rope. Mohini ran into the kitchen. "The cobra man is here," she shouted to Bayabai and sat in the windowsill of the sitting room, her fingers worked into a lattice across her eyes. Through the apertures she saw the man lower his basket to the ground as Bayabai placed a bowl of milk on the floor. The cobra slithered out, its body sleek and long. Mohini stumbled to the sofa. The front door banged shut and Bayabai was standing over her, holding out her cupped hands. Mohini flinched as though the snake were coiled in the empty bowl of milk.

"You are as bad as your mother," Bayabai said. "It's a good thing the snake man comes but once a year or the two of you would be prisoners in your own house."

"Has he gone?" she asked. "And you actually saw the you-know-what return to the basket?"

"No! I did not!" Bayabai hissed as Mohini shrank back.

Kamala was upstairs on Keshav's bed. Mohini walked into the room. "Don't tell me anything," Kamala pleaded. "I saw him leave the gate a moment ago. Can you hear him? Banging his stick on someone else's door. Keshav, come back—tell that woman who is opening her door to close it."

Mohini's eyes fluttered open. Balu was washing the clothes under the tap in the backyard. The air was still. The plants stood like sentinels, their shadows staining the terrace floor. A pigeon rustled its wings in preparation for flight. Kamala stood in the doorway of her room. "I'm awake," Mohini said.

Kamala sat on the bed, her expression serious.

"What's the matter?" Mohini asked.

"Early this morning we got the news that Samuel Marzello is no more."

"What!" Mohini lifted her head and supported her upper body on her elbows for a moment before she collapsed back against the pillow.

"The newspaper boy told your grandfather this morning. He and Baba have gone to the Marzellos' to pay their condolences."

"But he was fine yesterday!"

"There was some kind of an accident, the newspaper boy said."

Mohini was drinking her milk in the dining room when Keshav and Vishnupant returned. She called out to her father.

"Let him take his bath first. He'll talk to you later," Kamala said.

"Why must he take his bath first?"

"Because the body of Samuel was probably there when they went to pay their respects."

In his bedroom, after his bath, Keshav told Kamala and Mohini what he had learned. "Late last night two men knocked on the Marzellos' door. The servant girl told them that the place was closed to business. She could tell the men were drunk. She said she had opened the door only a slit so as not to let them in." Keshav glanced at Mohini.

She was tracing the pattern of Kamala's bedcover with her fingers.

He looked at Kamala.

Kamala nodded, murmuring, "She knows about it being a house of ill repute."

Keshav continued. "The two men pushed past the girl and saw Samuel. He was reading a book on the sofa. They demanded to know what he was doing there even though they had just been told that the establishment was closed. By this time, the entire household was up. Mr. Marzello asked them to leave. He did not recognize the men. They were strangers. He and Samuel walked out after them into the front verandah. It was at this point that one of the men shoved Samuel with both his hands. It caught the boy unawares and he fell down, hitting his head against the edge of the stone step. Mr. Marzello said death must have been instantaneous. Samuel did not move again, did not even open his eyes. Mrs. Marzello has asked to see you, Kamala, and Mohini too."

"What did you tell her?" Kamala said.

"I said I didn't know about Mohini, but that you would pay her a visit."

"Why is she asking to see Aai?" Mohini said. "She's never met her before."

"Actually, we have met before," Kamala said. "A long time ago. You were very small. I had taken you to the park. Jolly Marzello was there with Samuel. He would have been eleven or twelve. We spoke to one another. Shortly after that she became a recluse."

"I would like to go and see Mrs. Marzello, Aai. I'm not nervous or scared."

"Are you sure?" Keshav asked her.

"I like her and Samuel too. He was very nice."

"Go in a couple of days, then," Keshav said. "There will be fewer people paying condolences." He turned to go downstairs, then stopped in the doorway. "Kamala, you do remember I'm leaving tomorrow morning? First I have to go to Nasik and then to some construction site near Sangli."

"But they are in completely opposite directions. And no, you did not tell me."

"I know they are in different directions, but there's no point in me coming back to Bombay and then leaving for Sangli the very next day."

"You've become very absent-minded, Baba," Mohini said. "This is the second time you have forgotten to tell Aai until the last minute."

"I suppose I'm getting old," Keshav said. He turned abruptly and left the room. Mohini glanced at her mother. Kamala was picking Keshav's used towel off the floor and missed seeing the puzzled look in her daughter's eyes.

EIGHTEEN

When Kamala and Mohini stepped into the Marzello compound, the scent of frangipani was strong. Mohini drew Kamala's attention to the thick morning-glory creeper that sheltered the property from prying eyes: it was alive with lilac flowers. Yellow blossoms hung in bright clusters from a single flowering tree that stood at the south end of the lot.

Mohini followed Kamala into the front room, keeping her gaze averted from the corners of the steps, knowing that Samuel must have dashed his head against one of them. The shutters of the windows were closed and the room was dark. Two men were sitting on the sofa. One of them came forward when he saw Kamala shrugging off her sandals just inside the entrance. It was Mr. Marzello. He nodded at Kamala and caressed Mohini's cheeks. She let out her breath slowly as he stepped back. His palms were clammy and his body reeked of sweat.

"Follow me," he said, moving to the left and parting a curtain into an inner room.

Jolly Marzello was sitting in an armchair, facing a shuttered window. The lovebirds in the cage on the dressing table were twittering softly. The earthy smell of their feathers filled the airless room.

"Jolly, look who is here," Mr. Marzello said. His voice was hearty, but there was no accompanying smile, not even the pretence of one. Mrs. Marzello put out her hand. Kamala crouched next to her armchair and took it in her own.

"Give me your strength, Kamala," Mrs. Marzello said. "Even if it is just for a minute, transfer all your strength to me." She put out her other hand, and Kamala gestured to Mohini that she should take it.

Mr. Marzello placed a low stool next to the armchair so Mohini could sit down. He was about to pull forward another when Kamala eased herself into a cross-legged position on the floor without letting go of Mrs. Marzello's hand.

"It is very many years since we met, but do you know why it is that I remember your name?" Mrs. Marzello asked. Her voice was low and quavery.

Kamala shook her head.

"Because *kamal* means 'lotus.' I said to Marzello when I came home that afternoon, I told him that your name suited you. 'Just the way a lotus blooms in choked, muddy waters,' I said, 'Kamala Oek blooms in the midst of a burdensome fate.'"

"Do you know why I remember your name?" Kamala asked her. "Because when we spoke there was so much laughter in your voice. So jolly."

Mrs. Marzello smiled faintly and Kamala tightened her hold on her hand.

"And what does your name mean?" she turned to Mohini.

"One who is enticing."

"I see you have your mother's eyes, and her strength too." She let go of Mohini's left hand, which she had been tightly gripping. Suddenly, without any warning, she began to weep, tears running down her cheeks and into the corners of her mouth. She bared her teeth every few seconds, opening her lips to draw in some air. A rasping sound exited her throat. Her nostrils were streaming. There was a hand towel on the bed. Kamala passed it to her. Mrs. Marzello mopped her tears, then began to rub the towel vigorously against her face. Kamala removed it from her hand. Mrs. Marzello's light brown eyes were blurred and swollen, her skin looked raw and chafed. Mohini picked up a half-filled glass of water that was within reach. She passed it to Kamala.

Mrs. Marzello waved it away. "When will I see him again?" she said. "When will I again clasp him to my chest?" She sounded frantic.

"Soon," Kamala said.

Mrs. Marzello looked away from the window and turned towards Kamala.

"You will see him soon," Kamala repeated. "Compared to eternity, one lifetime for us is but a blink in the eye of our Creator, is it not? If you remember that, time will go quickly. And when it is your turn to pass away, you will be reunited with your Samuel and everyone else you have lost. Till then, take courage."

"But how?" Jolly Marzello's question was a moan.

"Survival is one game we have all been forced to learn. And however unkind life may be, there are always moments that are pure and devoid of pain. Keep faith that your deep suffering will lessen as time goes by."

"You give the advice of an angel, Kamala, but I am only human."

Kamala said, "Here, take a sip."

Mrs. Marzello took the glass and drank the water in great gulps. "We will leave Bombay," she said, "Go somewhere far away. I have been feeling dead for many years, Kamala. One makes choices, and one day, even if they are choking you, you cannot loosen their grip. My son was the only true thing in my life. Now, everything good has gone with him . . ." She wept into her hands. When she looked up, her eyes were glazed over, as though she did not know where she was.

"Why don't you lie down?" Kamala suggested.

Mohini stood up as Kamala helped Mrs. Marzello out of her chair and onto the bed. She immediately curled up and put her two fists against her mouth. Kamala removed a cotton shawl from a hook on the wall and draped it over her legs. She started to remove Mrs. Marzello's shoes.

"You don't have to do that," Mr. Marzello said, walking into the room. He aligned the shoes under the bed. His actions were deliberate.

"Come again, please," Jolly Marzello whispered.

"Whenever you want to see me, send your servant with a message," Kamala said. "Day or night, it doesn't matter."

The sun, which had been bright and fierce when they had walked into the house, was now covered with a thick blanket of grey. It had been like that all week: rumbling clouds gathering overhead within minutes, only to disperse just as quickly without opening their bellies over the heated city below.

At dinner that night, Mohini described to Vishnupant what had happened at the Marzellos'. She turned to Kamala and said, "Do you really think Mrs. Marzello will meet Samuel when she dies?"

Kamala nodded and glanced in the direction of Vishnupant.

Mohini was impatient for an explanation. "But how can you be so sure?" she asked her mother.

Kamala sat forward in her chair and quickly reached for her water. She drank from it slowly, her eyes trained on the dining table.

Sensing her discomfort, Vishnupant said, "I think your mother was referring to the Hindu pantheistic tenet, 'I am the universe and the universe is me.'" He pushed his chair away from the table, knowing that he was unprepared to have this discussion with Mohini.

"Where are you going?" she asked. "You haven't even finished your dinner."

Seeing the determination on her face to get an answer, he knew he wouldn't be able to leave the room until she was satisfied.

"So what does the tenet mean?" Mohini said.

"It's a long explanation."

"I don't mind."

"The 'I' in the tenet means all of us: you, me, all the people that inhabit the earth. What the 'universe' means is absolutely everything that comprises our existence: earth, wind, water, fire, and air. Also, animate things such as plants and animals and inanimate things such as pencils, paper, vessels, clothes, etc. Everything that we see, hear, touch, feel, smell, and even those things that are beyond our senses. Do you understand so far?"

Mohini nodded.

"So, what the tenet means is not only do we live in the universe and are a part of it, but also that the universe is contained within each of us. That is to say, there is no separation between the universe and us."

"But what has that got to do with Mrs. Marzello reuniting with Samuel after she is no more?"

Vishnupant took a last mouthful and chewed thoughtfully. He paused to add a few grains of salt to his buttermilk, then said, "Take a person before he is born. At that stage that person is a soul without a body. Agreed?"

"Yes." Mohini looked at her mother. Kamala was emptying a little of her drinking water into her steel plate so that the traces of food still remaining on its surface would not congeal.

"Now, when that soul is born into the world, it slips on a garment. That garment is the human body. From that point onwards, after the soul has slipped into its garment, the soul becomes 'I.' *I* am hungry, the baby cries, feed me. *I* am tired, rock me to sleep. *I* am wet, clean me. The moment the soul is born there is immediate separation between it and the universe. So far so good?"

"I think so."

"It is the 'I' that the soul has now acquired that classifies the world into various categories and makes us say: 'This is a book, that is the sky, these are my feet, that is my mother, that, my friend.' Instead of seeing unity in everything, the 'I' sees the differences. But when a person dies, the garment or the body is shed, as is the sense of 'I.' Relieved of its senses and its 'I,' the soul goes back to seeing unity in everything. So, when Mrs. Marzello is relieved of her body, she will be reunited with her son."

Mohini was silent. She opened her mouth, then shut it again.

"What?"

"But how will Mrs. Marzello who has no 'I' recognize Samuel who is also without?"

"That's a good question," Vishnupant said, pleased by Mohini's logic.

Mohini smiled and nodded for him to continue.

"It's like a river flowing into the ocean. It right away becomes part of that ocean. And once in the ocean, there is nothing to separate this river from that river: all the water is simply One."

He pushed his chair away from the table once again and finished his buttermilk, standing up. Mohini looked at her mother. Kamala was pouring herself another glass of water. Mohini got up and laid her cheek against Kamala's shoulder before leaving the room.

Lying in her bed that night, Mohini tried to think about what Vishnupant had told her. She found she couldn't concentrate. Every time she tried to recall her grandfather's words, all she could see was Mrs. Marzello's distorted face as she wept and said, "But I am only human."

A flash of lightning wakened Mohini. She sat up quickly as the thunder reverberated in the sky. Water streamed down in broad ribbons onto the terrace floor. She could hear it gurgle as it rushed into the drain.

"The rain woke me up as well," Kamala said, walking into her room. "Do you want to use the toilet? I can help you."

"I don't want to use the toilet."

"You weren't thinking of standing in the terrace door,

were you? The water is slanting in. The floor may be wet. You could fall."

"How much longer are you going to watch over me, Aai? How much longer are you going to protect me? And by protecting me, how much longer do you think you will be able to extend my life?" Mohini got out the last question before the tears could clog her throat. Her face felt hot and she was glad that the room was dark.

Kamala sat next to Mohini on her bed. Mohini thought, If Aai puts out her hand, I will place mine in it. But Kamala made no move to put out her hand, and Mohini laid hers on Kamala's lap. Her mother planted a loose fist on Mohini's palm.

"I am not the one who gave you life," Kamala said. "And I will not be the one who will take it away. But I will do whatever it is within my power to do in order to make sure that you do not suffer needlessly. I will do everything in my power to make your life as comfortable as I possibly can. If by helping you to the toilet, I can avoid a fracture, that is what I will do." Kamala got off the bed.

She was almost at the door when Mohini said, "You promised me, Aai, that you wouldn't keep any secrets from me, at least secrets that have to do with me."

Kamala turned around. "What secrets have I kept?"

"The astrologer in Hoshiarpur said my thirteenth and fifteenth years were bad for me."

Mohini heard a sharp intake of breath before Kamala said, "Who told you that?"

"I overheard."

"Who was talking?"

Mohini looked away.

Kamala moved forward and sat once again on Mohini's bed. "There is a reason, Mohini," she said, "why I do not believe in astrologers. I do not deny that many predictions made by them do come true. Nevertheless, astrology is an imperfect science. There are many that do not."

"But did you know what the Hoshiarpur astrologer had said?"

Kamala nodded.

"Then why did you not tell me?"

"I'm going to ask you a question. I want you to think very carefully before giving me your answer. Did you at any time during your meningitis attack believe that you were not going to recover?"

"No."

"Neither did I. Not through the injections, the massive headaches, the oxygen cylinder, the seventeen lumbar punctures, not through all that did I once get a feeling that you would not pull through. I do not need an astrologer to tell me what is going to happen."

Mohini lay down. Kamala placed the pillow that had fallen to the floor under Mohini's head. She unfolded the light cotton sheet and brought it up to cover Mohini's hips. The downpour that had begun swiftly had just as swiftly stopped.

"I'm sorry, Aai," Mohini said.

Kamala leaned her forehead lightly on Mohini's chest, and when she moved away, Mohini touched her petticoat where her mother's face had briefly rested. It was soaking wet.

No servant arrived from the Marzello household with a message for Kamala. By the end of the week, Vishnupant heard at the gymkhana that the Marzellos had sold their property. The next day someone said they were planning to buy another in the suburb of Santa Cruz. No one knew anything for certain. All Balu could report was that the shutters of their windows remained closed, night and day.

Shridhar arrived one evening. The first thing he asked Kamala was whether Keshav had returned from Sangli.

"Why? What's the matter?" she said, getting off the swing and closing her book. Mohini had pulled a chair to the outer wall of the terrace where she could look at the people as they went to and from Shivaji Park.

"Nothing."

"Your tone, Shridhar, you frightened me."

"It's just that when I was passing through Sangli three days ago, I thought I would drop in and see Keshav."

"And? How is he?"

"He's all right. I thought he would be back by now. That's why I asked."

"Yesterday we received a telegram that his work has been delayed."

Shridhar nodded and went and stood next to Mohini. Gulaam was chatting with his friends at the junction of Mill Road and Mohur Lane. White light from the Irani's shop spilled onto the footpath, illuminating Gulaam's cat, which was grooming its body in a leisurely fashion. It sat up suddenly, as the elongated tinkling of horns filled the air and people scrambled off the road to make way for three bicycles whose riders were hurtling down the lane without looking to the left or right.

"Is something wrong, Shridhar?" Kamala said, coming up to him.

"All I asked was whether Keshav had returned from Sangli and your mother is worried," Shridhar said to Mohini.

Mohini looked at Kamala.

"She doesn't look worried," Mohini said. "I think she thinks you are."

"Well, I'm not."

"You'll stay for dinner, of course?" Kamala said.

"How can I refuse?"

She left the terrace to go downstairs.

"Get up, Mohini, and sit on my lap," Shridhar said. "Is it my imagination or can I hear the sea in the background?"

"It's high tide," Mohini said, shifting positions. She looked at the moon. It hung limply in the air, as though dangled carelessly from a string by some invisible hand.

Keshav returned the following week, unaccompanied by the five blasts of his horn that preceded his arrival whenever he had been away on-site. Kamala and Mohini were alerted to his presence only when they heard the driver, Madanlal, call out to Balu. They hurried downstairs, Vishnupant already ahead of them in the car porch. Balu was piling Keshav's luggage at the bottom of the steps. He glanced every now and then at Madanlal as he helped Keshav out of the car. Keshav stepped out slowly, holding on to his arm. Looking at Keshav, Vishnupant leaned towards the railing of the verandah and clutched it. Mohini took a step forward and held out her walking stick. "Take this, Baba," she said.

"I'm better now," Keshav said, waving away the stick. "It was a bad bout of malaria." Mohini looked at Madanlal.

There was a small smirk at the corner of his mouth as he took the cane from her hand.

"Take it, Sahib," he said, thrusting it into Keshav's grasp.

Keshav handed it back to Mohini and, with the aid of Balu's hand, climbed up the shallow flight of stairs.

"Will he be able to walk upstairs?" Kamala asked Madanlal discreetly.

"I prefer the end room," Keshav said.

Kamala hurried into the back verandah. The end room had not been used since Nandini and Raghunathrao had left for Calcutta. With Bayabai's help, she threw open the shutters of the windows. Mohini switched on the ceiling fan in order to rid the air of its accumulated mustiness.

Balu helped Keshav into the chair. Kamala handed Balu the bed linen she had removed from the wooden cupboard. For the next few minutes, Keshav's laboured breathing and the unfolding of sheets were the only sounds in the room.

Keshav asked, "Where is Baba?"

Vishnupant stepped in from the verandah. He had never looked so nervous, Mohini thought.

"I'm all right," Keshav said, his tone light and casual. "You should have seen me a week ago."

"That telegram you sent? Did you say you would be delayed because of work or because you were ill?"

In the doorway, Madanlal coughed.

"You don't have to look so worried, Baba," Keshav said, avoiding a direct answer. "I've been ill before—gastroenteritis, a touch of typhoid another time—you remember."

"Your problem, Keshav," Vishnupant said, "is that you insist on going on-site when there is no real need to."

"I would not go if there was no need for me to go," Keshav said slowly, the irritability in his tone barely contained.

Behind them, Madanlal coughed again.

Keshav turned around swiftly. "Leave the car keys, take your things, and go!"

Keshav did not turn back until he had watched Madanlal leave.

"Look at your body, Keshav," Vishnupant said. "It is shaking. Turn off the fan, Mohini. And you must have lost at least ten pounds. Your cheeks look as if you have no teeth and your eyes are sunken."

Kamala left the room saying she would call Dr. Chitnis.

Keshav gestured for Mohini to come forward. She sat in the chair next to him. "How are you?" he asked.

"I'm fine," she said, leaning away slightly because her father's breath was stale and furred.

"Why don't you have a bath before Dr. Chitnis comes?" Kamala said, on her return. "I've told Balu to draw hot water for you."

"Now promise me, Keshav," Vishnupant said, "that you will not take any unnecessary on-site assignments."

This time Keshav did not bristle at his suggestion. "Even if they are necessary," he said, "I will send someone else."

Madanlal approached, a towel draped over his arm.

"I thought I told you to go home," Keshav said.

"Kamalavahini told me to stay in case Dr. Chitnis writes a prescription." He made a move to help Keshav to his feet, but Keshav waved him away. Madanlal glanced at Mohini as he stepped back, a shallow smile on his face.

Mohini grimaced, dropping her eyes. She had never liked Madanlal. There was something eerie about his presence, about his smile that was not a smile but a sneer. And she hated the reckless way in which he drove the car whenever Keshav was not with them. But most of all, what Mohini found intolerable was the disrespect he sometimes showed her mother. He repeatedly ignored Kamala when she told him to drive a safe distance from the footpath, and grinned his lopsided grin when she cautioned him to keep to the centre of his side of the road. He had had this nasty habit, the moment he saw a pedestrian walking alongside the road, of veering so close to that pedestrian that the man, woman, or child would be forced to jump out of the way. This disagreeable habit, however, had now been abandoned. He didn't dare pretend to run over pedestrians any more. Not after what had happened to him when he was driving Mohini and Kamala to Dr. Agarkar's in Nana Chowk, a month before Mohini's thirteenth birthday.

The car had been approaching the Tardeo junction, when Madanlal suddenly swerved from the centre of the road and directed his vehicle towards two men who were strolling along its side. He had every intention, Mohini and Kamala knew, even as he came within a hair's breadth of their bodies, of making them believe that they were about to be run over.

Unfortunately for Madanlal, the traffic light in front of him had turned red. As he braked and screeched to a halt, his two victims ran up from behind him, wrenched open his car door, pulled him out, and slammed him against the side of the hood. Their faces angry and distorted, they punched him repeatedly in the stomach. Mohini cowered back in her seat, terrified that they would kill Madanlal. They did not let him go until the traffic light turned green and the drivers behind them started blowing their horns. Madanlal stumbled back into the car badly shaken, and Mohini could tell by Kamala's expression that her mother would not repeat this incident to Keshav because she knew that Madanlal had finally learned his lesson.

Mohini looked at him now. His face was stony as he watched Keshav walk to the bathroom unaided. After Keshav had shut the door, he turned away, an unpleasant expression on his face. Thrusting his hands deep into his pockets, he left the room.

NINETEEN

Keshav was sitting up in bed by the time Dr. Chitnis arrived. In spite of a bath and a shave, his face looked gaunt. There were deep hollows under his eyes and his uncut hair curled disagreeably against his neck. Dr. Chitnis checked his blood pressure, listened to his chest, and after asking him to sit forward, applied a stethoscope to his back. The bones of Keshav's spine were like baby's knuckles pushing against his weathered skin. Dr. Chitnis lifted the end of the sheet that covered his feet. Mohini muttered that her father's ankles were not swollen. Dr. Chitnis nodded agreement. He looked up at Keshav. "Kamalavahini said something about a malaria attack. Have you been taking quinine?"

"We always carry it. The mosquitoes in those parts, they are like flies."

"Did you send for a doctor?"

Keshav shook his head.

"There must have been a town nearby."

"There were people to look after him at the daak bungalow, Doctor Sahib," Madanlal said, entering the room.

"Daak bungalow?" Dr. Chitnis asked. He knew that civil engineers were not accommodated in daak bungalows, which were government-staffed buildings with running water and sanitation. Instead, they occupied makeshift quarters that were rudimentary and more often than not erected as temporary structures.

"We've been commissioned to work on a railway project at the moment," Keshav said.

Dr. Chitnis covered Keshav's feet with the thin sheet. "Nevertheless, daak bungalow staff are not the same as—"

"You are right," Keshav interrupted him. "I should have sent for a doctor."

"How do you know you contracted malaria and nothing else?" Dr. Chitnis asked, crossing his arms across his chest.

"I have seen many cases of malaria over the years. I could recognize the severe headache, nausea, vomiting."

"Temperature?"

"It went up to one hundred and three degrees."

"For how long?"

"About three days. The other symptoms disappeared completely by the end of the week. Now I just feel very tired."

"Well, if it is malaria you had, you have probably become anemic as well. Any rigors?"

"Not too many. But I remember feeling very hot."

"How long were you away this time?"

"Seventeen days," Mohini said.

While drawing blood from the inside of his elbow, Dr. Chitnis told Keshav to take plenty of rest. "Drink lots of water. Eat light meals and when your stomach feels up to it, get Kamalavahini to make you her famous sweetmeats. You could do with some weight gain. I'll come and see you again in a day or two." He placed the vial of Keshav's blood in his doctor's bag. He turned to Mohini and said, "Malaria is not contagious. You'll be able to keep your father company while he recuperates."

Over the next couple of days, Mohini sensed that her father did not want her company, nor did he want anyone else's. At first, it felt strange having Keshav at home. The malaria had made him listless. The newspaper that Vishnupant placed next to his pillow often went unread. Sometimes, if he was in the mood, he asked Mohini to read to him the headlines. Even then, she was never certain whether he was paying attention or merely pretending to.

When Dr. Chitnis told Vishnupant that Keshav did indeed have malaria, and that it was of the malignant tertian kind, Vishnupant gave up his customary seat overlooking the front yard and asked Balu to move his armchair into the back verandah. He looked worried. Dr. Chitnis assured him that Keshav's attack was mild, and that in such cases the malaria subsided within a fortnight, although the weakness could linger. Vishnupant was not reassured. It was the word "malignant" that he did not like. And when Dr. Chitnis patiently explained to him that in *malignant* tertian there was no possibility of a recurrence whereas in *benign* tertian there was, his expression relaxed slightly.

After watching Keshav eat a quarter of the little Kamala had served him on his plate, Vishnupant asked her whether she thought Dr. Chitnis's prognosis was accurate.

"Would you like another doctor to see him?" she asked.

"I suppose you don't think it necessary." Vishnupant said.

"Baba will be all right!" Mohini said.

"And you are siding with your mother, as usual!" he grumbled.

Keshav was silent.

Mohini hid her laughter at her grandfather's nervousness behind the newspaper, which she hastily grabbed to cover her face. She wished her father would move back into his bedroom. It wasn't as though he was too weak to climb the single flight of stairs. Besides, for recuperation purposes, his bedroom was so much more pleasant than the downstairs end room, which was dingy and dark. The window facing north did not allow in sufficient light and the window in the east wall was permanently shut because outside stood two banana trees, and banana trees, as Bayabai constantly reminded everyone, bred mosquitoes.

Vinod and Sudha came to see Keshav a week after he had been diagnosed with malaria, bringing with them a small cardboard box that Vinod placed in Vishnupant's hand before bending down and doing namaskar. Sudha followed suit.

"What has happened that you have crossed less than one whole mile to receive my blessings?" Vishnupant asked, running his hands over the space above their backs.

Vinod looked embarrassed. "We should come more often to see you, Vishnukaka," he said. "Vasanti came over last Saturday." He turned to Kamala. "Bharati carries the bead coin bag you sent her as a birthday present wherever she goes."

"Aai made it," Mohini said.

He nodded. "Vasanti told us about Keshav's malaria so we thought we would come and see him." He turned to

Vishnupant. "And we have some good news. You know that we've been looking for a suitable boy for Swati. Well, a boy and his family came to see her only last week and just yesterday the boy's side said yes to her." He pointed to the cardboard box that was on the table. "Open it, Sudha, and give everyone something to sweeten their mouths."

"I'll call Baba," Mohini said. She entered the end room.

Keshav came out on the verandah and sat down in a chair. "Congratulations!" he said to Sudha as she gave him a sweetmeat. "Mohini just told me."

"Give Mohini two pieces," Vinod said, coming around to where she was sitting. He put his hands alongside her neck and massaged her shoulders. Mohini counted how many pieces there were in the box as Sudha held it out to her. There would be only two remaining after she had picked one: one for Bayabai, and the other for Balu.

"I'll have the second one later," she said to Vinod.

"So tell us about the boy," Vishnupant said.

"His name is Aniruddha Gokhale. He is a doctor and his family live on the other side of Shivaji Park, in the first gully leading towards the sea."

"When is the wedding?" Keshav asked.

"I think the boy's side wants it to be soon."

Sudha nodded. "Within two to three weeks," she said, looking at Kamala.

"You will be all right by then, won't you?" Vinod asked Keshav.

"Absolutely. I intend to go to my office next week."

Mohini glanced at Kamala, but she was looking at the lantern that Balu had hung from the ceiling for Divali and which he had forgotten to take down. It was swaying in the breeze, its coloured paper casting a mosaic on the floor.

"Just take it one day at a time, Keshav!" Vishnupant said, clucking his tongue.

It proved to be prescient advice because the following day Keshav was too weak to take a bath and had to be sponged down by Balu. It was also the day a lady who Mohini had never met before rang the doorbell and asked to see him.

"I am Mrs. Pendse," the lady said. "Dr. Chitnis is my brother-in-law. He has told me all about you."

Mohini smiled and moved aside to let her in. As they walked together to the back verandah, Mrs. Pendse said, "When you are ready to begin your lessons, send me a message through Dr. Chitnis. I'll come here and we can go over whatever is troubling you. All right?"

Mohini had no idea as to when she would feel strong enough to resume her studies. She remembered Dr. Chitnis had said that his sister-in-law was a retired headmistress, and that if Mohini wished to continue with her Standard Seven curriculum, then she, Mrs. Pendse, would give Mohini private tuition.

She led Mrs. Pendse to the far end of the verandah and asked her to take a seat. "I'll check if Baba is resting or whether he can come out," she added.

Keshav was sitting up in bed, twirling his glasses in one hand, pinning down a stack of unopened office files with the other. She told him that a Mrs. Pendse had come to see him.

"Sumatibai!" he said. "Dr. Chitnis said she might drop in. I'll be out in a minute."

Mohini waited for him to stand up to make sure that his dhotar was properly draped and that it was not too crumpled. He walked out to the verandah.

"You look black," Mrs. Pendse said.

"Malaria and sunburn: two hazards of the engineering profession," he said, smiling.

"Didn't they teach you in school to stay out of the noon-day sun?"

"I'm sure they did, but some lessons I have forgotten." His words were playful, but there was a sombre note in his voice.

"Have you told Mohini that you were the most brilliant in my matriculation class, but also the laziest? Look at you now! Burning candles at both ends. Always away on site, Dr. Chitnis tells me."

"Sumatibai taught me in school, Mohini. For three years in a row she was our mathematics teacher."

Mohini smiled. Something jumped in the periphery of her vision. She turned her head. Mina and Nina's two rabbits had entered the backyard. They sniffed the air before darting in the direction of the water tank. Mohini watched them until they disappeared around it.

"Well," Mrs. Pendse was saying, "it looks as though we are going to become related: your niece Swati is to marry Aniruddha Gokhale, I understand."

"Yes, Vinod and Sudha were here yesterday and they told us. But how are you related to the boy?"

"He is my brother's grandson. You remember my nephew? He was not in the same school as you, but he used to play regularly in the quadrangular cricket matches. He was a batsman. Vinayak Gokhale."

"Vinayak is your nephew?"

Mrs. Pendse nodded. "You may have met his sister, my niece, Charulata Pradhan. She married a boy from the CKP caste, outside our Brahmin community. She lost him and her infant son in a train derailment two years ago. Very tragic. She was one of the first women to graduate from Poona Engineering College. Have you come across her?"

"Yes, I have," Keshav said, glancing at Mohini. She was watching the rabbits that were now crouched next to the tank, their noses busy, bodies quivering. "Mohini," Keshav said. "Ask Balu to bring Sumatibai some tea."

Mohini turned to Keshav. Her father's face was unusually red. She started to say something, but his expression was forbidding. "Tea," he reminded her.

"I've already had my afternoon tea," Sumatibai said. "I was at the samaj just now. I didn't see Kamala there."

"She's in the kitchen," Mohini said. "I can call her if you want."

But Mrs. Pendse was standing up. She glanced at her watch. "I said I'd drop by for five minutes because that's all the time I have today. Tell your mother, Mohini, that I will see her at the samaj some other time."

"Walk Mrs. Pendse to the door," Keshav said.

When Mohini came back, Kamala was in the verandah, laying out Keshav's tea and snack on the table in front of him. Mohini told her about Mrs. Pendse's visit.

"I didn't know Sumatibai was here, or I would have come out," Kamala said, turning to Keshav, who was silent.

Mohini touched her father's forehead.

"What are you doing?" he said, pulling back.

"You are looking flushed. Just checking whether you have a temperature."

"I'm fine," Keshav said.

Mohini said, "Then when are you coming upstairs?"

He looked at her blankly.

"Upstairs. To your own room."

"Whenever your mother gives me permission."

Kamala silently handed him a steel jug of water, looking aggrieved and disbelieving at the implication that Keshav was choosing to remain downstairs because she had not yet granted him permission to return to his room.

"So you'll move, Baba?" Mohini asked. "Today?"

Keshav nodded as he washed his hands over the edge of the verandah, letting the water drip into the shrubs below.

Mohini smiled, looking at Kamala.

"Help me arrange the food on the table," was all Kamala said. While Keshav was eating, she said to him, "Sudha sent a message this morning. She asked whether your father and I could go to their house in the afternoon to meet the Gokhale family."

Keshav did not say anything.

"Baba!"

"Yes, go." He set down his cup of tea, seemingly lost in his own thoughts.

After lunch, Keshav followed Mohini upstairs. Everything was different. Kamala had got Balu to shift his desk to the opposite side of the room, and the beds had been moved to where the desk used to be. Since the room was in the shape of a rhomboid, the single beds were joined together in order to fit the side tables at either end. Keshav had wanted this arrangement for a long time: the way the beds were placed now, there was no tree outside the window to obstruct his view of the sky.

"Did you notice the wall above your desk?" Mohini asked.

Keshav looked up. It was the oblong village scene Kamala had begun to embroider soon after they were married and had finished before Mohini was born. Three parrots were perched on the banyan tree whose roots hung down from the branches like climbing ropes. The grass was an emerald green, the sky a delicate blue. In the right-hand corner stood a cream-coloured cow with jet-black eyes, a newborn calf nuzzling her underbelly, another grazing a little distance away. A bull stood behind the cow, its neck extended protectively over the cow's back. "Do you like the new arrangement, Baba?" Mohini said.

Keshav nodded. Kamala came into his room, carrying a fresh jug of water.

"What time do you have to leave for Sudhakaku's?"

"Not before three-thirty. You lie down on my bed, Mohini. I'll rest on the spare one in your room. Your office papers are on the side table next to your bed," she told Keshav.

"I think I feel well enough to do some work," he said, reaching behind him.

When Madanlal brought Kamala back, Keshav, Vasanti, and Mohini were sitting in the front verandah. They watched as Madanlal made sure that all the car doors were locked before handing Kamala the keys. He sauntered out of the car porch, his back hunched, hands in his pockets.

"Where's Vishnupant?" Mohini said.

"He asked to be dropped at the gymkhana."

"What did you think of the boy?" Vasanti asked.

"Very nice. Handsome too. He and Swati make a good pair. He is on the short side, so her being short does not matter."

"Handsome? How?" Mohini asked.

Kamala thought a moment. "Well, he has this very nice smile and he's always smiling." She turned to Keshav. "Madanlal asked me for money again."

"What!" Keshav's face turned red.

"Last week he said he wanted twenty rupees."

"I hope you didn't give it to him."

"Well, I didn't think you were well enough for me to bother you, so I gave him—"

"Kamala!"

"—only ten. Then just now, after dropping off Mohini's grandfather, he asked me for ten more."

"And?"

"I said he should talk to you because I don't deal with money matters. He said he did, yesterday, and that you refused."

"And rightly so. I already gave him twenty, when we were on-site. He owes us thirty rupees now. He has absolutely no business involving you. The next time he asks, tell him to go to the office if he wants an advance."

"I don't think he will ask me again. I was very firm with him this time," Kamala said.

"I said *if* he asks you." Keshav's voice was laced with irritation.

Mohini looked at her father. She couldn't understand why he was taking out his anger on Kamala. Her expression stricken, Kamala walked quickly into the house and hung the keys on the hat stand. When she came out again, her face was composed. "Sudha took me aside this afternoon when we were there. It seems there are no wedding halls to be had in Shivaji Park for the fourth of January, which Guruji has picked as an auspicious day."

"What would she like for us to do?" Keshav said. His voice was soft and smooth, an attempt he was making, Mohini could tell, to erase the effects of his earlier abruptness.

"How many guests are they expecting?" Vasanti said, her tone dry and detached. Mohini knew that her aunt was hurt because she had not been invited along with Vishnupant and Kamala to meet the Gokhale family.

"About a hundred to a hundred and twenty-five." Kamala turned to Keshav and said, "I offered her our house. For the wedding."

"You didn't, Kamalavahini, did you?" Vasanti said.

"I thought if we put up an awning," Kamala continued, "the backyard could be enclosed, making it suitable . . ." She looked at Keshav, who had fixed his gaze across the lane.

Mohini's eyes were shining. "I think it's the best suggestion ever."

"What is?" Vishnupant said, entering the verandah from the side of the car porch.

Kamala got up and hurried into the house.

Mohini told her grandfather about Kamala's offer.

"I agree with your mother," he said. "It's the least we can do for an Oek granddaughter."

"But, Vishnukaka," Vasanti said. "You know Sudhavahini and Vinoddada. If the wedding is here, they

will conveniently transfer all the responsibility of the planning onto Kamalavahini's shoulders."

"Kamala probably knew that when she made the offer."
He turned to Keshav. "And I can tell someone else is not
too enthusiastic about Koleshwar Nivas being turned into a
marriage hall, either."

"It doesn't matter one way or the other to me," Keshav
said, pushing himself up and out of his chair. He headed
upstairs.

The following day, Keshav felt well enough to go back to
work. He got a colleague from Bandra to fetch him on his
way to Fort so that Kamala could keep the car for the wedding preparations.

When Kamala returned home that afternoon after a
shopping expedition, her face was white and her eyes
looked hollow. Mohini was alarmed. She asked what the
matter was and Kamala muttered that it was that time of the
month for her.

Keshav returned from work early, a sheaf of papers
clutched in his hands, and more files stuffed into his bag.
Mohini told him that Kamala had a stomach ache and that
she was resting upstairs. When she followed him there
after finishing her milk, the interconnecting door between
their rooms was shut.

By dinnertime, Kamala said she was feeling much better, but Mohini thought she must still have a stomach ache
because she ate only a quarter poli and a tablespoon of rice.
Keshav worked late at his desk that night, and when he
finally switched off his lamp and went to bed, Mohini
found she could not sleep.

So as not to disturb him or Kamala, she entered the sewing room through the back verandah. Moving gingerly, she made her way to the window. A stray dog was stretched out on its side in front of the Irani's, head thrown back, throat exposed. A single bulb was burning in the front entrance of the Kulkarnis' home. The scent of frangipani drifted across the lane. The light from Vasanti's front room was like a golden shaft spilling across the compound wall. Mai was probably up. She often read late into the night because she could not sleep due to the increased ringing in her ears. Somewhere, a grandfather clock chimed twice. Kamala came and stood next to Mohini.

"I didn't mean to disturb you," Mohini said.

"Can't sleep?" Kamala asked.

Mohini nodded.

"Do you want me to change the position of your bed? You are facing the south now. If we rotate the bed by ninety degrees, you will face the east."

"Do you think that will help?"

"It might. Have you noticed how dogs sniff around the room before settling into a comfortable position? We don't do that. Maybe we should."

"I think I slept too much this afternoon," Mohini said. "When you were gone shopping."

Kamala looked away. "Don't stay standing for too long." She left the room. Mohini heard her switch on the light in her bathroom, and when she returned to her own room a few minutes later, the bathroom light was still on.

Inside, Kamala was sitting on the stool. After Mohini had gone to bed and all was quiet, she reached into the front of her blouse and opened for the first time since she had come across it earlier that evening, the letter she had found while clearing Mohini's cluttered desk. She began to read. "My darling Kamale . . ."

As she came to the end of the first paragraph, she let the letter fall to her lap. She covered her eyes with her hands as a once familiar but now distant sweet paralysis took hold of her limbs. She remembered how she used to wait for Keshav in the upstairs window, now and then moving back into the shadows in case one of the neighbours noticed her impatient yearning, only to return to her post when she thought sufficient time had passed and it was all right to resume her watch. She blushed when she thought about the night that she had fallen asleep sitting up in bed, when she had come awake to Keshav's mouth against her own, the familiar musky smell of him that she associated with red-dish brown earth and pale green leaves filling her nostrils, his one hand lightly gripping her thigh, the other cupping her chin.

She glanced down at Keshav's handwriting and flushed at the thought of Mohini having read this letter. She scanned the rest of its contents and was relieved that it was only the first paragraph that was unambiguous and intimate. Kamala did not know when she had last seen this letter or how it had gotten separated from the bundle of all the other letters she had secreted in a carved wooden box on top of her wardrobe. There was so much she had forgotten! So many little details about the first two years of her marriage. When she returned to her room, Keshav was lying on his back, fast asleep. Just as she was about to run her fingers through his hair, she remembered the thinly veiled insinuations that Madanlal had made that afternoon. She stumbled back onto her bed and sat there for a long time, staring at her lap, her clenched feet gripping the ground.

TWENTY

Signs of cooler days were everywhere. In the early mornings Mohini pulled up her quilt to cover her shoulders. Vishnupant got Balu to remove his sleeveless cotton jacket from the top shelf of his wardrobe. At night before going to bed, he donned his knitted monkey-cap that covered his ears and head and made him look like a clown. Kamala searched in the cupboard of her sewing room for an old sweater she had knitted for Keshav the first time he had visited Delhi in the winter. She gave it to Balu to wear. Bayabai, as usual, refused the offer of a shawl, but for the very first time she reluctantly agreed to bathe with hot water instead of the cold water she had pledged herself to bathe in when her husband had died some forty years earlier. Even Keshav, who was used to all kinds of weather, tried to get Mohini to lower the speed of her ceiling fan. She refused, reminding him that she needed the air to flow around her body.

"And, Baba, whoever asked you to sleep in my room?" she added. It was the third time she had seen him first thing in the morning, spread-eagled on the spare bed, a pillow placed over his eyes.

"You know my snoring disturbs your mother!" he said, seeming to plead for some kind of understanding.

"I don't mind Mohini's fan," Kamala said, walking into the room. "Why don't I sleep here instead?"

"No. I wouldn't dream of asking you to do that," Keshav said; his tone was formal.

Since Keshav had come home after his malaria attack, reticent, tired, and preferring to recuperate in the end room downstairs, Kamala's face had become difficult to read. Then later, her expression had become unfathomable. Watching her drink glass upon glass of water, Mohini wondered how her mother could imbibe so much fluid. It did not occur to her that water was a purgative, a purifying element, the ultimate remedy Kamala resorted to in times of worry and stress.

Her father, Mohini could tell, was making an effort to put things right, except she did not know what had gone wrong. If he suggested that Kamala stay behind after her embroidery class to chat with the samaj ladies and that there was no need to hurry back home, Kamala would shrug and say that she was not interested in chatting. Besides, had he forgotten? There was a wedding to prepare for.

Mohini would wait for Kamala in the front verandah, watching her mother as she hurried down Mill Road, her eyes drawn to the car porch even before she had crossed the junction. "He's back?" she would ask Mohini, even though the parked car declared that he was. When Mohini replied yes, she would nod in a relieved fashion and hurry on upstairs. But if Keshav asked her any questions relating to the samaj or her class, her manner would change abruptly. She would narrow her eyes and become mistrustful of the fact that he was taking all this interest in her. In some ways she might have been justified: Mohini had never until now heard her father inquire about Kamala's embroidery classes.

One evening, as soon as Mohini stepped into their room, she got the distinct impression that harsh words had been spoken in her absence. An ominous silence hung in the air. Keshav looked up from his desk and said to her, "What were Vishnupant and Balu talking about?"

"You heard them upstairs?" she said. "Vishnupant was trying to remember when it was that the pond in Shivaji Park was filled in, so Balu reminded him of the stoning incident that had taken place in the park just prior to the dismantling of the mill workers' huts."

Keshav turned back to the papers on his desk.

"What are you studying?" Mohini asked.

"Come and take a look."

It was a survey map of Bombay Presidency through the centre of which was sketched in the flowing Godavari River.

Keshav said, "The last time I was there I had the fortune of seeing a white tigress and her cubs drinking water from that very same river."

Kamala, who was reading her book, looked up and said, "That would have been the west-flowing tributary. People say white tigers are common there. It is the holy ground of Durga Devi and the peculiarity is that the person who sees a white tiger never sees one again." She looked at Mohini as she spoke.

Keshav said he had heard the exact same story. He seemed appreciative, as though he was proud and a bit surprised at the depth of her general knowledge.

But Kamala's lips became thin as she said, "I may not be an engineer and I may not travel anywhere, but my head is not empty and I do know a few things."

Keshav became still and his eyes widened, but he rapidly composed himself.

Mohini glanced at her mother. Kamala was staring at her book, now closed on her lap: she had missed seeing the startled expression on Keshav's face.

Ignoring the bitterness in Kamala's voice, Keshav said, "You may not be an engineer, Kamala, but that is not because you do not possess the intelligence to become one. I have often told Mohini that your grasp is excellent and your memory even better. Your knowledge about medicine is a case in point. Ask her if what I am saying is not true?"

"You don't have to flatter me," Kamala said a little unsteadily.

"If telling the truth means I am mocking you, then it is much better that I say nothing."

Ordinary conversations between her parents had assumed unpleasant nuances, veiled meanings, the kind Mohini had not been exposed to and did not understand. She found there was nothing she could say or do to ease the tension and she tried to keep out of their room when they were both in it.

She took to reading in her own room or on the swing or lying down on Vishnupant's bed. When she tired of that, she got Balu to dust the carom board and prop it up on two dictionaries on her bed. Hansa did not come as often as she used to because now there were final exams to study for. The last time she had visited Koleshwar Nivas, she informed Mohini that she had taken on the new girl Kanta as her studying partner. Her expression when she told Mohini this was apologetic. Even so, hurt by this information, Mohini did not tell Hansa, as she had been meaning to all week, that the inner core of the pink stone had begun to reveal golden nuggets.

After sitting on her bed, the carom board placed at its centre, Mohini would choose the white wooden discs for the imaginary Hansa, the black for herself, alternating the colours at the end of each game. She would take turns, first playing for Hansa, then for herself. She tried to be fair so that she did not end up winning every game. The more she played, the more she understood the geometry of flicking the cue disc at an angle—depending on the weight behind the flick—that would nudge or whip the black or white wooden disc into a pocket, sometimes sending two discs of the same colour flying into two pockets at the same time. Kamala scolded her for using too much boric powder on the carom board and limited it to a single sprinkling at the start of each game.

There were half moons of weariness under Kamala's eyes and sadness surrounded her gestures. Vasanti asked Kamala whether she was getting enough sleep, but Kamala's answers were so guarded and reserved that Vasanti knew better than to press the issue.

When Sudha came over to discuss wedding details (Kamala had earlier conveyed to Sudha that the Koleshwar Nivas venue would necessarily involve the inclusion of Vasanti in all discussions), Kamala was very heedful of the conversation, clinging to it like driftwood, as though paying minute attention to what was being said would carry her safely into the next moment.

As she sat opposite her mother in the dining room, her mind drawn to a conversation she had overheard, Mohini willed Kamala to forget whatever it was that Madanlal had told her.

"Did Madanlal give you any details?" Keshav had asked Kamala the previous night.

"No," Kamala muttered.

"And yet you choose to believe him? That man is in debt. There is some court case in his village and he needs the money. He's only trying to blackmail us."

"I know that," Kamala whispered. "But that does not alter the facts, does it?"

"The facts don't exist," Keshav said. "Please, for your sake, forget what Madanlal told you."

Now Balu came in carrying a small straw basket.

"What's that?" Kamala asked.

"Before he left for work, Mohini's baba told me to pluck *zaai* buds," Balu replied.

"You haven't made a garland for your hair in such a long time. I told Baba to remind me to tell Balu in the morning. He must have decided to remind Balu himself."

Vasanti and Sudha pushed back their chairs. Mohini and Kamala walked them to the front door.

That night, when Balu was turning down Mohini's bed after dinner, Kamala told him to pull a mattress from the spare bed into the terrace and make up her bed there, under the stars.

"But, Aai! You don't like the early morning dew and you get a funny feeling when you look up at all that vastness," Mohini reminded her.

Kamala looked at Balu. "You heard me," she said.

"Can I sleep outside too?" Mohini asked.

"If you wish. Now go and get changed."

Afterwards, Mohini waited for her mother on the swing. The night sounds were a blur, woven into a tight shroud, one sound indistinguishable from the other. The brief cold snap had long since broken, replaced by a humidity that made the scalp weep and itch, the skin continuously damp. Kamala came out and lay on the mattress, facing the wall. She had removed the zaai garland that Mohini had earlier fastened around her bun. She pulled up her quilt until only the top of her head was showing.

Mohini lay down on her mattress and placed her palm against the small of her mother's back, and though she could feel the occasional tremor in Kamala's body, there was no way she could read her thoughts. She could not hear the questions that were running through Kamala's mind: Why do wise men say learn to transcend attachment? Why not instead learn to transcend memory? My anguish and humiliation spring from the fact that I remember his cold- ness over the last few weeks. If I learned to transcend my memories, I would be calm and unruffled, like that plant, that tree, that sky, that road . . . Does Keshav really think that I am blind, or worse, stupid and dull, not to realize the meaning behind Madanlal's sordid words? Why can't he just admit to his lapse instead of denying it? At least then I can forgive him, knowing that his confession has showed him to be honest and repentant.

In the beginning of their marriage, some fifteen years earlier, Kamala had right away sensed that everything about her existence had fundamentally changed. She was no longer a girl in her parents' home, but a woman finding her way in a world lined by complete strangers. And by the time Mohini had come along and the visits to Dr. Merchant had become a weekly feature, Kamala had worked it such that the inside of her head had become a territory that she could control by moving the stakes that defined its boundaries. Sometimes, the soil underneath a stake was loose, and it was easy enough to move it when required. At other times, the stakes were so difficult to budge that it would take her weeks to move them into another spot, and then weeks again to get used to the new dimensions. And now that she was required to move them for a reason that was clearly Keshav's fault, she found that even if she could shift them, their sharpened ends caused her to constantly bleed. She shuddered.

"Aai, are you all right?"

Kamala turned onto her back and put out her hand. Mohini interlaced her fingers with those of her mother and watched Kamala stare back defiantly at the sky that looked down on them with a million glittering eyes.

Mohini wondered what Madanlal could have said to her mother to have upset her so. She couldn't come up with an explanation.

Kamala withdrew her hand from Mohini's grasp and turned to face the other way. Mohini's head was hurting, and her temples throbbed every time she moved. She cradled her head in her hand and found relief in the thought that this time her parents' misunderstanding had nothing to do with her. She carefully pulled her quilt over her ears so as to protect her face from the invisible bats she imagined would swoop out of the shadows the minute her eyes were closed.

"Are you all right?" Kamala asked. "Do you want to go back inside?"

"Do you?"

"Only if you want to."

"I'm all right . . . Aai, when the moon is overhead, it looks smaller than when it is rising or sinking. I don't understand."

"I don't either. Now go to sleep. And no questions until the morning."

Mohini nodded. If the moon was a fixed size, as it was, and the distance between the moon and earth was fixed, as it was, then the only thing different was that the head was tilted more when she looked at it overhead compared with when she looked at it when it was hovering over the horizon. She still didn't understand. All she understood was that if she closed her eyes, the moon and everything else would disappear.

Drifting off to sleep Mohini remembered that terrifying afternoon at the park when she had been six years old. Vishnupant was reading his newspaper on the bench, and Mohini and Balu were crouched at the edge of the pond. Suddenly, a blood-curdling yell was heard. Balu pulled Mohini to her feet just as two men burst out of a hut across the pond, their faces livid with anger. One of the men stooped and picked up from the ground a large boulder. He started to hurl it when Balu clamped his hand over Mohini's eyes. By the time she had pried his fingers loose, the wounded man was crouched on the ground, clutching his head. He was screaming in pain. Blood was running down his face and dripping onto his bare torso. His attacker was standing to one side, his triumphant face smouldering with gloating anger.

When Mohini woke up in the morning, the wet dew clinging unpleasantly to her body, the image of that fight was still with her, only now the wounded man's face was Madanlal's and the attacker's was hers. And Keshav's voice was saying, "But the facts don't exist."

TWENTY-ONE

Two days before the wedding, on the morning of the mehndi session, Swati, Shobha, and Bharati came to Koleshwar Nivas to fetch Mohini. A week previously, Sudha's Marwadi neighbour had suggested to her that the bride and her sisters get decorative henna applied to their hands. When Sudha rejected the idea, saying that it was not a Brahmin custom, Swati asked Kamala and Vasanti to convince their mother to change her mind. Vasanti offered her home for the application, and when she said that she would also pay for the session, Sudha finally gave in.

Mohini was finishing a late breakfast on the back verandah, watching the men set up the wedding marquee in the courtyard that had been swept and cleared. Behind her, against the wall, were stacked folding chairs and wide wooden slats that would be fashioned into a central podium on which the marriage ceremony would take place.

"Are you ready to come with us to Vasantiatya's?" Bharati said, entering the verandah.

Mohini said, "I still have to have a head bath. You go on ahead. I'll come later. Where's everyone else? Swati and Shobha?" She placed her hands over her ears as the men began to knock the poles into the ground, the ring of their metal hammers sharp and continuous.

"In the dining room."

Mohini got up and Bharati took the empty plate from her hand before passing her the walking stick.

"Look at Swati!" Shobha said when Mohini and Bharati entered the room.

Swati had covered her face with her hands. The back of her neck as she hung her head was deeply flushed. Shobha wrestled Swati's fingers away. Her eyes were overflowing and there was panic in Swati's face. Kamala moved away from the window and put her arms around her niece's shoulders and told her she would make the most beautiful bride anyone had ever seen. Swati, who was sitting on a dining chair, flung her arms around Kamala's waist and sobbed so heartily that her sisters and Mohini looked at Sudha in dismay. Bharati whispered harshly to Shobha, "Now look what you have done."

"I didn't do anything!" Shobha said.

"Ssh . . ." Kamala murmured into Swati's hair. "You will be all right. You are such a gentle girl. Your in-laws are bound to see that. It is only natural that you are nervous. I had just turned sixteen the month I got married and I haven't forgotten what it was like at the beginning. But you will get used to it."

Swati looked at her mother. Sudha's eyes were so full that when she nodded her tears fell into the bowl she was holding. Everyone laughed.

Watching Swati, Mohini thought it was just as well that she would never have to make an in-law family her own, that she would never have to get used to another house, another bed, another person, another room. But Swati's outburst was soon forgotten. She described to Vasanti the mustard sari with a crimson border that her uncle had given her for the wedding ceremony. She turned to Mohini and said, "What are you going to wear?"

"Aai has made me a parkar-polka. It's peacock blue with little gold peacocks in the body and a narrow gold border."

"I can't wait to see it," Shobha said. "And mind you don't cut your hair in the time left before the wedding."

Mohini's hands flew to her head. "It's not too short, is it? It's only in the summer that I ask Aai to trim it closer to my head."

"It's not at all too short," Vasanti quickly said, noting the self-conscious gesture with which Mohini was pulling down the ends of her hair.

"Vasantiatya," Bharati said. "You said we could have a look at the saris you wore during your wedding."

Vasanti looked at Mohini. "You'll come later?"

Mohini nodded.

"We'll go ahead, then," Vasanti said. "It's years since I gave Bebitai the key to my sari trunk, and knowing her, it will be a while before she is able to locate it."

"I'll ask Balu to find out how everything is progressing before I send Mohini over," Kamala said.

By the time Mohini entered Vasanti's flat it was afternoon. There was a fresh, green scent of crushed mehndi leaves. Three of Swati's cousins from her mother's side were sitting cross-legged against the wall of the verandah, their elbows on their knees, palms facing up. Shobha introduced Mohini to them. They lifted their hands so Mohini could see their palms. Mohini liked best the design that made the palms look as though they were holding circlets of ivy leaves.

When it was Mohini's turn, the younger of the two women who were applying the mehndi told Mohini to take a seat in front of her on the floor as she continued to mix the ground leaves and water in a bowl on her lap.

Swati, who had closed her eyes while the older woman was applying the design to her feet, now opened them and said, "Let her sit on the divan."

The young woman looked up. She clucked her tongue in sympathy at Mohini's short stature, her buckled legs, the greyness of her skin, her large face with its prominent fore-head. She moved on her knees alongside the divan after Mohini was seated. Mohini opened her palms. The mehndi-wali massaged them before starting the application. "So soft," she said, smiling into Mohini's eyes. "Just like butter."

Swati complained to Mohini that it was two inter-minable hours since the henna application had begun.

"You want to look like bride or bride's sister?" her mehndiwali said. "Close your eyes again and go to sleep. I'll tell you when I'm done."

"I don't think I can sit in one position for that long," Mohini said. "Half an hour maximum for both hands. Will the application be finished within that time?"

"I'll be like an express train jhat and pat. Now, what design do you want me to make?"

Mohini said she wasn't sure.

"Paisleys?"

Mohini nodded. She looked onto the balcony as the cousins burst out laughing. One of them loudly said, "I'm telling you. It's called the Mount of Venus."

Mohini looked at her palm where the mehndiwali was using the tip of her forefinger like a nib in order to drop thin lines of the design that she improvised as she went along. There was a central paisley and surrounding it squares, diamonds, circles, triangles, and smaller paisleys that showed their shape only from a very close range. From a distance the geometric figures looked connected, as though a maroon piece of thread had been unwound into an intricate pattern on the palm.

The old woman who was doing Swati's foot told Mohini that the design her sister was applying on her palms was a special one, and that on the day of the wedding everyone would ask Mohini to display her hands. She grinned. Her front tooth was chipped and her right nostril was pierced with a tiny gold blob. Mohini thought that instead of washing her hands after each application, the woman probably ran her fingers along the top of her head because the hair on her crown was an odd red colour and made her face look masculine and broad.

The cousins in the balcony were laughing again. "But let me finish my story!" One of them raised her voice. "As I was saying, this girl in my building was so bold that she told the mehndiwali that she wanted her left palm—you know, because it is on the same side as the heart—to be a maze. And the first letter of the bridegroom's name should be at the centre of that maze. She said she was going to, on their wedding night, ask the groom"—the cousins once again burst into laughter—"to trace the path of the maze and find that letter before she would let him, you know . . ."

The young woman who was doing Mohini's palms

stopped her application, winked at Mohini, and raised her head to look out on the balcony.

"Anyway, the wedding night came and my friend asked her groom to trace the path. He began at the centre of the left wrist, but the mehndiwali had done such a good job— the path going up and down, forwards and backwards, in and out, under and over—that halfway through the maze the bridegroom keeled over."

"What happened?" the other two asked, stopping their laughter.

"The four-hour wedding ceremony in front of the smoking fire and meeting all the guests and waking up at five in the morning had left him so exhausted that he fell asleep across her lap. My friend said she must have sat like that for several minutes, holding his snoring face in her palms."

The laughter became snorts. The woman who had finished doing Swati's feet turned around and said to the cousins who were walking into the room, "If your friend had asked the mehndiwali to trace a maze beginning at the ankle, I'm sure the groom would not have fallen asleep."

The cousins went forward to inspect Swati's hands. One of them said, "Look at Swati—she's gone white!"

Mohini sank her chin into her chest lest they comment on her face, which was red and burning. There was a strange throb at the bottom of her stomach. She slowly lifted her head, wondering whether Swati would burst into tears the way she had earlier that morning. But Swati's expression was animated now, and her eyes were shining as the cousins bent over her, admiring the design on her feet.

Vasanti brought some food on a large tray. "Everything is bite-sized so you can pop it into your mouth with a spoon without disturbing the design," she said, passing around the plates.

The girls ate in silence, smiles licking their faces every time they thought about the cousin's friend and her wedding night.

"Can you bring out Chhaya now? I'm finished eating," one of the cousin's said to Shobha, carefully holding her empty plate by its rim and laying it on the windowsill.

Vasanti said, "I'll bring out the baby."

Chhaya had been so quiet that Mohini did not know there was a baby in the flat. Vasanti placed the loosely swaddled bundle on the divan, next to the mother who was sitting cross-legged, her blouse hooks undone, ready to nurse her little baby.

Vasanti dangled her set of keys over Chhaya's face. "Aren't her eyes simply gorgeous?" she said to Mohini.

The irises were a deep black and luminous, and the red string, which was tied around Chhaya's plump wrists, was already getting too tight. Vasanti bent over Chhaya and laid her cheek against her forehead, then turned her face and kissed the baby over and over again as the mother waited patiently.

"Vasantiatya," Mohini softly said, as she gestured towards the baby's mother.

Vasanti looked up. "Oh!" she said, straightening her back. "I didn't know your mother was ready to feed you." She placed Chhaya carefully on her mother's lap.

Mohini, Swati, Bharati, and Shobha crossed the lane to Koleshwar Nivas, their hands bound in leaves. After applying a sticky mixture of lime juice and sugar to their palms—this to make the henna a deeper, brighter red—the women had wrapped leaves around their hands so that the design would stay in place and the henna, which had long since dried into a fine powder, would not fall off and litter the floor.

In the backyard, the workers were finished. They had stretched, fifteen feet high, red cloth walls around the poles. Only the cotton ceiling and the assembly of the central wooden podium remained.

"We've been sitting for so long that my legs feel stiff," Swati said, watching the men as they unfolded bolts of cotton along the floor of the courtyard.

"I feel like going for a walk along the beach," Bharati said.

"In this heat?" Shobha muttered.

"It's early January. How hot can it be? What do you think, Kamalakaku?"

Mohini looked at Kamala.

"Why not?" Kamala said. "I promised your mother that the driver would drop you home by four, but I don't think she will mind if you are late. The stroll will do us all good." She had stopped referring to Madanlal by his name.

The sea was awash in an aquamarine haze. A million suns bounced off the water in a million points. The collapsed sails of a grounded boat hung like a bedraggled flag. A small boy was doing somersaults over the slanted mast. He stopped his tumbling and looked at them. As Swati, Shobha, and Bharati hurried towards the sea, he came running up to Kamala and Mohini and held out one hand. They had brought no money with them, no loose change to place in his grubby fist. He raised his hand higher and opened his fingers. Inside the cup of his palm were nestled ivory shells, each one no bigger than the size of his fingernails. "Take them," he said. Kamala made a basket of the end of her sari and he opened his palm, scattering the shells from a height so that they caught the sun and took on a rosy hue. When his hands were empty he ran away and climbed back into the boat. A man was sitting cross-legged on its stern, his downcast gaze fixed as though mesmerized by the water.

Farther along the beach, clusters of people were seated on the sand, their voices drifting towards Mohini and Kamala every time the breeze fanned their way.

"I'll sit here, Aai," Mohini said, walking towards an area where the wind had flattened a dune. "You go and join the others."

The soft, dry sand, Kamala knew, had a tendency to drag down on Mohini's feet. It would be too much of an effort for her to walk across it. "I'll stay with you," she said.

"There's no need." Mohini pointed to her bulging pocket. "I've brought a book. Really! You better go quickly if you are to catch up with the others."

Kamala spread out her handkerchief on the sand and held Mohini's elbow as she lowered herself onto it. When Mohini was comfortably seated, Kamala stood tall and scrutinized the horizon. It was a clean, unbroken line. She started to walk towards it.

Mohini watched Kamala stroll along the seashore, in no hurry at all to catch up with the others who were small dots moving north in the direction of Mahim Bay. Water birds circled high above, squawking in a quarrelsome manner before settling on the ocean surface where they bobbed up and down, their bodies motionless as though anchored to the ocean floor.

Mohini wished Keshav could have come with them. These days she missed him at the oddest of times, even during the day when it was not usual for him to be at home. The last time that she had come here was over a year ago, when her father had wanted to see the spread of constellations undimmed by the unlit sea. The rising moon still behind them, they lay back against the sand, arms cradling their heads, the silence broken only by the lapping waves. Every now and again Keshav pointed out to her the few constellations that he could name. Down the beach some- one had built a fire, and whenever there was a gust, tendrils of woodsmoke would waft in their direction.

Mohini picked up her book. A piece of paper fluttered to the sand. It was the second item she had placed in her pocket on the afternoon she had sorted out the untidy bundle in Kamala's wardrobe. She unfolded this paper now, and as she had on the day when she had first found it, she laughed at the large and childish handwriting that appeared on both sides of the page. It was the will that she had drawn up after a widowed Vasanti had arrived at Koleshwar Nivas.

There had been some initial talk then, concerning Vasanti's inheritance, particularly because she had mar- ried into such a wealthy family. Vinod had brought up the subject in front of Vasanti the first time he had come to see her. Vishnupant told him that since it was he, Vishnupant, who had offered to bring Vasanti back with him to Bombay, the question of Vasanti's father-in-law bringing up the issue of inheritance had not arisen and nor was he,

Vishnupant, going to bring it up. His tone was stern and the subject was dropped.

However, around the time Vasanti moved in with Mai and Bebitai into Shiv Sadan, Vinod and Sudha had raised the issue once again. Did anyone know whether Babasahib had left a will? Vishnupant looked at his nephew coldly and told him that he would be permitted to reopen that issue on the day that Vasanti would cease to be looked after by her uncle. "Besides," he added, "a monthly money order has started arriving from Nagpur. It's in the bank in Vasanti's name." So, he warned, there would be no discussion whatsoever relating to any will.

It was the first time that Mohini had heard mention of a will and she asked Keshav what it was. She listened carefully to his explanation, and after giving it a fair amount of thought during the night, she sat on the swing the following morning and drew up a will of her own. After all, her measles attack of a year ago, although mild, still had had, she knew, the potential of carrying her away and there was no telling when she would contract another disease, or how severe it might be.

Sifting the sand through her fingers, Mohini glanced at the document on her lap. She had used a blunt pencil to itemize and allocate her possessions. She began reading.

The last will of Mohini Oek. Age: 10
Date: June 1944

1. *I leave Induaji's emerald brooch, which Vishnupant gave me, to Hema because she is Vishnupant's only other granddaughter.*

2. *I leave Helen Keller's book, which Dr. Merchant brought from England and gave me, to Hansa because she likes its smell and the gold lettering on the cover.*

3. *I leave the William Blake poems, which Babasahib gave Vasantiatya, which she gave me because she cannot read English too well, to Aai.*

4. *I leave my embroidery handkerchiefs made by Aai to Vasantiatya.*

5. *I leave Balu my fountain pen so that he will not be so lazy and learn to write.*

6. *I leave my small mirror to Vishnupant. When the barber does not come because he has body-ache, Vishnupant can hold it to his face and trim his moustache and nose hairs.*

7. *I leave the photograph of Aai and me when I was three years old taken by Shridharmama in front of Shivaji Park pond to Baba.*

8. *I leave the pressed jacaranda blossom in my dictionary to my Poona Aji. To my Poona Ajoba I leave all my ayurvedic tonics because Aji told Aai that the muscles inside his head are becoming weak.*

9. *I leave my history textbook to Shridharmama because he is always asking Aai to explain this and that.*

10. *I leave the thick, patchwork quilt (made by Poona Aji) to Bayabai. She is always walking with a limp in cold weather because her hip hurts.*

This will witnessed by—Hansa and Balu.

Hansa had signed her name in her characteristically untidy handwriting, and Balu had copied the letters of his name—which Mohini had written for him in English in block letters—next to Hansa's in a wavering hand.

"What are you reading, Mohini?"

Mohini looked up. Her cousins had returned from their stroll. "Where's Aai?" she asked.

"We passed her on our way back. She won't be long, she said," Swati replied.

"Can I see what you are reading?" Shobha asked, holding out her hand. Mohini hesitated for a moment, then passed her the will. The girls crowded around Shobha and read the piece of paper, peering over her arms. When they were finished they looked at Mohini.

"The things you do, Mohini!" Swati said.

"I've never seen Induaji's emerald brooch," Shobha said.

"Well, it is not made with real emeralds. When someone presented it to Vishnupant at the university, he gave it to Induaji. It looks like a sheaf of wheat, but it is made of small green stones."

"Item number six—what mirror?" Swati asked, looking up from the will.

"That was also Induaji's. Vishnupant said I could keep it. It's made out of steel. If you look into it, the reflection is very sharp, but it does not show colours properly."

Bharati took the will from Shobha's hands.

"The Helen Keller book is the one that Kamalakaku lent Aai," Bharati said.

"Did Sudhakaku read it?" Mohini asked.

Bharati shook her head. "But Swati did. She could not put it down. What do you mean, Shridharmama is always asking Aai to explain things?"

"He's much better now. But before, whenever he stayed

for dinner and Baba and Vishnupant discussed politics or history, he would not know what to say because he did not know most of the time what they were talking about. But the next time he came back, he would remember to ask Aai to explain this and that." Mohini grinned at the memory.

"How come you never left us anything?" Shobha asked.

"Shobha!" Swati remonstrated.

There was silence. Shobha dug a line in the sand with her heel. Suddenly, she knelt down and threw her arms around Mohini. When she moved back, her eyes were full, threatening to spill onto her cheeks. She turned away quickly and reached for her handkerchief that had slipped deep inside her bodice.

"Don't," Mohini, Bharati, and Swati cautioned together. But it was too late. She had already pulled out the handkerchief. The mehndi on her right hand was most likely smudged underneath the leaves. The girls looked at her, expecting the tears to well up again. But she smiled bravely and looked away and waved to Kamala, who was taking shape in the distance.

TWENTY-TWO

On the morning of the wedding, Mohini, Keshav, and Vishnupant stood in the back verandah, inspecting a courtyard that had over three days been transformed into a marriage hall. A white cloth had been stretched overhead to form a ceiling and the centre podium on which the ceremonial fire would be lit was being decorated with flowers. Kamala and Vasanti were hanging marigold streamers along the edge of the podium and Balu was disentangling the rose garlands, which the bride and groom would slip over each other's head.

The inspection party moved to the kitchen. The cooks had begun their chopping and peeling, and there was a smell of hot milk and coffee laced with cardamom and sugar as someone stirred a large steaming vessel over the stove. Bayabai had retreated across the lane to Vasanti's. A tall man, his chest and abdomen gaunt and concave, poured three cups of coffee and handed them to Mohini, Keshav, and Vishnupant. They went to the sitting room and sipped from their cups while sitting on the sofas and armchairs that had been pushed against the walls. A cotton dhurrie was spread on the floor to accommodate the guests.

The heady fragrance of the tuberoses standing tall in brass vases filled the room.

In the front verandah, Vasanti was supervising Balu as he stood two stalks of banana leaves on either side of the front door. On the floor lay the bunch of mango leaves that would be hung from the lintel before the guests arrived. The shoe stand had been moved away, as had the chairs. When Balu was finished, he handed Vasanti a three-compartment box, which contained red, green, and white powders. Vasanti sat back on her haunches and prepared to draw on either side of the door ancient symbols that represented fertility, good fortune, and abundance. She pinched the white rangoli powder between her middle fingers and thumb, and holding her hand steady, she defined on the swept floor a lotus, a swastika, a coconut, an elephant. She allowed Mohini to dot the designs with the red and green powders, saying, "Use the powders to enhance the beauty of the symbols. Other than that there are no rules as to which colour goes where."

After the entrance was decorated, all but Vishnupant went upstairs to change. Every Divali Kamala bought Vasanti a new sari, and this year Vasanti had preserved hers in the box in which it had come in order to have something new to wear for the wedding. She lifted the lid of the box now and removed the sari. It was made of cotton, with a small white-on-white check pattern, its thin black border accented by pale yellow thread woven into a design resembling fish scales. It was the first time Vasanti would be wearing a five-yard sari. Mohini was glad. She did not like nine-yard saris because she had seen too many women with broad hips and thick calves wear them. Draped the way they were, with the front of the sari brought back between the legs and tucked into the waist at the back, the hips had a tendency to look like fat gourds, the legs like tree trunks. But more to the point, nine-yard saris were old-fashioned. Mohini didn't mind Kamala's wearing them inside the house or when going to the Jijabai Samaj, but she pleaded with her to wear a five-yard sari when she came to school for a function or when Balu had gone to his village and she brought Mohini her lunch. Kamala had always obliged.

Mohini opened her wardrobe door and, standing behind it, changed into her peacock blue parkar-polka. Vasanti came out of the bathroom. She stood in front of the mirror and peered into her face. She raised one eyebrow, then the other, and ran her tongue over her teeth. She smiled and, glancing sideways at her profile, adjusted the end of her sari that fell over her left shoulder.

Mohini came out from behind the wardrobe door and said, "Vasantiatya, just for today, for my sake, will you not wear a single strand of pearls?"

Vasanti gave a start. "I didn't know you were there."

"So, you will wear it for me?"

Mohini could tell her aunt was tempted, but Vasanti shook her head. "This gold chain is fine. It's bad enough you talked your mother into giving me this five-yard sari."

"The pearls in Aai's strand are not even big. It is not as if you are exchanging your chain for a heavy gold or dia- mond necklace."

Kamala came into the room. "Mohini! Can't you see you are bothering your aunt?" Her tone was sharp. "Go quickly and see what jewellery you want to wear. Baba is waiting to return the jewellery box to the safe. Lay whatever you want carefully on the bed in full view so nothing will drop to the ground or get entangled in the bedcover. Now, go."

"It's all right, Kamalavahini," Mohini heard Vasanti say. "She just wanted me to wear the pearls. After all, it is the very first wedding in the next generation."

Although Vasanti did not ask Kamala not to be so hard on Mohini, Mohini knew that that was what her tone implied. She waited for Kamala to say something, but her mother was silent.

Once, many years ago, Vasanti had accused Kamala of being too strict with Mohini. They were on the swing and Mohini was sitting in the windowsill in her room, within earshot but out of sight.

Kamala had not replied.

"When Mohini emptied that water over Bayabai's head," Vasanti continued tentatively, "you were so cross with her. You've seen, we've all seen, how Bayabai nags her, useless little things. I know Mohini should not have done what she did. But you scolded her soundly and even made her touch Bayabai's feet in front of all of us."

"You want to know why I am so strict with Mohini?" Kamala said. "Because, if I allow her leeway on account of her illness, if I allow her to make her abnormal health an excuse for bad behaviour, then it will not be long before she will lose respect for herself and slide into self-pity. And if that happened, I would never forgive myself. She is only a child and it is up to me to make sure that I bring her up in such a way as to allow her to grow up with dignity and character."

"It was not my place to criticize—"

"What if something happens to me?" Kamala continued, ignoring the interruption. "She will then be at the mercy of someone who will have to perform all the duties that I, her mother, perform. I know what you want to say, Vasanti: 'But I am here, Kamalavahini, am I not?' Yes, you are here, and you will willingly take my place. But day in, day out, year in, year out—only a mother has a mother's heart, a mother's patience. It is not enough that whoever is looking after her in my absence stay the course because of a sense of duty. To stay the course because of a sense of pity would be infinitely worse. No, I am strict with her because when people visit her, ask after her, nurse her, are drawn to her, it is not out of pity or a sense of obligation, but because of her strength of character, the generosity of her heart, the sharpness of her mind. If I am to go before her, she must be able to live her life with her head held high."

Mohini slipped on the pearl bangles, afterwards holding out her wrist to Keshav so he could fasten the small gold screw. "You choose the necklace," she said to him. He picked up a string of pearls with a tiny crescent pendant studded with diamonds.

"Does it not match?" he asked triumphantly.

Mohini nodded and he fastened it around her neck. "This belonged to your grandmother," he said. "Pearls looked beautiful against her dark skin. Take out the diamond solitaire earrings and I will put away the box."

While slipping on the earrings, Mohini said, "Was it the most unexpected thing that ever happened to you—Induaji passing away so suddenly?" Mohini's grandmother had died in her maiden home in Belgaum of complications arising from a heat stroke.

Keshav nodded. "If only the onset hadn't been so sudden," he said. "Countless people survive heat strokes. But I'll always be grateful for one thing—she knew you were on the way. Your mother thinks your grandfather indulges you? Your Induaji would have been worse!"

Mohini dropped her hands to her side and stood up. "How do I look?" she asked.

"Like the darling that you are."

Mohini went to her room. Vasanti was sitting on the bed watching Kamala get dressed.

"Aai," Mohini said, "why are you not wearing the new sari Baba bought you for Divali?"

"I don't have a matching blouse."

"Since when have you started wearing matching blouses, Kamalavahini?" Vasanti said.

"Change, Aai," Mohini urged, as Keshav walked into the room. Mohini looked at him to back her up, but he was silent.

"I'll change into the new sari later," Kamala said. "Right now I must go downstairs. Guruji has been asking for the silverware all morning. Vasanti, will you lend me a hand? Mohini, mind you don't pull on your necklace or bangles. They are very delicate. If you feel too hot and they begin to bother you, give them to Baba to keep in his pocket."

"You should tell her to change, Baba." Mohini nudged Keshav.

Without replying he tucked her walking stick under his arm, gave her his hand, and together they followed Kamala and Vasanti downstairs.

Mohini was in Vishnupant's room when the guests started to arrive. Bharati and Shobha were straightening the pleats of Swati's sari. Swati looked at Mohini and smiled. She made a circle with her right thumb and forefinger, running her eyes up and down Mohini's parkar-polka to indicate how pretty it was. There was a dark line of kohl inside Swati's lower eyelids that accentuated the crescent shape of her eyes. Her face was slightly flushed and now and again she ducked her head, and when she looked up, there was a lingering smile on her face. She asked to see Mohini's mehndi, which had turned a beautiful red. And since the boy's side were yet to arrive, she held up her palms and bared her ankles to relatives who asked to see her bridal design. She looked at ease today, her eyes intermittently drawn to the window.

Bharati was the first to spot the bridegroom. "Swatitai! Here he comes!" she whispered.

Without haste, Swati sat back on the bed and patiently waited for the preliminary religious ceremonies to begin.

Mohini went and sat in the chair next to Vishnupant in the back verandah. Guests continued to filter through the house and into the marquee. After a while, Keshav came up to Mohini and told her that she should take one of the seats in front of the podium before they got filled up.

"Are you coming, Vishnupant?" she asked.

"You go on. I can see better from here," he said.

Mohini took a seat in the front row.

The previous evening at the prenuptial religious ceremony, the groom had introduced himself to Mohini. "You can call me Aniruddhadada," he said, "since you call Swati Swatitai. Dr. Chitnis has told me all about you."

Mohini smiled. She had been watching him during the ceremony. His face was narrow; a bushy moustache lined his upper lip. His hairline was receding into a widow's peak and his well-defined eyebrows seemed to have a life of their own, even when he was not speaking.

"Are you sure you are Mohini?" he said, a hint of doubt and laughter in his voice. "The Mohini I have heard about is quite talkative."

Before she could reply, Sudha came and took him away, telling him that there was someone else she wanted him to meet. Now, he came and took his seat on the podium. He glanced around, and when his eyes met Mohini's, he smiled.

Seated across the aisle from Mohini was a lady who was fanning herself with the end of her sari. Although the morning was temperate, her cheeks were flushed. She looked at Mohini and her smile was so warm that Mohini smiled back. Her cream-coloured sari was plain and simple, but it looked crisp and fresh against her dark complexion. Her hands, as she fluttered the end of her sari in front of her neck, were small and delicate, in contrast to the rest of her, which was plump and well endowed.

"Our bangles are similar," she said to Mohini, stopping the motion of her arms and displaying her wrists.

Mrs. Pendse, Keshav's mathematics schoolteacher, took the empty seat next to the lady. She leaned forward and looked at Mohini and said, "I see the two of you have already met."

"Not quite," the lady with the identical bangles said. "I know who Mohini is, but she does not know who I am."

"This is my niece, Mohini. She is also the groom's aunt. Her name is Charulata Pradhan."

Mohini remembered Mrs. Pendse's telling her father that Mrs. Pradhan had lost her husband and her infant son in a train derailment.

Mrs. Pendse started to say, "Keshav said he has met—"

"Your parkar-polka is lovely," Mrs. Pradhan interrupted.

"Aai made it," Mohini said.

"Your mother must be very talented," Mrs. Pradhan said.

"You should see her embroidery, Charu," Mrs. Pendse said. "And it was Kamala—Mohini's mother—who made the generous offer of Koleshwar Nivas because all the regular marriage halls were booked up."

Shridhar came and sat in the empty chair next to Mohini, to her left. An Oek member of the family, sitting to the other side of him, said, "It will be your turn next, Shridhar. Has the wedding date been set?"

Shridhar shrugged. "The original idea was to get married last August. In July, it was discovered that Suhasini's grandfather would have to get his gallstones removed. Since there were no suitably auspicious days for the operation until the beginning of December, Suhasini's parents said they wanted to wait until after the operation before fixing a marriage date. Now, their guruji says there is no auspicious wedding day until sometime in June, so they want a formal engagement."

"I thought you were already engaged," the Oek relative said.

"We didn't have a religious ritual. So, January 30 will be the day when Suhasini and I will become officially engaged."

"You have to have patience in these matters, Shridhar," the Oek cousin, a bachelor, advised with a chuckle.

Mohini nudged Shridhar. Shridhar leaned forward and picked up a handful of the coloured rice grains from the big steel plate Shobha was holding out in front of him. When she moved away down the aisle, he saw Charulata Pradhan was looking his way. She smiled at him. He swiftly sat back in his chair.

"Do you know her?" Mohini softly asked. "When Mrs. Pendse came to see Baba, she told him that she was one of the first batches of women to graduate from Poona Engineering College."

Shridhar said, "It's hot, Mohini. I'm going to find a pedestal fan so I can stand in front of it."

Before Mohini could tell him there were no pedestal fans because Sudha had decided that there was no need to rent any, he walked away towards the verandah. Vasanti was standing behind Vishnupant in the doorway of the end room. Mohini pointed to the chair left vacant by Shridhar and motioned for her aunt to come sit next to her.

"I'm all right here," Vasanti indicated with her hands, retreating farther into the room.

People stood up. Sudha's youngest brother was leading Swati to the centre of the podium where two gurujis were holding up a royal blue silk stole, intricately embroidered with gold thread. Aniruddha stood on one side of it, and now Swati took her place on the other. The gurujis held the stole so that it stretched like a curtain between the bride and the groom. The musicians stopped playing in preparation for the singing of the mangalashtaka.

Sudha's sister, who had a reputation of possessing the sweetest voice, began on the wrong note, then corrected herself by starting the first line all over again. Two fat boys in the audience tittered, covering their mouths with their hands. The mangalashtaka were rhyming verses especially composed by Sudha's brother-in-law for this occasion. They extolled Swati's virtues and those of her parents, who had been given the important responsibility of raising her in such a way that would one day enable her to become a dutiful wife.

When the verses came to an end, the gurujis resumed their chanting and brought the more significant part of the ceremony to a conclusion. The stole-curtain was lowered and the bridegroom garlanded the bride and she in turn garlanded him, and all those who had been preserving their handful of rice grains for this moment sent them flying in a torrent on top of the bride's and bridegroom's heads. Swati looked up, her expression demure and poised.

TWENTY-THREE

Mohini joined the circle of Oeks that was gathered at the back of the marquee. They ran their hands over her cheeks and asked her how she was and complimented her mother for the good job she had done with the wedding arrangements. Most of them had travelled from Poona to Bombay. Because there was no proper marriage hall and Vinod's flat was too small to accommodate out-of-town relatives, they had woken up at three that morning, in order to catch the five o'clock train.

One of her second cousins vacated her chair for Mohini. Mohini lowered herself and then shifted to one side so her cousin could sit as well. There wasn't enough space on the chair for both of them. Her cousin suggested Mohini sit on her lap. "Do you remember me?" she said. "I'm Naina."

"Of course I remember you," Mohini said.

Naina's lap was soft and her arms as they circled Mohini were dimpled and plump. She lightly touched the diamond of plaster inside Mohini's elbow and asked her whether it hurt.

"It doesn't if I pull it off quickly," Mohini said. She removed the plaster and scrunched it into a ball between her fingers.

"I meant the transfusion itself. Does the needle hurt?"

Mohini shook her head and looked up.

Someone was saying how cool and crisp Poona had become, now that it was winter, and what a pleasure it was to sit in the verandah after lunch, to bask in the sun's warming rays. Someone else remarked how very hot it had been on the day Keshav and Kamala were married, triggering off a discussion about other family functions and get-togethers.

When Vishnupant joined the circle, one of his cousins told him how on each subsequent visit to Bombay the city appeared to be rapidly changing, its population constantly on the rise. More buildings, more people, more noise, more cars.

Vishnupant said, "When we moved into Koleshwar Nivas, in 1933, there was no road in front of our house, only a footpath lined by gulmohur trees. That's how Mohur Lane got its name. Do you see any gulmohur trees now? All were cut down when they turned the path into a tar road."

"There is still one tree left," a young man said.

Mohini knew the one he was referring to. It stood directly opposite the side entrance of their school. The tree blossomed in the summertime, and Hansa never walked past it without collecting in her palms the flame-coloured flowers that had drifted to the ground. There were dried petals in Mohini's dictionary, the pages between which they were pressed, a mild saffron-pink.

Another cousin said that he agreed with Vishnupant, that Shivaji Park was, indeed, losing its trees. When he and his family had walked from the railway station to Koleshwar Nivas that morning, there was no shade to be found alongside the road.

Vishnupant said, "Around the time Koleshwar Nivas was built, the nearest street lamp was at the corner of Cadell Road and Ranade Road Extension. If the man in charge of lighting the lamp was late, he would be soundly scolded by the mothers who would say to him, 'Aren't you aware of your duty? When you light your lamp, it is a signal for our children to come indoors. What if a snake or a scorpion or a rat bites them? Who will take responsibility then? You?'"

"Are there snakes here still?" Naina asked.

Vishnupant looked at her. "They get flushed out every time a different property is prepared for construction. Koleshwar Nivas was the first cement structure in this neighbourhood. Around us were properties in which stood hundred-year-plus homes that were made of mud bricks with red Manglori roof tiles and palm trees that had been planted to keep the sandy soil from shifting."

"I wonder if you remember, Vishnu," a relative said, the same man who had not found shade that morning. "The one summer when I was here and we went to the Kulkarnis' across the lane because the grandfather had been asking for tobacco. There was a peaceful demonstration and all the shops were closed. They had buffaloes in their backyard and the old man was sitting on the edge of the well, talking to them, when we went up to him with the packet of beedies."

Vishnupant nodded. "The sound of their bellowing was familiar until they sold that side of the property to a developer who built Shiv Sadan. I also remember every property had a rooster. Each rooster could be identified by the cry it emitted at daybreak."

"Is all this true?" Naina whispered into Mohini's ear.

"Vishnupant"—Mohini raised her voice teasingly—"Naina doesn't believe you!"

"And why should she? Everything is changing so rapidly. Tomorrow's generation will say, 'What nonsense are my parents and grandparents talking? Why do we not see a single trace of the life they describe?'"

"Don't forget to tell them," Mohini reminded her grandfather, "about how at night people would—"

"That's Mohini's favourite memory," Vishnupant said. "Because there were very few street lights in those days, if anyone was returning home after dark, he would call out something to the owners of the various properties he had to pass in order to let them know that it was not a stranger walking by their property but a neighbour. There were very few cars then, and the smallest rustle from the direction of the lane sounded like a footfall. If Keshav's friend, Dadu Patil, was returning home late, he would call out as he walked past Koleshwar Nivas, 'How are you, Vishnukaka? You can let Keshav know I'm home.'"

"What if it wasn't anyone from the neighbourhood?" Naina's younger brother asked.

"If we heard footsteps without a greeting, then someone would call out to his neighbour and say, 'Gangadhar, are you expecting company?' And if Gangadhar was not, he would call out to his neighbour and so on until the man was identified."

"Were there any thieves?" someone asked.

"I remember one time a bhangi, a sweeper, from behind Crown Mills was caught trying to break into a house. That too in the middle of the day. The women of the household wanted the man to be taught a lesson. But the men released him with a simple warning." Vishnupant turned to his granddaughter. "Mohini, see if we can have something to drink. All this talk is making me thirsty."

Mohini got off Naina's lap. After passing on the message to Balu to bring out a tray of coffee, she went to Vishnupant's bathroom. There was a lineup of people waiting to use it. She went upstairs to her own.

"How was I supposed to know that one day she would be here, in Koleshwar Nivas?" Keshav's voice drifted in from the terrace, through the bathroom window. He was speaking softly and Mohini had to strain her ears to catch his words. "I didn't even know she was Sumatibai's niece until Sumatibai told me. Under the circumstances, what was I expected to do?"

Before Mohini could wonder to whom her father was talking, Shridhar said, "You should have thought about all this first, Keshav. Before it all began." His voice was harsh. Mohini gave a start. The swing creaked. One of them must have pushed heavily against the terrace floor with his feet.

"Does Kamala know?" Shridhar asked.

At the mention of her mother, Mohini's heart began to race. She lowered herself on the seat.

"I know Madanlal told her something, but she refuses to tell me his exact words. Knowing him, he must have simply hinted at what happened without giving any particulars. I think if Kamala knew more, she would have accused me with the details—"

"Why don't you just get rid of Madanlal?" Shridhar said.

"I have made arrangements for him to be assigned to the Works in Parel so he doesn't have to report to me or to my Fort office. I wanted him here for the wedding because

he knows most of the out-of-town relatives. I could tell
him to pick them up from the bus and railway stations
without needing to send Vasanti or someone else with
him." Keshav sounded weary. "I've already had a word
with Madanlal regarding the other business. I told him
that he has caused enough mischief and that Kamala
knows everything, and if he thought he could blackmail
me, then he was mistaken."

"Did he believe you?"

Keshav must have nodded because Shridhar did not
repeat his question or make any other remark.

Downstairs, a baby started to cry, and a few minutes
passed before it could be hushed. Shridhar was saying
something, but Mohini could not make out his words.

Keshav said, "I remember it was dusk and we walked
into a small clearing, which the trees had turned into a
bower. The last of the birds were flying home, the moon
was a silver crescent and night was unfolding slowly, like a
paper fan. The drone of the insects, the rustle of our
clothes, the treetops swooning against the sky . . ." Keshav
tapered off. Laughter floated up from the gathering below.

"That's hardly an . . ." Shridhar began, but Mohini
could not catch the end of his sentence. She shifted
slightly on the seat so that she was just a little bit nearer
the window.

"It's lonely, she said," Keshav was saying. "No husband,
no son, only a mother-in-law who has never recovered
from the shock."

"And?"

"And nothing, Shridhar. It was an interlude. It's finished now!" Keshav said. "It's never going to happen again.

She works for the railways and the collaboration with B & J was a one-time project."

"I suppose so," Shridhar said.

Mohini stretched her spine and sat upright in disbelief. Somewhere in the conversation, her uncle's tone had turned from berating to neutral to curious to accepting, as though now he wanted to know only the details. Whose side was he on?

"Keshavdada!" Vasanti called out, as Mohini heard footsteps entering the terrace through the upstairs back verandah. "They're about to serve the first lunch sitting. Kamalavahini wants you to look after the boy's side to make sure everything is running smoothly."

"Where's Vinod?" Shridhar said.

"I've sent Balu to look for him. Kamalavahini is in the kitchen. Sudhavahini is the only person from the immediate family who is there."

"Where's Vishnupant?" Keshav said.

"Are you coming or not?" Vasanti asked impatiently. "And what are the two of you doing upstairs when you should be attending to the guests?"

A cramp had taken hold of Mohini's big toe. She tried to wiggle it. She couldn't. She let the water trickle down between her legs. She prayed they would not hear her as they passed the bathroom: everything was so still. She was rinsing the soap off her hands when she remembered something Keshav had earlier assured Kamala: *But the facts don't exist.*

Mohini walked down the stairs carefully, lifting the bottom edge of her parkar with her left hand so as to keep it from becoming entangled between her legs. With her right she clutched the railing, aware that her fingers were numb and cold.

The chairs in front of the podium had been cleared and low sitting stools were laid out in rows, a banana leaf in front of each stool. Servers were going down the row, putting on every banana leaf the items each was carrying in his serving bowl: salt, half of a quartered lime, a teaspoon of curds, chili pickle, cucumber salad, fried brinjal-and-potato fritters, curry made of alu leaves and daal, curried cabbage, vaal lentils, rice, varan, and ghee. The smell of chili pickle made Mohini's mouth water.

She glanced down the rows. The boy's side were seated, with the addition now of Swati who sat next to Aniruddha, to his right. The kohl was smudged around her eyes. Her forehead was orange and yellow where so many women had dotted it with turmeric and red kunku before handing her their wedding presents. She had changed from her heavier yellow sari into a lighter one. She caught Mohini's eye and pointed to an empty place opposite her.

"I can't sit cross-legged on the low stool," Mohini said, pointing to her legs.

When the servers had finished serving the last of the five sweetmeats, Vishnupant shouted out the grace, "Har! Har! Mahadev!" and everyone began to eat. Keshav and Vinod went between the rows and urged all the seated guests not to be shy and eat to their heart's content. Sudha and Kamala walked down the aisle with sweetmeats, heaping generous second portions onto the emptying banana leaves.

Swati, Mohini could tell, was quite exhausted, and she barely picked at her food. But when it was time for the bride and groom to feed a mouthful from their own banana leaves to each other, she boldly said a prepared rhyme, which contained Aniruddha's name, and picking up a large ladoo, she stuffed it playfully into the bridegroom's mouth. When he had finished swallowing it, he returned the favour by pressing into her mouth a large coconut karanji, the largest he could find. Everyone laughed. When urged by his family to say a rhyme containing Swati's name, he turned to his sister. She whispered something into his ear. He held up his hand and everyone stopped talking. He repeated slowly the words his sister had said:

I put down my scalpel and
waited for a change of tide,
And it was sweetest fortune
when Swati was swept to me
And became my bride.

The wedding guests clapped their hands and some giggled, shocked by the boldness of the rhyme. Swati ducked her head and blushed and continued to look into her lap as the servers resumed their rounds and everyone went back to eating. And the next time Mohini looked at Swati, the banana leaf in front of her was empty and she was pushing back her low stool.

After the people in the first lunch sitting were finished eating, Kamala and Mohini stood in the verandah, handing out a vida filled with lime paste, betel nut, cloves, cardamoms, catechu, and fresh coconut to guests who had washed their hands.

When Aniruddha's parents came to receive their vida, Kamala introduced Mohini to them. "They've been asking to meet you since yesterday, Mohini," she added.

Mr. Gokhale said, "We keep hearing about you from Dr. Chitnis. You know he was Aniruddha's professor at Grant Medical College." He turned to Kamala and put out his hand to bring forward the lady who was standing to one side of him. "I don't think you have met my sister, Charulata Pradhan."

Mohini's walking stick clattered to the ground.

"What is it?" Kamala asked, taking Mohini's hand. Mohini's lips were dark, her complexion ashen.

"I'm hungry," she muttered.

"I'll get you something to eat," Kamala said, smiling at Charulata as she handed the stainless steel plate holding the vida to Bharati, then moved away in the direction of the kitchen.

Vasanti led Mohini to the end of the verandah where she could sit and get some fresh air. Mohini glanced sideways at the door leading into the house. Charulata Pradhan was slipping her feet into her sandals as she prepared to leave Koleshwar Nivas with her aunt.

Kamala climbed the shallow verandah stairs and placed a plate of food on the table in front of Mohini and told her to eat. "I must see to the rest of the guests," she said, hurrying away.

When Aniruddha walked up to Mohini, Vasanti quietly left. He pulled forward a chair, its back towards Mohini, and stretching one leg over its seat, straddled it. "You must not allow yourself to go hungry," he said, wagging a finger at her. "Hypoglycemia is no good."

"Dr. Chitnis already told me," Mohini murmured.

He smiled at her. Mohini noticed his cheeks were deeply dimpled. "Start eating!" he said. He sat with her patiently, silent, until the last grain of rice was finished and only the husk of the squeezed-out half-quartered lime remained. Swati brought Mohini a pitcher of water.

"Can I get you anything else?" she asked.

"No. You should wash your face," Mohini whispered into Swati's ear when she was pouring out the water into a glass. "Your forehead is all coloured."

"That's exactly what I said to your Swatitai," Aniruddha said.

Swati blushed and moved away.

After drinking deeply from her glass, Mohini rinsed her hands into her plate with the water that remained.

"I see you have a very good appetite," Aniruddha said.

"Very!"

His face became serious. "Dr. Chitnis says your headaches have increased after your meningitis attack. You are also getting body ache."

Mohini nodded. Kamala came forward and passed Mohini a towel.

Aniruddha looked at Kamala and said, "I don't know whether Dr. Chitnis mentioned this to you, but I suggested to him that Mohini try some homeopathic medicine. He agreed that it wouldn't be a bad idea." He turned to Mohini. "I understand you don't like to take medication every time you have a headache because it makes your stomach feel queasy?"

"And because it doesn't always work."

"So, would you be willing to try homeopathy for all your aches?"

Mohini hesitated and looked at her mother.

"Why don't you give the new medicine a try?" Kamala said. "It might bring you some relief."

"There is this friend of mine who is a homeopathic doctor," Aniruddha said. "He lives quite close, on the other side of Cadell Road. His name is Ramesh Natu and he's here today, although I don't see him now or I would have introduced him to you."

"It's all right," Mohini said. "I don't have to meet him today."

"I'll make an appointment for you then." Aniruddha pushed back his chair. "One other thing. Do you mind if I accompany Dr. Chitnis when he next comes to examine you?"

"He doesn't examine me on a regular basis. He does that only when something is wrong. Otherwise, he comes to take my blood in order to find me a match before a transfusion. And then for the transfusion itself."

"Do you mind if I come with him for the transfusion, then?"

"I don't mind," she said. "And if your hand is as light as his is, you can even administer it."

"Agreed. Now I think I'd better go and see if I can find a sofa to stretch out on. I ate too much!" He stood up, smiled at her, and followed Kamala into the sitting room.

A sharp pang tugged on Mohini's heart, a quiver of envy for Swati, who had returned to the verandah, her face washed and shining.

TWENTY-FOUR

Two days after the wedding, Aniruddha rang the doorbell of Koleshwar Nivas and handed Kamala a chit of paper on which was written Ramesh Natu's address, and the time and date of Mohini's appointment. Kamala pressed him to have a cup of tea but he declined, saying he was already late for work.

Dr. Natu's consultation rooms were located at the bottom end of one of the lanes leading from Cadell Road towards the sea. On the afternoon of Mohini's appointment, Bhaskar, Keshav's new driver, opened the car door for Mohini and Kamala, outside the clinic. He pressed downwards with his hands the air in front of him to indicate that he would wait in that spot until the appointment was finished. He had just arrived in Bombay from Kerala and could not utter a single word of Marathi or Hindi. He was very short, and when he was behind the wheel of the car, to give him some height, he placed under him on the seat an old eiderdown that he had obtained from Balu.

Mohini and Kamala waited until they had walked through the front gate of Dr. Natu's property before grinning at each other: after Madanlal, the courteous, open-faced Bhaskar was a breath of fresh air, a miracle, a find.

A path led to the front steps of the house. On one side was a circular bed filled with white flowers, on the other stood large wooden tubs holding various varieties of hibiscus.

Kamala and Mohini removed their sandals outside the front entrance and walked in through the wide-open double doors. The stone floor was cool under their feet. If this was the waiting room, there were no patients. The seating arrangement was Indian style; the mattresses placed on low divans, the large cushions, the bolsters, were all covered in clean, white sheets. The walls were a pale pistachio green. There was not a soul in sight. Opposite the door through which they had entered was another leading out into the back verandah. Kamala stepped out, Mohini close behind her.

There was a tulsi-house in the courtyard, next to which stood a life-sized statue of the monkey-god Maruti, from whose head sprouted two saffron flags. Sunbirds were flying in and out of the spreading rain tree, their busy twittering not masking the sound of pounding that was coming from one of the rooms to the right. Someone was making goda masala: the delicious aroma of coriander, sesame seeds, black pepper, cumin, and chilies filled the air.

"I don't think we are in the right place," Kamala whispered.

They turned around and came face to face with a man so pale and gaunt that it took Kamala a moment to collect herself. "We were given this address for Dr. Natu's clinic," she said.

"Did you not read the sign outside?" the man asked. His voice was as bloodless as his face.

Kamala faltered.

"Outside the front entrance with an arrow pointing to the left?" he said. He turned on his heels and they followed him through the sitting room, out the front door of the house, and to the right. At the end of the verandah he pointed to a square building with a flat cement roof.

"Dr. Natu sees his patients there," he said. He was still standing at the end of the verandah watching, when Kamala pushed open the door of the clinic and walked in. The waiting room was dark. Windows were cut into the upper half of the walls.

"Today, it is not patient day," said a man from inside a wooden cubicle to their left. There was a note of triumph in his voice, as though he was glad that their effort to keep their appointment would now be wasted. Kamala opened her purse and removed the chit Aniruddha had given her. After reading it, the man pointed silently to an inner door.

Inside his consultation room, Dr. Natu was sitting at his desk. Kamala said, "We did not realize today is not your patient day. We can always come back another time. Aniruddha Gokhale made the appointment for us."

"Come on in! I'm expecting you," Dr. Natu said, standing up. "Take a seat. You must be Mohini. I purposely said for you to come today because on regular patient days, at any given time, there are at least half a dozen patients waiting to see me."

After they were all seated, Mohini looked at Dr. Natu. He was not Aniruddha's age at all. His hair was quite grey and there were red blood spots on his neck and arms. He unscrewed the top of his fountain pen and opened a thick notebook to a clean page. He scribbled Mohini's name and the date. "Aniruddha has given me a good understanding of your medical history. The reason you are here, Mohini, is because of your headaches and body ache, is it not?"

She nodded. "Mostly headaches."

He readied his pen and said, "I'll make notes as you answer me. Let's start with the first question. Do you eat eggs?"

Kamala said, "Now and then. When her reserves are low and she seems particularly tired, I give her a raw egg."

Mohini grimaced.

"Cooked eggs taste much better," Dr. Natu said. "You boil them for five to ten minutes until the yolk is firm and then you unshell them and sprinkle lots of salt, pepper, some chili powder if you wish, before eating them with bread." He made the eggs sound tasty.

"Our cook is very particular," Kamala said. "I have to give Mohini egg on the terrace, far away from the kitchen."

"Life is full of unnecessary complications, is it not?" Dr. Natu said, removing his glasses and rubbing his eyes vigorously. His hands were long and lean like those of a surgeon.

"How frequent are your headaches?" he said, picking up the pen.

"Almost every day," Mohini said. "Sometimes they go away for a few days."

"What areas of your head are affected the most?"

"All areas."

"When are they the most acute? Morning, noon, night?"

"I can't say, but sometimes I wake up with a headache."

"Where does it ache then?"

"On the right side of my temple, behind my eye. Sometimes even my right ear feels as if it has a headache. Those headaches last for one or two or three days. One moment they are there, then suddenly they are gone."

"Apart from your tingling ear—I'm supposing it is a tingling sensation—do you experience any other kind of discomfort?"

"Sometimes I feel nauseated. And . . ."

"Yes?"

"I don't think it happens when I am having a headache, but sometimes it feels as if the whole world has become very sharp."

"What do you mean?" Kamala said.

Mohini looked at her and thought for a moment. "If you say, 'Here, take your tablet with this water,' I will put out my hand and swallow the tablet as usual, but to me it feels as if I am grabbing the glass from you, swallowing the tablet hastily, and the sounds of my swallowing will be very loud against my ears."

"You never told me this," Kamala said.

"Does everything seem to be more exaggerated at those times?" Dr. Natu said.

Mohini nodded slowly.

"Sounds, movements, smells?"

"I haven't noticed smells."

"How long do these exaggerated spells last?"

"Not long."

"Try and be more specific, Mohini," Kamala said.

"Well, when I used to get them in school, maybe part of one period."

"Next time you get this sensation, I want you to note whether it is preceded or followed by a headache."

There was a knock on the door. The man from behind the cubicle entered the room. "Can I go now?" he asked.

"And what if she needs medicine?"

The look on the man's face was stolid.

"Go. And make sure you lock the medicine cabinet and leave the keys in the big house."

The man withdrew.

Dr. Natu scanned the notes he had written thus far.

"Apart from the exaggerated feeling, anything else?"

Mohini looked at Kamala.

"You can tell the doctor anything you want," Kamala said.

"I get this whoosh-whoosh in my left ear sometimes when I am lying down. As if waves are breaking against my eardrum."

"Are they spaced at regular intervals?"

"Yes. Sometimes the whoosh seems louder, then it fades and becomes loud again."

"You didn't tell me, Mohini."

"You never asked me, Aai."

"Have you told Dr. Chitnis?" Kamala said.

"He didn't ask me either."

Kamala looked alarmed.

"It's her anemia," Dr. Natu said to Kamala. "Because Mohini's blood count is particularly low, her heart has to work harder. The whoosh that she then hears is the increased pumping action of the heart as it works to push the blood through her arteries and veins. Let's get back to your headaches, Mohini. Do you get them when you are particularly upset about something?"

Mohini looked at Kamala.

"Only you can answer that," Kamala said.

"No, not because I am upset."

Kamala said, "The times I have noticed she gets them is when she has gone for a long period without eating, or before her transfusions, or under the direct sun, or when she has been reading for too long."

"Tell me, Mohini, are you short-tempered?"

"No, I'm not."

"I expected you to say that. Let's ask your mother."

"She's not," Kamala confirmed.

"Do you get along with other members of your family?"

Mohini nodded.

"Do you quarrel with them?"

She shook her head.

"But you must disagree with them sometimes. You must argue—"

"But I don't quarrel," Mohini said resolutely.

"She becomes quiet when she is angry," Kamala said. "Won't say a word. She sulks."

Mohini glared at Kamala. How could her mother accuse her of sulking when she herself had specifically told Mohini that she would not tolerate her arguing with her elders?

"Watch out, Mohini," Dr. Natu said, "or you will show us that you can sulk."

Mohini ran her clammy hands against the front of her frock and deliberately looked away from Kamala.

"Food—is there anything in particular that does not suit your stomach?"

Mohini shook her head.

"How do you sleep?"

"All right. Baba says that since I have no activity and since I doze off during the day, I cannot expect to sleep through the night."

"Do you dream?"

"Sometimes."

"Do you remember your dreams afterwards?"

"Sometimes."

"Any recurring dreams?"

She shook her head.

"Menses?"

"Only once."

"Very little bleeding," Kamala added.

Dr. Natu pushed back his chair. "I will go through the information that Aniruddha has obtained from Dr. Chitnis regarding Mohini's thalassemia and I'll send you word when the medicine is ready."

Kamala opened her purse. "How much?" she murmured.

"When you send your driver or servant to pick up the medicine, the compounder will have the bill ready."

Mohini and Kamala stood up. "I'm grateful to you for seeing Mohini even if it is not your patient day," Kamala said.

"Not at all. Mohini, give your grandfather my regards. I introduced myself to him the day of Aniruddha's wedding."

At home, Mohini related to her grandfather Dr. Natu's message. "He is Pantoji Natu's son," Vishnupant said. "A stricter and more disciplined man I have yet to meet than Pantoji. He was a regular bridge player at the gymkhana before he passed away at the ripe old age of eighty."

"But Dr. Natu seems almost as old."

"It runs in their family," Vishnupant said. "They all have prematurely grey hair and ancient faces. Ramesh Natu's older brother looks like Pantoji's brother, not his son. So, what does your new doctor say?"

"He didn't take my pulse. He didn't listen to my back or chest. He didn't ask for my blood count. He didn't examine the glands around my neck. And if he had a stethoscope, I didn't see it." Her tone was dismissive.

"No one is going to topple Dr. Chitnis from his exalted position," Vishnupant said. "But you will give the new doctor's medicine a try, won't you?" Vishnupant wanted to tell her to keep a positive attitude but something in her expression said that she didn't need to be reminded.

"Dr. Natu did not check my blood pressure either," she added, before leaving his room.

TWENTY-FIVE

It was the season for marriages. The day after Dr. Natu's appointment, Balu received a short letter from his mother telling him that she had fixed the date for his marriage for the twenty-fourth of that month. Balu showed the letter to Kamala who, after reading it, passed it to Mohini.

"Your mother has beautiful handwriting," Mohini said.

"What, Mohinitai? Do you think my mother can read and write? There is this one man by the bus stop that everyone goes to when they want letters written."

Mohini read the letter again. "Your bride, Shevanti, have you met her?" she asked.

Balu nodded.

"How come you did not tell us?" Kamala said.

"There was nothing to tell, Kamalavahini. Our horoscopes had to match first, did they not? Before that, how could I say anything?"

"Do you want to get married?" Mohini said.

Balu grinned. "You will like her, Tai."

"The wedding is in less than two weeks time," Kamala said. "How long will you be gone this time?"

"Three or four days only," Balu said. "Narya has promised to come, and if he doesn't, I won't go."

Kamala smiled and said, "All I ask is that in the event your cousin does not show up, then please return on the day you say you will return. You can bring Shevanti back with you, if you like."

This time Narya, whom Kamala addressed by his full name, Narayan, was as good as his word. He came the night before Balu was to leave. Mohini had a headache, and she and Kamala were sitting in the terrace swing where Kamala was massaging into her scalp oil that had been previously boiled with curry leaves. They could hear Balu in the courtyard, itemizing for the benefit of his cousin all the jobs Narayan would be expected to do. Balu's last sentence was a threat: if his cousin did not do a good job, if there were any complaints about him from either Kamalavahini or anyone else in the house, then he, Balu, would not cough up the money he had promised to give Narayan for his services. If Narayan did make any assurances, they must have been of the silent kind because all Kamala and Mohini could hear in response was his spitting into the bush.

"Tobacco?" Mohini murmured.

"I'll have to tell Narayan that he cannot chew any while he is working here."

But Balu must have already told him because in the morning, when Narayan presented himself, his teeth were rinsed. And apart from the redness of catechu on his tongue from previous paan chewing, his mouth, every time he opened it during the following days, did not have the customary pinch of tobacco stuffed to one side of it. Balu's threat regarding his duties, however, was quickly forgotten.

Narayan was lethargic as he went through the motions of sweeping and mopping and ironing, and set to work without any order or plan. No one, not even Bayabai, reprimanded him for his sluggishness. "Some help is better than no help," she muttered to Kamala as she kneaded the dough.

At the end of the first day, while they were eating dinner, Narayan entered the dining room and said he would prefer to return to Wadala where he shared a small tin shack by the railway tracks with three other men from his village.

"Go if you must," Kamala said, "but have dinner before you leave. And have you finished turning down the beds?"

"I was just about to do that," Narayan said, leaving the dining room.

When Vishnupant left the table after he was finished, Bayabai complained to Kamala that Narayan ate too well. "For lunch he ate twice the amount that Balu eats and he adds much too much milk to his tea."

Kamala patiently said that his eating "too well" meant only that he was probably hungry most of the time, and now that he had the opportunity, he was making up for all the nights he had gone to bed on a half-empty stomach. Bayabai shrugged as she left the dining room. And later, when Mohini found some excuse to go into the kitchen at the time Bayabai was ladling food onto Narayan's plate, she noted that in spite of Bayabai's begrudging him his big appetite, the serving she was making was large and generous.

When Mohini reported this to her mother, Kamala said, "Bayabai's bark has always been worse than her bite. Now, are you going to tell me which clothes you want to take for Shridhar's engagement? I want to put them to one side so Balu can iron them as soon as he returns." She was in her dressing room, sorting out the saris she would be taking to Poona.

Balu came back on the day he said he would. He gave Mohini a newspaper bundle containing six ladoo made of puffed rice, chana daal, and jaggery. "My mother sent these especially for you," he said, trying very hard, but unsuccessfully, to control the grin that opened up his face every time he referred to his wedding.

"When will I get to see Shevanti?" Mohini asked, picking up a ladoo and biting into it.

"Soon," he said with a grin, and quickly brought in a high stool to remove from the top shelf of Mohini's wardrobe the bags Kamala had said they would be taking with them to Poona.

Kamala did not want to leave the packing until the very last moment when there was a likelihood of forgetting some item or the other. Everything, therefore, was ready to be loaded into the car a day prior to their departure. Dr. Chitnis came in the afternoon to administer Mohini's transfusion. It went smoothly, and by the time he had dismantled his equipment and instructed Balu to load it into his car, Kamala came upstairs with a large tray containing samples of various savoury and sweet preparations she had made to take with them to Poona. Mohini and Dr. Chitnis ate well, and before leaving he instructed her to have a good time at the engagement and to tell him all about it the next time he came to see her.

However, within an hour of Dr. Chitnis's leaving Koleshwar Nivas, Mohini's temperature began to rise. She told Kamala that she felt itchy everywhere and that her back was starting to ache. When Keshav came home in the evening, he reminded Mohini that this was the second episode of a reaction to a transfusion she had suffered in as many months. He was troubled. Mohini told him not to worry so much. "Aai has already given me medicine to reduce the fever," she said. "And another tablet for my backache."

All night long, every two hours on the hour, Kamala checked Mohini's temperature. The mercury hovered around 103 degrees, never dropping below that mark. Mohini's breathing became laborious, and every time Kamala asked her whether she needed a drink of water or a back rub, Mohini shook her head without opening her eyes. Then, towards the early morning hours, after a great deal of perspiring on Mohini's part, Kamala took her temperature again. The mercury had settled into its normal range.

"You and Baba go to Poona for Shridharmama's engagement," was the first thing Mohini said to Kamala after her mother gave her the latest thermometer reading. Mohini's eyes were clear, her voice was strong. "I'll be fine," she said.

"I'm not leaving you, Mohini, not in this condition." Kamala rinsed the thermometer in the bathroom basin and returned it to its case. Mohini had fallen asleep.

Looking at the wall clock, Kamala whispered to Balu, "It's six-thirty. Not too early to call Dr. Chitnis and let him know about Mohini. You wait with her while I go downstairs and make that phone call."

Balu finished sweeping the room, glancing at Mohini's chest now and again to make sure it was moving. He noted with satisfaction that her breathing was regular.

At eight o'clock, Shridhar rang the doorbell. When Balu informed him that Mohini had been ill, he hurried upstairs, clutching in his hands a large box of sugary sweetmeats Kamala had asked him to pick up to carry with them to Poona.

Mohini was awake and sitting up in bed.

"You better take the train to Poona, Shridhar," Kamala said as soon as she saw him. "We won't be able to come."

He went to Mohini and felt her forehead. "As cool as a cucumber," he said to her, removing his hand.

"That's what I told Aai, Shridharmama. All of you go. I'm fine now."

Kamala shook her head.

"I suppose I have no choice but to catch that train since it is my engagement," he said. He knew that Kamala's mind once made up had a tendency to stay made up and that it would be futile now, not to mention frustrating, to try and change it. He ran his fingers along Mohini's eyebrows.

"That feels good," she said.

He sat next to her on the bed. "When I return," he said, "I'll bring back some sweetmeats for you. All right?"

Mohini smiled.

One hour later, when Dr. Chitnis came over, Mohini's temperature was still normal. He took her blood pressure. It was only slightly elevated. "How is the nausea?" he asked her.

"I didn't have any this time," she said.

He told her to drink sweetlime juice, and because her body was still itching, he suggested she apply to her skin a generous amount of talcum powder.

"Dr. Chitnis," Mohini said. "Is it all right for Aai and Baba to go to Poona without me?"

"I don't see any reason to hold them back," he said, crossing his arms across his chest.

Mohini looked at her mother.

"Your father has gone to get some medicine. Let's see what he says when he comes back," Kamala said.

Mohini knew Kamala was stalling. She looked at Dr. Chitnis. Ever since Madanlal's departure Mohini had sensed a slight thaw in the way her parents addressed each other, and now she was eager for them to go to Poona together.

"It's all right if you go, Kamalavahini," the doctor said. "We're here, Vishnupant, Vasanti, and I." Before leaving the room, he told Mohini to keep track of her symptoms and to ask Balu to call him if anything changed.

Around ten o'clock, when Mohini was sitting up in bed once again, reading a book, Kamala finally relented. Vasanti got off the raised ledge of the terrace door, saying, "You better leave quickly if you are to make the four o' clock ceremony in good time. Meanwhile, I'll tell Bayabai to pack a tiffin carrier for your lunch." She hurried downstairs before Kamala could change her mind.

Mohini said, "Nothing is going to happen to me, Aai! And tell Aji I will definitely make it for the wedding."

"We'll try to be back tomorrow," Kamala said.

Keshav entered the room. "Kamala, Vasanti just told me to get ready to leave."

Kamala nodded.

He turned to Mohini and said, "Make sure you tell that temperature of yours not to rise. At least not until after we are back. Let's see . . . today is Friday, so we should return latest by Sunday evening. I expect your grandmother will insist that we spend an extra night."

———

By lunchtime, Mohini's temperature was on the rise again, and she was racked by chills. Vasanti heaped cotton blankets on her body and fed her from a tablespoon a steaming concoction Bayabai had prepared: lemon grass, cloves, garlic, a small quantity of onion, all brought to a boil. It was a bitter medicine, malodorous and unpalatable, but Mohini drank it without complaining.

"Shall I call Dr. Chitnis?" Vasanti said.

"No! And don't say anything to Vishnupant about my temperature. He'll worry unnecessarily. Especially since Aai and Baba are not here. Besides, you know how my temperature comes and goes during a reaction. By evening I'll be fine."

"No, I don't know how your temperature goes up and down, Mohini! And I didn't say anything to Vishnukaka when he asked me why you did not come down for lunch. I merely said you weren't feeling hungry."

"Did you send Balu for some lime? I'm beginning to feel a bit nauseated."

"He went and got some from the market, and while he was away, his cousin Ganpat's roommate came to fetch him. It seems Ganpat met with some kind of an accident in the granary. Nothing serious, but he has been admitted to hospital. So Balu's gone there."

"But Ganpat lives in Sewri."

"Balu did say he wouldn't be back until sometime tomorrow. He just left a few minutes ago."

Mohini told Vasanti that she wanted to go downstairs. "I don't feel cold any more. In fact, I'm hot and sweating. Also, my eyes are too sore to read and I'm fed up with playing rummy. Please, Vasantiatya? It's late afternoon and in the front verandah, at least I'll be able to see people."

Clutching her aunt's arm, Mohini made it down the stairs without feeling too faint. The medicine Dr. Chitnis had left for her had lowered her temperature but hadn't done anything for the weak, woolly feeling inside her limbs and head.

"Has Vishnupant gone to the gymkhana?"

"I think so. He's not in his room," Vasanti said, leaving the verandah.

Mohini leaned her walking stick against her chair. She looked across the lane. Nina and Mina's rabbits were on the roof of their hutch, and the sisters were sitting in the windowsill, their noses pressed against the iron lattice-work. They looked like monkeys from afar, their knees drawn up to their chests, their arms extended up to clutch the bars. Mohini turned her head. The Irani's tea shop was busy. She could hear the tinkling of cutlery against glass, and now and then the sound of a raised voice and muted laughter. Gulaam was sitting behind the counter at the till. Mohini shifted her gaze to the left. Mai was standing in their verandah. Mohini waved to her. On the floor above Mai, the Tikekar brothers had occupied their habitual evening spot in their east-facing balcony. Their wives were seated grandly on either side of them, their buns decorated with flower garlands, their expressions staid yet alert, as though posing for a family portrait.

The Marzellos' compound was dark. The family had locked up their house and left for Vasai just before the new year, hiring to look after the property a Nepalese Gurkha watchman who had moved into the shed behind the guava tree with his two dogs. Sometimes, Mohini could hear the dogs in the middle of the night, baying at the moon, or barking at someone or something, perhaps the large rats that still made their home in the lushness of the garden.

The hushed silence was broken by loud, piercing cries. Mohini turned swiftly to her left, the noise of running feet and alarmed shouting from the direction of Ranade Road Extension becoming stronger as a knot of men came into sight and dashed down the lane, in the direction of Shivaji Park. She strained forward as they ran past Koleshwar Nivas. "Bapuji . . . Bapuji," they called out, as they disappeared down the lane. Vasanti came out on the verandah and hurried to the front gate. People were exiting from the Irani's, scattering in various directions as soon as they stepped out. Mina and Nina were no longer in the windowsill and Mai was gazing at the sky, oblivious to the shouting men who could still be heard in the distance. There was a rasping sound as Gulaam started to pull down the steel shutters of the tea shop. He paused for a moment to let those still trapped inside crouch under the shutters and hurry away.

"It must be true," Vasanti said, walking up the shallow steps.

"What? I couldn't hear what the men were shouting. Only 'Bapuji! Bapuji!'"

Her aunt looked at Mohini, her eyes unnaturally big in her triangular face. "Gandhiji has been slain," she said, tears running down her cheeks. "That's what I heard them say from the kitchen. 'Bapuji is slain! Bapuji is slain!'"

"What do you mean?" Mohini asked. "Did someone kill

him? Is he dead?" She covered her mouth with her hand as she waited for Vasanti's reply.

"That's what those men were shouting."

The lane had become very quiet. Mohini wrapped her hands around her shoulders, suddenly furious at Vishnupant for going to the gymkhana when he knew she and Vasanti and Bayabai were all alone in the house.

Vasanti looked across the lane, at the Irani's tea shop. It was now fully shuttered. "It must be true," she repeated.

"Was it a Muslim, do you think?"

"I don't know, Mohini, I don't know. Let us pray not, or the bloodbath at the time of partition will seem like child's play."

Mohini shivered. Vasanti handed her the cooling cup of tea from the tray she had hastily deposited on the shoe stand. Mohini drank it quickly as Vasanti gulped hers.

"We should go in," Vasanti said.

"I prefer to wait here for Vishnupant."

Vasanti held out the ladoo to Mohini. The tears of shock that had run down her aunt's face had dried up. Apart from a breathy catch in her voice, she was now quite composed. Mohini ate absent-mindedly and kept her ears pricked up for Vishnupant's footfall. Across the lane, Mai had left the balcony, as had the Tikekar brothers and their wives. Vishnupant appeared under the corner street lamp, walking into his shadow as he crossed Mill Road.

"It was a man by the name of Nathuram Godse," were his first words as he entered the front verandah through the car porch. "A Chitpawan Brahmin from Poona. Gandhiji was shot three times on his way to a prayer meeting."

Mohini tried to get up but found she couldn't. The hollow

feeling she had felt ever since Kamala and Keshav had left was now sweeping through her whole body. "Aai, Baba?"

"I already thought of putting a call through. But your grandparents do not have a telephone. I could call Ashok, but he lives two miles away, and I don't know whether he will be able to get a message to Keshav. Not tonight. Do we have any other contact number?"

Vasanti and Mohini shook their heads.

Vishnupant removed his sandals and went to the sitting room. Mohini and Vasanti followed him in. They sat on the sofa, the silence from the lane spilling into the spaces between them. Mohini removed from her pocket the walnut-sized pink stone that Hansa had given her. She carried it around these days, hoping that one day more of its inner core would be revealed. She held it up to her eyes. The stone looked opaque, dull. Vasanti had switched on the single ceiling light, leaving the wall-mounted lamps unlit. The corners of the sitting room were dark. Even though Mohini wanted to ask her grandfather something, anything, just to break the silence, she could not think of a single thing to say. The world was spinning out of control and they could do nothing about it. Vishnupant was sitting upright on the sofa, his hands enclosing the handle of his walking stick planted firmly on the ground between his knees. Now and then he leaned back, only to sit forward again.

When Bayabai told them that dinner was served, they washed their hands and filed wordlessly into the dining room. The table was laid as usual, but Bayabai had left the plates empty. "I didn't know what everyone wanted to eat," she murmured, standing inside the doorway leading to the kitchen.

Vasanti asked Bayabai to bring out some rice. That's all they could manage to eat that night: rice mixed in with curds and a dash of lime pickle to help ease the food down the throat. Afterwards, they sat in the dark in the front verandah.

At the time the beggar brother and sister were expected to walk down the lane, Bayabai did not wait for them to come around to the back but stood at the front gate instead, the food package wrapped and ready, still warm from having just been taken off the stove.

"I'll sleep upstairs tonight," she told Vishnupant, as she climbed the shallow stairs of the verandah.

Vasanti told Mohini that she should go to bed.

"Are you coming inside?" Mohini asked Vishnupant.

He was silent.

"What are you thinking?" Mohini said.

"Not thinking. Just wondering when, if ever, the book I am writing will be finished. Every time I think I have reached the final chapter, there seems to be, sadly, yet another item to add."

Vishnupant got to his feet and motioned for Mohini and Vasanti to come indoors. He bolted the front door and entered his bedroom. Mohini and Vasanti followed him in.

"What are you doing, Vishnukaka?" Vasanti asked, as he rummaged inside the top drawer of his desk.

"Looking for my notebook and pen."

"It's right there, underneath the newspapers," Mohini said, pointing to his bed.

"Make sure that the doors leading into the back courtyard are bolted, Vasanti," he said, before going into the bathroom.

After checking the doors, they waited for Bayabai until she had switched off the kitchen light. Vasanti carried her bedding up the stairs. Bayabai said she would sleep in Keshav and Kamala's room. Vasanti dropped her bedding there, then took the tray containing the small bananas, a glass of buttermilk, and two ladoo from Bayabai's hands and placed it on Mohini's night table.

She shook the thermometer until the mercury dropped back into the bulb, and carefully centred it under Mohini's tongue. When she removed the thermometer, the temperature read 102 degrees.

Even though they were not in the mood to read that night, Mohini and Vasanti each picked up a book. They skimmed the pages distractedly. They expected something to happen without knowing exactly what it was that they were waiting for. They lay on their sides, now and again looking out into the darkened terrace, Bayabai's steady snoring piercing the lifeless quiet of the night.

"What time is it?" Mohini asked.

Vasanti turned around and looked at the wall clock. "Almost midnight," she said. Her eyes were so heavy-lidded that the book slipped from her hands.

"I'll turn off the light," Mohini said, reaching for the lamp.

It wasn't until Mohini heard Bayabai clearing her throat sometime in the early morning that she opened her eyes. Even though there was a bitter taste of sleep inside her mouth, it felt as though she hadn't slept at all. Bayabai's bones cracked as she got off her pallet and cracked yet again as she bent over and rolled up her bedding before carrying it downstairs. Mohini sat up in bed. She looked over at Vasanti, who was looking at her.

"Did you sleep, Mohini?" Vasanti asked, snuggling deeper under her quilt.

"A bit. I could lower the speed of the fan, if you want."

"I don't mind," Vasanti said.

Mohini lifted her walking stick and reached behind and adjusted the dial.

"It's amazing how you can do that," Vasanti said, stifling a yawn. Outside, the first birds were chirping.

"Do you think Aai and Baba will come back today?" Mohini asked.

"Difficult to say."

"I wonder if they went ahead with the engagement."

"They must have. The engagement was scheduled for four o' clock. Vishnukaka said the radio bulletin carrying the news of the assassination came on at six." She sat up, adjusting her sari across her breast. Her hair was flattened on one side of her head. The areas under her eyes were smudged. She hadn't slept much either. She went to the bathroom and afterwards took Mohini's temperature.

"How much?" Mohini asked.

"Ninety-nine point eight. How are you feeling?"

"Hurting everywhere. Other than that, I'm fine. Can you switch on the hot-water geyser in Aai's bathroom? My geyser is not working."

"No, Mohini, no," Vasanti said, shutting her eyes for emphasis. "I'll help you to the toilet. You brush your teeth and then I'll sponge you down later."

Mohini was steady in the toilet and even steadier standing at the washbasin while brushing her teeth. "Vasantiatya," she said, after being led back to her bed, "as long as I'm not feeling dizzy, which I'm not, Aai lets me

have a bath in the bathroom even when I have a slight temperature. A bath will make me feel fresh. Really. The
reason why my body is aching so much is that I need to
move it a bit. Last day and half, except yesterday evening, I
lay in bed, remember?" It was only when she saw Vasanti's
resolve start to break that Mohini stopped talking.

Vasanti helped Mohini to Kamala's bathroom before
lighting the flame in the kerosene geyser. After settling
Mohini on a stool, she went out to get Mohini's change of
clothes, and when she returned, she tested with her finger
the trickle coming from the tap. "Still not hot," she said,
sitting back on the raised lip between the bathing area and
the rest of the bathroom.

"Do you think Gandhiji suffered much, after he was
shot?" Mohini said.

"I don't know."

"In that last second or even half-second—what must it
be like to know it is the end?"

"They say Gandhiji was expecting death all his life, that
right from his early days in Africa he thought he would die
from an assassin's bullet. I read that somewhere."

"I wonder why he thought that."

"I don't know. I read somewhere else that Gandhiji
thought that if he died like a martyr, he would have earned
his name and reputation of 'Mahatma,' Great Soul."

"Do you think it mattered so much to him?"

"That's what they say. But who can tell? Maybe an
astrologer predicted Gandhiji's end when he was very
young and he knew all along that he'd die this way."

"Vasantiatya?" Mohini asked, as Vasanti dragged the half-
filled bucket from under the tap that was now gushing hot

water and steam. She pulled up an empty bucket and placed it under the running tap. "Do you believe in astrologers?"

"No."

Mohini glanced up from the bucket and looked at her aunt.

"Not one astrologer," Vasanti said, "told my parents that I would be widowed at such a young age. The face reader who lived next to us in Poona said something would happen to me when I was nineteen, something irrevocable that would change my entire life. A great upheaval is how he described it. And when my father was alarmed and asked him what he meant, he assured him that he saw no shadow of death on me or on those around me. Just a great upheaval." Vasanti shifted her gaze to the bathroom window, which was covered by an opaque pane of glass. "The astrologers, the face reader who had predicted right for so many people, were completely wrong about me. That's why I don't believe in them." Vasanti turned off the geyser. She ran the cold-water tap. She crouched against the wall next to Mohini. After a few moments she said, "Babasahib was always talking about going away for further education, right from that first day after we were married." Her voice was low, barely audible. "He always spoke about how much he admired and respected the British. How he was in complete awe of the fact that such a small island-nation could rule almost one-third of the world." She crouched forward and removed the filled bucket and pulled into its place the first bucket of cooling water. She turned down the cold-water tap to a trickle. She looked at Mohini resolutely and said, "There is something I want to tell you, Mohini. Something Babasahib said to me before he sailed for England."

"Go on."

"'You are an intelligent girl, Vasu,' he said to me. 'One day, you will understand why I had to leave you.' I remember his words all the time." She looked at Mohini's blank face. "Think, Mohini! Think what he could have meant!" Her voice had risen and her complexion appeared sickly, white, and the freckles on her chin looked like pierced blemishes.

Mohini shook her head, mesmerized by the moist earnestness of her aunt's eyes.

"You have so much imagination, Mohini," Vasanti continued. "I was counting on you to come up with a conclusion similar to mine."

Mohini stared at the wall. Babasahib had said that one day Vasanti would understand why he had to leave her. But Vasanti already knew that everything about England fascinated him. He was curious to go there. Besides, other people had gone abroad for further education and Babasahib obviously wished to do the same. What other thing was there to understand? Vasanti's face crumpled when Mohini shook her head yet again.

"I don't need any help figuring it out, really," Vasanti said, her eyes squinting unnaturally as though she were preventing a dam from bursting. "He didn't just say I would understand why he had to leave, he said I would one day understand why he had to leave *me*. I think Babasahib is still alive."

"What?"

"He is not dead. He had decided never to return to India even before he left Chafekar Wadi, long before we were married. He could have changed his mind, of course, after our marriage, but he didn't." The tears ran down Vasanti's face. "I know that's got something to do with his landlady, that woman, who wrote to inform us of his demise, she has something to do with all of this. Or else why can we not find her? I know he is still alive." Vasanti's words tumbled out of her mouth like a memorized theorem. A conclusion not self-evident but arrived at by a chain of reasoning. She pushed back against the wall and got up.

"Do you think that is why no astrologer mentioned death?" Mohini said. "Because there was no death?"

"I knew you would give it the same interpretation," Vasanti said. She stopped abruptly, her throat beginning to fill up. She stuffed her fist into her mouth so she could contain her sobs. Her body was heaving as she stood there, hunched forward. Mohini leaned back on the stool, the cold tiles soothing against her back. Suddenly, the context of her aunt's angry, desolate, hopeless reaction during the discussion of Brahma's dream became clear. Mohini put out her hand, but Vasanti did not see it. When she could bear her aunt's anguish no longer, she pulled on Vasanti's sari until Vasanti was once again crouching next to her. Mohini took her aunt's hands away from her mouth. There was a ring of teeth marks on Vasanti's right knuckles. She brought forward the end of her sari to cover her face and held it there until her breathing was back to normal. Mohini carefully peeled away the sari from her aunt's head. Vasanti reached forward and turned off the tap above the bucket that was now overflowing.

After a long silence Mohini said, "Do you think you will ever try to look for him?"

Vasanti shook her head.

"You must tell Aai all this."

"I already have. A long time ago. Now she and you are the only people who know."

"What about his family? Would he have contacted them in all these years?"

"I asked my sister-in-law, when she was last here, whether the family had heard anything about Babasahib since I had met her last. She repeated that there was nothing new to report. I believe her."

"What did Aai say when you told her that you think Babasahib is still alive?"

"Kamalavahini said that if what I believe is really true, then I should do my best to forget him, and every time I think about him, I should remember that he abandoned me and for that there can be no excuse."

Vasanti held out her hand and helped Mohini to her feet. "The water is turning cold. Do you want me to bathe you?"

"I'm almost fourteen, Vasantiatya."

"Don't lock the door, then. I'll wait outside until you are finished. Be careful. The floor is very slippery."

After Mohini was done bathing and getting dressed, Vasanti walked her to her bed and sat her down and peeled a banana and popped a slice of it into her mouth. Mohini ate the rest of the food by the time Vasanti was finished her bath. She watched her aunt as she sat on the bed, combing out her wet hair before twisting it into a loose knot at the back of her neck. Her actions were mechanical. Without looking at Mohini, she lay back on her bed and within moments was fast asleep. Mohini switched off the fan and covered her aunt with a quilt. She walked out to the terrace and sat on the swing. The morning air felt cool and clean.

Down the road someone had turned up the radio, the crisp tones of the newsreader all but drowned out by a sonorous chanting of prayers as a funeral procession passed Koleshwar Nivas on its way to the cremation ghats.

TWENTY-SIX

 Mohini and Vasanti went downstairs. It was late morning, and Vishnupant was in the dining room, sipping from a cup of tea. "Do you think Aai and Baba will come back today?" Mohini asked him.

"I don't think so," he said. "Now sit down and eat."

Mohini picked at her second breakfast, after which she and Vasanti joined Vishnupant in the front verandah. He was talking to Mr. Kulkarni, who stood up as soon as he saw Mohini and Vasanti step out through the door. "Just thought I'd let you know," he said to Vishnupant, before hurrying down the path and crossing the lane.

Mohini waited for him to enter his house before asking, "Let you know what?"

"He says that there has been some retaliation in the eastern parts of Bombay Presidency."

"Retaliation against whom?" Vasanti asked.

"Brahmins."

There was a long silence. Mohini leaned back in her chair and looked up at the ceiling where the white paint was peeling away from the edges. Damp patches created by the last rains stained the entire length of the verandah.

359

Mohini's eyes grew heavy and she dozed off. "Who's crying?" she muttered, sitting up quickly as an ominous wailing filled the air.

Six or seven women were walking down the narrow lane that ran along the right wall of Mr. Kulkarni's property. They were beating their chests and weeping so loudly that Mohini was sure they could be heard in Shivaji Park. They belonged to the Gujarati community, as made evident by the end of their saris that were brought forward from behind their right shoulders. The kunku on their foreheads was smudged as they slapped their faces in anguish. They stood in the middle of Mohur Lane, repeating, "Our very own Bapuji is slain! Our esteemed father is no more! The world has lost a holy man!"

Vasanti closed her prayer book and hurried to the far end of the verandah to get a better look. Across the lane, the Irani's shutters were half open. Gulaam's two sisters were squatting under them, almost toppling onto their faces as they craned their necks to watch the women who continued to stand in the middle of the lane, beating their chests.

Mohini glanced at Vishnupant. He was looking at the scene thoughtfully, his hand rubbing the back of his neck. She turned her attention to the women. Now they were being joined by their menfolk. Mohini rose to her feet, thinking that the men had come to contribute to the public mourning. But instead of beating their chests and weeping alongside the women, they steered the ladies back down the narrow lane from which they had emerged.

Slowly, silence returned, occasionally broken by the

high-pitched twitter of parrots as they flew away in batches from the trees inside the Marzellos' yard.

"There must be scenes like this all over India," Vishnupant said, looking across the lane. "Vasanti, I think Mai and Bebitai are waving to you."

"I better go and see what they want," Vasanti said, slipping into her sandals.

Vishnupant waited for her to cross the lane, then said, "I've been thinking about sending her to college."

"Who? Vasantiatya?"

"Yes. She is a matriculate and should have no difficulty in continuing her studies."

"You'll let her go alone?"

He smiled but said nothing.

"What! Tell me."

"What if your mother were to go with her?"

Mohini looked at her grandfather in disbelief. "Does Baba know?"

"Not yet."

"Do you think he will agree?"

"I don't see why not. But the more pertinent question to consider is this: Do you think *they* would want to go to college?"

"Which college?"

"I don't know yet. There are a couple in our area. Most likely one of those."

"I know Aai would like to go to college, and if she went, I suppose Vasantiatya would want to go as well. But, Vishnupant," Mohini said, swallowing the dryness in her mouth, "who will look after me?"

"You can look after yourself. And I'm here, aren't I?"

"But Aai already goes to the samaj to teach embroidery."

"She needs something for her head, Mohini. It's not enough to do this and that merely to pass the time. The mind must have stimulation."

"What about me, then?" Mohini said, looking away.

"What about you?"

"I don't go to school. Doesn't my mind need stimulation too, or don't I matter?"

"The rivers inside your eyes are rising," Vishnupant said. He tossed his handkerchief onto Mohini's lap. She let it fall to the floor. She used the edge of her frock to dab her eyes.

"Everyone tells me I have this fine granddaughter whose agile mind is filled with all kinds of wonderful things," Vishnupant said.

"Don't exaggerate."

"I'm only reporting what I hear, Mohini." He put out his hand and Mohini pulled her chair closer and laid her small fist on his palm.

They looked at the Irani as he swept the footpath in front of his shop. Mai and Bebitai were still talking to Vasanti by the side of the lane.

"Vishnupant?" Mohini said. "You know when I asked you why Brahma was having such nightmares? You went into the dream business, but you never did answer my question."

"The fact is, Mohini, that I had no answers then and I don't have any now." He let go of Mohini's hand. "And whenever I think I have a possible answer, twenty other questions arise from that possibility. That does not mean, of course, that one stops asking questions."

A car trundled past, its exhaust spraying a plume of grey smoke into the air.

"But here's what I do know," Vishnupant continued. "I know there is light, and the absence of it, goodness, and then the absence of it, virtue and vice, wealth and poverty. And countless other converse, obverse, and opposite phenomena. Why is the sky blue and not yellow, the sun yellow and not blue? Questions I want to ask Him and most definitely will ask, if and when He grants me an audience. But until then, it will have to remain a mystery— Here's Vasanti now. Don't say a word to her or anyone else about this college business, all right?"

"I won't," Mohini said.

After lunch, Vishnupant's friends from the gymkhana brought him more news. There had been trouble in the Girgaum area of South Bombay. Bricks had been thrown into Brahmin homes, and one man, who was sitting inside reading his newspaper, had had his skull broken open.

In the late afternoon, before the street lamps were switched on, Vishnupant turned to Vasanti and told her that he would personally go across and tell Mai and Bebitai to keep their verandah door bolted during the night.

"Also tell them that on no account are they to open the front door should anyone come knocking or ringing the doorbell," Vasanti said.

After dinner, because Balu still had not returned from Sewri, Vishnupant inspected the ground-floor doors and made sure they were securely bolted, even though Vasanti had told him that she had double-checked them herself.

He called after Mohini as she climbed the stairs, "I'm not expecting your parents to come home before tomorrow evening. So don't worry about them and sleep well."

———

"Are you planning on reading tonight?" Vasanti asked Mohini upstairs, after their teeth had been brushed and they had changed into their nightclothes. "If not, I will switch off the light."

"Leave it on, if you don't mind," Mohini said. "I won't be able to sleep unless I have read at least a few pages. Did you hear the Gurkha's dogs in the Marzello compound last night?"

"Yes. But that's because I was awake. Otherwise, you know me. Once I'm asleep, nothing wakes me up."

Mohini fetched from Keshav's desk the engineering book she had found earlier that afternoon under her father's pillow, while resting on his bed. It was a slim volume containing a brief summary of the history of road building. It explained how ancient people relied on animal trails to cross a forest or forge a river because animals were born with a natural instinct, one that allowed them to seek the shortest, most navigable route between two points. It spoke about the importance of roads in the evolution of man. How they facilitated in the transportation of peoples, goods, and ideas, resulting over time in the flowering of civilizations and the growth of human intellect. Accompanying other nuggets of information were hand-sketched illustrations of Roman aqueducts, wooded lanes, forest paths, wooden bridges, seaside docking yards, mountain trails. On the very last page was a sketch of an arching span of a highway dipping and disappearing into the horizon from which buildings grew tall and brushed the sky. Mohini's eyelids grew heavy. The book slipped to the floor.

"What is it?" Vasanti said, without opening her eyes.

"My book fell, but I can reach it." Mohini leaned over the side of her bed and picked it up. The outer flap had separated. Inside, on the yellow hardback cover was a central indentation in the shape of a hexagon. Someone had written in a neat and concise hand, "Even Arjun had to leave Uloopi and return to Draupadi." There was no signature. Mohini wondered whether Keshav had seen the inscription. She opened the book to the front page. Keshav's initials were in the upper right-hand corner. They were written in his own hand. Under his name he had penned in the month: "December." There was no date and no year. Mohini slipped the cover back on and placed the book under her mattress. She stared out into the terrace.

Arjun was Prince Arjun from the Mahabharata. Princess Draupadi was the beautiful wife he shared with his four brothers. The story, Mohini remembered, went like this:

One day, Arjun had entered the quarters of Draupadi and Yudhisthir, his oldest brother, in order to retrieve his weapons, because they were hidden there and he needed them to slay some marauders who were harassing the common folk. Remembering afterwards that the brothers were forbidden to enter the living quarters of the brother whose turn it was to consort with Draupadi, Arjun had become penitent. He said he would pay for his transgression by going away for a period of time. It was during his ensuing travels that Uloopi had seen him at a riverside, kneeling over the water's edge as he bathed his face. So enamoured was she of his princely bearing that she captured him and took him to her father's kingdom under the sea. But she knew she could not keep him there forever, and later, when it was time for him to return to his family, she had had no choice but to let him to go.

Mohini switched off her lamp.

Although she tried as much as possible to shut out of her mind the terrace conversation between her father and Shridhar, there were times when she was unable to do so. It gave her a bad feeling, remembering Keshav's admission, and even though she knew that she had to side with her mother in this situation, she could not get herself to feel anger or animosity towards her father. It had by now become clear to Mohini that the estrangement between her parents was the direct result of the worry and anxiety caused to Kamala during her meningitis attack. It was Mohini's fault.

Her dreams were jumbled that night. Snakes leaping over walls. Her mother and father in a bullock cart, the road uncoiling its glistening body under their dangling feet. Vasanti waiting for a bus to take her to the Scottish Highlands. Hatted women wearing high heels and gathered frocks pointing to Babasahib Chafekar's turban abandoned on top of a hedgerow, the dripping magenta of its silk staining the dull leaves.

Mohini's eyes flew open. The sky above the terrace was dark. Running footsteps were approaching the junction from the direction of Ranade Road Extension. The Gurkha's dogs were barking and a man was shouting, "We'll split up. Look for them in all directions. You know what to do when you find them! Wring their necks! Kill them!" Mohini heard the sound of bamboo sticks being dragged along the tarmac as the men dispersed. Terrified, she closed her eyes. They flew open again. Much nearer, directly under her window,

was the sound of jagged breathing, as though someone's
lungs had run out of air. The men must have posted a lookout. Mohini shivered and blocked her ears with her hands.
A minute later she removed one hand to check whether all
was still again. The heavy breathing she had earlier heard
had subsided into an occasional, erratic sob. Clamping the
pillow against her ear, she counted slowly to ten. She loosened her hold. Everything was quiet: the lookout must have
left his post. Even the dogs had settled down—she couldn't
hear their rattling chains or their impatient scrabbling. She
closed her eyes and held her breath.

The dogs began to bay. Startled, she sat up. The men
were back in the junction. Sticks were being dashed against
the tarmac, accompanied by the resounding ring of metal,
as though some of the sticks were iron bars. Someone
shouted above the barking of the dogs, "No use waiting for
them here. We'll wait for them to cross the park. Sooner or
later they will have to go home. And when you find them,
don't spare them! Chutney is what we want . . ."

Mohini stared at a single point between Vasanti's eyebrows, willing her aunt to open her eyes. Vasanti stirred.
She straightened her legs and turned onto her back before
facing the other way. Too frightened to call out to her,
Mohini peered around for her walking stick: she would use
it to prod Vasanti's back. The stick was leaning against the
wall, out of Mohini's reach.

In order to gain courage, she forced herself to recite the
Ram Raksha, all thirty-eight stanzas. Just as she was about
to begin a second recitation, her heart started to thump:
there was a stealthy rustling under her window, as though
someone was moving from left to right on the roof of the

car porch, towards the outer wall of the terrace. There was a scrambling noise.

Mohini froze as footsteps advanced across the terrace floor and came to a halt outside her door. She lifted her eyes. A man was standing in the moonshine, his broad, squat figure silhouetted against the terrace plants. He stood there looking in, his hands clutching either side of the door.

Mohini pressed her palms to her cheeks as a hunched figure glided left to right across the terrace, moving crab-like towards the swing. The man in the doorway turned abruptly and made his way back to the outer wall. Mohini could hear him haul something in. It must have been another man, for now two men crept across the terrace and joined the third by the swing. After a few moments, during which they softly whispered to one another, they stood up and moved out of sight, making their way into the house. There was a scraping noise, immediately followed by three loud thumps and a groan: they must have jumped into the courtyard below. Then silence. Seized by an exhaustion that had been threatening to catapult her into a deep sleep all day long, Mohini closed her eyes and didn't open them until the dogs were barking once again. It was morning. Vasanti was sitting on the spare bed, massaging oil into her scalp.

"Why are the dogs barking?" Mohini asked.

"They always bark and whine at the time of their morning feed," Vasanti said.

"Didn't you hear anything in the middle of the night?" Mohini's voice was thin.

Vasanti quickly shifted to Mohini's bedside and laid the back of her hand across her forehead. "You called me? I didn't hear you."

Mohini moved away and the two tears that had been forming inside her eyes ran down either side of her face and onto her pillow. Vasanti removed her hand as though stung, water forming in her own eyes.

"It's not your fault," Mohini mumbled.

Vasanti searched her face. "What is it, then? A bad dream?"

"I don't think so." Mohini sat up in bed.

Vasanti got to her feet and held out her hand.

"I'll need my walking stick," Mohini said.

After passing it to her, Vasanti followed Mohini out to the back verandah. Mohini leaned over the railing and pointed to the unplanted flower beds beneath the terrace window. They were deeply smudged. And halfway between the flower beds and the water tank lay two overturned sandals.

"Whose sandals are those?" Vasanti asked.

Mohini briefly told her about the events of the previous night. Vasanti listened aghast, and when Mohini was finished, she scolded her niece for not waking her up.

"It's not as if I didn't try," Mohini said.

They hurried downstairs. The front door was still bolted and Vishnupant was drinking tea in the dining room. Mohini started to tell him about the men.

"Not now, Mohini," he said sternly, holding up his left hand. He drained the tea with his right. "That was my second cup, so whatever it is that you want to say, it must wait until afterwards." He pushed back his chair and stood up.

Vishnupant did not like to be disturbed in his morning routine. Right away after his second cup of tea he would head to the toilet, after which he would go in for his bath. It was only after his morning prayers were completed that he would allow anyone to approach him. The fixed sequence of these activities was sacred to him, and he did not like to be interrupted until all four had been completed.

"But you must listen to her, Vishnukaka," Vasanti said. "Some men forced themselves into our house last night. They climbed in from the terrace."

"Did they harm you?" Vishnupant said, quickly dropping back into his chair.

"No," Mohini said. She told him what had happened.

"I thought I heard some commotion in the middle of the night, but I must have fallen right back to sleep." Standing up once again, he hurried to the back verandah and unbolted the door.

A garland of sparrows rose into the air as he strode outside, followed closely by Vasanti and Mohini. The water tank was oozing water where Bayabai must have forgotten to shut off the electric pump. Vasanti shut it off now. Someone was moving behind the tank. "Who is it?" Vishnupant boomed in his sternest voice.

Mohini gave a start and Vasanti clutched her hand.

"Come out at once and show yourself!" Vishnupant barked.

Slowly, a man stepped out from behind the tank. It took Mohini a moment to recognize Master Rajaram. The last time she had seen him he was outside the Shivaji Park Gymnasium, wearing stiff, knee-length khaki shorts and a pearl-white cotton shirt, its top button undone. His feet had been bare. He was facing rows and columns of young men, using his eyes and voice to command rigour and discipline as they exercised to his count.

Now, he was dressed in a white dhotar. It was mossy

green in places where it had rubbed against the tank. A close-fitting red turban ringed his head and his white shirt was fastened at the cuffs with rectangular ruby-eyed cuff-links. On his feet were mojadies, the kind worn at weddings and formal occasions. The delicate gold threads on their upturned fronts were cut through, as though they had been snagged on something sharp.

Mohini looked at Vishnupant. His face was cast in stone.

Dr. Ramesh Natu was the next to walk out from behind the tank. A deep gash, the length of a thumb, spanned the left side of his face. He stood beside Master Rajaram, his lips a closed slit. Only the right part of his face moved when he finally said, "Forgive us, Professor Oek, for intruding in this way. Please allow me to explain—"

"You had better come inside, then," Vishnupant said, turning on his heel and entering the house.

Dr. Natu indicated the outside tap to Master Rajaram. Vasanti removed the cooking vessels that had been washed the previous night and left there to dry.

"The toilet is there," she said, pointing to the outhouse.

Master Rajaram said, "I'll go first."

Dr. Natu looked over his shoulder and softly said, "You can come out now."

Mohini nodded. She knew she had counted three of them.

A boy crawled out from behind the water tank. He stood up slowly, his stiff rickety legs unfolding from under him like a newborn calf's. He shook his head as though to rid it of excess water. When his gaze settled on Vasanti, he grinned.

"Why, Chotu Bumbavale!" she exclaimed. "I didn't expect to see you here." She was outraged, shocked.

Chotu clasped his hands in front of him and pleaded, "Don't tell my father, please. None of this is my fault. I swear! Ask Dr. Natu if you don't believe me . . ."

"I believe you," Vasanti said, ready to melt at the slightest sign of distress.

Chotu's mother was Vasanti's friend, and the one sentence Mohini had repeatedly heard in connection with him was that Chotu had an unerring ability to be in the wrong place at the wrong time.

Vasanti ushered Master Rajaram and Dr. Natu into the house and came out once again. Mohini lowered herself into a chair as Chotu walked to the outhouse. Afterwards, he turned to its maximum the handle of the tap and let the water gush forcefully over his hands and feet. Minutes later Vasanti had to remind him that he was done. When he had finished drying himself, Mohini got up and together they led him into the sitting room, where everyone else was assembled.

TWENTY-SEVEN

Vishnupant's face had not softened. He made no attempt to pick up the glass of water that Bayabai had placed on the table in front of him. He did not look at Mohini when she sat next him on the sofa.

It was Chotu who broke the long silence. "They said they would kill us, Oek Ajoba," he said, his voice cracking. "If we had not hidden on the roof of your car porch, they would have."

Mohini swallowed. "I heard them too," she said, wishing to change the expression on her grandfather's face. Vishnupant did not acknowledge her assertion.

Master Rajaram and Dr. Natu looked at each other. Dr. Natu nodded and Master said, "I went to Girgaum yesterday to attend the naming ceremony of my nephew's son. After the ceremony I was waiting at Charni Road Station for the train when I met Ramesh Natu and Chotu. Ramesh told me he had gone to visit his sister in Thakurdwar. We travelled back together in the same compartment."

"It was late," Dr. Natu said. "The train was more or less empty. Hardly anyone got off at Dadar Station."

Chotu gave a deep shudder, verging on a sob.

Vishnupant sternly cleared his throat.

Master Rajaram said, "We left the station and started walking down Ranade Road. We had almost reached the Gokhale Road junction when I heard people stepping out of the Virkar Building behind us. I turned around, wondering who it could be at that hour of the night, especially since the building had been dark when we had passed it just a moment before. I saw two men, perhaps three, stepping back into the darkened stairwell as I turned around."

Dr. Natu said, "We crossed Gokhale Road. Halfway down Ranade Road Extension, we glanced over our shoulders. Now there was a cluster of them. Perhaps five or six men. They were keeping their distance. I asked Master whether we should wait for them to catch up to us and confront them, but Chotu here started to run."

"I was scared," Chotu said. "They had sticks in their hands. They were banging the sticks against the pavement."

Master continued to explain: "We crossed the road and hurried after Chotu. We could hear the men closing in behind us. The deserted plot at the end of Ranade Road Extension, the one with the abandoned well—I thought they would likely corner us there. Chotu was waiting for us at the mouth of Mohur Lane. We turned into the lane in order to avoid the empty plot."

Dr. Natu said, "We were walking past your house when the dogs inside the Marzello compound began to bark. The men must have heard the dogs too because now we could hear them running into the lane. I remembered the car porch from the time I had come here for Aniruddha's wedding. I quickly scaled the wall, Master and Chotu following closely behind me. We had just dropped onto our bellies behind the parapet wall of the roof when the men ran into the junction."

Master Rajaram said, "We never meant to come inside the house, Professor Oek. That is, not until Chotu started to loudly wheeze. I believe the men would have come looking for us on your property if a suspicious noise was heard from your compound."

It was Chotu's wheezing that Mohini had heard. She thought someone had been sobbing. She shivered at the memory.

Vishnupant spoke for the first time. "Why were you being followed? What did those men want with you?"

Master Rajaram and Dr. Natu shook their heads.

"Are you saying it was a random attack?" Vishnupant said.

Master Rajaram said, "You must have heard about similar attacks against Brahmins across Bombay Presidency in the wake of the assassination."

Vishnupant made no reply.

"Professor Sahib," said Master Rajaram, "Ramesh and I have been residing in the Shivaji Park area for a very long time. Everyone knows who we are, which caste we belong to, even where we live. Everyone knows I teach lezim and bodybuilding at the gymnasium. Everyone knows that we are members of the Rashtriya Swayamsevak Sangh and that the ruling Congress party and the RSS differ on several matters, be they political, social, or economic. That is not a secret because we never thought of keeping it a secret. There is no ban on having differing opinions. But to answer your question, Professor Sahib—yes, I think those men were ready to attack any Brahmin, and we happened to be walking down Ranade Road late last night."

Vishnupant got to his feet just as Bayabai walked into the sitting room carrying a tray with steaming cups of tea.

"Serve the tea to the others," Vishnupant said. "I must go for my bath." He left the room abruptly, his jowls dark and unshaven, the strain of having his morning routine disturbed showing on his face.

Dr. Natu took his teacup and stood by the window. Looking out into the street from where the strident call of the knife-sharpening man could be heard, he said, "They say villagers would walk miles and miles if they knew he was passing through. On railway platforms and open fields where the crush of bodies was so thick, sometimes they caught only a glimpse of him. And yet they trekked across the countryside to see their Mahatma's face, to touch their Mahatma's feet. How could it all go so wrong?"

Chotu sat upright and said, "Baba says Gandhiji has—had a very big heart, and that if he had given *all* his energies only to social work, India would be ready for self-rule today." Chotu had been too shy to speak in front of Vishnupant, and now, with all eyes trained on him, he fluttered his knees.

"What else does your father say?" Dr. Natu asked.

Chotu twisted in his seat and looked at Dr. Natu by the window. Satisfied that the doctor was not making fun of him, Chotu turned around. He fixed his eyes on the wall above the sofa and said, "Baba says Gandhiji should recognize—should have recognized—British society for what it is. Baba says we may have a caste system here, but in England they have a class system of their own."

"You obviously listen very closely when your elders are speaking, Chotu," Master Rajaram said, placing his empty cup on the armrest.

Chotu grinned and looked at Mohini, who was listening intently. "Baba says Gandhiji should not have gone to British Parliament to meet the king—"

"To Buckingham Palace," Master Rajaram corrected.

"—wearing only a loincloth," Chotu continued, as though he had not been interrupted. "And woollen shawl mended with khadi, his feet and thighs uncovered except for flimsy sandals. Baba said Gandhiji was meeting the king on behalf of all Indians. He should have dressed properly. That's why they didn't take him or the Indian people seriously. Anyone looking at him would have thought that all Indians were poor and dressed like that."

"What should he have worn instead?" Vasanti asked.

He grinned at her and said, "He should have dressed like Prime Minister Nehru. In a long, black jacket, with proper shoes and socks, and a rose in his lapel. He could have worn a Gandhi cap if he wanted."

Everyone smiled. While describing Nehru's clothes, Chotu's face had acquired a haughty, regal expression as though he would have met any number of kings if only properly attired.

Vishnupant returned. He had bathed, but his face still looked drawn. "I'll have breakfast before I sit for my prayers," he said.

Master Rajaram stood up immediately. "We should be going. Thank you for your hospitality, and I hope you will accept our sincere apology for entering your home without first asking your permission."

Vishnupant nodded.

Master Rajaram joined his hands in a namaskar and inclined his head respectfully before leaving the room.

"Chotu, was your mother expecting you home last night?" Vasanti said, concern in her voice.

"It was a last-minute decision to come back with me to Shivaji Park," Dr. Natu said. "His mother probably thinks he's still at his uncle's in Thakurdwar."

"Nevertheless, you better go home," Vasanti said.

Chotu rose to his feet and followed Master Rajaram out the front door.

Dr. Natu looked at Mohini. "How are you doing?"

"All right."

"She's recovering from a reaction to a transfusion," Vasanti said. "She's had high fever and a body ache the last two days."

Dr. Natu laid the back of his hand against Mohini's forehead. "Still a slight temperature," he said. "You are taking the headache medicine I had my compounder prepare for you?"

Mohini nodded.

"Is it working?"

"Sometimes."

"You are doing very well for someone who so recently has had an adverse reaction," Dr. Natu said. "Get something to eat, then go and lie down." He turned to Vishnupant. "Taking shelter here probably saved our lives. Once again, please forgive us for intruding in this way." He bent down and touched Vishnupant's feet. Before leaving the room, he looked at Mohini and said, "Thank you for not raising the alarm when I stood in the terrace door last night. If the men had left even one person on watch, any unexpected commotion inside Koleshwar Nivas would have led them to our hiding place. I sincerely hope I did not frighten you too much." He quickly left the room.

"When he stood in the terrace door, you recognized him?" Vasanti asked in disbelief.

"Not right away. But, yes," Mohini said. "Only I wasn't certain it was him until he came out from behind the water tank."

Bayabai stood in the doorway and told them to come to the dining room because breakfast was ready.

She had spooned a generous amount of food into three bowls, along with a side serving of curds and pickled lime. After they had finished eating, she came and stood next to Mohini. She caught Mohini's chin between her thumb and fingers and said, "You go upstairs now and sleep. No need to worry about Aai and Baba. They came to me in my dreams last night. They told me they will soon be back in Koleshwar Nivas."

Upstairs, even before Vasanti could close the shutters of the verandah door in order to block the sun that fell across the beds in a bright lozenge, Mohini felt the tug of sleep. Its gentle arms pulled her into its magnetic field, encompassing her in a diffused light whose source she could only sense because it remained invisible, unseen.

TWENTY-EIGHT

 Keshav and Kamala were back at six o'clock that evening. Mohini and Vasanti were in the front verandah when Keshav's black Morris Minor pulled into the car porch.

Kamala hurried to where Mohini was sitting and put out her hand, "How are you feeling?" she said.

"Fine. No temperature and very little body ache. Aniruddhadada and Swatitai came to see me this afternoon. He said Dr. Chitnis told him to find out how I was."

"Where is Vishnupant?" Keshav asked.

Mohini said, "He's gone to the gymkhana."

"You heard what happened on Friday, of course?" Keshav's tone was grave.

Vasanti nodded. "We were more worried about you in Poona because we heard there was lots of trouble outside Bombay."

"I'm so glad that you are back," Mohini said, still holding her mother's hand.

"I wish we could have come home sooner."

"Mohini would have liked that, Kamalavahini," Vasanti said. "She was worried about you. But tell me. What were you doing on Friday when you heard the news?"

"We'll talk about it later," Keshav said. "When Vishnupant is back."

"How did the engagement go, Kamalavahini?" Vasanti asked.

"It went off very well and everyone was asking why Mohini could not come." Kamala turned to Mohini. "Ajoba said no transfusion for at least three days before Shridhar's June wedding. That way, even if you have a reaction, you'll be able to travel by the fourth day." Kamala looked rested. The cool Poona weather had brought a slight bloom to her cheeks.

Keshav caught both of Mohini's hands in his dry palms and said, "We missed you. Everyone missed you."

Bayabai came out and took from the new driver, Bhaskar, a large cloth bag filled with fresh vegetables. "Hope you brought back some carrots, Vahini," she said to Kamala. "Poona carrots are a lovely red, not like the anemic orange ones we get here."

"Carrots and much more," Keshav said. "This time I told Vahini to buy as many vegetables as she wanted and she did. There is another big bag just like that." He left the verandah.

Kamala noticed that Mohini wanted to say something. "What is it?" she said to her daughter. "I see you are bursting with some news."

"Tell them, Mohini," Vasanti said. "I'll help Bayabai sort out the vegetables."

"Let's go upstairs," Kamala said.

Keshav was in his bedroom, sitting at his desk. He was opening and closing the drawers. "What can you not find?" Kamala asked. Mohini's heart gave a little jump: the Poona trip seemed to have formed a reconciliation that she had been hoping for. Kamala was actually talking to Keshav and there was a familiar exasperation in her voice because he had once again misplaced something.

Keshav turned around and looked at Mohini. "I'm missing a book," he said. "This thin." He held his fingers an inch apart.

"Your history of road building?" Mohini asked.

"Yes."

"Do you want it right now? I found it in your room and took it to read."

"No. Keep it as long as you want. I was just wondering where it was."

"The cover came off, so I glued it down. Is that all right?"

"I suppose so," he said. "It's not important."

"Baba, you want to sit out on the swing?"

"She has something to tell us," Kamala said.

The stars were out. Keshav tilted back his head and examined the sky. The Gurkha's dogs were silent and Gulaam's sisters were singing a song, clapping their hands in unison during the chorus.

Kamala and Keshav listened intently as Mohini related the events of the previous night. When she was finished talking, Kamala said, "We should never have gone to Poona. They took a risk. They should not have come inside the house. What if the men had seen them climb onto the roof? What if they had seen them climb into the terrace and followed them in?" Her voice was small.

"I know what you are saying, Kamale. But don't go worrying yourself over something that could have happened but did not," Keshav said. He took Mohini's hand and laced his fingers through hers.

"I suppose you're right," Kamala said. She got off the swing. "If you've finished telling us everything, Mohini, I would like to go downstairs to light the samayi in the puja room."

"I've finished," Mohini said, leaning against Keshav. Kamala left the terrace. "I missed you, Baba, more than I've ever missed you before. You aren't planning another on-site visit, are you? Tomorrow or next week?"

Keshav crossed his arms across his chest and stretched out his legs. "I've already issued instructions," he said. "From now on I intend to work only out of my Fort office."

They sat in the front verandah after dinner, eating vida. Kamala had found fresh betel leaves in Poona, and Balu, the expert vida-maker, had folded half a dozen, stuffing into their tops fresh coconut that was juicy and sweet.

"Did you see any trouble in Poona or on your way here?" Vishnupant asked.

"None on the way here. But this afternoon, we heard about some trouble at the tank that is a mile from Kamala's parents' home. It's a large tank, with quite a few residences built around it. Sometime this morning, a mob entered one of the houses and hammered on the door and told everyone to get out because they were going to torch the property."

"Why?" Mohini said.

"Because on the first floor lives the youngest brother who is a staunch Rashtriya Swayamsevak Sangh man, and as you know, Nathuram Godse, the assassin, is also an RSS member."

"So they burned it to the ground?" Mohini asked.

"The oldest brother is a civil servant. He is well known as someone who has high regard for his office and the law. But really, Kamala, you should fill them in on the background of that family."

When Kamala remained silent, he said, "Go on, at least tell them what you told me, about the civil servant's daughter."

Kamala looked at Mohini. "One day, about twenty-five years ago, the oldest brother's daughter took part in one of Gandhiji's prabhat pheris, public assemblies. Girls and ladies would meet in the early morning hours in a nearby playground and walk around its periphery in order to protest British rule." Kamala's voice faded away.

"Go on," Mohini urged her.

Keshav smiled. "Go on, Kamala," he said.

Kamala continued. "When the girl's father found out about her participation, he told her that she was never again to join any protest or demonstration no matter how non-violent it may be. He reminded her that he was a civil servant, an employee of the British government, and she was never to betray his office again. Then he beat her with a stick across her legs so she would not forget what he had said. I was only a little girl then, but I remember her showing the welts on her calves to your grandmother so she could apply some ghee to them."

"So what happened this morning, Baba?" Mohini asked.

Keshav said, "The oldest brother, the father of the girl Kamala just told you about, went downstairs and met the mob and told them that the property belonged to him, and not to his youngest brother. So, instead of torching the whole building, they entered the youngest brother's first-floor rooms and ransacked them. They threw out all his furniture, and when we passed the tank on our way here, we could see tables, chairs, and stools floating in the shallow water."

"Tell them what happened on Friday night," Kamala murmured. "That was quite frightening."

"Tell us, Baba," Mohini said.

Keshav said, "After the engagement, when we were getting ready for bed, around nine o'clock, there was a loud knock on the front door, which had been left wide open. Tukaram, the servant boy, was busy sweeping the end of the verandah, so Kamala went to answer."

"I still had on my good sari," Kamala said to Vasanti. "The one I had worn for the engagement."

"We were right there behind her, of course," Keshav said. "Umabai, Anantrao, Shridhar, and myself. The verandah was quite dark, so I reached for the switch. Before I could turn it on, someone said in menacing tone, 'No light!' I moved forward to see who had spoken. Eight or ten men were standing there. Some of them had tied handkerchiefs low around their foreheads. One of them pointed to the banana leaves against the door, and to the rangoli, which had not been swept away, and said, 'Are you offering a thanksgiving puja because he is dead?'"

"'The father of our nation is dead and now you are offering a thanksgiving puja,' is what he said," Kamala murmured.

"Another man pointed to Kamala, his manner insolent and threatening. 'Are those her purified silk garments? The type you Chitpawan Brahmins wear before you sit for your prayers?' Kamala had already moved behind me and I glanced at Umabai. They hurried into the inner room. Kamala's father gestured for me not to speak. He stepped out on the verandah and very patiently and calmly explained that we had just celebrated his son's engagement. 'Our neighbours will verify to the truth of what I am saying,' he said, pointing to the residents of the building who were standing behind the men. The men turned around, saw the crowd, and instead of moving away, they took a step forward. Just then Kamala's aunt Kusummavshi walked into the front room and said, 'I've been telling these people all along that the thirtieth is not a good day to hold an engagement ceremony. It's an inauspicious day, I kept telling them. But does anybody listen to an old woman?'"

"I think Kusummavshi said that purposely. She wanted to distract the men," Kamala said. "Nothing frightens her."

Keshav nodded. "I was looking at her as she was grumbling. Her hair was awry, as it always is, her tone fierce."

"Then what happened?" Mohini urged.

"I continued to look at her, waiting to see what she was going to do or say next. When I turned around to face the door, all but two of the men were walking towards the compound wall. The neighbours were dispersing back to their homes. The two men who remained behind could easily have forced their way into the front room if they had wanted. I doubt Anantrao, Shridhar, or I could have done anything to stop them. So the three of us just stood in the doorway, without moving. Suddenly, a series of sharp whistles pierced the air. I think the rest of the gang was impatient to move on. The two men turned and walked away, one of them muttering that we wouldn't be so lucky next time."

The silence was broken by the tinkling of Kamala's bangles as she moved her hands restlessly on her lap, still agitated by the memory of Friday night.

"Does anybody know yet why Gandhiji was killed?" Vasanti said.

"We will have to wait for Godse's testimony. There is some speculation, of course," Vishnupant said. "At the gymkhana someone was wondering whether it was to do with Gandhiji's recent fast, the one he went on two weeks ago."

"In order to coerce Nehru and Patel into giving Pakistan the agreed-upon compensation of fifty-eight crores?" Keshav asked.

"The same one."

"So what is wrong with that?" Vasanti said. "Money once promised should never be withheld."

Keshav said, "Who knows? Maybe Patel was going to use the money as leverage in order to settle the Kashmir issue or the refugee issue or any other issue, for that matter. There are so many these days. But who can tell?"

"Still, that money was owed," Vasanti said.

"No one is disputing that," Keshav said. "But applying pressure tactics is not a fair way of making one's point."

She turned to Vishnupant in dismay, "But fasts were Gandhiji's trusted weapons, were they not?"

"Except this time, Vasanti, he was using his weapon against his own government and not the British."

A deep gloom hung over Shivaji Park and the rest of India in the following weeks. As the days passed, more news trickled in from the various parts of Bombay Presidency, which appeared to have been the worst hit. There were stories of looting and ransacking and lynching and murders as some of those bearing the same last name as the assassin were attacked. Stores owned by Chitpawan Brahmins were burned to the ground. A sugar factory was saved when the maharaja of the district went to the factory premises and stayed in the managing director's bungalow, daring anyone to destroy the factory in his presence. The maharaja of Sangli was unable to save another establishment, this time a film company. When the mob told him that they would burn down the buildings right there in front of his eyes, he chose to leave.

At her sewing class, Kamala heard of ladies who had been harassed, businesses that were forced to shut down, properties that had been destroyed. Slowly, law and order was restored, and the confrontations resulting from the events of January 30, 1948, became less and less.

February was cold that year. It was snowing heavily in the Himalayas, and the breezes sweeping down from the north carried a hint of ice. Hansa came to visit Mohini, wearing a striped cotton sweater that was too small, a skirt that was too short, and a blouse whose buttons were stretched to the limit. Kamala looked at her and said, "You will have to get your mother to stitch you some new clothes—you've grown so much."

Hansa said, "I'm very unlucky that all my cousin sisters are older than me."

"But why is that unlucky?" Mohini asked.

"Because I have to wait for them to outgrow their clothes before they can pass them on to me. What were you doing when I arrived?"

"We were counting the snagged kites in Mr. Kulkarni's bhendi tree," Mohini said, pointing across the lane.

"Will you have something to eat, Hansa?" Kamala said.

"What have you made Mohini this afternoon?"

"She felt like eating potato fritters. Bayabai must be frying them right now."

"It's almost a year since I tasted your fritters, Kamalakaku. And the chutney."

"I'll go in and tell Bayabai to bring out two plates, then," Kamala said, getting up. "I have to put the finishing touches on the chutney as well."

"How is school?" Mohini asked.

"Not bad. It's boring this week because all we're doing is revisions. What about the tutor Dr. Chitnis said you could have? Do you think your mother will ask Mrs. Pendse to teach you?"

Mohini shook her head.

"Does that mean you may come back to school?"

"I don't think so, Hansa."

Kamala came out and handed each girl a plate, the fat fritters steaming. Before sitting down, she laid the back of her hand against Mohini's forehead. "Cooler," she noted.

"Temperature?" Hansa asked.

"It's this glandular fever I've been getting."

"So how are you feeling today?" Hansa said.

"Not too bad. Just a slight headache and my right eye feels a bit sore. Do you want more?"

"Let me finish this one first," Hansa said. She licked the chutney off her spoon.

There was a tinkle of anklets as Shevanti came out with glasses of water. Hansa looked at Mohini and raised her eyebrows. "Oh!" Mohini said. "This is Balu's wife."

"I thought she was in their village."

"Shevanti," Mohini said, "this is Hansatai. She is my best friend." Shevanti grinned until the ends of her mouth curled up, revealing her back teeth.

"When did you come to Bombay?" Hansa asked.

Shevanti stood there shyly without replying.

"Only last week," Kamala said. "She likes it here. Isn't that so?"

Shevanti nodded and said, "She told me to ask you whether you wanted more to eat."

"Her name is Bayabai, Shevanti," Kamala said. "And yes, you can bring out some more."

"Not for me, Aai."

"No more?" Kamala asked. "All right, bring some for Hansa."

Shevanti went into the house.

"She seems quite smart," Hansa said. "Will she be staying?"

"That's up to Mohini," Kamala said. "The woman we engaged for her massage didn't work out."

"She was too sullen," Mohini told Hansa. "I always felt she resented giving me a massage."

"Now I'm urging Mohini to try out Shevanti," Kamala said. "There's not much work for her to do here otherwise. I'm reluctant to break the Bayabai-Balu partnership in the kitchen, and something tells me that Bayabai will not take too kindly to a change of partners after all these years."

"Actually, Aai, Shevanti massaged my head and neck this morning. She's good, and the best thing is that she doesn't talk too much."

"But, Mohini, you are the one who loves talking and asking a hundred and one questions," Hansa said.

Shevanti returned with more fritters for Hansa. Hansa ate hers quickly and got off her chair. She went inside to wash her hands. When she came back, Mohini was holding a thermometer under her tongue.

"I just looked at the clock," Hansa said. "It's getting late. Aai said I absolutely must be home before it gets dark."

"That's right," Kamala said. "You're a big girl now." She removed the thermometer.

"When will you come again?" Mohini asked.

"Soon," Hansa said. "And next time I come, you better not have a fever."

She gave the swing a hard push before running down the verandah stairs and through the car porch, turning right into Mill Road. A minute later she was back. Without saying a word, she crouched on the floor and opened her satchel. When she could not find what she was looking for, she clapped her hand to her head and said to Mohini, "This morning, before I left for school, Aai reminded me again to take the bottle of tonic she made for you last week. I must have forgotten to put it in my satchel."

"Bring it the next time you come," Kamala said.

Hansa looked stricken. "Aai has been reminding me all week."

"It doesn't matter, Hansa," Mohini said. "There's no hurry."

Hansa brightened. "That's true. But I won't be able to come until the first-quarter exams are finished. Not for another fortnight at least. Not before mid-March."

"Come after your exams," Kamala said. "Now hurry home before it gets too dark."

TWENTY-NINE

Mohini was waiting for Vishnupant in the front verandah. Although it was only April, it felt like early monsoon season. The air was dense and sultry, the trees dusty and dull. There was shallow water inside the hollows in the footpaths, a dark sprinkling on the roads. Pink blossoms from the rain tree drifted down and scattered in the garden, dislodged by a mellow breeze. Gulaam's dog, tethered to a long rope, was crouched on its haunches, sniffing and inching his nose into a pile of debris the municipal sweeper had pushed into a high pyramid at the side of the lane.

Mohini went to her grandfather's window and peeped in. The room was empty. She could hear the sounds of running water from the direction of the bathroom. He must have purposely told her and Kamala that they should be ready to go to the Kulkarnis' at eight-thirty because he wished to make sure that they would not be late. It was now eight forty-five.

Mohini looked across the lane at the Kulkarni property. Two men were sitting in the front verandah. They were bare to their waists, the holy thread running diagonally across their chests in a thin white line. This morning would be the first time she would enter the Kulkarnis' home. In the past, when she had accompanied Kamala to Chitra Kulkarni's haldi-kunku functions, they had gone directly to the back garden. There, Kamala had introduced Mohini to a group of samaj ladies who were seated on a thick cotton carpet spread under the shade of the single banyan tree, some branches of which had rooted themselves in the dark soil below. The ladies had worn fine saris reserved for such occasions, and gold bangles and necklaces that had been removed from a velvet-lined jewellery box. Their hair was lustrous and well groomed. Sitting next to her mother—as opposed to joining girls of her own age who chattered and played at the end of the garden—Mohini had enjoyed listening to the ladies chat about this and that. Recipes, servants, incidents involving children and relatives, the blouses they were sewing, wartime rationing, the shortage of cooking oil. Mohini liked Chitra's unvarying menu and looked forward to these afternoons.

She walked away from Vishnupant's window now and sat in his armchair. At breakfast that morning, which she had eaten while sitting on his bed, Vishnupant had told Mohini that they had been invited to the Kulkarnis' to meet Swami Siddheshwar.

"Who is he?" Mohini had asked.

"He is a religious man. He took his vows after completing his education in Poona."

"Why is he staying with the Kulkarnis?"

"I believe he is a distant relative of theirs. He was in Gujarat and is now passing through Bombay on his way back to the ashram. He founded it himself. It is somewhere off Satara Road."

Mohini was curious. She had never met a swami before. She had seen pictures of various saints beside some prayers in Kamala's prayer book. There was Sant Tukaram, dressed in a dhotar with a frock-like jacket, a broad sash tied around his waist, a turban on his head, a one-string instrument in his hands.

There was Sant Gora Kumbhar, a potter-saint, wearing a similar low turban, the whites of his eyes predominant as he danced in religious ecstasy, and unwittingly trampled into the clay beneath his feet his son who was playing among the heaped earthenware in the courtyard. Mohini liked the Gora Kumbhar story. His connection with the Almighty had been so strong, his faith so great, that upon seeing the trampled, lifeless body of his child, he had fallen to his knees and begged Lord Vitthal to restore to him his son. And as soon as life had returned to that crumpled body, Mohini imagined, Gora Kumbhar must have handed the boy to his horror-stricken mother for safekeeping, for what guarantee was there that the father would not once again harm the boy the next time that he went into a trance? Moksha, or salvation, once achieved, Mohini had heard, was difficult to renounce.

In another cluster of illustrations in Kamala's prayer book was Sant Namdev; he was holding up a bowl of milk to Lord Vitthal, dark eyes in his tonsured head fixed on the Lord standing on a narrow brick, His arms held akimbo in order not to lose His balance. On the opposite page was Sant Ramdas, wearing only a narrow loincloth, a double string of wooden beads hanging around his neck, a single string around each wrist and upper arm. Then there was Sant Janabai, sitting in front of her grinding stone, the bun at the back of her neck unloosed from strenuous labour, a strand of hair falling across her cheek, as she looked in disbelief and adoration at Lord Krishna who had cast aside His shawl and necklace in order to help her, His hands holding alongside hers the grinding stick. And on the final page, Sant Mirabai, her long tresses tumbling to her hips, flowers around neck and wrists, daisies in her ears, lovely face lifted to Lord Krishna, her friend, her lover, her father, her mother, her god.

Kamala stepped out on the verandah, her lips pursed into a thin line. She carried in her arms half a dozen oranges, which she placed in the chair next to Mohini. Kamala went inside and returned with a paper bag into which she piled the fruit. Her actions were deliberate, tense.

"Who are the oranges for?"

"Your grandfather told me to carry some," she said curtly.

"What's the matter?" Mohini asked.

Kamala shook her head and said nothing.

Vishnupant was ready. His dhotar was so white and new that it dazzled Mohini's eyes. His moustache was combed; his tonsured head gleamed with oil. Mohini stood up. She took Kamala's hand and together they followed Vishnupant to the front gate and across the lane.

The men who were earlier seated against the wall of the railed verandah were no longer there. In their place were Mina and Nina, their resemblance to their mother so slight that for the longest time, before Kamala had dispelled her assumption, Mohini had thought them to be adopted. Seated on the narrow arms of the wooden bench, the sisters kept their balance by pushing bare legs into the opening under the armrests. They stood up as Vishnupant, Mohini, and Kamala walked up the narrow path, the queen of the night bushes on either side brushing against their legs. They ran to Mohini and hugged her, their sixteen- and seventeen-year-old strapping bodies enveloping her slight frame. After a few moments, Kamala stepped forward and gently pried loose their arms. They sat back on the bench and told Kamala and Mohini to go inside. A rolling heaviness of the tongue accompanied their speech; there was a hint of remoteness in their eyes.

"You can go in," they repeated, bursting into laughter, amused at their own synchronicity. When they saw the paper bag Kamala was holding, they held out their hands. Kamala told them that the fruit was for someone else and that she would send some especially for them when she returned home. They nodded and perched on the arms of the bench as before. Mina laid a palm on Mohini's head as Mohini stepped into the rectangular front room.

Two mattresses had been placed together against the far wall. Chitra Kulkarni was changing the sheets on them. Kamala handed Mohini the paper bag and went to help Chitra tuck in the ends. Together they slipped new covers on the bolsters. A threadbare cotton carpet, its colours and pattern faded beyond recognition, was spread on the floor in front of the mattresses. The sofa and two armchairs covered in black leather were pushed against the eastern wall.

After she was finished helping Chitra, Kamala joined Vishnupant and Mohini who were standing in the middle of the room. Chitra Kulkarni greeted Vishnupant, then turned to Mohini and said, "I remember coming to your naming ceremony." This was at least the third time that she had addressed Mohini in this way. "Till today I can recall the fragrance of tuberoses the minute I stepped inside Koleshwar Nivas. You were only thirteen days old. It was a grand affair." Chitra turned to Kamala. "Such a tiny bundle she was. Too small even then." She swung to Mohini again. "But you slept the whole time. Did not cry even once."

There was a nervous quality to Chitra's voice, the ends of her sentences sinking and subsiding so that she had to pause and take a deep breath before continuing on with the next. And from the beginning of that very first pause, Mohini would wait in growing discomfort for that moment when Chitra's thoughts would dry up altogether and Mohini would be spared the ordeal of having to wait for the next sentence, the next intake of breath.

Chitra dropped her voice a few notches and said, "Swamiji is so accurate—"

"Who?" Kamala interrupted. She sounded puzzled.

"Swami Siddheshwar," Mohini prompted her.

"That's right," Chitra continued. "Mina and Nina—everything happened exactly the way he described it. Right from the beginning, as far back as my difficult pregnancies. But now, he told us last night, there is nothing to worry about. No major health concerns. They are strong, Kamala. The other day Mina came running towards me, I fell to the ground. Such force with which she hugged me. They get no colds, no coughs, no fevers. Swamiji wants me to be grateful for their health." She took a deep breath and her voice dropped even lower. "As you know, I am not supposed to eat sweets but cannot resist them, and their father, there is this condition in his family, some kind of hole in the heart. Who will look after them after we are gone, Kamala? That is why, when searching for a girl for our son Madhav, we must find someone kind and suitable who will be willing to take on the responsibility of her sisters-in-law when neither of us are left."

Chitra's eyes were sweeping in Mohini's direction. She whispered to Kamala, "Ask Swami Siddheshwar for guidance for her. Everyone says that just like his uncle, Swamiji can look not only into the past, but into the future as well."

Kamala's mouth reset itself into a thin line, but she was saved from replying by Mr. Kulkarni, who came up to them and said, "Have you put out the water? Here they come." Chitra hurried into the inner room.

Swami Siddheshwar entered through the verandah door, followed by two men. Vishnupant bent down and touched his feet. After straightening up, he introduced himself, then introduced Mohini and Kamala. Swamiji nodded at them, then turned to the two men and said, "You may as well go to the seafront before it begins to rain." By the deferential look on their alert faces, Mohini thought they had to be his disciples, their heads shaved into a pale smoothness, their ribs showing through thin, bare torsos.

"Where are the oranges?" Kamala whispered. Mohini took them from the sofa where she had placed them and handed the bag to her mother.

After Swamiji was seated on the mattress, Kamala removed the oranges and placed them on top of the smoothed-out paper bag at his feet. She bent over and did namaskar, and when she moved away, Swamiji made a sign for Mohini to come forward. She crouched down close enough to touch him and joined her hands together. His dark eyes were moist as he looked at her, the whites shining and clear. His cheeks were smooth and unwrinkled, but underneath his eyes drooped several folds of skin that gave him a benign, dog-like appearance. His forehead was a bed of narrow, thread-like crevices; his neck was unlined and taut. His lips, the insides of his palms, the beds of his fingernails, the soles of his feet were a light pink. They formed a contrast to the mahogany darkness of his skin. He wore the holy thread diagonally across his chest, and hanging around his neck was a rope of wooden tulsi beads held together with thick, red string. Mohini's gaze was drawn back to his eyes.

Swami Siddheshwar reached out and lightly touched the top of her head. Removing his hand after a minute or so, he turned towards the open side doors leading into the verandah. The sky was blue. Waiting for Swamiji to say something, Mohini became aware of the movement of breath inside her body. When her legs started to feel heavy—she was still crouching—she looked at Vishnupant, who indicated with his hand that she could move back. "If it is too difficult for you to sit on the floor," Swamiji said to her, "sit on a chair."

"I'm all right," Mohini said. She joined Kamala, who was seated cross-legged on the carpet to the left and in front of Swamiji, and placed both her legs to one side: it was the only way she could sit on the floor. By now there were several people in the room, some of whom Mohini recognized. Inside, everything was hushed. Outside, the world flowed with sound: the sporadic cawing of crows, the frantic warning of a bicycle bell, the footfalls of pedestrians, the repeated flapping of wet cloth being shaken out to dry.

Swamiji looked away from the door. "It is the first time they have seen the ocean," he said, referring to his two disciples. "We have a river, of course," Swamiji continued. "Not too near. Not so we can hear it flow." He looked at Vishnupant. "I understand your son is building roads and bridges in our area."

"That project will be completed by the end of this year," Vishnupant said. "He couldn't come this morning because he had to go to work."

"Now that we have achieved independence, it is good that there are among us engineering experts, people like your son. This country of ours is so ancient that endless knowledge and energy must be employed if it is to meet today's demands. We have made some progress"—he glanced around the room again—"nobody can deny that. Nevertheless, we are still covered in centuries of lethargy that breeds procrastination and laziness. We see it in our district all the time. It takes three men to do the work of one. And providing all this inefficiency a certain legitimacy are our superstitious beliefs." He wiped the sweat from his neck with a hand towel. "This heat of ours does not help. It saps the energy, dulls the brain." He smiled. His words were unhurried, their intonation conversational. Yet nobody in the room offered any response.

Kamala let out a deep breath. Her mouth was not pursed any more, her body was relaxed. Her eyes fixed on Swamiji, she put out her hand towards Mohini. Mohini placed hers in it and leaned against her mother. "Sit straight," Kamala murmured. Mohini thought she heard a distant peal of thunder.

"Although there is much we do not know," Swamiji continued, "the answers to the how, where, what, when, and why of life, its origins and continuing purpose, there are other things we do know or, alternatively, can learn from the rest of the world. This country of ours must now give undivided attention to those other knowable things." He raised his eyes. "Come and sit down," he said, patting the mattress. Mohini turned around. Mina and Nina were standing in the doorway. They came forward and sat to his left.

Swamiji said, "Throughout this millennium our subcontinent has been repeatedly conquered and carved up and divided, and now that the British have left, we must seek ways to understand the pluralistic nature of this land." Swamiji looked up once again and smiled. Mohini turned around as people who had gathered in the doorway entered the room. Vasanti came and sat next to her.

After everyone had settled down, Swamiji looked out the window. A child asked his mother how much longer it would be. She hushed him. From the inner room, Chitra said, "Someone do a head count so we know how many cups of tea to make. We should have put out a pedestal fan."

Mr. Kulkarni stood up and opened the remaining side doors before sitting down on the carpet once again. Swamiji looked at him and asked, "Everything all right?"

Mr. Kulkarni nodded.

From outside came the pleasing sound of wind rustling through trees. Clouds were moving across the sun. The verandah was dappled in light and shadow. The two disciples were back. Swamiji asked them to come forward. They sat cross-legged to his right, facing his profile, the length of their thighs resting comfortably on the floor. Swamiji reached for the water. Chitra left the doorway of the inner room and, bending forward, poured him a glass. Tilting back his head, he held the glass high above his mouth and deftly directed the stream between his teeth. Afterwards, he looked out the window. It had grown dark. Rain was falling, and but for the verandah that ran alongside the house, it would have entered the room. A pigeon was perched on top of an opened side door, small head nestled in a sleek, plump body.

Without shifting his gaze, Swamiji said, "It is written in our scriptures that all this is Brahma's dream." His eyes briefly roamed the room. "However," he continued, "it is not a random dream. Not one where cause is not followed by effect, every action by a reaction."

Mohini waited for Swamiji to continue. When he did not, she glanced behind her. The child who had asked the question had stopped fidgeting. Most people had closed their eyes. She looked at Swamiji. He was dabbing his neck and temples with a hand towel. Vishnupant was looking down into his lap, and Kamala was resting her chin on her raised knee. Mohini closed her eyes, but her mind was too alert to keep them shut.

Swamiji had fixed his gaze directly above everyone's heads. He sat so still that he could have been mistaken for a statue, a statue in which the eyes were alive, reflecting the light. The minutes ticked by as Mohini listened to the rain. She closed her eyes once again. This time she could keep them closed. Swamiji had referred to the fact that the Indian subcontinent had been repeatedly plundered during the previous millennium. Vishnupant had once said to Mohini that the conquerors could have come for, had they known its value, the Indian mind that for centuries had delved into the mysteries of science, nature, and philosophy with such success. But they had come for something else of course: diamond-studded palanquins, elephants trained in warfare, armouries in which every inch of wall space was covered with shining weapons, abundant granaries, floor to ceiling stacked with sifted provisions, aromatic spice. They wished to experience the pleasure of cultivated gardens in which prancing peacocks spread iridescent wings and girls danced with feet so delicate and dainty that it seemed as though their bodies never touched the ground.

A dull ache began to spread through Mohini's limbs. She opened her eyes. Mina and Nina were standing in the doorway leading into the inner room, making urgent hand signals for her to join them. Grateful for the opportunity to get up off the floor, she flattened her palms on the carpet and pushed herself to her feet. Kamala's eyes were closed.

She hobbled to the door, unable to straighten her knees. Leaning against the door frame, she waited for the stiffness and pain to ease before following them into a long, high-ceilinged hall. Seven cots were placed along parallel walls and tall, intricately carved mirror-fronted almirahs graced the four corners. The oblong-shaped house running east-west in a single wide corridor was divided into rooms by wooden partitions that ran from ceiling to floor. She followed Mina and Nina into the dining room, where the dining chairs were lined away from the table against the walls, the rope latticework on their seats sagging and frayed. They stepped into the kitchen. The tea was ready and the cook was pouring it into cups that were ranged on a large steel tray. "What do you want?" she muttered sourly, continuing to pour. After she was done, she lifted her eyes.

Upon seeing Mohini, she forced a smile and said, "Give the child some khadi sakhar!"

Mina poured a spoon of rock sugar out of a jar into Mohini's hand. Back in the dining room, the sisters looked at her and she evenly divided the sugar into three parts. She popped hers quickly into her mouth before it could become sticky on her palm. It melted on her tongue too swiftly and left behind a tingling aftertaste of cloves. "Tell your mother tea is ready," the cook called out. Mohini remained seated on the chair while the girls went to fetch their mother. When they returned they sat across from her, on the other side of the dining table. Glancing at their vacant faces, Mohini remembered a discussion that had taken place in Koleshwar Nivas a long time ago. Someone—Mohini could not recall who—had posed the question as to which part of the body it would be the most difficult to live without. Vasanti said she would hate to lose her ears because she had seen first-hand how loss of hearing had isolated Mai from the rest of the world. Shridhar said he would hate to lose the use of his legs because inactivity would drive him so crazy that he would have to be committed to a madhouse. Kamala said the loss of her hands would be unbearable. Keshav said the eyes were the most important part of the body because without them the world would be plunged into darkness and the idea of living in a dark world was just too frightening to bear. Mohini agreed with him. Vishnupant said that he could imagine living in a world without his eyes, ears, hands, and feet, but he could not imagine living in a world where his mental faculty was extinguished. "Of course," he said, "if I were to lose my mind due to an illness or an accident, the saving grace would be that I wouldn't know that I had lost it. And if I were born mentally deficient, I wouldn't know what I was missing. Nevertheless, if one of them has to be weak, I prefer a strong mind and a weak body as opposed to the other way round."

Watching Mina and Nina as they got up and leaned back against their chairs so as not to be in their mother's way as she carried the tea out into the sitting room, Mohini now changed her mind and thought that Vishnupant had been the most right.

By the time the emptied teacups were returned to the kitchen, the rain had subsided. The air was heavy with the scent of wet earth. Mohini followed Mina and Nina to the front room. Vishnupant was sitting on the sofa and Swamiji was standing by the side door, surrounded by a knot of people. Mohini joined Vasanti at its periphery.

Swamiji was saying, "Not only in ancient times, even today Brahmins are employed in different branches of science, engineering, medicine, mathematics, accounting, and teaching."

Mostly Brahmins were gathered there. Perhaps Swamiji had been asked to define the role of a Brahmin within a caste system whose unrecorded beginnings were formulated—so Mohini had heard—in response to the need to organize and accommodate the various polyglot tribes that had, through the centuries, poured into the Indian subcontinent from the north. In order to provide everyone a valid place and a sense of identity, society had been classified into four groups: the Brahmin or the priestly class, the Kshatriya or the warrior class, the Vaishya or merchant or business community, and the Shudra or the servant or peasant working class. Ever since the assassination of Gandhiji, society's attention seemed to have become focused on the Brahmin community. Perhaps someone had alluded to that in some form or the other and asked a question and now Swamiji was making his reply.

"Why don't you sit down, Swamiji?" Mr. Kulkarni said. Swamiji glanced at the disciple to his right.

The disciple indicated the room. People had returned to their seats.

Swamiji conceded with a small nod and took his place on the mattress. Mohini sat on the sofa next to Vishnupant.

Swamiji waited for the room to become quiet, then said, "In early Vedic times, Brahmins were priests, philosophers, poets, singers. In the Mahabharata, Brahmins were ranked with divine beings. They were considered divine, albeit mortal, because they studied the Vedas. Their asceticism separated them from the other groups." He looked around the room before continuing. "So then the question arises, How did these people, who were given more to the spirit and intellect, become so exploitive, so superstitious, so tradition-bound?

"Examine what I am about to say, then decide for yourselves whether there is some truth in my conclusions. Just like today, in those days, not every Brahmin possessed the intellectual capacity to be a poet or a mathematician, a scientist or a metaphysician." People nodded. Swamiji held up one hand and said, "Nevertheless, these Brahmins, shall we say of lesser intellect, had household duties to perform, expenses to meet, families to clothe, stomachs to feed. Perhaps it was these Brahmins—failed poets and mathematicians—who, over a period of time, devised religious rituals that only Brahmins could perform. They had good knowledge of astronomy by which they could set up elaborate altars. They had enough time on their hands and sufficient intelligence to memorize lengthy sacred texts. And because of their superior status in society, they possessed the confidence to state with certainty that unless rituals were performed in the prescribed manner, those same rituals would bring bad tidings to the performer." Swamiji smiled. It transformed his face. "There is an English saying, 'Necessity is the mother of invention.'" Those in the room who understood English nodded and returned his smile.

"By the same token then, Swamiji," someone said, "those Brahmins that had neither a good memory nor knowledge of astronomical data must have taken to begging."

Swamiji's eyes twinkled and everyone laughed. There was a long silence. This time Mohini could shut her eyes with ease. When she opened them, Swamiji was joining his hands together in leave-taking. He looked at his disciples. They led him out the side door, down the verandah, around the back of the house, and into the garden.

Slowly, people started to leave. Chitra and Mr. Kulkarni were standing outside. Kamala thanked Chitra for inviting them. Chitra smiled and said, "We told only your family and the Moghes. But the news must have spread throughout the neighbourhood. I could not believe the crowd."

Mohini would not let go of Vasanti's hand outside Koleshwar Nivas. "I can come in only for a few minutes," Vasanti said. "Mai and Bebitai are expecting me home for lunch."

They went upstairs to Kamala's room. She changed her sari and joined Mohini and Vasanti on the bed.

"Had you met Swamiji before, Kamalavahini?" Vasanti asked.

"When Mohini's grandfather told me this morning that we were going to see the nephew of the famous astrologer R. S. Talwalkar, I thought the nephew was also an astrologer. I did not even know his name until Chitra mentioned it."

"But I knew it, Aai."

"Your grandfather told you we were going to see Swami Siddheshwar?" Kamala asked. "Then why did you not tell me?"

Mohini shrugged. "I thought you knew."

When they went downstairs, Vishnupant was sitting in the verandah, writing in his notebook. He stopped his pen and said, "So, Kamala, tell me whether or not you were in a bad mood this morning because you thought we were going to get our horoscopes read?"

"You purposely did not tell her, Vishnukaka," Vasanti said.

"But Mohini knew," he protested. "The whole neighbourhood knew. Swamiji has a doctorate in philosophy and history. I thought Kamala would find him interesting."

"But you told her we were going to see Talwalkar's nephew," Vasanti said, slipping into her sandals.

"Don't underestimate your Kamalavahini," Vishnupant said. "Tell me, in spite of the fact she thought we were going to see an astrologer, did she carry our horoscopes? She saw my hands were empty. Wild horses would not drag her into doing something she does not want to do." He chuckled into his handkerchief.

Smiling shyly, Kamala went inside.

"Is that the bibliography?" Mohini asked him, pointing

to his notebook. The tome he had begun to write after his retirement was almost finished and now only a few insertions remained.

"No."

"Can I see what you have written then?" Mohini said.

Vishnupant passed her his notebook.

The greatness of Mohandas Karamchand Gandhi lies in the fact that he introduced to the world the notion that political ends and peaceful means are not parallel concepts, but can be made to intersect by using the latter to achieve the former. In a century where world leaders have sought to exert control through fascism, racism, and imperialism, Mr. Gandhi was the notable exception in that he chose to wield power by introducing the Jain principle of ahimsa or non-violence into the freedom struggle, and instead of endorsing aggression and retaliation, he promoted a message of tolerance and peace.

THIRTY

Mohini woke up to a typical pre-monsoon day, the late-April air so laden with moisture that it assumed shapes in her still, incandescent room. It was the paperweight that pinned Hansa's geography notes to the glass-topped desk, the restraining fingers that caused the overhead fan to move so sluggishly, the sound barrier that prevented the elongated cry of the vegetable vendor from reaching her ears. Outside, the sky was blue and the clouds had dispersed. Bebitai must be gloating, she thought.

The previous evening, when Kamala and Mohini had gone to see Mai at Shiv Sadan because she was suffering from yet another wheezing attack, Vasanti said that it looked as though it was going to be an early monsoon season. A grey blanket of clouds had obscured the sun for three whole days, and the air was so still and sultry that it was impossible to sleep at night. "You mark my words," Bebitai said, raising her voice so that Mai could hear her. "The clouds are a false alarm. The first rains will be here not a day before the fifth of June."

Mohini looked out into the terrace. The clouds might have dispersed during the night, but the air had not lost its denseness. There was not even a hint of breeze in the motionless leaves. She went into the bathroom and turned on the cold-water tap. Sitting on the stool, she undressed, throwing her nightclothes on the pile of dirty laundry Shevanti had heaped on the floor in one corner. After her head bath, she went downstairs. Shevanti was pounding goda masala in the front verandah. "Why aren't you doing that in the kitchen?" Mohini asked.

Shevanti sniffed, her chin creasing into fine lines with the effort of restraining herself from saying anything. She and Bayabai must have had another disagreement, Mohini thought.

"Where is Aai?"

"Vasantitai came early this morning," Shevanti said. "Mai had another attack. I heard Vasantitai tell Kamalavahini that Mai was insisting that she would not feel better until Vahini held her hand."

"Can you get me something to eat?" Mohini said.

Shevanti got up and went inside the house. Mohini stood in the verandah and watched the parrots as they lifted up from the rain tree and disappeared into the banyan tree, behind the Irani's tea shop. She picked up the pink stone from the railing and held it up in front of her eyes. She was about to put it down when she noticed that the sunshine was streaming into the south end of the verandah. She leaned over the railing and opened her palm. The kernel of the stone was ablaze. Astonished, she held up the stone and turned it this way, then that, but no matter how she held it, the inside remained lit up with solid bolts of gold. She curled her fingers around its coolness and waited for Shevanti to bring out her breakfast.

Later, as she was reading a book in the verandah, she heard the front gate creak. She looked up. It was the sugarcane-juice vendor.

"Where have you been?" she called out. "I've been waiting for you since the beginning of last week."

The juice vendor smiled and removed his turban and walked down the path towards Mohini. He could have been mistaken for an actor. His eyes were deep and luminous, his moustache luxuriant and neatly combed, his skin bright.

"I had to go to my village," he said.

"Another daughter?" Mohini asked.

"A son!" He looked at her with pride, his moustache quivering.

Mohini smiled. "When are you going to set that up?" she said, pointing to the juice equipment he had left standing outside the front gate.

"In fifteen minutes you can come and get it," he said.

She pointed to her feet. "I don't think I can walk all the way to the park."

"Then I'll draw you a glass here," he said. "Tell Balu to bring out a jug." He turned away.

"Is the sugar cane Rasavanti variety?"

"All the way from Miraj," he said. "Just taste it and you will know whether or not I am speaking the truth."

Kamala did not like Mohini drinking from the juicewala's small ribbed glasses because they were not properly washed. He cleaned the used ones by immersing them into a bucket full of murky water before drying them with a rag that had seen whiter days. Whenever Mohini felt like sugarcane juice, Kamala reminded her to carry her own glass.

Mohini looked at Shevanti, who was standing in the front door, and told her to bring out the tallest jug. She watched the juice-wala from the verandah as he held long sticks of sugar cane against the outer side of the iron crusher and cranked the handle. The polished brass funnel through which the juice was slowly trickling glinted in the sun.

"Don't forget to add some ginger and lime juice," Mohini called out, her taste buds doing a dance as the jug frothed up with the straw-coloured liquid. "Gold-coloured," Vasanti would have corrected Mohini if she had been here, loving the juice too.

When Shevanti was walking back up the front path, taking in deep breaths of the bouquet of the juice in the jug that she carefully held against her breasts, Mohini told her to tell the juice-wala that she would send the money later on with Balu. He heard her and called out, "There's no rush, Tai." He hoisted his equipment onto his shoulder and crossed Mill Road in order to take his customary position on the footpath outside the gymkhana. His back was ramrod straight, the loose end of his turban hanging between his shoulders like a decorative tassel.

As Shevanti handed Mohini a filled glass, Mohini said, "Bayabai does not eat or drink stuff touched by outsiders. Vishnupant cannot have the juice because it has too much sugar. The doctor said he must not eat sweet preparations. Pay attention, Shevanti. I'm telling you this so that you will give Vishnupant only the smallest helping when he asks you to bring him jaggery or anything sweet. You understand?"

Shevanti nodded.

"Go into the kitchen and pour out two more glasses. One for yourself and one for Balu. Whatever is remaining, take to Shiv Sadan."

Shevanti nodded again. Mohini returned to her book, sipping her drink slowly, making it last as long as she could, holding the glass close to her chest so that the flies would not settle on its rim. When Kamala approached an hour later, Mohini was sleeping peacefully, the open book turned face down on her lap in order to hold her page.

After lunch, Mohini said she would go upstairs to finish the profile of Kamala that she was in the process of sketching. She had found an old studio photograph of her mother's taken soon after she and Keshav were married. A couple of weeks previously, when she was grumbling to Vishnupant that there was nothing to do, a friend of his who was visiting suggested that she draw something to pass her time. When she said that she did not know how to draw, he said he would teach her. She knew that he painted portraits in his spare time, and readily agreed.

She was shading in Kamala's mangalsutra, the necklace she had worn since her marriage, when Shevanti ran into her room and told her that Hansa was downstairs.

"What's that in your hands?" Mohini asked.

"Some medicine, I think."

"It's the tonic Hansa's mother made for me weeks ago. It's taken Hansa this long to remember to bring it. Place it on my desk. Why didn't Hansa come upstairs?"

"She's talking to Vasantitai."

"Is that Baba's voice I hear? Is he home already?"

"It's Saturday, Mohinitai."

"I'll come downstairs," Mohini said, placing her feet on

the floor next to her bed. She made sure the pink stone was in her pocket because she couldn't wait to show it to Hansa. "But first I have to use the bathroom."

Shevanti waited to one side as Mohini got to her feet before handing her the walking stick. Outside the bathroom, Mohini gave the stick back to Shevanti to hold. As Mohini was closing the door behind her, her foot slipped on the wet floor and she fell on her back, the rush of pain squeezing the air out of her lungs. Shevanti shouted out to Mohini, and hearing no answer, she pushed open the bathroom door. Mohini was lying in a pool of water, her head turned towards the clothes that Shevanti had only recently rinsed and twisted to get rid of the excess water before hanging them over the side of the bucket to drip. The grill on the drain was still covered in soapsuds. Her mouth blanched with fear, Shevanti held out her hand to help Mohini to her feet.

"Get Aai," Mohini whispered.

Shevanti ran out of the bathroom. Within seconds Keshav was crouching next to Mohini, sliding his arms under her body. Kamala, Vasanti, and Hansa moved back as he carried her out of the bathroom and propped her up on the spare bed, holding her against his chest. Kamala knelt in front of Mohini and lifted very gently her daughter's arms that were dangling lifelessly by her side. Mohini fainted as a searing pain sliced through her body.

When she regained consciousness, the desk lamp was casting long shadows across the ceiling, a pedestal fan was whirring behind her head, and Keshav's watch was ticking beside her ear where he had laid it.

"Are you awake?" he asked Mohini, getting off the spare bed.

Mohini briefly closed her eyes.

"Dr. Chitnis came earlier on," Keshav said. "He said to leave the planks of wood just the way they are, strapped to your arms and legs."

There was a question in Mohini's eyes.

Keshav understood, for he said, "It was my idea. The workers who are painting our house left the unused planks of wood in the terrace. Balu stripped them down to size, and between us we tied them to your arms and legs to give the limbs some support. Is the cotton rope too tight?"

"No," Mohini said.

"The humidity must be very high. In spite of the two fans you are still sweating." He picked up his handkerchief and crouched beside her bed.

As plumes of pain spread through her body, Mohini concentrated on her father's sickle-shaped scar as he leaned over her and reached with his handkerchief behind her neck. The scar was brown and slightly wrinkled, its evenly spaced stitches the colour of milky coffee. It had been a long time since Mohini had noticed the scar on the underside of his chin. It was many years since she had asked him to tilt back his head so she could see that curved grin, muddy teeth neatly bared. The feel of Keshav's wide, dry hands against her skin was unfamiliar. She didn't remember when last he had tended her. He wiped the back of her neck with his handkerchief, its checked, faded cotton soft but inadequate where it was already damp with the perspiration he must have carefully dabbed earlier from her brow and throat. Mohini said nothing. It made him feel good, she knew, to be of assistance to Kamala.

"Aai?" she said.

"She's gone downstairs just for a minute."

Mohini closed her eyes.

"Here she comes." There was a rustle of clothes as Kamala came and stood by the bed.

"I think she's fallen asleep again," Mohini heard Keshav whisper.

When Mohini opened her eyes hours later, the muscles in her arms and legs were throbbing and her head felt as though it was going to burst. She lifted her gaze and saw Kamala in the periphery of her vision. She was sitting on the raised ledge of the terrace door, early morning sunshine framing her body. Without looking up, Kamala shifted to the left so that now she was within Mohini's range of vision.

"Thirsty?" she asked, raising her eyes. Mohini did not need to say anything for Kamala to know that she was not thirsty, that the inside of her head was burning fiercely, that her limbs, supported by the wooden planks whose hardness she could feel against her skin, gave little trouble, but only if she held her body very still.

Even though she wanted to look down at her arms and legs just to see how the planks had been strapped on, she knew it would be too much of an effort, too painful for her, to lift her head. She had felt her bones crumble when she had slipped and fallen on the bathroom floor.

Kamala looked in the direction of the window. Mohini's Poona grandmother came from behind the spare bed and stood next to Kamala. She smiled. Mohini closed her eyes briefly and said, "When?"

"Last night your father put a trunk call through to Ashok with a message for us that you had fallen. We took the midnight bus and came. Your grandfather is here as well."

Mohini rolled her eyes to the other side of her bed.

"He's downstairs with Vishnupant," Keshav said. "They arrived only half an hour ago."

"Sit on the bed," Kamala said to her mother. Leaning forward, she heaped together the newspapers that were fluttering under the ceiling fan. Umabai sat down and leaned across the bed and put out her hand towards Mohini.

Mohini turned towards her grandmother. The pain caught her unawares. The echo of her cry was still inside her ears as Keshav, Kamala, Umabai, and Vasanti ran to her bedside, their eyes narrowed in concern. It was the first time Mohini had seen Vasanti since Keshav had carried her out of the bathroom the previous afternoon and propped her on the spare bed. But, slipping in and out of consciousness over the next eighteen hours, Mohini had heard Vasanti's keys jangling at her waist when she had shifted positions in the windowsill behind Mohini's bed. Ever since the bulldozers had begun to level out the Marzello property in order to construct two four-storey buildings, the windowsill had become Vasanti's favourite spot. She liked to watch the parrots fly in and out of the one guava tree left standing inside the compound wall. The thatched house had been demolished, and the garden buried under mounds of excavated debris. The four coconut trees, which Mohini imagined to be sisters, the taller three leaning protectively over the smaller, losing their composure only in the lashing monsoon weather when they swished their heads from side to side, were now four stumps. Vasanti told Kamala and Mohini that she was happy that the guava tree was left standing because now at least the parrots would continue to have a perch. But Kamala had said it was only a matter of time—with Shivaji Park developing at the rate it was—before various birds would disappear, leaving behind the hardier pigeons, sparrows, and crows.

"Breathe deeply," Kamala softly repeated. Mohini closed her eyes, then opened them again: a desert wind was searing through her body, rearranging her bones as though they were shifting sands, slicing into her like rolling gusts of flame. There burst through her mind an image of lions leaping across her torso, teeth dripping, claws bared. She closed her eyes. A narrow glimmer of light, a slit into a partially open, illuminated room, beckoned. A concerned voice said, "She's slipping into a coma." It was Induaji as she must have looked before her heat stroke, her face heart-shaped and smiling, cardamom mole prominent under her left eye, eyebrows forming a weak bridge above her nose. Mohini recognized her from the photograph on Keshav's desk. Vasanti and Vinod's father, Sitarampant, was standing next to her, a distant expression on his face, as though he were thinking about the annual yield or the failed monsoons. He dropped his gaze and noticed Mohini looking up at him. Grinning at her widely because he had not seen her in such a long time, he reached into his pocket and brought out a flat, silver box. The accompanying smell of snuff entered Mohini's nostrils and her eyes flew open, expecting to see a ring of faces holding out handkerchiefs under her chin. Instead, Kamala was sitting on the spare bed, cross-stitch roses tumbling every which way on her lap, an open prayer book in her hands. Her lips were moving silently. The lamp was tilted towards the ceiling. Next to Kamala, on Mohini's desk, stood a large jug of water, its contents undrunk.

"Better deep maroon and not pink roses," Mohini said.

Kamala looked up, startled, flinching as the needle she had attached to her blouse pierced her shoulder when she moved forward and knelt by Mohini's bedside.

"Where's everyone?" Mohini asked.

"Sleeping." Kamala very carefully placed her hands against Mohini's cheeks and cupped her face. She applied no pressure and after a moment or two removed her fingers.

"What's the time?"

"Five in the morning."

Mohini turned her eyes very slowly and looked into the terrace. The bougainvillea was colourless, the sky a nameless blue, and as she stared at it, stars moved forward and speared its softness.

"Aai?"

Kamala locked her eyes into Mohini's.

"Baba's letter—did you find it?"

"I found it where you had left it on your desk. It was such a long time ago, Mohini. Reading it, I felt as though it was another Keshav who had written to another Kamala."

It was the first time Mohini had heard Kamala take Keshav's name. "But you, him, you are still the same," Mohini said.

"You'd think I'd know better at my age, and moreover because He gave me a daughter like you . . ." Tears streamed down Kamala's face and fell rapidly on the sheet. She did nothing to wipe them away, but continued to look into Mohini's eyes.

When Kamala's tears became sobs, Mohini said, "Remember what you told Mrs. Marzello?"

Kamala nodded, unable to speak.

"Aai?"

"Don't talk. The effort is too much."

"I'm sorry for all the trouble I have caused you."

The tears ran even faster down Kamala's cheeks. After a minute or two she settled back on her haunches and pulled up her knees. She rocked herself back and forth, her forehead buried deep in her lap. When she looked up, her face was dry and her eyes were clear. She cupped her hands very gently, soft and hovering like weightless feathers, over and under the fingers of Mohini's strapped hand.

Keshav came into the room, followed by Vishnupant, Anantrao, Umabai, Vasanti, Vinod, Aniruddha, Hansa, Bayabai, Balu, and Shevanti. Kamala did not move. When Dr. Chitnis entered a bit later, a coral glow was fanning the east. Gulaam, who was carrying Dr. Chitnis's bag, came up and, looking at Mohini, raised his hand to his forehead.

Dr. Chitnis said, "What a stately picture you make, Mohini. One person to move your foot, another your hand, still another your head. Just like—"

"Royalty," she said with a smile, looking out into the terrace. The swing was moving although there was no one in it.

"Try to be like the blind," Vasanti's Chafekar Wadi Guruji had said to her when she had become widowed. The blind do not see. "Be like the deaf." The deaf do not hear. "Be like the dumb." They do not speak. "Like those without a tongue." They do not taste. "Like those with no hands." They do not touch. "Become one who has neither hands, nor mouth, nor tongue, nor eyes, nor ears."

Be like the swing . . . The tenuous thought that had occupied her for so long took tender shape. She closed her eyelids. The room retreated slowly, and she understood in a way that she had never understood before that that which she was about to enter was a formless, timeless unity and the world she was rapidly leaving behind . . . nothing but the lingering remnants of a temporal dream.

GLOSSARY

Family Relationships

Aai	Mummy, mother
Baba	Daddy, father
Atya	father's sister or father's cousin sister
Aji	paternal or maternal grandmother
Ajoba	paternal or maternal grandfather
Dada	older brother or cousin brother
Tai	older sister or cousin sister
Vahini	sister-in-law or cousin sister-in-law
Kaka	father's brother or father's cousin brother
Kaku	Kaka's wife
Mavshi	mother's sister or mother's cousin sister
Mama	mother's brother or mother's cousin brother
Mami	Mama's wife
-pant	suffix denoting respect
-rao	suffix denoting respect
-ji	suffix denoting respect

ACKNOWLEDGMENTS

In bringing this book to life, there are many to whom I owe a debt of gratitude. First and foremost I would like to express love and heartfelt thanks to my mother, Manjoo Modak, for her moral fortitude, her constancy, and her ability to face with courage and compassion the unique and unforeseen circumstances that have marked her life. Many thanks to Mhatre Kaka for recalling so vividly and with such enduring love the neighbourhood of Shivaji Park as it was in the 20s, 30s, and 40s. Thanks to my cousin, Ashok Joshi, for his steady willingness in helping me ferret out obscure figures and facts. And to Kaka Shinde: a special thank you for re-creating for me the life of an engineer as it was both before and immediately following Independence.

Special thanks to Joan Clark for her generous friendship and continuing support, and to Daphne Marlatt for her unwavering encouragement at a critical juncture in the manuscript drafts. Sincere thanks to Ven Begamudre for sharing with me so unstintingly his vast knowledge of the writing art.

To Dean Cooke, my agent, for his firm endorsement and early response: my gratitude. Many thanks to Maya Mavjee at Doubleday for her immediate support and enthusiasm, to Bernice Eisenstein for bringing to the manuscript an informed and meticulous eye. And heartfelt gratitude to my editor, Martha Kanya-Forstner, for her commitment, acuity, and for making long-distance editing an unexpected pleasure.

This book is a work of fiction; however, I am greatly indebted to the many historians and authors who have analyzed, studied, recorded, and reported extensively and intensively the unique entity that is India. I would like to make special mention of the following: *A New History of India* by Stanley A. Wolpert; *Maharashtra 1858–1920* by B. R. Sunthankar; *Witness to an Era: India 1920 to the Present Day* by Frank Moraes; *In Light of India* by Octavio Paz; *A Search in Secret India* by Dr. Paul Brunton; *The Proudest Day—India's Long Road to Independence* by Anthony Read and David Fisher.

Finally I would like to thank the Canada Council, and The Banff Centre Writing Studio for their timely support.

ABOUT THE AUTHOR

Shree Ghatage is the author of the short story collection *Awake When All the World Is Asleep*, which won the Thomas H. Raddall Atlantic Fiction Award and was nominated for several other awards. Ghatage and her family came to Canada in the early 1980s. She spent fifteen years in Atlantic Canada and now makes her home in Calgary.

A NOTE ABOUT THE TYPE

Brahma's Dream has been set in Filosofia,
a typeface designed in 1996 by Zuzana Licko,
co-founder of Émigré Fonts. The face is a modern
interpretation of the classic Bodoni, allowing for
applications that Bodoni's extreme contrasts
cannot address, namely good readability
in smaller text sizes.